brutal CONQUEST

LILITH VINCENT

This book is dedicated to everyone who felt weak at the knees when Daemon Targaryen ordered his niece to "Turn around," and from that moment on gleefully supported his many, many crimes.

BRUTAL CONQUEST: A FORBIDDEN STANDALONE ROMANCE

She stole my birthright, so I'll claim her by any means possible.

I was banished from my family two years ago by my *Pakhan* and brother, and any mention of the Belyaevs makes me burn with red-hot anger. I'm no longer heir to the Belyaev crime family fortune.

But she is.

Zenya Belyaev, the most beautiful girl I've ever seen. She's the mirror of my soul. The second half of my treacherous heart. The key to my future as the most powerful man in the city.

Our love is forbidden fruit. Zenya burns from the shame of wanting me, but I will sink my teeth into her heart and make her lick the juice from my lips. She thinks one taste is enough for me after wanting her all these years?

Princess, I'm only just getting started.

Author's note: Brutal Conquest is a standalone MF romance with forbidden themes, breeding, an eighteen-year age gap, a jealous and possessive alphahole uncle (no blood relation) and a sweet but strong virgin heroine. The story is dirty and delicious, so please read at your discretion.

PLAYLIST

One Woman Army – Porcelain Black
Dirty Thoughts – Chloe Adams
Dark Horse – Katy Perry
Queen – Loren Gray
R.I.P 2 My Youth – The Neighbourhood
People You Know – Selena Gomez
the hills – Aidan Alexander
Walls Could Talk – Halsey
Figure 8 – Ellie Goulding
Fire For You – Cannons
Devil – Two Feet
I Wanna Be Yours – Arctic Monkeys
Are You That Somebody – Aaliyah
Heat Waves – Glass Animals
Love Me Again – John Newman
Into You – Ariana Grande
NFWMB – Hozier

Search "Brutal Conquest by Lilith Vincent" on Spotify or go to
https://spoti.fi/3OfvDDH

A NOTE TO READERS

Dear readers, this story is going to squick some of you out, but I love to set up camp between squick and sexy and live there. While Kristian is Zenya's uncle, he and Zenya aren't blood related, though Zenya grew up with him spoiling her and she believes they were related for a long time. There are some dark themes, birth control fuckery, breeding, sexual assault of a side character, attempted sexual assault of the heroine (not by Uncle Kristian), violence, and manipulation dubcon (by Uncle Kristian). There is also depiction of cancer and cancer treatments.

There are no harems, cheating, manwhores, or sharing. Uncle Kristian is a one-woman man and turns into a jealous and possessive monster every time another man so much as breathes near his sweet little niece. He pledges his life and his heart to Zenya waaay before he should and the impatient-for-her-to-grow-up-so-I-can-make-her-mine trope is strong with him. He keeps his hands to himself while she's underage, but if a grown-ass man looking at a fifteen/sixteen-year-old and thinking "that's my future wife" makes you rage, this is not the book for you.

Chapter One

ZENYA

"Cut her face."

"Rip her eyes out."

"Shove a knife up her cunt."

"All of that at the same time."

The four men advance on me, two holding guns, another swinging an axe, and the last with a baseball bat propped on his shoulder. I've already felt the vicious blow of the bat. My ankle is throbbing like it might be broken, and I'm covered in blood and crouching over my last surviving ally.

Andrei lifts a shaking hand and seizes my wrist. His face is pale beneath his tan, and his trembling lips are turning blue. "Zenya. *Run.*"

I have my hands pressed over an axe wound on Andrei's chest, and blood is bubbling up between my fingers. If I run, he'll die. My other two men are already dead, their body parts littering the floor of this dingy warehouse, along with three more corpses. I killed a man tonight. The first time in four years that I've taken a life.

I shake my head rapidly. "I'm not leaving you."

Andrei's been working for my father almost as long as I've been alive. He has a son. For the last two years, he's stepped up and helped me while Dad has grown sicker and sicker. Andrei is as good as family, and family is all I have.

Andrei's hand slips from my wrist and falls to the floor. His face slackens and he stares fixedly at the ceiling.

Pain slices through me and I can't breathe. Every day, it feels like my family is growing smaller and smaller. I keep losing people. Mom. Uncle Kristian. Dad's fading away to a brittle skeleton before my eyes. Now I'm responsible for Andrei's, Radimir's, and Stannis's deaths, because I asked them to come here with me tonight.

I take a shuddering breath and lift my hands from Andrei's chest. He deserved better than dying on a cold concrete floor in a warehouse. All three of them did.

"Aww, is she going to cry?" one of my attackers taunts in a hideous baby voice. "Is the widdle girl going to fall apart?"

I stand up and glare at the advancing men, and nearly slip on the blood covering the floor. There's so much blood. More than I've ever seen in my eighteen years, and I once witnessed four men being tortured to death.

2

There's no point screaming for help. There's no one around for miles on this wet and lonely night to hear me. I scan the floor feverishly for a weapon. My gun is out of bullets and I throw it aside.

I spy a knife laying in a pool of blood just a few feet away, and my heart leaps. I take a step to one side, and my injured foot skids on someone's trailing intestines. Pain blazes through my ankle and I grit my teeth on a scream.

"Dumb fucking Belyaev bitch," a greasy-haired man taunts me. "Your family is finished. It's our time to rule this city."

"Like hell we're finished," I snarl in reply. "The Belyaevs aren't going anywhere while my father and I are still breathing."

The man holding the bloody axe brandishes it at me with a grin. "Troian Belyaev's a walking corpse, and we're going to fix the other half of that problem right now."

They mean every word. Rival families and gangs have been circling Belyaev territory like vultures ever since Dad's sickness returned. If these men get their hands on me, I'm dead, and they won't be quick or merciful about it either.

I desperately want that knife. If I go for it, they'll be on me, so I make myself wait. I drop into a crouch and curl my hands into fists. It's not much, but it's all I can do right now. I'm only five-foot-three, and someone used to tease me that a strong breeze could carry me away like a dandelion seed. My insides convulse with hurt and anger as they do every time I think of Uncle Kristian. My father's brother. He loved to trail his fingers through my silky, silvery hair and call me his dandelion. His princess. When he was banished from the family two years ago, he left me struggling with my head barely above water, just when I needed him most.

But I don't need him now. What I need is a weapon and a clear head, and so I push the memory of my tall, dangerous uncle away.

I wince as I slowly back away from the men in front of me. All right, I wouldn't say no to Uncle Kristian's muscle, ruthless energy, and creative violence right about now, but he's not here, is he?

So fuck him.

I'm not giving up without a fight.

Even if I don't survive, I'll take one or two of these shitheads with me.

I study the four men before me, hunting for recognition in their faces, tattoos, jewelry, but nothing seems familiar. My men and I came here to collect a shipment of black-market goods, but these assholes got here first and ambushed us.

The man closest to me runs his tongue over his teeth, his eyes glinting with malice, and I see he has a jeweled tooth. "Shall we kill her? Or shall we send her back to the Belyaevs bleeding from every hole?"

The greasy-haired one on the left sniggers. "Keep her on this side of death so she has time to tell Troian Belyaev everything we did to his precious baby girl."

A third man leers at me. "With your daddy's flesh wasting from his body before he's even dead, your family is finished. Just give up, *devochka*." *Girl.*

I am no girl. I might be young, but I turned eighteen yesterday, and I'm the next in line to lead the Belyaev clan, the most prominent Bratva family in the city. With my father so dangerously ill, I already

4

am running it, in all but name. I am my family, and my family is me.

The man brandishing the baseball bat steps toward me. "I think I'll break her legs first."

My whole body tenses. If I can get that bat away from him, or dive for the knife, I might stand a chance. I get ready to dodge his strikes and use all the self-defense and hand-to-hand fighting skills I've drilled again and again.

"Bring it on, asshole," I snarl.

Over the rain pattering on the tin roof, a crunching sound reaches our ears. Heavy footsteps growing louder.

Two of my aggressors glance over their shoulders along the darkened warehouse. Shadows have swallowed everything, but the footsteps are getting louder.

And louder.

So loud that even the man intent on breaking my legs frowns and turns around.

While they're distracted, I bend down and snatch the knife and shove it into my boot.

The shadows thin about thirty feet from us. A man steps into a shaft of streetlight that falls through a dirty window and stops where he is.

The stranger is huge. Over six-foot-four and wearing black clothes that cling to his muscular frame. I can't see his face. He's wearing some kind of tight-fitting face covering that conceals his head and neck. I can make out his jaw and nose beneath the material, but that's all.

He looks like a walking threat.

What in the fresh hell is this?

Apparently my attackers don't know who he is either, as one of them calls, "Hey, Batman, this is a private murder party."

The others laugh in response, but the stranger doesn't make a sound. I can't see his eyes, but I can tell from the way his head turns that he's staring at the men one after another. Sizing them and their weapons up.

He hasn't looked my way once, and I wonder if he sees me. It's possible that he's come here tonight to settle a score with these four men, and I'm caught in the crossfire.

With any luck, I can escape while he's fighting these *mudaki*. *Assholes.*

But the stranger still doesn't move, and the tension is killing me. If he wants to attack them, why did he announce his presence like this? Either he's cocky, or he's stupid.

One of the men seems to wonder the same thing as he shakes his head and says, "Look at this dummy, just standing there."

The stranger is outnumbered and outgunned, but he doesn't move. Seconds tick past. A full minute.

All four men glance at each other in confusion. Two of them even send baffled stares my way, but I don't know what the hell is going on.

The greasy-haired man scratches his cheek. "Uh, buddy? You seem lost. Why don't you just fuck off?"

The silent man doesn't move a muscle. There's something regal about the way he stands there. He's built like a warrior, all strength and control, and I have a feeling he doesn't make a habit of doing what people tell him to do. I get a sudden mental picture of myself on my knees before this unknown man while he strokes his thumb slowly over my lips and murmurs, *Good girl*.

I shake myself. Where the hell did that thought come from? *Zenya, focus on getting the hell out of here.*

Greasy-haired guy strolls over to the stranger. "You want to join our group or something? Sorry, but we don't hire silent idiots."

The stranger doesn't respond. Not one flicker of movement.

Greasy-haired man gives a puff of derisive laughter, and he reaches up to wave his fingers in front of the man's face.

The stranger suddenly grabs his wrist. I hear the *schhwick* of a switchblade and the stranger plunges the blade between the man's ribs. The greasy-haired man gives a gurgling cry, and his eyes open wide in shock and pain.

The stranger yanks the knife out and the blade is covered in blood. More blood spurts from the injury, and the wounded man's knees buckle. The other men shout and raise their weapons.

The stranger grabs a fistful of the man's clothing and uses him as a human shield as bullets fly. He takes his victim's weapon and returns fire, all the while advancing on the other men.

Holy forking shirt balls.

There's something familiar about this man's movements and singular focus. Perhaps it's an attitude that I've witnessed before. He's not cold and calm, but he's not frenzied and chaotic either.

Two more of the men topple to the ground, screaming, both with bullet wounds in their legs. One of them drops his axe. The stranger could have killed them, so he either wants them alive, or he wants them to suffer. Every line of his body speaks of hate. This man is steadily taking down his enemies with silent and controlled rage.

The men on the ground have run out of bullets. The fourth man has his gun up but he's not firing as he backs away, the whites showing all the way around his eyes.

Still holding on to his very dead and bullet-ridden human shield, the stranger stalks closer to him. When he's six feet away, he throws the corpse at the last man standing, who fires, but it's too late. He goes toppling to the ground under the weight of his dead friend, and his gun skitters away into the darkness.

The stranger stares down at the man and slowly transfers his weight from one foot to the other as if he's savoring this moment. I can't see his face, but from his exultant attitude, I'm certain there's a smirk on his lips.

I thought I'd witnessed all the carnage I was going to tonight, but as the stranger turns around and heads for the axe, I realize how wrong I was.

Still ignoring me, he scoops up the weapon and hefts it in his gloved grip, testing its weight and balance. He must notice as the uninjured man throws his friend's corpse off, but he doesn't react until his victim is nearly on his feet. As he starts to run, the stranger takes two long paces while raising the axe above his head, and he brings it down on the man's back. There's a crunch of bones breaking, and the man screams. He rips the axe out and lifts his enormous arm once more, bringing the weapon down on the man's skull. As the blade penetrates bone and brain, the man's scream is cut off, and he falls to the ground.

The stranger gazes pitilessly at the bleeding corpse for a moment, and then turns away, leaving the axe buried in his skull.

He's not in a hurry now. The wounded men are crawling on their bellies through all the blood toward the door, whimpering and sniveling. I'm edging in that direction as well, hoping he somehow hasn't noticed me or he just doesn't care that I'm here.

The stranger examines the two bleeding men on the ground, contemplating them like they're cockroaches he wants to crush underfoot. He seems to be enjoying their pathetic attempts to escape. There's a machete strapped to his back, and he reaches behind his head to pull it free.

One of the men's flailing legs connects with the stranger's black boots. The stranger lifts his foot and brings it down on the man's ankle, pinning him in place. He raises the machete and brings the blade down as fast as lightning, severing the man's leg mid-calf.

The man screams, an inhuman sound of someone out of his mind in pain and terror.

The stranger kicks away the severed limb, and then raises his machete and cuts off the man's other foot. He takes one long step over the wriggling body and gives the other man the same treatment. I wince every time the blade hits bone and concrete. My hands lift to cover my ears, but they hover over either side of my skull. He means to go on cutting little pieces off these men while they die slowly.

I can't take the carnage and the screaming any longer. "*Just kill them already.*"

The stranger freezes. The seconds tick past painfully as I wonder if he's about to attack me.

He flips the blade in his hand until it's pointed downward, and then thrusts it through one of the men's rib cages and straight into his heart, before dispatching the other man in the same manner. The screaming stops.

The man raises his machete and gives it a downward flick, and the blood coating the blade spatters against the floor.

Silence reigns in the warehouse. I can hear the pattering of the rain overhead once more.

I need to get the hell out of here.

Though it makes pain blaze through my ankle, I make one tiny step to my left—

The stranger swings around and faces me.

I wish I could see his eyes. Is he wondering what to do with me, or has he already decided that I'm a dead woman?

There's no way around this killing machine to the exit, so if I want to leave, I'm going to have to persuade him to let me.

The stench of all these dead bodies is almost overwhelming, but I straighten my shoulders, lift my chin, and declare, "My name is Zenya Belyaev. I came here tonight to collect that delivery." I nod at the pallets which are off to one side. "Radar jammers and detectors. Illegal in this country and worth half a million on the black market. They're yours if you want them. I never saw you here. I'll walk away and you'll never hear from me again."

It's a good deal. Any sane criminal would take it.

The stranger doesn't even glance at the pallet. Instead, he starts to walk slowly toward me. I thought he was intimidating as he was slaughtering four men, but nothing compares to his predatory advance. He moves like a panther, that bloody, glistening weapon brandished in his gloved hand.

I want to back away. I want to *run*, no matter how much it hurts, but the second I do he'll break me like a doll.

I refuse to let him see that I'm afraid of him.

I'm Zenya Belyaev, and I refuse to be afraid of anyone.

The stranger stops right in front of me, and I force my chin up to stare at his face covering, right where his eyes must be. I fix an expression of proud dislike on my face, and I'm pleased that I'm able to hold it there.

Then my injured leg starts to shake. The stranger's gaze drops and he tilts his head to one side as he contemplates my trembling ankle.

I sense amusement from him. Mockery.

I lift my heel half an inch more to take pressure off it, and my leg stops shaking.

"I'm not afraid of you," I tell him. "The stench of blood is making me sick. What are we doing now? I'm a busy woman, so attack me or piss off."

Those are the only two options. I sense there's something else he wants from me, but I'll die before I give him that. He can fight me and kill me, but I won't let him humiliate and destroy me like that.

The stranger lifts his machete and gazes at the blade like he's considering his two choices. Then he throws it aside.

I inhale sharply.

Shit.

I liked it better when he was armed.

I won't let him—

He reaches for me, gloved fingers outstretched, seizes my wrists, and drags me against him.

"Don't you fucking touch me! Let go of me. *Let go of me, you asshole.*"

I scream and thrash around in his grip. His hands are as tight as manacles, and I know I don't stand a chance against him, but I refuse to stop fighting.

The stranger hooks one arm around my waist and one under my knees, lifting me into the air. A moment later I settle against his broad chest and he turns and starts walking. He carries me through the warehouse bridal style, stepping over body parts and through puddles of gore.

All the fight goes out of me, and I gaze up at him in surprise. Suddenly I sense nothing threatening coming off this man. He holds me like I'm precious.

"Where are you taking me? Who are you?"

The man finally replies, but he does so in a whisper, and I can barely hear him. "A friend."

I blink in surprise. "He speaks."

No reply. The stranger keeps walking through the darkness, carrying me like I weigh nothing.

Like I'm what he came to get.

"If you were my friend you'd show me your face."

"I can't do that," he replies in a gruff whisper.

My eyes narrow in suspicion. "Why are you whispering? Do I know you?"

The stranger laughs softly, and I can't tell if he means *of course* or *of course not.* He shoulders his way through a door, moving carefully so my feet don't knock against the doorframe, and carries me up some steps.

We emerge into what must be the warehouse break room. There's a sofa, and he takes me over to it and sets me down gently.

"Are you hurt?" he whispers, and to my surprise, he brushes my long hair back from my face and runs his fingers down my arms to check for cuts and bruises. Then he reaches for my legs and his fingers brush my injured ankle. I realize he's about to feel the knife in my boot, and I jerk my foot away.

"I'll ice it later. Am I your captive?"

He settles beside me on the sofa and gazes at me. I wonder how much he can see through that thing over his face. "For now."

The room is illuminated with streetlight, and I study the shape of his face once more. A strong jawline and brow. A long, straight nose.

He sounds amused as he whispers, "Well, do you know me?"

My back is against the arm of the sofa and my feet are pressed against his thigh. Strong thighs. This is a man who never skips leg day. From the looks of him, he never skips anything day. The man is pure muscle.

"Um, I don't know," I murmur, reaching down like I'm going to scratch my ankle. My fingers slip inside my boot, yank out the knife, and I lunge for him.

I was intending to hold the blade to his throat and demand he takes his mask off. He snatches my wrist with one hand, tugs the knife from my fingers, and throws it across the room.

"Stop that. Be a good girl."

Good girl. Those two words send shivers through me. "I just want to see your face."

Tentatively, I reach for his mask, but he grabs both my wrists and drags me onto his lap. My whole body tenses as I ready myself to fight him again.

But he doesn't do anything but gather me close and press my palms against his chest. I stare at my hands, feeling his taut muscles beneath my fingers. My thighs are hugging his hips.

"What are you doing?"

"I like you close to me," he purrs.

I draw in a shaky breath as his words vibrate on a very personal level in a very personal area. Butterflies erupt in my belly, and I can't tell if this man is my white knight or a black dragon. "Why can't I take your mask off?"

The stranger lets go of my wrists and tugs my knees higher up his hips and settles his arms comfortably around me. "You won't let me hold you like this if I take it off."

"Do you have scars? Are you missing an eye?" Not that I would care. Plenty of men I know have scars. They're an occupational hazard in our line of work.

He shakes his head. "Nothing like that."

"Are you going to let me go?"

"Soon. But first I want payment for saving your life."

At last we're getting to it. As a Belyaev, I understand that what people want from us isn't always stackable on a pallet. They want favors, introductions, alliances. "Name your price, and I'll tell you if it's something I'm willing to give you."

The stranger's focus moves from my face to my breasts to my

thighs, and he takes a long, deep breath. The energy in the room shifts and crackles. The man holding me in his arms is hungry. Incredibly hungry.

Anger throws a blanket over the butterflies in my belly. "You think I'm going to fuck you in thanks for killing those men? I'm not a whore."

But the stranger shakes his head. "I don't want that."

"Oh. Then what do you want?"

He reaches out and runs a lock of my platinum blonde hair through his gloved fingers. His voice is a caress as he murmurs, "A taste."

My eyebrows shoot up. "A kiss?"

He leans closer until I think he's going to press his masked lips to mine. "Not a kiss. I want a real taste of you."

"What's a real…" Heat flames in my cheeks as I realize what he's asking for. He wants to take off my clothes, put his mouth on me, and lick me like an ice-cream cone. "Are you crazy? No way."

"You've seen what I'm capable of. You like a man who's a fighter, Zenya Belyaev. You crave a man you can respect. Downstairs, you couldn't take your eyes off me."

"What else was I going to do while a stranger murdered four men in front of me? Play *Lily's Garden*?"

"What's *Lily's Garden*?"

"Wow. How old are you?"

He sounds amused as he replies, "Older than you. Busier than you as well if you have time to play games."

I'm busy, but I'm also an insomniac some nights.

The stranger runs a gloved forefinger gently across my

collarbone. His featherlight touch is enough to send sparks of fire shooting through me.

"You're so beautiful, Zenya," he whispers, and there's so much longing in his voice that a pang goes through my heart. This might be the first time I've met him, but he's known me for a long time from the sounds of it. Perhaps from a distance. Maybe I have a stalker and didn't know it.

I didn't know anybody outside my family cared about me this much.

Crap. I'm finding this romantic? My loneliness is plumbing new and sordid depths.

"I'm engaged," I lie. "My fiancé's insane, and he'll kill you."

He picks up my left hand and shows it to me. "I don't see a ring."

"We haven't had time to get one yet," I say, but it's plain that he doesn't believe me. I suppose a stalker would know if I were engaged or not. I haven't been around many men socially apart from my father in two years.

"I want one taste of the proud and beautiful Zenya Belyaev. I've waited a long time, and tonight I saved your life. Give a starving man one moment of heaven, and then you'll never see me again. You won't even know who I am. Not my face. Not my name."

"You'll have to take your mask off if you're going to do that," I challenge him, burning with curiosity to see his face.

He reaches into his pocket and pulls out a blindfold. "I already thought of that."

I stare at the blindfold hanging from his fingers. His grip on my waist tightens and his body heat seems to scorch me. I can feel his lust. He wants me badly, but willingly. I'm not in any danger from this man. In fact, I feel safer than I have in a long time.

Which is *insane*.

He's a killer. Alarm bells are ringing distantly in my head, but the clamoring desire to let this man do whatever he wants to me drowns out everything else.

He takes advantage of my hesitation to turn on the sofa and drop me onto my back on the cushions. I gasp in shock as he hovers over me, one hand braced by my head.

The blindfold is still dangling from his fingers. "Put it on, Zenya."

I glance down, and my thighs are hugging his body.

My shaking fingers are moving on their own. Am I really this lonely? This desperate for pleasure and affection?

Apparently I am, because I reach for the blindfold, pull it down over my face, and settle it over my eyes. The world is enveloped with velvet darkness.

"Perfect," he breathes, stroking my hair back from my face. His hands disappear, but a moment later they're back. They feel different, and I realize it's because he's taken off his gloves, and he's touching me with bare skin. I moan as he strokes his fingers over my lips and down my throat.

"That's it. Just relax and let me take care of you." His whisper is heavy with desire.

It's been a long time since anyone told me to relax. Usually it's, *We need this, Zenya*, and *What next, Zenya?* and *There's another problem, Zenya*. On and on until I want to scream.

This stranger isn't making demands of me. He just wants to caress me while I float in warm, cozy darkness.

The stranger strokes his hands down my body to the button on my jeans, which he pops open. He continues down my legs and unlaces my boots, carefully slipping them off my feet along with my socks. He's especially careful with my injured foot and touches a place close to where the baseball bat connected with my ankle.

"If they weren't already dead, I'd make them pay for this," he growls softly.

I feel the zipper on my jeans parting, and then he tugs my pants and underwear down my legs.

If I'm going to stop this man, now is my last chance.

But I don't move.

And then my whole lower half is naked beneath him.

"You're more beautiful than I imagined," he breathes, and presses a kiss to my ankle. He's freshly shaved and I feel the faint rasp of his stubble.

He kisses my calf. Then the inside of my knee. My inner thigh. I can feel him devouring me with his eyes.

Both my hands come up to cover my face, overwhelmed by the fact that a man is looking at my almost completely naked body. Putting his mouth close to my most intimate parts.

He moves from my thigh to my hip. I feel his lips against my hip bone as he presses a kiss there. A moment later, he strokes me with his tongue and moves lower.

Kiss. Lick. Kiss. Lick. Inching closer to my sex.

He kisses the top of my slit. I gasp and my whole body jumps, and he laughs softly. "You're so sensitive there. Wonderful."

He kisses me again in the same place, and my whole body

floods with heat.

"You smell delicious, Zenya. I've always wanted to know…" But whatever he was going to say is lost as his tongue slips between my folds and strokes firmly against my clit.

Both my hands fall away from my face as I cry out. Loudly.

The stranger groans as well, as if this is giving him as much pleasure as he's giving me. I've never heard a man sound like that before.

I didn't know a man could sound like that.

His tongue surges against my clit again, and I arch my body into his soft, wet tongue.

As he licks me, he pushes the tip of one finger into my core, and then another. Just one knuckle deep, but it's enough to drive me wild.

"So perfect and tight. How lovely you are, Zenya."

I start panting hard, and I scramble to get purchase on something, anything, with my legs. The stranger wraps my thighs firmly around his shoulders. He feels incredible to cling onto, and I wonder what it would be like to drag him up to my lips, press a feverish kiss to his mouth, and beg him to sink into me.

I know his dick is big. I know it. I know it's big.

One of my hands grips his shoulder. The other holds on to the back of the sofa for dear life. I'm making noises I never thought were possible.

"That's it, princess," he whispers coaxingly, devouring me like I'm fruit. "Come for me. I want it so bad."

No one wants this orgasm more than me. I'm rising up a wave so powerful and unstoppable that everything feels out of control. Red-hot fire is roaring within me, and I'm going to burst apart.

I crest the wave.

And plunge down the other side with a loud cry. My head flies back. My body arches against the stranger's mouth. My nails dig into his muscular shoulder. The intensity goes on and on, until it finally releases me.

The stranger stops licking me and hungrily kisses my sex, every touch of his lips sending residual sparks through me. I don't want it to be over. I never want to come back to earth. I just want to be free.

But the pleasure fades away, and I return to earth with a thump. I open my eyes, and for a moment, I'm confused why I can't see.

Then I remember the blindfold.

I remember my name.

Where I am.

Oh, shit. I just let a complete stranger go down on me while there are dead bodies downstairs. What the hell was I thinking?

Who *is* he?

I have to know. I pull my blindfold off and blink rapidly. The stranger has drawn the mask up to uncover his jaw and mouth and he's pressing kisses to my inner thigh.

I freeze as I stare at him.

I know that jaw.

I know that mouth.

He knows I'm looking at him and he doesn't care. A smile touches his lips as he presses yet another kiss against my inner thigh.

No.

It *can't* be.

It's a trick of the light.

"Let me see your face," I say in a strangled voice.

"But I want to go on kissing you, Zenya," he replies, and he's not whispering now. A familiar deep voice twines through my senses.

With a shaking hand, I reach out, grasp his mask, and pull it off.

White-blond hair tumbles around his face. His handsome, smirking face. Pale blue eyes flick up to meet mine.

My blood turns to ice in my veins.

I'm imagining things.

This isn't happening.

I sit up with a shriek. "Uncle Kristian?"

He grins wickedly up at me and takes another swipe at my sex with his warm tongue. "Hello, princess. Did you miss me?"

Chapter Two

ZENYA

Uncle Kristian was adopted by my grandparents when he was a baby, but you wouldn't know it to look at him. We all have similar features and hair, though Dad's and mine is ashier than Uncle Kristian's. No one ever bothered explaining to me that Uncle Kristian isn't actually Dad's biological brother. I found out when I was eleven when I overheard my dad's cousins discussing it. My favorite person in the whole world wasn't my real uncle? I burst into tears and ran into the garden. I was distraught. After Mom died, I clung to Uncle Kristian. He was my biggest comfort. He knew how to make me smile even on my worst days. I adored my uncle. I loved his smile and the way my heart lit up whenever I saw him. I was too young to know what charisma was or understand that he was good-looking. What I did understand was that he was always happy to see me. Energy crackled around him, and he commanded everyone's attention without even trying whenever he entered a room.

He found me sobbing my heart out in the garden. "Dandelion, what's the matter?"

Dandelion was what he used to call me when I was a child. He said my platinum hair reminded him of a silky dandelion puff.

I could barely get the words out. "You're not my real uncle? Are you going to leave me, too?"

Uncle Kristian drew my chin up and made me look at him, and until that moment, I'd never seen him angrier in my life. "Who's been saying I'm not your real uncle? Who dares to spew such lies to my niece?"

I explained about overhearing my aunts talking about him—they were really my cousins, but I called them my aunts because they're Dad's age—and he ground his teeth together.

"Technically, yes. I was adopted into this family."

"Why didn't you tell me?"

He got down on one knee and gripped my upper arms. "Because it doesn't make any difference to me. I'm a Belyaev just like you. I don't remember any other family. *You're* my family. You and your father are my life."

My sobs finally started to subside, and I wiped my eyes, gazing at his stricken face.

"I'm sorry I didn't tell you, dandelion. Can you forgive me?"

"You won't leave me, will you?" After Mom died, I was terrified of people leaving me. Being abandoned by the people I loved most in the world and left in a lonely, dark hole. Mom suffered a massive stroke one day while she was gardening and collapsed. Uncle Kristian picked me up early from school and took me to the hospital. Mom was in a coma for a few days, and then she just slipped away.

"I swear it," he promised. "I'm not going anywhere."

I believed him.

Then five years later, he left.

Only to explode back into my life in the most shocking and wicked way possible.

My chest starts to heave. Black spots swarm before my eyes. My throat locks up so tight I can barely speak. "You—you put your mouth—*you made me—*"

I can't say it.

Can't catch my breath.

I think I'm going to pass out.

Uncle Kristian sits up, his brows drawing together in concern. "Zenya? Are you all right?"

I push my fingers into my hair and clutch my head. How can he even ask that after what he just did?

"I'm going to ask you one question." I grip Uncle Kristian's sweater in both my hands, pull him close, and shriek, "What the hell were you thinking?"

Instantly, his expression darkens. "Don't raise your voice to your uncle. What are you talking about, Zenya? You knew it was me the whole time." Uncle Kristian glares at my hands like he can't believe

I'm disrespecting him like this. He even uses his *listen here young lady* voice on me.

I gape at him. "I did *not* know it was you."

His eyes flash wickedly. "Well, now you know. Let's do it again and you can enjoy it even more this time."

Uncle Kristian slides his warm hands around my thighs and lowers his mouth toward my sex.

I make a choking noise. My legs are still parted and my entire everything is bared to him. I snap my legs shut, grab my underwear, and yank them up my legs. If Dad hears about this, he's going to be furious, and my face burns at the thought. "I can't believe you tricked me. Don't ever mention this to anyone."

His pale blue eyes flash, and I have a split second's warning before he grabs me, scoops me onto his thighs, wraps both arms around me, and pulls my sex tight against his hips. I'm trapped within his arms. Even though I haven't seen him for more than two years, I remember well that Uncle Kristian allows no one to talk to him like this, even his favorite niece.

"Don't tell me what to do, Zenya. Your uncle doesn't like that."

I squirm in his grip. He's hard. Oh, my God, he's got an erection like a rod of iron and it's right there against my underwear. I press my hands against his chest, trying to push myself away from him, but he's too strong and he won't let me go. I feel hot all over. My flesh is erupting with embarrassment.

"The second you saw me downstairs you knew it was me," he murmurs huskily. "I could see it in your beautiful eyes. You wanted me, so what was I supposed to do? You know I've never been able to deny you anything."

Sure, I've always been able to twist my uncle around my little finger, but so he'll buy me candy, let me stay up late, and teach me to drive his overpowered car when I was only thirteen. I wasn't making eyes at a stranger in black.

Was I?

I have no freaking idea, but if I was, it was because I didn't know it was my uncle.

Uncle Kristian plants a slow kiss on my throat, but I jerk my head away from him.

"Don't do that."

He grits his teeth in frustration, and I can tell he's itching to tell me off again. "You know I live to spoil you, princess. I've got a lot to catch up on now that I'm back."

He's back?

"You are?" I whisper, hope surging through me, and hating that I'm so needy for the man who abandoned me.

Uncle Kristian smiles. "I am. I missed you, dandelion."

Dandelion.

I groan and drop my head onto his shoulder. "Where the hell have you been all this time?"

He strokes his fingers through my hair and gathers me closer against his chest. "Missing you. I'm so sorry. Leaving you was the last thing I wanted."

Warmth cascades through me and a post-orgasm haze dulls all my reasoning. No one's hugged me in such a long time. Dad's too sick, and sure, my brothers and sisters jump into my lap for cuddles, but that's me holding them. I grew up being spoiled in Uncle Kristian's strong arms.

My arms wrap slowly around his neck. He breathes in deeply, savoring this moment, as if he really has missed me as much as I've missed him. The room is dim and quiet. There's no one around for miles. No one alive, anyway.

There's just the two of us.

His body feels like heaven, all warm flesh and strong muscles. The rich, familiar scent of his signature cologne and the musk of his body reaches my nostrils, making me moan in pleasure.

I've always loved the way Uncle Kristian smells.

I sit up slowly and gaze into his eyes. This feels like a dream.

Uncle Kristian takes my chin in his hand and plays his thumb over my lower lip. "After missing you for so long, how could I not want to kiss you, Zenya?"

He tilts his face up to mine, inviting me to kiss him. Heat trickles down my body to pool between my legs.

"Because..." I manage in a whisper, and then lick my lips. Suddenly my mouth is dry. "Because..."

The most handsome man I've ever seen is inviting me to kiss him, but it's Uncle Kristian. It doesn't matter that his hair is rumpled and longer than it used to be, and the shadows are playing over his face in enticing ways, it's *Uncle Kristian*.

His thumb runs down my chin and caresses my jaw. "Look at you. I always did like you covered in blood."

My fingers tighten on his sweater. Nails dig into his shoulders. The only other night he saw me covered in blood was the night I started feeling differently about myself. That I was a true Belyaev, and I was going to become a fully-fledged member of this family, not a daughter who would be petted and spoiled and live in luxury and ignorance before leaving to marry a bland and wealthy man.

Is he saying that's when he started seeing me differently, too?

Uncle Kristian tilts his chin up to kiss my mouth.

I suck in a breath and turn my face away. "Don't do that."

Anger flashes over his face. *He's* angry with *me*? That's not fair.

But Uncle Kristian has never cared about what's fair. I love him as much as I love Dad, but I'm not blind to his faults. He's arrogant. Surly. Manipulative. Dangerous. Violent. He's a walking middle finger to absolutely everyone.

Except me.

I've always been special.

"I haven't seen you for two years and you're already crossing lines."

Uncle Kristian tilts his head to one side and smiles at me. "Don't you think it's more fun on this side of the line?"

I take a deep breath and try to think. I need to distract him from looking at me like I'm food. "What are your plans? Are you going to see Dad?"

"Of course. As soon as I take you home."

"Please don't upset him. He's not strong enough," I implore.

A concerned line forms between Uncle Kristian's brows. "Is he in pain?"

"With cancer riddling his lungs? Of course he is. You'd know that if you'd bothered to be here these past two years."

"You know I wanted to be here," Uncle Kristian says, and there's genuine sorrow in his eyes.

My hands are resting on his shoulders, and I fiddle with the fabric of his black knit sweater. My heart cracked in two when I watched him leave, and all the love I carried for my uncle drained away. He never tried to come home. I imagined him out there living a carefree life while I was left behind to shoulder the burden of Dad's illness and family responsibilities at just sixteen years old.

"Then prove it. Swear you'll never breathe a word of what happened here tonight."

Uncle Kristian strokes his fingers through my hair with a smile. "Sure. I'll keep your secret, princess."

"My secret? You're the one who did this."

"For a price."

"What price?" I feel a thrill of trepidation and something hotter as I wonder what he's going to ask for. A kiss? Another taste of me?

He nods toward the door. "Let me take care of what's downstairs. I have men with me. Mikhail is here, of course. We'll clean up the bodies and get the merchandise to the Silo. You've had enough for tonight, and I want you home in bed."

The Silo is where we store all our illegal goods for sale.

"I'm fine," I say automatically. It's what I've said every time someone's questioned whether I could carry on these past two years. With Uncle Kristian gone and Dad bedridden, I've had to put on a strong front. I'm the eldest child, and when Dad passes away—which won't happen for a long, long time; I won't believe otherwise—he's named me as his successor.

People are starting to wonder whether Dad will survive this

latest bout of cancer. That's probably why I was attacked tonight. We seem to be weakening, which means our territory and power is up for grabs.

"I wasn't asking," Uncle Kristian replies.

I glance at the door and shake my head. "I can't believe they're dead. Andrei. Radimir. Stannis."

"They were good men. We'll make sure their families are taken care of."

"Because they were family to us," I whisper. For a moment my eyes sting, but I fight for control and rein in my emotions.

I get up off Uncle Kristian's lap and reach for my jeans, but he gets there first, picking them up and shaking them out for me. As natural as if he's always done that.

I take my jeans back from him, my cheeks reddening at how forward he is. "I can dress myself."

I manage it mostly, but it's hard with an injured foot. Uncle Kristian holds me around the waist to stop me from toppling over. I refuse to look at him as I sit down and pull on my socks and shoes, but his presence is impossible to ignore. I can feel my cheeks heating even more as I remember that just a few minutes ago, I had my head flung back and my legs open while Uncle Kristian hungrily licked my clit.

Like he's always wanted to do it.

Oh, Jesus.

Don't think about that right now.

In fact, never think about it again.

I look toward the door. All those dead bodies. The merchandise.

There's so much to do, and I can barely walk. How am I going to—

I gasp as Uncle Kristian scoops me into his arms and carries me downstairs. "I told you, I'll take care of it after I get you home."

I'll take care of it. I can't remember the last time anyone said that to me.

I don't need anyone to take care of me. I can take care of myself.

As if he can sense my thoughts, Uncle Kristian puts his lips against my ear and murmurs huskily, "You love it when I take care of you, princess."

My toes curl in my shoes as his double meaning shoots straight to my clit. Tonight feels like a fever dream that I can't wake up from.

There's a black Corvette brooding on the far side of the parking lot. Uncle Kristian makes a beeline for it, and it unlocks automatically as we approach.

"Open the door for me. I've got my arms full." He leans down so I can reach the handle.

I stare at it, and then over at my car. I couldn't drive it even if Uncle Kristian did put me down and let me hobble away from him, and so I pull the door open.

"What are you even doing here?" I ask him as he settles me in the passenger seat.

"I'm back. I'm rejoining the family."

Panic flames through me. If he rejoins the family, someone might find out what happened between us tonight. Maybe it's better that Uncle Kristian just stays gone. Dad probably won't even let him come home after what he did.

I pin him with a glare. "Do you think you can decide to come back all on your own? Dad's going to have something to say about this."

"I don't give a fuck what your father has to say." There's that anger simmering beneath the surface again. If anyone has the right to be angry, it's Dad with Uncle Kristian.

Unless there's something I don't know about?

"Why now? What's changed?" I ask.

Uncle Kristian pulls the seat belt across my body and buckles me in. With his face just inches from mine, he gives me a dark smile that makes me blush red to the roots of my hair.

"Everything. Happy birthday, princess."

ZENYA

TWO YEARS EARLIER

I loathe the smell of hospitals.

Cold, sharp disinfectant. The whiff of industrial strength bleach from the floors and bedsheets. Carts of bland, sad food on ugly plastic plates that look like they're for overgrown toddlers but are really for despairing and trembling adults.

As I walk down a wide hallway tinged faintly green, I pick up on another scent.

Fear.

This place reeks of it.

Uncle Kristian is up ahead, his long, lean body propped against the wall as he stares into a hospital room. My eyes lock onto his strong, handsome profile to keep myself grounded. He has the face of an angel chiseled from cold, pale marble, but there's nothing angelic about Uncle Kristian. I've witnessed him do things that would have Satan himself giving him a round of applause.

As I draw closer, I see that his black shirt is open at the throat, revealing the crossed guns tattoo on his chest and the silver chain he wears. His fine, platinum blond hair is falling into his eyes.

As I near his side, he turns his head and his pale, wintry eyes meet mine.

"*Kak plokho…?*" *How bad…?* My voice catches in my throat as I speak in Russian. The two of us often speak in the language of the Old Country when we don't want people to understand what we're saying. It keeps dangerous, violent, and secret things private from my seven younger siblings and random members of the public.

Asking about Dad is not dangerous, violent, or secret, but right now I crave the intimacy of our private language. Seeing Uncle Kristian and gnawing on my inner cheek are the only things keeping me from losing it and screaming the place down.

I can't lose it right now. Or ever. I'm a Belyaev, the eldest of Dad's children, and we have nerves of steel.

Uncle Kristian nods silently at the doorway, indicating I should go in and see for myself.

Ten months ago, Dad was diagnosed with lung cancer. He smoked heavily as a young man but he gave it up so long ago that I don't remember ever seeing him hold a cigarette.

I have seen Dad in so many hospitals, clinics, and waiting rooms since then. Four months of chemotherapy only made him sicker, though I tried to be grateful for the powerful medications that were being pumped into Dad's body week after week as they would hopefully mean I would be able to keep my father. Dad's hair fell out, he lost a dramatic amount of weight, and he was so tired that he could barely form sentences.

But he's survived, so far. In the six months since the chemotherapy ended, Dad's regained a lot of his strength and vitality. His hair's grown back and there's life in his blue eyes once more. The cancer has remained localized to his lungs, which means his five-year survival rate is thirty percent.

Thirty percent.

A heart-stopping, nail-biting, sweat-inducing number, though the doctor was smiling when he told us. As if the fact that there was a seventy percent chance that my father would be dead within five years was supposed to be amazing news for his family.

But today it's not the cancer that's landed him in a hospital bed. Today it's a motorcycle accident.

A grin breaks over Dad's face as he sees me standing in the doorway. His right leg is strapped up in a temporary cast, and there's a bandage stuck to his forehead. "There's my favorite girl."

He's awake. He's not been smashed to pieces. I grab the doorframe to steady myself and struggle not to tip my head back from sheer relief. It's better to pretend I wasn't worried. That I truly believe the Belyaevs are unshakable.

We *are* unshakable.

I stare at Dad's happy, almost gleeful expression, and then at his oncologist, Doctor Webster, who's glowering at him.

Doctor Webster clears his throat and moves toward me. "Zenya, it's lovely to see you again, but I must ask you to remind your father that he needs to take better care of his health. He won't listen to me."

I press the sleeve of his shirt. "I will. Thank you for coming to the hospital in the middle of the night to check on Dad."

"Of course. I hope I never see any of you in here again." The oncologist flashes a final peeved look at Dad and then leaves the room.

I really hope so, too.

My stepmom, Chessa, is clinging to Dad's hand. My siblings who are closest to me in age, Lana and Arron, are perched on each arm of the blue vinyl armchair.

I like Chessa as much as someone can like a stepmom she wishes she didn't have to have, and I shoot her an apologetic look for being called Dad's favorite girl. Chessa gives me a smile and a small shake of her head, telling me she doesn't care as she clings to Dad's hand. Chessa knows Dad loves her, and he treats her and her children from an earlier marriage with care and respect. They've had two children of their own since they were married five years ago, and he loves them dearly.

But I'm Dad's eldest child, and I'm part of his world. Unlike my brothers and sisters, I know that Troian Belyaev is *Pakhan* of the Russian mafia in this city, and quite a lot about how my family makes its money.

I don't know everything yet because I'm sixteen, and Dad isn't sure how much he should reveal to a teenager—and a girl, no less.

There aren't a lot of women in his line of work, but I don't see that it matters. Bullets are just as deadly when they're fired by a five-foot-three girl as they are a six-foot-four man.

"Where does it hurt?" I ask Dad, approaching his bed.

"I have no idea. I'm on enough morphine to make an elephant see pink elephants. I need an operation on my leg, apparently. The orthopedic surgeon says she hasn't seen a break as bad as mine in years." There's pride in his voice, as if he's thrilled he was injured doing something dangerous. Dad hasn't been able to do anything dangerous since before his diagnosis.

"We saw the X-ray," my younger brother, Arron, tells me with wide, shining eyes. He's twelve years old and fascinated by everything grisly. "Dad's bones were all smashed up. It was so cool."

Lana, who's fourteen, sticks her tongue out and grimaces. "I didn't look. Gross."

My mouth twitches as I look from Arron to Dad, who both wear the same boyish grins, though Dad's is slightly woozy from painkillers. I haven't seen Dad smile like this in such a long time.

"Troian's also got a concussion. I don't know what he was thinking, getting on a motorcycle when he's not fully recovered from his chemotherapy," Chessa says, and darts an angry look out the door into the corridor.

Dad glances that way too, and then lowers his voice and says, "Zenya, take Kristian home, will you? He says he's not in pain, but you know how proud he is."

Uncle Kristian is hurt as well? I whirl around and stare through the door at him. He's still leaning against the wall with one shiny leather shoe propped up and his hands in his pockets, trying to appear casual, but now I look closer, I can see from the muscle ticking in his jaw and the beads of sweat on his brow that something's wrong and he's trying not to show it.

I raise an eyebrow at him. *Are you in pain?*

He lets out a short, defiant huff, as if he's never even heard of being in pain.

Oh, yes. I know how proud my uncle is.

I kiss Dad goodnight and tell Chessa, Lana, and Arron that I'll see them at home. Then I walk out into the corridor and stand in front of my uncle, amusement making my mouth twitch.

"A motorcycle? Dad doesn't own a motorcycle," I say in Russian. "Was it yours?"

He lowers his eyes and peers down his long, straight nose at me. "*Net*. We borrowed it from the assholes we were beating up."

Of course they did.

"What happened tonight?"

A smirk slides over his handsome face. "*Shkola.*"

School. That's code for delivering a beating to someone or a group of someones who have overstepped our boundaries.

Uncle Kristian explains in Russian how the two of them went to confront some rival gang members who were infringing on Belyaev territory. They could have sent foot soldiers instead of the *Pakhan* and his younger brother showing up personally, but that's what my dad and Uncle Kristian are like. Or they used to be before Dad's diagnosis. If they can't handle things on their own sometimes, they don't deserve to lead.

Apparently, teaching the gang some manners was going well

until some of the gang's friends showed up, and Dad and Uncle Kristian had to escape quickly. That's where the motorcycle came in. Dad was driving and Uncle Kristian was on the back, and they crashed on a wet and slippery side street.

Switching to English, Kristian mutters, "Shout at me if you want to. I know you're mad at me for getting your dad all fucked up."

I stare at him in silence for a long time. My uncle is lean, muscular, and fast. I've seen him swimming in our pool and working out without his shirt plenty of times to know that his body is a weapon. He escapes from trouble before it has a chance to touch him.

Dad, though? Dad's tough and strong and leads our family, but his strength is being our unshakable rock. He weathers trouble and withstands storms, but sometimes he takes damage in the process. Lately, he's been taking a lot of damage, and it hurts my heart to see it. It was devastating for me to see Dad in misery and pain day after day. It must have been devastating for Uncle Kristian, too. The two of them have always been inseparable.

Behind me, I can hear Dad joking with a nurse that he's fine and he walked off worse injuries as a young man. For the first time in months, he sounds happy.

I fix my uncle with a severe look, as if he's the sixteen-year-old and not me. "Dad's oncologist is appalled that he's only just recovered from cancer treatment, yet he's running around at night crashing motorcycles. Did you at least show those *mudaki* who's boss around here?"

The ghost of a smile touches Uncle Kristian's lips. "Princess. Troian and I had them on their knees swearing to be good little boys until their shithead friends showed up."

I don't like seeing my dad surrounded by medical staff yet again, but at least this time, it's for something I know he'll get better from. He seems enlivened by the experience, like racing around on a motorcycle was the adventure he needed to feel like himself again, which was probably Uncle Kristian's intention all along.

If Uncle Kristian knows one thing better than anyone else, it's how to feel alive.

Chessa will be angry with him for a week straight, though she won't dare say anything to his face. I haven't forgotten how my uncle stepped up as the head of this family and kept the business running while Dad was too ill to get out of bed. He kept me going, too. I had to be strong for Chessa and my brothers and sisters, but Uncle Kristian was strong for me.

I tilt my chin up and smile at my uncle. "Then what do I have to be angry with you about?"

A smile breaks over my uncle's face. He laughs and then winces in pain. "Oh, fuck."

Uncle Kristian's black shirt is sticking to his chest with what I presume is blood. His tattered black suit jacket is draped around his shoulders like he can't lift his arms to put it on properly.

I step forward and peel his jacket and shirt back from the right side of his chest and see semi-dried blood over nasty scrapes. The deeper gashes are still bleeding. He must have slid across the gravel on his shoulder. "That looks painful."

"My shoulder feels like it's on fire," he mutters, wincing as he lifts it carefully to test the damage.

"Come on, I'll take you back to our place and clean you up. I've already said goodnight to Dad."

"What would I do without you, princess?" he asks as he follows me down the corridor.

The house is silent when we get home because I drove my four youngest siblings to their Aunt Eleanor's before going to the hospital. I take Uncle Kristian to the kitchen and get the first aid kit from out of a drawer.

He tries to take it from me. "I can do it. I'm used to patching myself up."

I hold the kit out of his reach. "One-handed? You'll make a mess of yourself. Sit down and let me do it for you."

Uncle Kristian sits down on the kitchen table with an expression of resignation, but there's a hint of a smile on his lips. "If I had been driving, we wouldn't have crashed. Your father hasn't been on a motorcycle in decades."

"Then why did you let him drive?" I ask, opening the kit on the table and pulling out antiseptic, tweezers, cotton pads, and bandages.

Uncle Kristian flicks me a dark look from beneath his lashes. "Are you serious? There are only two people in this world who I let order me around. One of them is the total boss of me in every way. I live for them. I would die for them." He touches beneath my chin. "The other is my brother."

After sixteen years of being as close to Uncle Kristian as I am my own father, I'm aware that he's not exaggerating when he says he would do just about anything for me. Uncle Kristian bought me my first handgun and my first pair of diamond earrings. The handgun came first, of course. Handguns always come first in the Belyaev family. My father is dependable with an iron will, but Uncle Kristian is the one who makes me feel alive and pushes me to be better, stronger, braver.

I shake the antiseptic bottle and smile. "You can charm me all you want. I'm still going to cleanse every single one of your cuts."

He shrugs out of his jacket. "You delight in torturing me, my sweet little niece."

I put down the bottle and help unbutton his shirt. Uncle Kristian often gets into fights and accidents, so this is a dance we've done many times before. I peel what's left of it from his shoulders and wince in sympathy at what I see. His entire right shoulder is scraped and bleeding, and there are pieces of gravel stuck in the cuts. Still, compared to Dad's multiple fractures and concussion, he got off lightly.

There's a silver chain around his neck, the same one he always wears, and I reach behind his neck with both hands to unfasten the clasp. "Did you know Dad's been saying you should settle down?"

Dad's been saying it more and more since his diagnosis. Uncle Kristian is his heir, and Dad believes a *Pakhan* should be a family man. According to Dad, a leader who is a father is more thoughtful in his decisions because he understands the value of other people's children.

Uncle Kristian gazes at me through the blond fringe that's falling into his eyes. "Oh? Why should I?"

"So you can have a family of your own." Uncle Kristian is thirty-four, and there are plenty of women who'd kill to marry him and have his children. In our world, dangerous men make the best husbands because they're willing to cross any lines to protect their families.

He runs his gaze over my face and murmurs, "You're my family, princess. Any daughter of mine could never be as clever and adorable as you."

I'm having trouble with the clasp of his necklace, and my arms are still around his neck. "Don't you want a wife? I've never even seen you with a girlfriend."

He puts his hands on my shoulders and rubs the tension in my muscles with his strong fingers. "There is no space in my heart for another woman. It's already full of you."

"Flatterer," I tell him with a smile, and my eyes close for a moment as I enjoy the way he finds all the tension I've been carrying and makes it melt away.

"Why are you asking me about a wife? Are you thinking about a husband?"

It feels good here, standing between his spread knees and basking in the heat coming off his broad chest. The house is silent and dark all around us. I rarely get Uncle Kristian all to myself these days. It's going to be hell for him to have me pick all that gravel out piece by piece, so I'll have to distract him.

I open my eyes and flash a teasing smile at him. "I'm sixteen. Of course I am."

The clasp of his necklace pops open and I lay the chain on the table next to him.

"Liar," he counters immediately, and then frowns. "Who?"

"Someone handsome," I say slowly, reaching for the tweezers. Uncle Kristian is studying me so intently that he barely notices as I pick a piece of gravel out of a scrape and set it on the table. "Strong and clever, too."

"How have you been meeting handsome, strong, and clever men behind my back?" he demands to know.

My father and Uncle Kristian have strong opinions about who I should be dating and the man I might marry. Both of them agree that any teenage boy who lays a finger on me should be put up against a wall and shot. Any prospective husbands should be dealt with in the same brutal way, according to Uncle Kristian, and before his diagnosis, Dad would have agreed with him. Since facing his mortality, I think he's warming to the idea that I should get married as soon as possible so I'm protected if anything happens to him. I don't agree with him, because I'll always have Uncle Kristian if anything happens to Dad, but it's a good distraction right now to wind up my overprotective uncle.

I smile mysteriously at Uncle Kristian and stroke my fingers along his bare shoulder until I come to another piece of gravel and dig it out. He doesn't even wince.

"He's wild but always dependable. He commands the attention of any room he walks into without even trying."

I pluck another piece of gravel out of his shoulder and then another. Soon his cuts are free of debris, and the pieces lay shiny red with blood on the table as Uncle Kristian's shoulder bleeds more than ever.

"Oh, you poor thing," I murmur, picking up a cotton pad to soak up the droplets.

Uncle Kristian doesn't seem to mind. In fact, he's smiling as I dab at his cuts.

"You're teasing me, aren't you? I would have noticed if a man like that had been sniffing around my niece. You're making him up out of thin air."

I cast him a look beneath my lashes. I'm not making him up. I have in all but name and the color of his eyes and hair described my Uncle Kristian. It's a pity that I already know exactly what I want in a future husband, but the man I'll someday marry will never measure up.

"You caught me," I say with a smile, and reach for the bottle of antiseptic. This will be worse than picking out the gravel, so I'll have to distract him even more. "I'll have to settle for someone weak or stupid who can't protect me or our children."

"Like hell you will. You're not settling for shit, princess. Now quit winding me up and get on with that antiseptic."

I look at him in surprise. "You knew what I was up to all along?"

"I always know what you're up to. Now get that stuff in my cuts."

"I hate hurting you," I mutter, putting a cotton pad over the bottle and upending it until the cotton is soaked.

"Don't worry. I like it when it's you."

My eyes widen. I understand the words he just said, but there's some meaning I'm missing. The answer is glimmering in his bright blue eyes, but I can't tell what it is.

"What do you mean?" I ask, and for some reason, I feel my cheeks heat.

"What I say, princess," he murmurs, stroking my long hair back from my neck so it falls down my back. "I like it when it's you."

I apply the pad gently to one of Uncle Kristian's cuts. He hisses through his teeth and his body tenses. As I keep working over the scrapes, he leans back on his hands and breathes harder. The rise and fall of his chest and the muscles of his stomach clenching and flexing against the pain are so distracting that I can't stop glancing at his body. I work slower and slower, but Uncle Kristian doesn't seem to mind one bit.

He looks…good. He looks different somehow, and he sounds different, too. I've seen Uncle Kristian without his shirt plenty of times, so why should today feel unusual?

He sinks his teeth into his lower lip and groans as I press the pad into the deepest scrape. The sound shoots straight down my spine and makes my knees weak.

What sound would he make if you dug your nails into his back?

I quickly look at what I'm doing, wondering where the hell that thought came from. I might not know what *I like being hurt when it's you* means, but I've seen enough movies to know what nails digging into men's backs signifies, and it's not a thought anyone should be having about their uncle.

Silence stretches between us as I keep dabbing at his cuts, and it's not one of our comfortable silences. It's filled with tension strung so tight it could launch a volley of arrows. Out of the corner of my eye, I see Uncle Kristian's gaze fixed on my face. I'm casting about desperately for a way to continue the conversation, when we hear the front door open and close, and I know my stepmom, brother, and sister are home.

Uncle Kristian glowers in the direction of their voices. "I thought they'd be longer."

As Chessa comes into the room with Lana and Arron behind her, she takes in Uncle Kristian perched shirtless on the kitchen table with me standing between his knees and purses her lips in disapproval. She and Uncle Kristian exchange looks that are downright hostile.

It's not only because of the motorcycle accident, but I don't understand what caused this rift. The two of them have never been the best of friends, but lately they seem to hate each other.

Chessa seems to be waiting for him to get off her kitchen table, but Uncle Kristian doesn't move.

"Hello, Chessa."

Instead of greeting her brother-in-law, Chessa turns to me. "Zenya, hurry up and finish what you're doing and go to bed. It's late."

I glance at the clock on the wall as Lana opens the refrigerator and gets out some juice. It's nearly two in the morning.

"My niece is busy," Uncle Kristian tells her in a voice as hard as granite. "Zenya can go to bed when she's finished so lovingly tending to me." He reaches up and tucks a strand of hair behind my ear, smiling at me.

For some reason, annoyance burns even brighter in Chessa's face, but instead of saying anything, she marches about the room, slamming kitchen cabinets and aggressively wiping down counters.

"Your stepmother is angry with me," Uncle Kristian says in Russian.

"*Da*," I reply, and continue in Russian, "she thinks it's your fault that Dad got hurt."

"That also."

I reach for the bandages to wrap them around his shoulder, but stop. "What else would she be angry about?"

"What isn't that woman angry about?"

Chessa is shaking out a fresh bag to line the trash. "Kristian, it's anti-social and inappropriate to carry on a conversation with Zenya in Russian when Lana, Arron, and I can't join in."

The muscle in Kristian's jaw flexes, a sure sign he's close to losing his temper. I place a placating hand on his chest and give him a meaningful look.

He glances at my hand and then murmurs, "I was asking if my beautiful niece minded that I've made her stay up late tending to my wounds."

Lana puts down her glass of juice and pretends to gag. "Stop calling her beautiful, Uncle Kristian. She's so full of herself already."

I smile as I unspool some bandages. Lana likes to tease me while other people can hear, but in private, she's told me several times that I'm never ever allowed to leave home, no matter what, because they all need me.

Kristian shoots her a glare. "Zenya *is* beautiful, and your sister isn't conceited. She has poise and grace beyond her years."

"Poise and grace beyond her years," Lana mocks, tipping her head from side to side as she rolls her eyes.

I smile a little at my sister's antics as I wrap the bandage around Uncle Kristian's shoulder.

"You see?" Uncle Kristian says to Lana, but not looking away from me. "You mock Zenya, but there's not a flicker of annoyance on her beautiful face. Your sister will be able to face down enemies who threaten her with death, things worse than death, and she won't bat an eyelash. Nerves of steel, this girl."

Chessa mutters something that sounds like *God, give me strength* and then walks out of the kitchen.

"Whatever," Lana says, flouncing off in pursuit of her stepmother.

I carefully wind a bandage around his bicep. "It's just my sister teasing me. It's hardly proof that I have nerves of steel."

Uncle Kristian raises a sardonic eyebrow at me. "And yet, in all my years, no one has enraged me more than my own brother."

"Brothers and sisters tease just to make you react. It's bait, and you shouldn't fall for it."

"But how will I sleep at night if I argue with Troian and I don't have the final word?"

I laugh and shake my head. "You're such a youngest sibling."

"You're such an eldest sibling," he throws back with a grin.

"You're a troublemaker, and this part of you is the worst." I touch his lips with my fingertips, and he kisses them, still smiling.

"You have no idea."

Butterflies flutter in my belly.

Arron yawns noisily and heads for the stairs.

"How was your dad when you left the hospital?" Uncle Kristian calls after him.

"He was telling us all about the motorcycle accident until Chessa told him to stop. She's mad about the whole thing. Goodnight, Zenya. 'Night, Uncle Kristian."

We call our goodnights after him. Switching to Russian, even though we're alone, Kristian says, "Chessa doesn't understand what it means to be a Belyaev. You only understand it if you were born to it, like you and Troian. Or raised in it like me."

I feel a tug in my chest, the same one I do every time I remember that Uncle Kristian and I aren't really related. I don't know why. I must be disappointed that he's not my real uncle and his powerful blood doesn't run in my veins. He's the one in my family whose skin truly feels like my skin. When his commanding aura brushes against mine, it feels like he's making me stronger. More daring. Braver. His thoughts are as readable as a book to me—just as mine are to him. In a crowded room, far apart and not speaking, when our eyes meet, we can have whole conversations.

That person is weak.

We should take advantage of this new development.

This place is boring. We should leave.

It's the sort of connection I've heard of twins sharing, and so the fact that Uncle Kristian isn't actually related to me is confusing. Frustrating. And—and—

I give a small shake of my head. I don't know what else it is or even how to put this restless feeling into words.

Uncle captures my chin briefly between his thumb and forefinger. "What's up, dandelion?"

I draw a bandage slowly through my fingers. The worst thing in the world would be to lose anyone else. I don't think I'd be able to bear it. "You'll always be my uncle, won't you?"

I expect him to reply with an immediate, defiant, *Of course I will*, but when he remains silent, I stop what I'm doing and stare at him in shock.

He considers this, and he's smiling. "Yes. Or no."

I blink at him in confusion. "What?"

"If I had my way it would be both yes and no."

"What's that supposed to mean?"

He just goes on gazing at me with that same speculative look in his frosty blue eyes. An expression that's close to wolfish.

I shake my head and go back to bandaging him. "Normally, I know exactly what you're thinking, but right now, I have no idea what's going on in that mind of yours." Except there's a warm feeling spreading low in my belly that makes my heart beat faster. My body is picking up on something my brain can't.

"That's probably a good thing for now," he murmurs, brushing his fingers through my hair.

I feel a familiar spurt of annoyance, the same as when Dad tells me he'll fill me in on something when I'm older. "You're starting to sound like Dad."

Uncle Kristian gives a low chuckle, and the warm feeling in my belly glows brighter. "I doubt that very much."

I finish pinning the bandages in place and testing to make sure they're secure, puzzling over Uncle Kristian's words. I'm always asking him and Dad to teach me more about what it means to be a Belyaev. To let me quit school and join them full time. Both of them say I have to get my high school diploma, but maybe Uncle Kristian is hinting that he's willing to let me in on a few more of their secrets.

If anything happens to Dad—please don't let anything happen to Dad, but that thirty percent chance is haunting me, and I can't help but think that if anything *does*—Uncle Kristian will step up and take over the family, and he'll need a second-in-command, just as he was second to Dad. Kristian is close with another man who works for us called Mikhail, but Mikhail isn't a Belyaev. If anyone should take their place by his side it should be me.

Uncle Kristian has always told me that it doesn't matter if I'm a girl. It's what's in my heart that matters. My strength and determination to protect this family and help us prosper.

When I'm finished, I wrap my arms around Uncle Kristian's neck and move closer to him, carefully embracing where he's not injured, and rest my forehead against his temple.

With my eyes closed, I whisper in Russian, "You're not allowed to be reckless from now on, and I don't want to hear about how you might not be my uncle one day. That's not allowed."

"But if I'm not reckless, I won't be me anymore, whether I'm your Uncle Kristian or not."

I draw away a little so I can look into his bright, hard eyes. We're mere inches from each other. "You can't be a little more careful, even for me?"

His eyes run over my face. My eyes. The tip of my nose. My lips. "Not even for you. But you don't want me to stop, do you, princess?"

Stop being Uncle Kristian? "Well, when you put it like that…"

Dad is my home, but my heart beats faster for Uncle Kristian.

So, no.

I don't want him to change.

I never want him to stop being exactly who he is.

"I didn't think so." Uncle Kristian draws me closer, stroking the nape of my neck and embracing me tighter in his strong arms.

"I said bed, Zenya," Chessa calls from the next room, and I realize she's been calling out to me for several minutes.

Uncle Kristian and I smile as we disentangle ourselves from each other and he scoops all the bloody bits of gravel into the trash while I pack up the first aid kit. I fetch him one of Dad's shirts to wear home and he orders a car for himself.

At the front door, he turns to me and touches my hair. "Tomorrow, I'm going to meet with our men and tell them what Troian and I saw when we went to take care of that gang. How many men. The exits. Their weapons. Everything they need to know to finish the job for us. Want to come with me?"

I gasp in delight and grab his arm. Dimly I'm aware that an offer to hear the kill orders for half a dozen men isn't what's supposed to excite a teenage girl, but after seeing Dad lying in that hospital bed and picking gravel out of my uncle's shoulder, I'm burning for some Belyaev justice. "Yes, please. I'd love that."

Uncle Kristian smiles and kisses my cheek. "Goodnight, beautiful. I'll pick you up at eight tomorrow night," he whispers in my ear, before heading out the door into the darkness.

I watch him go with a broad smile and then close the door and head upstairs to bed.

I've showered and changed into my pajamas, and I'm sitting up in bed brushing my hair when Chessa enters the room. She looks tired and worried, but she smiles at me.

"I'll be going to see Troian at seven-thirty in the morning before picking up the kids from Eleanor's. I can take you, Lana, and Arron with me and drop you at school afterward if you like."

"Yes, please. I'd love to see Dad again before he has his operation."

We discuss the scheduling and details of his surgery for several minutes. I expect Chessa to say goodnight after that, but she hesitates and then sits down on the bed.

Placing her hand on my leg over the blankets, she says, "Zenya, there's something I wanted to talk to you about."

I wait, terrified of what she's going to say, the word *cancer* looming in my mind. Please don't let the doctors have found tumors in Dad's leg.

"Why does Kristian switch to Russian whenever I enter the room?" Chessa asks.

I sigh in relief. Oh, is that all? Still, it's a little annoying that she's bringing up the Russian again. That's my thing with Uncle Kristian, and it has nothing to do with her.

"He doesn't always switch to Russian," I say, evading the question.

Chessa won't be evaded. "What Uncle Kristian does in his own house is up to him, but I feel like he's undermining your father's authority and mine by having secret conversations with you."

It's like she's implying there's something inappropriate about Uncle Kristian and me simply talking to each other in Russian. We're doing what he and Dad have done together a million times when my brothers and sisters are in the room.

"We talk about Belyaev business. It's important that the kids don't overhear what we're talking about because they might get scared."

Chessa fixes me with a concerned expression. "You're a kid, too, Zenya. You're sixteen and still in school. I feel like your uncle forgets that sometimes."

Good.

I want him to forget it.

"Secrets are important to Belyaevs," I say quietly, twisting the corner of a sheet with my fingers. It makes me uncomfortable to argue with Chessa because she's only ever been kind to me, but she should know by now that a lot of our business has to be done in secret because it's dangerous and illegal.

"I'm not talking about family business. I'm talking about you and Kristian."

I frown at her. "What about me and Uncle Kristian?"

"You two are always whispering to each other. I have to say your name ten times before you notice anyone in the room but him. If it were up to me, that man would learn some boundaries if he wanted to keep entering foot in this house."

"What boundaries?" I ask, confused by the idea that someone in our family would attempt to tell Uncle Kristian what to do when he does so much for all of us.

Chessa passes an exasperated hand over her brow. "A grown man shouldn't have secret little talks with a sixteen-year-old girl, even if she is his niece. It's not natural. Hasn't he got anything better to do?"

As much as I love Chessa, I feel anger spark to life in my chest, though I struggle not to give in to it and raise my voice. I was wondering whether to tell her where I'm going with Uncle Kristian tomorrow night, but now I know I won't be volunteering the information.

"I'm not really interested in what's natural. I haven't had a very natural upbringing, remember?"

Of course she remembers. She was there, and she should also remember that Uncle Kristian and I are the reason things didn't get much worse that night. It could have been carnage.

55

Well, it was.

Just not for the Belyaevs.

"And as for him having better things to do, how can you be so ungrateful, Chessa? Who's been looking after all of us while Dad's been sick?"

Chessa takes a deep breath as if she's struggling to keep her own temper under control. "I just worry about you, Zenya. I feel as if your father and Kristian made a mistake sharing so much with you at such a young age. Fourteen was too young to—"

"That wasn't their decision, was it?" It's on the tip of my tongue to say I'm glad it happened, but that would be cruel considering what that night did to Chessa and my older brothers and sisters. They all still have nightmares about it.

My stepmother shakes her head sadly. "No, it wasn't."

I reach forward and take her hand. "I'm fine, and I'm happy with the way things are. But thank you for worrying about me."

Chessa doesn't look happy, but she kisses me goodnight and leaves me to sleep. I lay down, pulling the blankets up and snuggling them around my chin.

With my eyes closed, I run through my plans for the following day. I'll see Dad before his surgery and then I have school, which will be dull, but there's nothing I can do about that. In the afternoon, I'll head over to the Silo and take inventory, and then after dinner—I smile in the darkness—I'll be doing some real Belyaev work with Uncle Kristian.

Uncle Kristian will be giving orders and I'll be standing by his side, which is exactly where I crave to be, always.

Chapter Four

KRISTIAN

The moment I step foot in Troian's house on New Year's Eve, Chessa locks hostile eyes with me. She's standing with her sister, Eleanor, and both sisters are wearing spangled party dresses and high heels. I can tell that Chessa has confided every terrible thing I've done lately to her beloved Eleanor by the way the sisters glare at me like I'm the big, bad wolf who's come to blow the house down.

They can give me as many sulky bitch looks as they want. Troian's the one in charge in this house, and I'm his beloved brother, so Chessa can kiss my ass.

"There's my scoundrel of a brother." Troian's voice booms out across the living room. The crowd parts, and I see him seated in a recliner with his leg in a cast extended in front of him. "Kristian's always breaking rules, and now he's breaking bones as well. Have you been causing trouble tonight, Kristian?"

I smile as cousins and various family members and friends laugh at Troian's joke, though I'm not sure my smile reaches my eyes. I want to remind Troian that he was the one who insisted he drive, and if he'd let me take charge of the motorcycle, we wouldn't have crashed.

But that's not my role in this little performance. He's the reliable one and I'm the fuck-up. These are the parts we've been cast in all our lives.

"Not as much trouble as I'd like to cause," I say with a broad smile, and then glance around the room for Zenya. Everyone thinks I'm joking, and the room erupts with laughter again.

I can't see my niece anywhere, so I step forward and embrace my brother. "*S Novym Godom.*" *Happy New Year.* "How are you?"

He gestures at the cast in annoyance. "I can't get up the stairs to my own bedroom and I can't do anything else that a man is supposed to do. I'll live, I suppose," he finishes grudgingly.

The adventurous clout of being in a motorcycle crash seems to be wearing off. If I know my brother, he'll make life hell for me, Mikhail, and every other man who answers to him over the coming weeks, venting his frustration to us at being confined to the house. My brother is a good *Pakhan* when all is well, but when he's aggravated, he can be as bad-tempered as a bear with a thorn in his paw.

"Apparently you're unkillable," I say, patting his shoulder. "Aren't we lucky?"

I walk through the crowd of party guests looking for my niece, but before I can move deeper into the house, Chessa strides across the room toward me, high heels clacking on the marble tiles and murder sparking in her eyes.

"You are unbelievable, Kristian," she hisses. Over her shoulder, Eleanor is watching me like a hawk, daring me to even look the wrong way at her sister. As if she has any say in what happens in this house.

"So I've heard." I slide my thumb along my jaw and smile sardonically at Chessa as I try to move past her.

Chessa steps in front of me. "I didn't mean that as a compliment. How dare you take Zenya to a meeting where you were discussing—" she peers left and right and whispers "—*felonies*."

"She told you about that, did she?"

"Only because that girl still has enough decency not to lie to her own stepmother, but I can assure you she didn't want to."

It's sweet that Zenya still believes you shouldn't lie to the people you love. I almost hope she never loses that innocence. My brother's second wife continues to lecture me in angry whispers about what I do with my own damn niece. Zenya is a straight A student, exceptional at running the Silo, and a perfect role model for her brothers and sisters. What's more, she's hungry for new and exciting things. If it weren't for me, Zenya would be bored out of her mind and she'd never have any fun, either.

I feel a warm glow as I remember sitting down to a poker game with her and some of the boys after the meeting. They were all fooled by her innocent, slightly confused expression as we played, but I wasn't. She purposefully threw three hands and then went in for the kill, winning an enormous pot and taking all of Mikhail's and Andrei's chips.

What a little vixen. I couldn't be prouder.

Chessa starts on about the motorcycle accident yet again, and my warm glow vanishes. "Wrap it up, Chessa. I need a drink."

Chessa bristles with anger. "Troian is sick, remember?"

I glare at her. I wasn't likely to forget that my brother has lung cancer.

"And you. Don't you think you behave too recklessly for a man of thirty-four?"

"Not really," I say, trying to signal the waiter with champagne at the other end of the room to come this way.

"If you have to carry on like a complete id—"

I flash her a glare, and she closes her mouth. She might be my brother's wife and rightfully angry with me, but she knows better than to start calling me names.

Chessa takes a calming breath and tries again. "Just leave my husband and stepdaughter out of your schemes from now on."

I laugh as if she's told a joke for the benefit of people passing us in the hall and embrace her like I'm about to wish her a Happy New Year. In her ear, I say, "Fuck off, Chessa. I'll do whatever the hell I want."

Chessa pushes me away, her face white with anger while I laugh and straighten my cuffs. Go on, say you'll tell on me to Troian.

I dare you.

But Chessa won't because she and I both know that she's already overstepped the line tonight by sticking her nose into family business. Marrying Troian doesn't make her a fucking Belyaev. Not in the true meaning of the name.

I watch in amusement as she flounders in front of me, and then she turns away and greets one of her newly arrived friends with a sparkling, "Thank you so much for coming! Happy New Year."

I grit my teeth and make my way through the party guests. If Chessa dropped dead tomorrow, I'd fucking celebrate. She's been busting my balls ever since she married Troian five years ago. We're not accountants or shopkeepers. We're in the Bratva, as she well knows, and there's risk that comes with that. If Troian isn't willing to get his hands dirty once in a while, he'll lose the respect of our men.

The living room is filled with family and dozens of children. I can see Zenya's younger brother and sister and Troian and Chessa's small children. Several of my nephews and nieces rush over and cling to my legs, and they squeal with laughter as I walk around the room pretending I don't know they're there. They're joined by some cousins' kids and soon I have five small children hanging off me.

Zenya enters the room, looking like an angel in a snow-white chiffon dress, and that's the end of fun Uncle Kristian. I stop walking and tell them, "Off you go. All of you. I want to talk to Zenya."

They pout and whine but let go of me, running off to continue the game with a cousin of mine. I turn toward Zenya, but Chessa steps in front of me yet again and grabs my arm.

This woman is testing my fucking patience.

"Why don't you leave her alone tonight? Let the girl have some fun instead of always being with you. There's a young man I want her to meet."

A man?

Over Chessa's dead and rotting corpse.

"What do you mean? I'm fun Uncle Kristian." I glare at Chessa until she removes her hand from my arm.

No one tells me what I can and can't do with my own niece.

I keep glaring at my sister-in-law until she turns away from me. Then I grab her arm and yank her back to me so fast that she gasps. My fingers dig viciously into her arm as I whisper through clenched teeth, "If Zenya talks to any man but me tonight, I will make you cry, and that's a fucking promise."

Just then, one of her children runs past us, a boy of seven or so. I don't know his name. I can't keep up with all her children. She brought three into her marriage with Troian and has had another two since they wed.

I let my gaze follow him significantly, and Chessa turns pale.

I wouldn't hurt one of her brats, but she's never been sure of what I'm capable of since the home invasion two years ago. For four hours she listened to the screaming, and she never once said thank you. That's gratitude for you.

Not that I did it for her.

I did it for Zenya.

Chessa wrenches herself from my grip and hurries away from me, clutching her hand to her chest.

I don't even need to move toward her. Zenya spots me all by herself and hurries to my side. My dark thoughts vanish immediately, and I smile down at her. "Hello, princess. Have you got a kiss for your uncle?"

She gazes up at me with a wretched expression. "I had to tell Chessa where you took me last week. I didn't want to, but she demanded I tell her and…"

I place a finger over her lips. "You couldn't lie to Chessa. It's all right, I understand."

I don't blame Zenya. Chessa should mind her goddamn business.

Zenya takes my hand and holds it tightly. "I'm sorry. Was she really angry with you?"

"I didn't notice."

Zenya gently touches my shoulder, her doll-like blue eyes filled with worry. "How are your scrapes?"

At last, some sympathy in this house for my war wounds.

"Don't worry about me. Let me take a look at you." I raise her hand over her head, turning her in a circle so I can admire her from every angle. Her waist-length silvery hair hangs in long, loose curls down her back. Diamond earrings are sparkling in her ears, and I feel a thump of pleasure as I realize they're the ones I brought back from Russia for her birthday.

"You're beautiful, Zenya," I murmur, drinking in every detail of her.

"I suppose I'll have to stay home next time there's anything really interesting to do," she says, finishing her turn and looking crestfallen.

I lower her hand and tug her into my arms, catching her lightly about the waist. "No. I want you with me."

She smiles, and a faint pink blush blooms across her cheeks, making her look even prettier. My niece is my delight. She's my favorite of Troian's children, and I'm her favorite person in the world.

"Chessa says you're putting me in danger."

"And what do you think?" I murmur, tucking a curl behind her ear. Her body is flush against mine and her slender fingers are stroking my shirt. Her lips are glossy and wet-looking. Fuck, I would give anything to kiss her right here in front of everyone, but that would be crossing one line too many for my brother.

"You wouldn't let me be in any danger," she replies.

"You're right, I'd die first."

Across the room, a boy I don't recognize is staring at Zenya, and I presume this must be the young man Chessa wanted her to meet. He's around eighteen and he's got the sort of looks that teenage girls seem to fawn over, judging from the hundreds of pop music videos I've been assaulted with over the decades in this house.

A hot, prickling sensation stabs my flesh. Zenya's only allowed to be devoted to me. If she marries, her husband is going to be my constant envy. I don't know how I'll keep my jealousy under control. I haven't ruled out making his death look like an accident the night before the wedding.

If she ever gets engaged. I haven't decided whether I'll let her because Zenya belongs to me. I shouldn't have to share her with anyone else. The only reason Troian doesn't get on my nerves is that he barely has time for his daughter. So most days she's all mine.

The boy takes a step toward us. I loop my arm around Zenya's waist and draw her toward the double doors. "Let's go outside. It's nearly midnight."

Fireworks have been set up all along the river at the bottom of the lawn that sweeps down from the mansion. We walk around the garden together, looking at the flowers in the moonlight as the music and the laughter of the party recedes behind us.

"Do you think Dad's looking well?"

I look at her sharply, my stomach in free fall that she's about to tell me that Troian's cancer is back. But no, he would have told me himself if that was the case. His prognosis is dire, but it's not necessarily a death sentence. We just have to wait and hope that the worst doesn't happen.

It would be terrible to lose my brother, but it would fucking destroy Zenya.

I get a flash of memory from her mother's funeral. Ten-year-old Zenya clinging to a numb and silent Troian on one side and me on the other, crying pitifully all the way through the service. I've never felt so helpless in my life. Ever since then, she's anxious to protect her little brothers and sisters and has moments of being clingy with Troian and me.

Fuck, I like it when she's clingy with me.

I like it a lot.

"He's looking better than ever," I assure her. "I'll probably take him out to crush more skulls this weekend."

"Where? Whose skulls?"

I give her a sidelong smile. "Wouldn't you like to know?"

"Yes, I would! I want to know everything."

I'm completely making it up, but my plan was to distract her from thinking about Troian's cancer and it's working. "Ah, sucks to be you, because I'm not telling."

"Uncle Kristian, you tell me right now." Zenya pokes me in the ribs and tugs on the T-shirt I'm wearing beneath my suit jacket, insisting I tell her everything. I let her do whatever she wants to me because it's an excuse for me to touch her while pretending to fend her off. She smells warm and sweet in my arms, like tropical flowers, and I'm laughing for the first time all week.

She has a hand beneath my T-shirt on my bare stomach when the countdown begins. People have lined up on the terrace.

Zenya turns and glances over her shoulder. "Should we join everyone else?"

I stare at the outline of her hand beneath my clothing. "Let's stay here."

A moment later, fireworks burst overhead.

Zenya looks up with a gasp of delight, and a smile spreads over her face.

Nothing that's happening up there could draw my attention away from the girl standing next to me. My eyes drop to her mouth. I gave myself a talking to earlier, that under no circumstances am I to kiss my niece on the mouth at midnight, no matter if we find ourselves alone or how pretty she looks with all the colored lights painting her face.

But that doesn't stop me from wondering if she'll kiss me. I've imagined that about a thousand times. How I'd laugh like I'm surprised and pretend that it hadn't occurred to me in a million years that the two of us might ever kiss.

Oh, Zenya, you shouldn't do that. I'm your uncle, remember?

Then, as she's blushing and apologizing, I'd draw her beneath a tree out of her family's sight and kiss her again. Harder. Deeper.

And confirm myself to be the terrible person everyone thinks I am.

"Happy New Year, princess," I murmur, taking her in my arms and kissing her cheek.

She throws her arms around my neck and hugs me. "Happy New Year!"

I turn her to face the fireworks and wrap my arms around her from behind, one forearm around her waist and the other across her chest. She reaches up and holds on to me as she gazes at the burning colors overhead, and her slender fingers slip into mine.

I'm not actually going to do anything with my niece. That would be messed up. Holding her like this? Obsessing over every little thing about her and inhaling her scent like a man addicted? It's fine. I've got my shit locked down. Zenya will never know.

I tuck a lock of her silver hair behind her ear and gaze admiringly at her profile. That adorable turned-up nose. Her Cupid's bow mouth shining with lip gloss. Troian's always so busy with work, his wife, and his younger children, so it falls to me to make sure Zenya's happy. She sees me as her uncle and that's all I'll ever be to her. Trying to change her mind about that would be wicked.

I'm not going to do that.

But if Zenya kissed me...

Chessa comes out into the backyard with a tray of champagne glasses, smiling as she hands them around. She sees me with my arms around my niece and glowers at us. Then she catches my murderous glare and she stumbles and nearly drops the tray.

I give her a hard, sarcastic smile and drop it before I look away. Fuck off. I can hug my niece if I want to.

I meant what I said about making her cry if that boy comes near my Zenya. It would be a pleasure coming up with a way to make Chessa suffer.

Two days later, I'm blissfully unconscious when my ringing phone drags me from slumber.

I fumble for my phone on the nightstand and squint at the screen. It's just past seven in the morning, an obscene hour of the day, but I have to answer if it's Troian, and I always answer if it's Zenya.

It's Mikhail, my friend, and the foot soldier I trust the most.

He can fuck off.

I stuff the phone under my pillow and go back to sleep.

But Mikhail rings again. I yank the phone out and answer it. "This better be important or I will use your balls for target practice."

"It's Chessa. She's dead."

I blink hard, wondering if I'm still asleep. "What?"

"You heard me."

I sit up slowly. "How?"

A car accident? Did I get drunk and put a hit on her? I know I've fantasized about it before.

"She must have got up in the middle of the night to eat some leftover Chinese food. A dumpling got stuck in her throat. She choked to death. Troian found her body on the kitchen floor this morning."

My mouth twitches. "She choked? The woman who's never been able to shut the fuck up choked on a dumpling?"

I burst out laughing.

"I knew you would laugh," Mikhail says with a heavy sigh. "That's why I wanted to tell you before your brother did. She's a mother, you know."

"I know, I know. But you have to admit it's funny."

"You're one dark motherfucker, Kristian," Mikhail mutters in an undertone, and I realize he must be calling from the house.

"How's Zenya?"

"She seems fine. Right now she's making breakfast for the kids. I don't think she was very attached to her stepmother."

You and me both, princess.

I'm sorry for Troian. I'm sorry for Chessa's kids. But I'm not sorry I never have to look at that irritating bitch ever again.

"Troian's a mess," Mikhail adds. "But I have to head off."

I throw the covers off and swing my legs out of bed. "I'm on my way."

Feeling pleased with the day so far, I take a freezing shower to wake myself up, dress in something somber, and head around to Troian's to give him my deepest, deepest condolences.

I find my brother in the living room with several of his older children, along with Chessa's sister, Eleanor. She's crying with the kids, but Troian just looks shell-shocked.

Troian's leg cast is covered in colored marker, courtesy of all the kids. I clasp him around the shoulders and then sit down next to him, and we watch Eleanor on the opposite sofa with the children.

"She was only twenty-nine," Troian says hoarsely. "I thought she'd fainted when I came out of the downstairs guest room this morning. Then I saw her face."

"At least one of the kids didn't find her," I murmur, thinking of Zenya.

Troian gives me a tired smile in gratitude for my uncharacteristic sensitivity. "Thank you for being here, Kristian. Will you check on Zenya for me? Her brother and sister don't remember much about the day their mom died, but she does."

"Of course I will," I reply, getting to my feet.

I find Zenya in the kitchen with the younger children. Her blonde hair is in an untidy pile on her head and her beautiful face is pinched with emotion, but she manages a small smile when she sees me.

She's making chocolate chip pancakes and pouring cups of juice, her hands fluttering from frying pan to juice carton to cooking utensils as if she's afraid to stop moving.

I turn the heat down on the stove and turn her gently to face me. "Are you okay, dandelion?"

Zenya locks her arms around my waist and buries her face in my chest. She stands like that for a moment, breathing hard, her whole body rigid.

"I'm fine. I am. I'm fine." She whispers it over and over as if she can make herself believe it.

Zenya's always been afraid of giving in to one moment of weakness. Most of the time she's not bothered by anything. Blood. Violence. Torture. Death. Even—

I grit my teeth hard, because while the memory of that man on my fourteen-year-old niece doesn't bother her, it makes me rage so hard I might spontaneously detonate and take out the neighborhood.

But other things have the power to shatter Zenya's heart in a second, and one of them is the memory of her mom dying. This is why she needs me, because I can tell when she needs extra support and love even when she won't ask for it.

A moment later she lets me go and turns back to the stove, turning the heat up and continuing with the pancakes. Brushing a strand of hair away from her face, she shoots me a wobbly smile and whispers, "I'm fine, really."

"Sure, princess," I murmur. But I'm not going anywhere.

I eat three of her pancakes because none of the kids are very hungry, and she's worried that she made them wrong, then I help her clean up.

It's usually bedlam in this house in the morning with so many kids. There's Zenya and her brother and sister, Lana and Arron; three kids from Chessa's first marriage, Felix, Noah, and Micaela; and two more that she had with Troian, Nadia and Danil. This morning there's mostly silence, punctuated by crying.

Zenya's face is pale as she stacks the dishwasher, but no matter how many times I tell her to sit down, she shakes her head.

Chessa's youngest, Danil, is just sixteen months old, and Zenya scoops him out of his highchair when he starts to fuss.

"I know. You want your mom." Zenya's face crumples and she starts to cry silently. I feel my heart turn over in my chest because Zenya almost never cries. She won't let herself, and sure enough, a moment later she takes a shuddering breath, blinks hard, and squashes her feelings down.

I stroke her cheek with my forefinger. This must be hell for her. The eldest child. The responsible one who has to hold it together for everyone else. I can't relate because that person has always been my brother Troian, but I admire Zenya so much whenever she takes the lead for her siblings. It's impressive. It's—

Don't think it, Kristian.

It's sexy.

Well, it is. I can't help the way I feel. It doesn't mean I'm going to act on it. I'll just admire her every chance I get and murder any man who looks at her. What's wrong with that?

I slide my hand around the nape of her neck and gently draw her closer to me. "Dandelion. Beautiful girl. You're allowed to cry."

"I'll do it later," she whispers thickly. "I'll set the baby off if I do it now. Distract me, please?"

I go on stroking the nape of her neck while she rocks the baby in her arms.

"You'll make a wonderful mother one day," I murmur, trying not to sound too interested in the idea. At thirty-four, it's about time I fathered a few children. Too bad the woman I want to be the mother of my children is my niece and only sixteen years old. Too bad she can never actually be mine.

Not that I haven't thought about it. God, she'd be perfect as a mother. She's already a little tigress around all these children.

She gives me a tired smile. "I hope so. I feel like I've had a lifetime of experience with babies already."

I run my thumb slowly along Zenya's jaw. "Whereas I have no

idea about children."

"You're not so clueless. You looked after me sometimes."

My eyebrows lift in surprise. "You remember that?"

Troian and Anna would occasionally drop her off at my house for me to look after while they went out in the city.

Zenya rocks the baby slowly in her arms as she talks softly. "Of course I remember. We would play hide-and-seek. When we went out, you'd let me steer your car while I sat in your lap. My first memory is of you. I must have been three, or even younger. Mom or Dad said you were on your way over, and I stood on the sofa so I could see out the front window, waiting for your car to pull into the driveway. I remember it was red."

I think for a moment, trying to remember a red car. Then I laugh because I do remember it. "The Mustang. I took you to a diner and you drew horses in crayons because you liked the horse on my car." I only had that car for a few months because it got rear-ended.

Zenya smiles up at me. "You remember."

"Of course I remember."

Whenever I came to the house, Zenya would shriek with pleasure and run into my arms the moment she saw me. Troian would scold me for playing favorites with his children, and I would insist that I wasn't while secretly giving her another present.

"You took me to a shooting range for my sixth birthday. Mom and Dad were furious with you."

"I probably shouldn't have done that," I say ruefully, rubbing my hand over my jaw. It's rough with stubble because I didn't have time to shave this morning. I remember Zenya in a Little Miss Messy

T-shirt wearing safety goggles and ear protectors. I didn't actually let her hold a weapon, but she sat on the barrier between my arms as I fired a Glock 17.

"I'm glad you did. I'm a very good shot now. You set off my competitive instincts because you were always perfect."

I give her a smug smile. "Well, I wouldn't say perfect." Who am I kidding? Yes, I would.

Speaking of perfect, I stroke Zenya's cheek. She closes her eyes and leans into my touch.

"You'll make a wonderful father one day," she whispers.

I nearly groan and cover her mouth with mine. Zenya shouldn't say shit like that while she's holding a baby and so very obviously enjoying my touch. I need to stop thinking about fucking my sixteen-year-old niece and getting her pregnant like a goddamn psycho.

But I can't help myself. Zenya has a plush mouth that was made for kissing. I just know that she sinks her teeth into that full lower lip while she's touching herself. What I wouldn't give to see her in that state. Tits bare. Fingers working her clit. Flushed and breathing hard, her beautiful eyes sparkling with pleasure.

"A good father? Maybe I will," I murmur, tucking a loose strand of her silvery hair behind her ear.

I want to go on standing here with Zenya and talking to her for much longer, but Troian calls for her, and then her brother does as well. Everyone always needs Zenya for something. Don't they understand that I was here first?

A few hours later, Zenya takes the youngest children upstairs for a nap, and I can tell I'm not needed here anymore. I wait for her to come back downstairs and then ask her to walk me out to my car.

Outside, it's overcast and breezy, and we watch heavy clouds scud across the sky.

Zenya wraps her arms around herself as the wind cuts through her thin dress. "Yesterday Dad was talking about teaching me more of the family business. He's seen how good I am at coordinating the Silo."

The Silo is our stock of illegal goods, though the location often changes. Zenya's been tracking incoming and outgoing merchandise for the last year using a series of encrypted spreadsheets on a hidden server. She's so efficient at it that she can keep on top of it alongside going to school and doing her homework.

"Finally. I'm glad to hear it." I've been telling my brother to get her more involved since she started asking him to include her.

"I was hoping you might teach me a thing or two as well." She shoots me a sideways glance with a smile on her lips.

"Me, princess?" I return her smile, knowing she means the criminal activities her dad thinks she's too young to know about.

"Who better than my dangerous uncle?"

Absolutely fucking no one. "Sure, you and I can talk about it as soon as things settle down here." I glance back at the house. "Who's organizing the funeral?"

"Eleanor is going to figure things out with Dad. Will you come back tomorrow?"

I stroke her cheek with my thumb. "Of course I will. Until then, take care of yourself and get some sleep tonight. Don't let everyone exhaust you."

Zenya suddenly throws her arms around my neck and holds

me close. "Thank you, Uncle Kristian. I don't know what I'd do without you."

I take advantage of the way she's pressed close against me to swiftly plant a kiss on her slender throat. My teeth want to follow my lips, but I make sure the impulse stays just an impulse. "Of course. Where else would I be?"

She pulls away slowly, letting her fingers run down my forearms and across my palms, before heading back toward the front door. I feel a pang as she goes, wishing I could take her away from the suffocating grief in that house. But they all need her too much.

Zenya's strong, I remind myself. She'll be okay until tomorrow.

I lean against my car watching Zenya until she gets safely back inside the house and closes the front door. There's a light feeling in my heart. Things are going to be better now. No more Chessa picking up on my over-interest in Zenya. No more Chessa trying to push other men at my girl.

I'll take Zenya out soon, just the two of us. Give her some fun for a change. Let her breathe. Make her smile. And keep other men far away from her because they're unworthy clods who have no business breathing near Zenya, let alone looking at her.

We'll be working together more as well. Who knows what might happen in some dark warehouse at midnight with the scent of blood in the air…

I groan and pull my phone from my pocket and place a call. Don't even think about it, Kristian.

Mikhail answers. "What's up? How's the family?"

"Not great. Get some of the boys together. We're going out."

"We are? Why?"

I get into my car and start the engine, and a grin spreads over my face. "Why do you think? The bitch is dead. We're celebrating."

I wake up at ten in the morning with a pounding headache, still wearing my clothes from the night before. Out of habit, I check my phone, then wish I hadn't. There are half a dozen messages from Troian telling me to get around to the house immediately.

I groan and roll out of bed.

Duty fucking calls.

Maybe I shouldn't have celebrated quite so hard last night. I seem to remember leaving the strip club with the boys around three. We went to one of their apartments and ordered food, but then someone opened a bottle of vodka and I don't think I ate anything.

I blast the shower at full heat, and then freezing cold, hoping it will sober me up. Today is going to be painful.

I still feel a little drunk from last night, so I grab a coffee from the shop on the corner, swallow some painkillers, and order a car to take me to Troian's house instead of driving.

By the time I arrive, the painkillers and caffeine have kicked in, and I'm starting to feel human again. The plan for today is to support Troian, make sure that Zenya is all right, and try not to keel over.

I knock on the front door, and a moment later, it opens. It's Zenya on the other side, and I smile at her. "Hey, princess. How are you…"

My smile dies as I see how red raw her eyes are.

Tears spill down her cheeks and she asks in a choked whisper, "How could you, Uncle Kristian?"

I gaze at her in astonishment.

Me?

What did I do?

"What's wrong? What's happened?" I reach for her hand and she lets me take it, but her grip is loose.

My Zenya, not holding me back?

As we stare at each other, I run through all the interactions I've had with my niece and the thoughts I've had about her recently. My fantasies have been depraved, but I haven't acted on them or even mentioned them to anyone. I've never told anyone about wanting Zenya. When I left her yesterday, she was tired and sad, but she smiled at me.

The only thing I can think of that might have upset Zenya is that Troian knows I made a vague threat toward Chessa two days before she died. What does he think I did, crept around here in the middle of the night and shoved a dumpling down her throat?

I know better than to start volunteering information that might get me into even deeper shit, so I play dumb. "You're going to have to help me out here. I don't know what I'm supposed to have done."

Zenya steps back with her head down, allowing me inside. "Dad's in the living room. He wants to talk to you."

I stare at my niece as I pass her. Not once in all her sixteen years has she not greeted me with a hug.

I make my way down the hall and turn into the living room. Troian's sitting in an armchair in an empty room, his crutches leaning against the arm of the chair.

My older brother turns his head slowly to look at me. There's grief on his face, but something else that wasn't there when I said goodbye yesterday.

Burning fury.

And it's directed at me.

"Is there anything you want to tell me, Kristian?"

I never tell him anything if I don't have to, so I play for time. "You sounded just like Dad then."

Explain yourself, Kristian. Why can't you be more like your brother, Kristian?

Troian slams his fist on the side table next to him. "Don't be smart with me. Answer the fucking question."

"I would if you'd stop being so goddamn cryptic. What is it that I'm supposed to have done?"

Troian pulls out his phone, unlocks it, and holds it out. I step closer and see that he's showing me a photo on his screen.

I realize I'm looking at a picture of myself in the strip club last night. I'm sitting on a red velvet sofa with my crew all around me. There's a girl on my lap, a brunette wearing lots of makeup, a spangled G-string and nothing else. Across her bare tits is a word scrawled in red lipstick. *CHESSA.*

My expression in the photograph is nasty. Vindictive. Both my hands are around the stripper's throat as I pretend to choke her.

Shit.

That.

I'd forgotten about that.

I was on my fifth or six bourbon on top of several glasses of champagne, and I'd just been ranting to Mikhail and some of the other boys about how much I hated my brother's wife. Someone had found a lipstick between the sofa cushions and it was lying on the table. On a whim, I picked it up and wrote *CHESSA* across the stripper's tits and pretended to choke her to make the boys laugh. To make myself laugh.

Now that I think about it, I remember being momentarily dazzled at the time, but I didn't connect the light with a camera flash. It was over in a second and then I forgot all about it. It was just one moment of a six-hour drinking session and was far from representative of the entire night.

But someone in the club took my fucking picture.

How do I play this? My brain is still sluggish with too much alcohol, but I know it didn't fucking mean anything. I was blowing off steam after a long day of seeing my girl and my brother utterly miserable without being able to do anything about it. Zenya was the most upset I've seen her since she was ten years old, and it got to me. I never wanted to see her like that ever again, and in my mind it was all Chessa's fault for not being able to chew a dumpling like a normal fucking person.

I'm tempted to make light of what I did or brush it off, but I can see from Troian's face that he's not going to be able to brush this off when his grief over Chessa's death is so raw.

I put my hand over my heart and meet his gaze with my sincerest expression. "*Mea culpa.* That was a terrible thing that I did. I have no excuse."

"No. Not *mea culpa*. That's not going to cut it, Kristian. This photo," he seethes, brandishing his phone at me, "has been shared by every business contact and associate I have in this city and beyond. Everyone in the family has seen it. All our men have seen it. I've been made a laughingstock by my own brother. I'm grieving, my children have lost their mother, and you went out and did the most disrespectful thing anyone could fucking think of. Why must you give me yet another massive headache?"

Oh, here we go. We've had this conversation many times over the past two decades.

Why did you start that fight, Kristian?

Why must you piss everyone off, Kristian?

Why did you rip that man's guts out and strew them all over the basement floor, Kristian? I was trying to close a deal with his father, Kristian.

I know I'm just about no one's favorite flavor in the ice-cream shop, but I don't give a damn about anyone's opinion of me except for my niece's, and she thinks I'm fucking wonderful. Troian's business contacts don't care that I'm a cunt. Having a crazy, unpredictable brother probably helps him.

"I fail to see how this matters. It's just a picture and I already said I'm sorry."

"It matters because you've disrespected my family and my dead fucking wife!" Troian shouts. He grips the arms of his chair, frustrated he can't get up and swing a punch at me because he's got a broken leg. He didn't blame me for crashing the motorcycle at the time, but I can feel all my recent misdeeds stacking up against me. It's tempting to go all in and tell him what he should really be angry about.

You think that's bad? Well, listen to this. I want to fuck your daughter. I want to fuck her so bad some days it's all I can think about. I can't function without seeing her. I want to fuck my baby into her and make her my wife. I've spilled so much cum fantasizing over this girl I could fill three Olympic-sized swimming pools. Waiting for her to turn a reasonable age while I dream about making my move is. Killing. Me. Slowly.

That's something he could be rightfully angry with me about.

Not this stupid shit with Chessa.

"Chessa got on my last fucking nerve, and yes, I was an asshole last night, but if you also remember, I avenged that ungrateful woman when she was gang—"

"Don't you dare bring her suffering up now!" Troian roars. "I can't even look at you, Kristian. I want you out of my sight and away from my children. I want you out of this fucking city."

This city? His children? He's going to stop me from seeing Zenya? "What are you saying?"

Troian glares at me, anger and grief stark in his face. My normally easygoing brother can be pushed and pushed, but I should have remembered that when he snaps, he loses all sense of perspective. "I'm disinheriting you."

"You're what?" I ask in a cold and deadly voice.

"I could die next year. Next month. Will you piss all over my grave before I'm cold as well? I'm giving everything to Zenya. She's already been proving herself worthy of taking over from me. She's smart, and unlike you, she's responsible. She'll grow into an extraordinary and powerful woman."

Of course she will. I've been thinking the same thing myself. Relishing the prospect, in fact, but with me to help her. I've envisioned leading this family with her at my side. Not for her to lead all by herself. "Zenya will take what you've built and make it a thousand times better, but she needs me like you've needed me. What this is really about is your pride. Your so-called *legacy*," I snarl. "You're facing your mortality and you're wondering how everyone is going to talk about you once you're gone."

I've humiliated Troian, and I know I should be going down on one knee before him and promising to do whatever it takes to make this right, but the threat to take Zenya away from me has me seeing red.

"You always did care far too much about what other people think of you," I rant. "The great and powerful *Pakhan*. You know who lies awake at night worrying what people think about a picture? Weak people. Stupid fucking people."

"Get out of my sight," Troian shouts, gripping the arms of his chair.

"Make me," I shoot back, glancing meaningfully at his broken leg. He's recovered from last year's chemotherapy, more or less, but I know he's sensitive about appearing less than he was. "Better yet, admit you lost your temper and take back what you just said."

He can't throw me out of this family.

These days I am this fucking family.

I'm the one who gets his hands dirty, protects everyone, and metes out justice. Troian might be the figurehead, but I'm the one who gets things done.

"I've made my decision. If you don't leave this city, I'll put a bounty on your head at midnight tomorrow. You won't live to see the sunrise."

A bounty on his own brother? Our parents would be turning in their graves. The Belyaevs have never allowed issues of pride to weaken us as a whole. "Are you fucking insane? You proud asshole. So I'm to be discarded after thirty-four years? The adopted brother. The disposable brother."

"This has nothing to do with you being adopted. This is all because you're a piece of shit who doesn't know when to stop." Troian reaches inside his jacket and pulls out a gun, placing it on the side table.

Grief and anger are raging in his eyes, and I doubt he's slept since he found Chessa's dead body. He's lost all sense of perspective.

"Now get out before I kill you myself."

I stare at the gun. My own brother is threatening me with a gun. He really thinks he can run this family and the business without me?

He'll be crawling to me in no time and begging me to return. Six months, tops.

I glance over my shoulder, and then stroll closer to my brother, leaning over his chair and lowering my voice so what I have to say doesn't travel beyond this room. "So much for loyalty, Troian. Be thankful that one of us still believes in what this family stands for, otherwise, I wouldn't merely threaten to kill you like you just threatened me. I happen to know who the main beneficiary of your will is right at this moment, and it's not Zenya."

I let that threat marinate in the air for an angry minute.

Then I stride out of the room and run straight into my niece in the hall. She's been listening to our entire conversation with tears pouring down her face.

I take her hand and pull her through the house and into the back garden so we can have some privacy. Beneath a jacaranda tree, I pull her into my arms and hold her tight.

"I can't believe this is happening. You're really leaving?" Zenya lifts her tear-streaked face to mine.

This doesn't feel real. I'm going to lose Zenya because of a stupid fucking joke that no one should ever have known about. "Your father doesn't make idle threats."

She clutches my shoulders and gazes up at me imploringly. "You can fix this. Just tell Dad you're sorry. He's not mad at you. He's just afraid he's losing everyone."

So his solution is to throw me out of this family? Zenya wants me to go in there and beg on my knees, but if I look at my brother again with this much rage pumping through my veins, I could very well beat him to death. "I can't fix this right now."

I watch Zenya's face crumple, and unlike yesterday, she doesn't have the strength to control her tears. As they flow freely down her face, I feel each one scorched into my soul.

"But how am I supposed to live without you?" she sobs.

I shake my head hopelessly. I don't know how I'm going to live without her, either.

Zenya cries harder. "This isn't happening. This is a nightmare."

I wish it were. I wish I could turn back time and hurl that tube of lipstick across the room. Or that I had been sober enough to recognize that flash of light for what it was and beat to death whoever took that photo. Or that I hadn't been a piece of shit and gone out celebrating at all.

"Where are you going to go?" Zenya whispers.

If Zenya follows me, it will make Troian even angrier, though it's tempting just to fucking take her. That really would finish off the Belyaevs. The only thing that stops me are the constant lectures I've been giving myself to be a good man around Zenya for the past year. "It's best you don't know for now."

Zenya's fingers tangle in my hair and she looks desperately up at me. "Why do I feel like I'm never going to see you again?"

I've been called heartless a dozen times in my life, and I wish it were true. As I gaze down into Zenya's stricken face, I can't breathe because everything hurts so much.

This is all Troian's fault, the proud fuck. He doesn't appreciate how hard it's been for me not to do anything about my obsession with Zenya. It would tear him apart to know his own brother wanted to get his filthy hands all over his innocent daughter. I've been a fucking angel with her, yet he's throwing me out of the family like I'm trash.

I take Zenya's face in my hands, breathing hard.

So why am I bothering to hold back?

I lean down and press my lips to Zenya's. Our first kiss, and there's so much of her to savor, but all I can taste are her tears. It's barely a real kiss, just a press of my lips to her soft ones. A promise for later. Something for me to remember and for her to think about until my return. "I promise I'll be back."

Zenya's so distraught that she doesn't seem to notice I've kissed her. My thumbs stroke the tears from her cheeks, but they just keep coming.

"People keep leaving me," she sobs.

Pain and regret flash through me as I lean my forehead against hers. "You're my most beloved person in the whole world, and it kills me to leave you. It won't be for long, but you have to let me go."

She wraps her arms around my waist and her sobs reach a fever pitch. "No, I won't."

"Please, Zenya."

In the end, I have to force her to let me go, and every second she fights me, I want to stab myself through the heart for causing her all this unnecessary pain.

As I drive away from the house, Zenya's cries are piercing my soul. I'll leave this city, but not because I'm afraid of Troian or anyone he sends after me. I'll leave because if I don't, I'll murder my brother and cause even more pain for Zenya.

But I won't stay away forever, and when I return, I'll make Troian pay for this.

I'll take what he loves the most and make it mine.

His money.

His power.

But first, I'll steal his precious daughter from right under his nose, and I won't ever give her back.

Chapter Five

KRISTIAN

PRESENT DAY

The Corvette purrs along familiar streets. Streets that I've missed in the two years I've been absent from this city. Belyaev territory.

My territory.

Or it will be once the girl next to me in the passenger seat is wearing my ring and carrying my baby. I've wasted two years when I could have been making her fall in love with me. When I went to the warehouse tonight, I thought I might be able to coax Zenya into closing her eyes and letting the stranger in black blindfold her and kiss her, but she was just so intrigued by me. Hungry for me to devour her. She claims she didn't know that it was me beneath the mask, but I think she did. She knows my scent and the shape of my body. Maybe she just didn't *want* to know.

But she craved what only I can give her.

She'll put up some resistance at first. I saw the shock in her eyes when she realized it was me between her legs. Unless she thought I was someone else? If so, I'll hunt down whoever dared to put his hands on my baby girl in my absence and crush his fucking skull.

Either way, Zenya's been missing her favorite uncle, and now I'm back. One reunion down, one to go.

Troian.

Anger surges through me as I grip the steering wheel.

Fucking Troian.

Before he dies, I'll make sure my brother knows I took my revenge on him by making his empire mine, piece by fucking piece, starting with his daughter and ending with every square inch of this city. Two years ago, if he'd backed down and let me return, I might have been gentle about taking the reins. I thought he'd get over that photo with the stripper and beg me to return to his side, but weeks slipped by and then months, and my phone stayed silent. My brother's stubbornness has always been world class, but this time his pettiness reached a new level. Taking away control of the Belyaev family is an insult that still burns, and I'm never leaving again. This is my home. My streets. My city. And that girl on the passenger seat beside me?

That's my fucking wife.

"You look pleased with yourself," Zenya says, staring straight ahead through the windshield with a troubled line between her brows. Her long silver hair is cascading around her shoulders and it's spattered with blood. Though her face is pale against her black clothing, there are two small spots of color burning in her cheeks.

She's angry with me? Or she's flushed with the memory of what we just did together?

I run my tongue against the roof of my mouth, recalling every detail and sensation of her sex against my mouth. The scent of her arousal. The cries she made as she came. I'm not pleased she gave me her pussy with a little coaxing. I'm fucking delighted.

After three years of ceaseless yearning, I've finally tasted her. "Of course I'm pleased. You know that I'm never happier than when I'm with you."

I reach over to take Zenya's hand, but she pulls away and turns to look out the window.

"You could have fooled me," she mutters.

Slowly, I draw my hand back. That burns, but I suppose she can't help but be angry with me when she doesn't know the full story about where I've been all this time and why.

"I've missed two of your birthdays," I murmur, turning left down a familiar street. "Two Christmases. All your happy days. All your sad days. All the days you needed me and some days when you were so angry with me that you couldn't breathe. But I'm back now, princess, and I'm going to spend every second making up for being gone for so long."

Zenya makes an angry *tch* noise and shakes her head. "It's not that simple."

I get it. She's angry with me for leaving and then staying away, but it wasn't by choice. I sense how much Zenya wants to shout at me, scratch me, unleash her fury on her uncle. I'll admit I've been a terrible man when I've got her pinned to a mattress, but only then. She can forgive me louder and louder as I make her come again and again. If she needs to weep she can do that on my bare chest while I kiss away her tears.

It's nearly one in the morning when I pull into the driveway at my brother's huge house. The mansion-like facade is lit up. The hedges are beautifully manicured, and as I set my booted foot on the white gravel, there's not a dead leaf or twig to be seen.

I open the passenger door and lean down to pick up my niece.

"No, don't, I can walk—"

But I've already gathered her into my arms. Her warm, sweet scent washes over me as I pull her close against my chest. I'm going to have my fill of holding her tonight. I've been aching for this for too long.

When we reach the front door, I lean down so my niece can unlock it, and then I'm standing in the marble hall for the first time in two years. I stop just inside the door and look down at Zenya. She's gazing up at me, her beautiful blue eyes filled with wariness and confusion.

I can taste *us* in the air that we're breathing.

I feel like I'm home, and my lips drift toward hers.

Zenya sucks in a soft breath and her fingers tighten on my shoulders.

Troian's voice calls down the hall from the lounge. "Zenya, is that you?"

My niece and I stare at each other, and I wait, one eyebrow raised, for her to announce that I'm here. When she doesn't say anything, I murmur, "Go on, Zenya. Tell your father where you've been and who you've been with."

She shakes her head slowly, her eyes narrowing. "If you tell him what happened tonight, I will never forgive you."

I smile slowly at her.

I won't.

Not tonight.

Not yet.

My plan has to unfold step by step. By the time Troian finally finds out that Zenya's pregnant with my baby and adores me with all her heart, I'll have his entire empire in the palm of my hand.

Zenya puts her head on one side, considering me. "Then again, maybe I'll tell Dad right now. Have you thrown out of this house—again. That is, if he doesn't shoot you for touching me."

Oh, she'd expose us, would she? I grin wickedly at her. "Go right ahead and tell him how you came all over your uncle's—"

"Zenya!" Troian shouts.

"Why doesn't he just come out here himself instead of shouting like an asshole?" I growl, stalking down the hall with Zenya in my arms.

When I round the corner, I stop dead.

I even take a second look around the room, because the man sitting in that armchair can't be my brother. What's left of his hair has turned white and his cheeks are sunken and wasted. His presence has been diminished along with his size. Claw-like hands clutch the arms of the chair.

There's thin plastic tubing beneath his nose connected to a portable oxygen tank that sits at his side. Troian's breathing is labored.

I look at Zenya, communicating with her silently. *I didn't realize he'd relapsed.*

Her hands tighten on the back of my neck, telling me about her fear, her worry, her heartache.

"Zenya, what happened to you tonight?" Troian only has eyes for his injured daughter and he hasn't noticed who is holding her.

"It was a disaster. Can you please put me down, Uncle Kristian?"

I don't move as Troian's attention snaps to me, and the expression of concern on his gray face morphs into fury. "You. What the hell are you doing here?"

I feel Zenya flinch in my arms. "I'll take Zenya upstairs and call a doctor for her, then you and I can talk."

"You will do no such thing. You will put my daughter down and get out of here right now. You're not welcome in my house."

"Dad, Uncle Kristian saved my life tonight." Zenya bites her lip as if surprised by how quickly she's sprung to my defense.

I squeeze her in my arms, hugging her in silent thanks for standing up for me. Zenya glances at me uncertainly, but I give her a reassuring smile. I'm not here to fight. I'm here for her.

Without seeming to realize she's doing it, Zenya strokes the nape of my neck as she gazes at me, her lower lip softening.

"I'll take you upstairs and call you a doctor. I'll be back in a moment, Troian," I say over my shoulder as I carry her out of the room.

"I—" She squeezes me tighter, confusion raging in her eyes, but she falls silent as we climb the stairs.

Her bedroom hasn't changed since I've been gone. She sleeps in the same canopied bed made of dark polished wood with a blue bedspread the same shade as her eyes. The thick carpet is cream and so are the net curtains.

"Is Nader still the family doctor?" I ask Zenya, laying her on the bed. My knee sinks into the mattress as I hover over her. She nods, and I run my forefinger down a lock of her ashy blonde hair. She's so beautiful that I can't tear my eyes away from her. Even more beautiful than before.

"Uncle Kristian, my ankle, and Dad's waiting for you."

Reluctantly, I get out my phone to make the call. Doctor Nader has been looking after this family since Zenya was a baby, and he's made dozens of house calls over the years. He sounds half asleep when he answers the phone, but he promises to be right over without complaint. He has no need to complain. Troian keeps him on a generous retainer.

"He'll be right here," I tell my niece, and reach for the button on her jeans.

Zenya clutches my wrist. "What are you doing?"

Our faces are very close together, and I murmur, "Helping you undress. I've already done it once tonight. Let's not take two steps back, princess."

She pushes my hands away, her cheeks burning. "I told you, we're pretending that never happened. Go talk to Dad."

I smile and stroke my finger down her cheek. She cares what happens between me and Troian tonight. That means she wants me to stay. "I'll make sure everything is sorted out at the warehouse. Call the men's families. You're not to worry anymore tonight. I'll come and kiss you goodnight after Doctor Nader leaves."

I leave her on her bed, gazing at me apprehensively. I would like a *Thank you, Uncle Kristian*, but she's still hesitant to give me her gratitude.

It doesn't matter. Soon enough, I'll have everything I want.

I wait by the front door until I hear a knock so I can let Doctor Nader in and point him upstairs, then I return to the living room.

Troian has gotten to his feet and is standing in front of the empty fireplace. It's the most impressive place in the room, but it doesn't escape my notice that he's clinging to the mantelpiece with one hand in case his legs give out.

I stand in the middle of the room with my hands in my pockets, gazing at him. "How bad is it this time?"

The cancer.

From the looks of my brother, he's got one foot in the grave.

"It's been rough, but I'm stronger than I look." Troian glares at me. "Why are you back? I changed my will two years ago, and it's final. I'm leaving you nothing."

"I'm well aware of that. I didn't come back for your money. I'm back for my niece."

The truth.

A lie.

And my destiny.

Troian's fortune is not as safe as he thinks it is if he still plans on giving everything to his daughter.

"Zenya is doing fine without you. That girl has been flourishing."

"Zenya was seconds away from being torn to pieces when I found her tonight, and from what I heard, those men were going to take their time about it. The *Pakhan's* own daughter. It seems that people are no longer afraid of Belyaev retribution. I wonder why that could be?"

I let my gaze run meaningfully over Troian's wasted frame.

If it's possible, my brother's complexion grows even more ashen, and his voice is shaking as he says, "Impossible. Where were Andrei, Radimir, and Stannis?"

"I'll show you later if you like. I'm going back for their body parts when Zenya is asleep." I relate to my brother how I returned to the city tonight and discovered from one of his men where I could find Zenya. I intended to watch her from afar for a day or two until I could talk to her alone, but she needed me sooner than I anticipated.

From the way I tell it to Troian, I was her knight in shining armor.

Troian drags his hand down his face, and for once, he's lost for words. "I…thank you for saving her life, Kristian."

"It was an honor and a privilege. You know I love my niece. I would do anything for her." I step closer to my brother, tension radiating from my body. "You can threaten me with the Grim Reaper himself as my assassin, but after what I've seen tonight, I'm not leaving her side. She's in too much danger."

If the wolves are circling the Belyaevs in the hopes of toppling our power in this city, then Zenya's going to get hurt without me. Troian's not strong enough to protect her anymore, so that man will have to be me.

Troian glances at me uncertainly. He knows he needs me, but

pride is preventing him from admitting it.

I make my expression sincere and put my hand over my heart. "I brought a dozen men with me. Loyal men who will do whatever I ask them to do, and that includes swear themselves to you. They're yours. They're Zenya's. The two of you can command us as you please."

"How did you find a dozen loyal men?"

I hear the scorn in my brother's voice. He thinks I can't inspire loyalty? I drop my hand from my heart and clench my jaw, but I manage to curtail my temper. "Do you think I've been doing nothing for two years? I'm a Belyaev. I always land on my feet."

I found plenty of ways to make money in my temporary city. All I had to do was find a crew with a weak leader, crush him, and take over. I was doing so well that many men in my position would have stayed there.

"If you were doing so well, what is there for you back here?" Troian asks.

Everything.

There's *everything* here for me.

"I'm a Belyaev, and this is where I belong. I crave to leave my mark on the world as you have. I want a beautiful and clever wife. I need sons and daughters, and they should know where they came from."

Zenya's going to be that wife. Her body craves mine as much as I crave her. I'll be the luckiest man on earth once my pretty niece wears my ring on her finger.

Troian considers me with a frown. "I always wanted you to be a family man, but I was beginning to think you'd stay a bachelor."

I shrug as if it's no big deal. I deserve an Oscar for my performance.

"It's something I've been thinking about for a while, and I've decided that now is the time."

Troian shakes his head in disbelief. "I can't believe my little brother is going to settle down at last. Have you got a woman in mind?"

I rub my hand over my jaw, smirking at my brother. "I shouldn't say just yet. I've only just started to make my move, and she's going to need some persuading. But she'll be mine in the end."

Troian laughs. "You always could be charming when you put your mind to it."

"I'm grateful for your confidence in me, brother," I murmur with a smile. Zenya hasn't witnessed one tenth of my charm. The poor girl doesn't stand a chance. She'll be looking at her uncle in a whole new light in no time, but that's only if I can persuade Troian to allow me to stay.

My moment has arrived. I step forward and put both my hands on my brother's bony shoulders and gaze deep into his eyes. "People need to rediscover their fear of the Belyaev family. Let me remind them who we are for you, and no one will dare touch a hair on our sweet girl's head ever again."

Making this about protecting Zenya works like magic, and my brother's resolve to hate me shatters.

Troian glances past me. "We should talk to Zenya about this."

I step back and hold out my arm, allowing him to lead the way. "You know I'm always happy to talk to Zenya."

Troian insists he can manage the stairs on his own, and he laboriously puts the oxygen tank on one step before clambering up behind it. It's slow going. By the time we reach the top of the staircase, his face has turned white and there are beads of sweat on his brow. He's doing his best to hide how much of a struggle this is for him, so I do him the courtesy of pretending not to notice.

We pass Doctor Nader in the hall and he tells us that Zenya has a bad bruise, but nothing is broken or sprained, and she'll be perfectly fine in a few days.

When Troian and I enter her bedroom, she's sitting up in her canopied bed, wearing pajamas and a quilted dressing gown, and there's an ice pack on her ankle. Her jewel-like blue eyes flicker from her father's face to mine, hungry to know what we've been discussing, but worried about it as well.

Troian sits down on the bed and pats Zenya's uninjured ankle. "Your uncle told me what happened tonight. I'm so sorry, sweetheart. This was all my fault."

Zenya glances quickly at me. I'm standing by Troian's shoulder, my hands in my pockets. No, princess. I didn't mention what else happened between us.

She turns to face her father. "You can't blame yourself for what happened. I was the one who was taken by surprise and got everyone killed."

Troian shakes his head sadly. "Your attackers should have been too afraid of me to try and hurt my daughter. Word must be out that I'm…" He gives her a sad smile and gestures at his ruined body.

Zenya leans forward and grabs his hand. "You're going to be *fine*."

She says it with such force that I wonder who she's trying to convince. I haven't heard anything about my brother's prognosis, and I make a mental note to find out later.

"It doesn't matter how I will be in the future, it matters how I appear now. Your Uncle Kristian wishes to return to us and put on a show of strength for our allies and enemies, and I think that's a good plan." He hastens to assure her, "But you're still my heir. Nothing will change that."

Zenya's face is blank with shock, and then she splutters, "You want him to stay? Have you forgotten how he mocked Chessa after she died? How many times have you been humiliated by that photograph when it's reappeared again and again these past two years?"

Where's the niece who sobbed so prettily in my arms, begging me not to leave her? She was never angry about the photo at the time.

Troian frowns at his daughter. "You pleaded with me for months to let Kristian come home. I thought you'd be happy about this."

Over his shoulder, I shoot her a sly grin. Oh, did she? How pleasing.

Zenya turns pink and leans forward to adjust the ice pack on her ankle. "Yes, well, more recently, I've been thinking about how Uncle Kristian likes to pretend to strangle strippers with my stepmother's name scrawled across their chests."

There's a flicker of agreement in Troian's eyes, and I decide now is the time for me to speak up. "Chessa sometimes got on my nerves, but I didn't hate her or wish her harm. I don't hate anyone, and I'm sorry for what I did. I'm a new man since I've been gone."

She gives me a sharp look. "I'm not so sure. You're very disrespectful. You don't seem to like women very much."

I flash her a heated smile, making sure her father doesn't see it. "I like one woman."

Troian pats Zenya's foot again. "Apparently your uncle wants to get married. He's already got his bride picked out." When Zenya goggles at him, he laughs and says, "Yes, I couldn't believe it either. You'll have to be the one to get that secret out of him, sweetheart, because he won't tell me who she is."

Zenya's hands tighten on the blankets. Finally, she says to her father, "May I please speak to Uncle Kristian alone?"

Troian gets up and kisses her cheek. "Of course. I'll say goodnight, and we can talk further on it in the morning." He gets up and shuffles slowly out of the room.

"You're a snake," Zenya says as soon as we're alone.

I narrow my eyes at her. "Don't speak to your uncle that way."

Her beautiful blue eyes flash. "You gave away the right to reprimand me when you did what you did in that warehouse."

I wait for Zenya to look down or instantly apologize like she would have done two years ago if she dared talk back to her beloved uncle, but to my surprise, she holds my gaze.

"Why am I a snake?"

"I don't know what you said to Dad to make him forgive you after all this time, but I know you must have lied to him and manipulated him."

"I told him the truth."

"And that is?"

"You need me, Zenya. Don't bother to deny it after I killed for you tonight." Just thinking about her at the mercy of those four moronic thugs makes my blood boil.

She sits back with an angry shake of her head and folds her arms.

But she doesn't argue with me.

"There's no shame in needing my protection. You're powerful and important, and I live to protect you." I reach out to touch her cheek, but she jerks away from me.

"Where have you been all this time?"

I sigh and drop my hand. "Nowhere special. I was building a new life for myself, seeing as Troian didn't want me in his."

"What kind of life? Where have you been? With whom?"

Is that a spark of jealousy I see in her eyes? I sit down on the bed beside her. "I promise you I haven't been happy. It was an empty life because I didn't have my favorite person with me."

This time, when I lift my hand to stroke my fingers through her hair, she lets me. The soft silver strands flow through my fingers like water, though Zenya watches me cautiously.

Suddenly she gasps and sits up. "The warehouse. All those dead bodies. I can't just leave them like that."

I take her shoulders and settle her back against the pillows. "Where do you think you're going with an injury? I brought men with me. I already said that I'll take care of everything."

She frowns at me, studying me with suspicion. "Why have you returned now? Why one day after my eighteenth birthday?"

A slow, heated smile spreads over my face. She can draw her own conclusions about that. "Just be thankful I showed up when I did. I haven't heard you say, *Thank you for saving my life, Uncle Kristian.*"

Zenya presses her lips together. "That's because I still remember you saying, *It won't be for long. I swear I'll be back.* Two years. Is that your idea of not long?"

I reach out to take her in my arms, but she lies down, pulling the blankets up to her chin. "Don't touch me. I'm so angry with you. Now go away because I want to sleep."

I wait until she's settled down on her back and then I lean over her, bracing my hands on either side of her pillow. "I know you're angry, but I'm angry, too. If it had been up to me, I never would have left in the first place."

Zenya's face softens, but she doesn't say anything.

You love your Uncle Kristian, remember?

"I'm going to work hard to make it up to you."

"How?"

"We have so much to catch up on, you and me." I let that rest in the air while I stare into her eyes. Then I let my gaze drop to her lips. I'm so close I could kiss her.

But I stay where I am. I just want to remind her that I once did, two years ago, and if she's a very, *very* good girl…

I might do it again.

"Night, princess," I murmur, a smile curving my lips. "Dream of me."

It takes me, Mikhail, and half a dozen other men until dawn to dispose of the bodies in the warehouse, hose away the blood, and collect the merchandise. Once it's been delivered to the Silo, I drive Zenya's car back to Troian's house and leave it in the driveway for her.

Then Mikhail and I meet at our favorite dive bar to get a drink.

It's dark and seedy and hasn't changed a bit. The carpet is sticky and the bourbon is excellent, just the way I like it.

"To being home," I say, raising my glass to my friend.

Mikhail knocks his drink back and gives me a tired glare. "What a welcome fucking home. Come home, he said. It will be fun, he said. And then we're up to our armpits in blood and body parts on the first night."

I swallow my bourbon, welcoming the refreshing burn at the back of my throat. "I don't enjoy scooping up human entrails either, but it's an important means to my ends."

"What ends exactly?"

I shoot him a mysterious look. "Getting everything I deserve."

Mikhail signals to the bartender for another bourbon. "You've been cagey about what we're doing here. The others don't care. They're just happy being part of the Belyaev crew, but I remember when you were thrown out two years ago, and it makes me wonder what you're really up to."

"Oh, didn't I say?" I ask, even though I know for a fact that I didn't breathe a word about my intentions to anyone.

"You don't tell me shit," Mikhail says, but he smiles good-naturedly at me.

I shake my head when the bartender tries to refill my glass because I need a clear head this morning. I wait until he pours one for Mikhail and walks away before I continue.

"I didn't come back to be my brother's lickspittle again. For him to order me around. Do his thankless bidding. Be grateful with what little he gives me. I want everything. I'm going to sit at the head of the

Belyaev family and control our fortunes and our destiny."

Mikhail gives a low whistle. "Ambitious. How are you going to get Troian to change his will back to favor you?"

I smile as I picture Zenya's perfect body beneath mine. Fuck, I can still taste that girl on my tongue. "I'm not."

"Then how?"

"Zenya."

"What about Zenya?"

"I want her."

Mikhail lifts his eyebrows. "You…want her?"

I toy with my glass, enjoying the confusion on Mikhail's face. It feels good to finally say it out loud. "I'm going to make Zenya fall in love with me. I'm going to marry Zenya. Through Zenya, I can take everything that's precious from Troian and make it mine, as it always should have been."

Mikhail shakes his head, his expression baffled. "Why in the hell would you want to do that to your own flesh and blood? You're brothers."

Anger burns through me at the memory of what happened two years ago. The humiliation. The grief. The pain.

I grip my empty glass and growl, "Because my brother took everything from me, and I'll never, ever forgive him."

Mikhail stares at me in bewildered silence. "Okay, fine. You want revenge. But Zenya's your niece. You're seriously telling me you're going to try and screw your niece? You make one move on her and Troian will put a bullet in your head."

"Zenya won't do anything that puts her beloved uncle in danger.

Don't worry about how I'll seduce her. I'm halfway there already."

All I need to do is make myself indispensable in Zenya's life. Her protector. Her unconditional lover. The man she's always adored, the dangerous rogue who's sweet only for her. I'll bet millions that Troian's been working that girl hard with barely a word of praise. She's starving for someone to lavish her with affection, and that man is going to be me.

"Halfway there?" Mikhail asks. "Bullshit. She grew up with you, and there's no way a sweet, innocent girl like Zenya Belyaev is going to let her uncle get his hands all over her."

"Yes, she will. That girl will become addicted to me."

Mikhail slowly shakes his head. "You're crazy."

"Who's going to stop me? You?"

"Oh, fuck no. I prefer my head attached to my body. I'm not getting in your way."

"Then you and I are fine."

"You're still fucking crazy, and I'm not drunk enough for this conversation." He knocks back his bourbon and calls for another.

"I was adopted, remember? Zenya and I don't share any blood."

"So? You look like her uncle. You act like her uncle. You held her hand at her mother's funeral. She thinks of you as her uncle and she always has. I doubt it's even legal for you to marry her."

"I looked it up. We'll need permission from a judge, but that's a technicality. My money can bribe any judge I choose."

"Wouldn't it just be easier to get Troian to change his will back to you? Less…messed up?"

I shake my head and laugh. "You don't get it. Zenya's my priority. She's been my number one since she was born. My favorite niece, and then…" I remember my pretty little niece covered in blood. "We're the same, she and I. I'm the only man for her, and she's the only woman for me."

He opens his mouth but closes it again and shakes his head.

"Go on. Say what you're thinking."

"No thanks. I like having all my teeth."

I turn and gaze at him with a serious expression. "Speak your mind. I won't lay a finger on you."

Mikhail flashes me a dark look. "You're sick. That's what I think."

I pat his shoulder. "I don't need you to like it. I need you to keep your mouth shut and help me when I need you."

"Yes, please. I'd love to help you fuck your niece."

"Marry my niece," I correct him.

"Don't bullshit me. I don't even think you're that interested in her. You just want revenge against your brother, so you're going to fuck that girl just to hurt him."

"Yes. I am going to fuck her, and there's not a thing Troian can do to stop me. But that's not all. I'm going to possess her. I'm going to consume her. And you know what?"

"What?"

I get to my feet and put some bills down for my bourbon because I have places to be this morning. Not one second of Zenya's life is going to pass without her seeing me, thinking of me, craving me.

I straighten the lapels of my jacket and adjust the silver rings on my pinkie fingers. "She's going to love me so hard I'll be all she can think about."

Chapter Six

ZENYA

I wake to the sensation of pressure on my mouth and sit up with a gasp. There's no one in my bedroom. I stare around at the carpet, the curtains, the closed door, and run my fingers across my lips.

I've had that dream before, that a man has taken my face in his hands and kissed me, but it's never been as vivid as it was just now. I felt the briefest press of his lips once, and it awoke a burning hunger in my body that rages as I sit here trying to catch my breath.

There are keys sitting on my bedside table. My car keys. I never leave them there, so why—

I remember.

The warehouse.

Andrei, Radimir, and Stannis being murdered in front of me.

A stranger in black killing my attackers, and then oh-so sweetly persuading me to reward him with a taste of my body that quickly spiraled out of control. Coming back down to earth and removing the blindfold, only to see that it was Uncle Kristian between my thighs.

I put my hands over my face and moan. The ancient Greeks wrote tragedies like this. The Belyaevs are filled with hubris, and now we're being taught a hard lesson to make us humble again.

I throw the covers off and swing my feet out of bed. I haven't got time to think about that right now. Mornings are my busiest time of day.

Doctor Nader told me that I should try to walk around on my foot today as long as it doesn't cause me too much pain. Carefully, I put weight on my injured foot. It hurts, but it's bearable, and I hobble to the bathroom.

I take a shower, dress in jeans and a tank top, and scoop my hair into a ponytail. Downstairs, the house is still silent as I turn the coffee maker on and open the blinds in the kitchen. The sun has just risen, and I get to work packing school lunches for my brother and sister, Arron and Lana; Chessa's kids, Felix, Noah, and Micaela; and finally, Nadia and Danil, my half-siblings. Then there are seven breakfasts to prepare, and while I set the table, I hear Arron and Lana calling for the younger children to get out of bed.

A few minutes later, Lana is sleepily twisting her fingers through her silvery blonde hair as she takes a seat at the table and pours herself some cereal. She notices I'm limping and frowns.

"What happened to you?"

"I tripped last night."

"What were you doing last night?"

A vision of a stranger dressed head to toe in black bursts into my mind, looming over me as I lay on the sofa in that warehouse. I can still feel his chest muscles against my palms. Hear his soft murmurs in my ear and feel his lips moving against my sex.

You smell delicious, Zenya. I've always wanted to know...

Always wanted to know. He definitely said that. *Always* wanted to know. What the hell does that mean, Uncle Kristian? Always wanted to know what I taste like?

I scrape butter over my toast without looking at my sister, my cheeks burning. "Working. Doing inventory."

As far as my siblings officially know, there's nothing criminal about our family. Unofficially? Who knows what Lana and the other kids overhear at school. Thanks to my Uncle Kristian, I never had any illusions about how my family makes its money. As the eldest child, he thought I should know as soon as possible, and after Mom died, Dad reluctantly agreed with him.

When all the kids are eating at the table, I get out Dad's medications and start counting his morning pills. These ones to treat the tumors. These ones to manage his pain and the plethora of chemotherapy side effects. I hate seeing Dad swallow down all these chemicals because they make him nauseated, foggy, and drowsy, but I remind myself that the alternative is far worse. The alternative is a swift and painful death. But it won't be forever. Dad will go into remission soon and then he'll start to regain his strength and become the strong leader this family needs.

My foot is aching by the time I reach Dad's bedroom and go in, but I'm careful not to let the pain show on my face as I pass him the pills and a glass of water.

Dad slowly and with a lot of effort sits up in bed. I stay where I am because he hates when I try and help him.

"Morning, Dad. How did you sleep?"

He makes a noncommittal sound as he props himself against the pillows. I hand him a glass of water and his medications and he starts swallowing them down. As he finishes and passes the water back, he asks, "What did you and Kristian decide last night?"

A thrill goes through me at the sound of his name. "Me? Why would I decide anything with Uncle Kristian?"

Dad gives me a tired, sad smile. "You know why."

The bottom falls out of my stomach. For a moment I feel nothing but panic and shame—Dad knows what we did?—and then anger surges on its heels. Of course he doesn't know. Dad's just being fatalistic again. "I don't want to hear that kind of talk from you. Your oncologist said that you're responding well to the chemotherapy and it's working."

"He said that he's seen *some* indications that *some* of the tumors were responding, but it's too early to say."

I busy myself tidying up his already tidy room and straightening the covers on the bed. "Exactly. It's a good prognosis. I haven't had time to think about Uncle Kristian. You should probably talk to him again and make up your own mind about whether you want him around."

But Dad's eyes have drifted closed and he's fallen back asleep. I gaze at him with sadness. His medications always knock him out again, and he's in no condition to make decisions about anything. It's down to me and Uncle Kristian what happens next.

In the hallway, out of earshot of the kids downstairs and Dad if he wakes up, I call Andrei's girlfriend. They've been together for six years and they have a baby son. She already knows what happened to her partner in the warehouse. Uncle Kristian talked to her last night, but that doesn't make her grief any less raw, and my words of sorrow and condolence do nothing to help her. There are tears in my eyes when I hang up.

Whoever did this to my men is going to pay.

Downstairs, I open my laptop at the kitchen table and check over emails and spreadsheets while the children swarm around me, eating and laughing and squabbling. I'm so used to the antics of seven young siblings by now that I'm able to focus under just about any circumstances, only today, I can't focus. I feel restless and off-kilter, and I keep glancing toward the door, expecting to see a tall, muscular man in a tailored black suit, a silver chain around his neck, and careless white-blond hair falling into his eyes.

I rub both my hands over my face and groan under my breath. I should just call him and find out where he is. What he's doing. What happened in the warehouse and where my merchandise is. I'm going to run into him sooner or later, so it's better to make the first move.

I reach for my phone but put it down again. It's way too early in the morning for Uncle Kristian. That man loves to sleep in.

Excuses, excuses. The truth is, I'm terrified of how I'll react when

I hear his voice.

Arron slams the dishwasher closed, making me jump, and then all my brothers and sisters start kissing me goodbye and grabbing their lunches off the kitchen counter.

"Bye, Zenya!"

"Have a good day, Zenya."

I brush crumbs from sweaters and straighten hair barrettes as I tell everyone goodbye, giving the kids smiles and kisses and telling them to have good days at school. One by one they run out of the kitchen.

Just as their voices fade away and I anticipate the sound of the front door closing, I hear Felix exclaim, "Uncle Kristian! What are you doing here? Where have you been?"

My heart rebounds around my rib cage, and I nearly knock my laptop to the ground. I stare at the clock on the wall like it's betrayed me. Uncle Kristian is here already? It's only just past eight in the morning.

I grip my coffee cup as I listen to his deep voice greeting all his nephews and nieces. I can picture them clustering around his long legs, gazing with upturned faces at this unexpected delight.

"Is your big sister in the kitchen?" Uncle Kristian asks. There are a few chirpy replies of "Yes," and then the front door closes and the house falls silent.

Footsteps sound in the hallway, growing louder and louder as Uncle Kristian approaches. Should I ignore him? Should I get up and greet him? I feel an insane and almost irresistible urge to run and hide.

If he hadn't devastated and abandoned me two years ago, at this moment I would be bounding to my feet to greet him in the hallway. With a huge smile on my face, I'd wrap my arms around his neck and pepper his cheek with kisses, enjoying the sensation of his warm skin and the slight rasp of his clean-shaven cheek beneath my lips. We were always affectionate, touching each other as often as we could. I used to slip my hands beneath his shirts and hug his bare waist. I would fall asleep in his lap when we watched TV, long after it ceased to be appropriate, though it never occurred to me that it wasn't.

And Uncle Kristian used to let me do all these things. He never once stepped away from me, told me to chill, or did anything else to discourage me from touching him. No wonder we'd crossed a terrible line last night. We were barreling toward it for years and I was too naïve to realize.

All these thoughts are raging in my head and my cheeks are burning when Uncle Kristian appears. He stands in the doorway wearing a suit jacket over a V-neck T-shirt that clings to his muscular body. Black looks good on him. It sets off his pale blue eyes and silver-blond hair, and it accentuates the long, muscular lines of his body.

A smile spreads across his handsome face. "Morning, princess."

Did he always say *princess* in that velvety purr? I can't remember. Years ago, I used to be his dandelion. If I was especially silly or grumpy or sad, I was his dandelion puff. From the year I turned fifteen he started greeting me with his head on one side, an unreadable smile on his lips as he murmured, "Hello, princess."

It made me feel special and grown up to hear him say that. I wasn't a floaty, feathery dandelion seed, I was special. His princess, and he was my prince.

Now he's giving me an intense look; hungry and possessive of me in ways that an uncle definitely shouldn't be.

He raises an eyebrow slowly. "Do I get a hello in return?"

My gaze lingers on details about him that I've never noticed before. How that mouth of his is tilted at the corner as if he's having wicked thoughts. How his jaw catches the light. The way a few strands of hair falling in his eyes have me itching to brush them back.

He shifts his weight from one foot to the other and rests his shoulder against the doorframe, and the swaggery way his body moves is so Uncle Kristian. I've seen him move like that a thousand times before. I witnessed him make that exact movement last night in the warehouse, and I didn't recognize him.

"Do I not even get a hug anymore, Zenya?" he murmurs, pushing away from the doorframe and sauntering around the counter to stand by my chair. He runs his forefinger along the underside of my ponytail and lets the heavy strands slip through his fingers. "Or a kiss?"

I'm Zenya Belyaev, and men do not fluster me. I've suffered my share of harassment, dirty jokes, and wandering hands. Not once have I crumpled before a man, and I'm not about to start now.

"Bad uncles don't get anything," I tell him, gazing at him from beneath my lashes. I nearly slap a hand over my mouth as I realize how suggestive that sounded, but instead I dig my nails into my palms and make myself hold his gaze.

Commit to it.

Uncle Kristian wants me flustered in front of him, so I don't give it to him.

His lips twitch as he gazes down at me. "In my experience, bad uncles get whatever they want. I'll make my own coffee, shall I?"

He turns away to the machine, and I can breathe again.

I tap a few numbers into a spreadsheet, pretending I'm not hyperaware of his body with his broad back to me just a few feet away. This man is as familiar to me as my own father, so why am I obsessing over him like he's a shiny new toy that I'm not allowed to play with? He moves to the fridge, and I can see his strong profile. He has the same proud, straight nose and pale blue eyes that I do. Grandma and Grandpa either chose a baby to adopt that resembled them on purpose, or it's purely a coincidence that Dad and Uncle Kristian look like blood brothers.

There are differences, though. Before he got sick, Dad was always soft around the middle and cheerful, whereas Uncle Kristian is lean, dangerous, and sharp like a sword. During the year or two before he left, I would be out with friends whose eyes widened at the sight of someone approaching me over my shoulder. "Wow, your dad is crazy hot."

I would answer without even bothering to turn around, "That's not my dad. That's my uncle."

People would stop and stare at Uncle Kristian, men and women alike. Mostly women. Laughing, I would always point out those who were particularly dumbstruck by my uncle.

"That woman is gawking at you so hard that she nearly walked into traffic."

Uncle Kristian would smile down at me, only paying attention to me, and reply, "Is she, princess?" Like he didn't give a damn about other people. He only cared about who I was looking at.

While I'm taking surreptitious glances at him, he finishes making coffee and places a fresh latte by my elbow. I know without asking that it will be made with an extra shot and half a teaspoon of sugar stirred in, just the way I like it.

My uncle draws out a chair and sits down beside me, holding his own coffee.

"These are pretty," he murmurs, taking my hand. I'm not sure what he means until he runs his thumb over my nails, which are painted dark red and filed into tapered points. His eyes run over me. "You're different since I last saw you. A little taller. Cheeks finer. Hair longer. You're even prettier, Zenya. I didn't think that was possible."

My hand looks so small in his large one, and because I'm admiring the way we look together, I tug my fingers from his grip. "You're different, too."

"Me? I haven't changed at all."

But he has. Uncle Kristian use to possess the power to make me feel safe just by being close to me. I sensed how dangerous he was, but I was never afraid of him because he was only a threat to other people.

Now? I'm terrified of him.

Last night. I want to beg him, *Please tell me it was a terrible mistake so I can forget about it and be happy to see you.* I want to wrap my arms around the strong, beautiful man that I love and soak him up like sunshine.

Uncle Kristian picks up his coffee, but he moves too quickly and some of the foam slops over the edge. "Damn it." He frowns and licks the foam from the rim of his cup, and I catch sight of his tongue. Time slows down as I watch it move across the ceramic in a firm, deliberate swipe.

Heat washes over me.

I *felt* that.

I swallow hard as I remember the stranger dressed in black who persuaded me to let him take off my jeans and use that tongue to bring me to climax. But it wasn't a stranger at all.

He's sitting right in front of me, smelling like aftershave and looking like a loaded weapon.

I cross my legs and feel a telltale slipperiness at the apex of my thighs.

Shit. I'm wet.

You sick girl, Zenya. You let a masked stranger get his mouth on you, and now you're all messed up because he turned out to be your uncle.

Uncle Kristian swallows, and even the way he swallows is entrancing, the muscles of his throat moving his Adam's apple. I wonder how those muscles move when he's breathing hard. When he tips his head back and groans. When he grips your hair hard and growls, *Fuck yes, princess, just a little deeper.*

Uncle Kristian notices me staring at him and smiles. "Penny for your thoughts?"

I suck in a breath and turn quickly to my laptop. "I wasn't thinking about anything." So defensive. So obviously flustered by the man sitting too close to me.

He laughs softly. "Liar."

I type a few things into my spreadsheet, and then my fingers hover over the keys.

"The merchandise in the warehouse last night..." I begin.

"It's secured. I took it over to the Silo early this morning. That was the last thing I did before coming here, after showering and changing my bloodstained clothes."

The Silo is where we store all our black-market goods before they're sold. We trade in anything people want but can't have thanks to the laws of the United States of America. Absinthe, Cuban cigars, radar jammers and detectors, anabolic steroids and other prescription drugs, weapons tech and blueprints, unpasteurized French cheeses, and short-barrel shotguns.

People in my world want the finest things. The most exclusive things. The forbidden.

My gaze lingers on Uncle Kristian.

We just love what we shouldn't have.

If the merchandise is safe that's one good thing I can tell Dad. I shoot my uncle a curious look. If he's been clearing up bodies and moving those goods then he must have been up all night. "Don't you need to sleep?"

He shakes his head. "All I need is you and this cup of coffee. I have about a thousand questions about what you and the family have been up to in my absence."

"Ask away." I'm pleased at how nonchalant I sound. How professional. If he wants to be here, then I'll keep him at arm's length, as is appropriate for an uncle.

"How is Troian? I spoke to him last night, but how is he really?"

I flinch a little. Is he dying, is what Uncle Kristian means. Pressing my lips together, I wonder what to say. In front of Dad and the kids, I'm firm, almost fanatical, about Dad being fine, but I don't know how to lie to Uncle Kristian. I don't want to lie to Uncle Kristian. He was always the one person I could share the whole truth with without worrying I'm letting everyone down.

I take a deep breath. "He's not great. We don't know—the oncologist says—"

I turn away and press my hand over my mouth.

Don't cry.

Don't cry.

Uncle Kristian loops an arm around my shoulder and pulls me against him. Before I know what's happening, I'm in his arms and his lips are against my temple.

"Hey," he says softly, and that one syllable is filled with strength and comfort. "You know you don't have to sugarcoat anything for me. Tell me what's worrying you and I can share the weight of it with you."

"I'm not weak," I whisper fiercely. My eyes are wide open as he tucks me beneath his chin, and I stare determinedly at the silver chain around his neck that disappears inside his T-shirt. The barrels of the crossed gun tattoos on his chest.

"Of course you're not. I know that better than anyone, remember?"

My eyes close, and I clench my hand on his T-shirt. He's so warm and strong. So solid, when lately everything's felt like Jell-O beneath my feet.

"I think about that night every day," he whispers.

Silence stretches as I remember the stench of blood and death.

"Me, too," I finally confess.

I should have known it was Uncle Kristian beneath that mask last night because I saw him murdering men once before, when I was fourteen.

I don't remember much about what happened earlier that day. It was a normal day, I suppose. I must have gone to bed at nine or ten, and I awoke just after two o'clock in the morning in my canopied bed not understanding why.

Did someone shout?

Did I hear heavy, unfamiliar footsteps in the halls?

As I sat up, Chessa screamed, a shrill sound but quickly smothered. My brothers and sisters started crying, and over all that was the sound of angry male voices.

I wanted to run to my family, but Uncle Kristian had taught me never to run blindly into danger. Get a weapon or get backup. I snatched my phone from the nightstand and dove into the closet. Ever since I found out that my family makes its money by less than legal methods at the age of eleven, it was ingrained in me that we don't call the police. Cops aren't to be trusted. Cops aren't on our side.

So I called someone way better than the cops.

Uncle Kristian answered after the first ring, his voice hazy with sleep. "Zenya?"

I cupped my hand around my phone and whispered, "There are men in the house."

Uncle Kristian didn't ask questions. He didn't even reply. A split second later I was listening to dead air, but it didn't fill me with hopelessness or panic. Uncle Kristian wasn't going to waste time talking when he needed to get to me as fast as possible.

A moment later, the wardrobe door was ripped open, and a huge man reached in and dragged me out. I screamed and thrashed in his grip. My bedroom was dark, and I couldn't get a good look at my assailant, but he smelled like sour beer with a heavy layer of cheap body spray. He was laughing as he threw me on the bed. He played with me the whole time, letting me go only to grab me again and throw me back down. I was terrified, but I was getting angrier and angrier as well. I could hear Chessa screaming. I could hear more men laughing down the hall. They were hurting my family, and it was *fun* for them. I couldn't hear Dad at all, which made me terrified that he was dead.

My attacker ripped off my shorts and undid his belt. I knew what was coming as much as a fourteen-year-old could know, and I nearly turned inside out from terror.

Then I remembered something.

The knife in my nightstand.

Uncle Kristian put it in there *just in case* six months ago and told me not to tell Dad and Chessa about it. Dad had old-fashioned ideas about girls and weapons, and Chessa worried about anything sharp that her babies could accidentally get hold of.

I flung my arm out and yanked open the drawer, and scrambled for the weapon among my diary, a spare phone charger, and half-empty tubes of lip gloss. My fingers closed against the hilt and I cried out with relief. In one movement, I yanked my arm back and drove it point-first straight at my attacker.

And it plunged deep into the side of his throat.

His eyes went wide. He scrabbled at the hilt. Then he realized what I'd done to him, his face darkened with rage, and he got his hands around my throat.

As he started to choke me, I remembered what Uncle Kristian told me about stabbing people.

Make sure you pull the knife out so they bleed.

I reached up and yanked the knife from his neck, and blood spurted all over the bed. All over me.

A moment later, the man toppled onto me.

The next thing I remember, I was beneath the man, stabbing and screaming with fury. There was the sound of breaking glass and someone came crashing through my bedroom window. He tried to grapple the knife from me.

"Zenya. *Dandelion.* He's dead."

I finally let go. Uncle Kristian pulled the blade from my fingers, stared at it with a jolt of recognition, then a surge of vindication. He threw the knife aside, heaved the body off me and pulled me into his arms.

"You're okay. I've got you. I've got you."

He held me tight and rocked me back and forth in his arms. I wanted to scream the house down. I wanted to go on stabbing. White noise was blaring in my ears.

I felt Uncle Kristian look toward the door and realized that every second he spent with me was a second longer the other men were hurting my family. I pulled myself from his arms and pushed against his chest. "Go help them."

Uncle Kristian took my face in my hands and peered desperately at me. "Are you okay? Are you sure? Did he hurt you?" Realizing I was half naked, he pulled a blanket from my bed around me.

I nodded quickly. I didn't want to scream anymore.

I wanted revenge.

Over the years, I'd heard whispers about the sorts of things my uncle was capable of, and now I was going to get to see it for myself. "Can I help you kill them?"

He stared at me in surprise. Then a slow smile spread over his face. "Please, dandelion. You've already claimed one kill. Give me a chance to catch up."

He planted a kiss on my nose and sauntered toward the door. I pulled my shorts back on, peered around the doorframe and watched him enter the room where Chessa was screaming.

The noises changed after that. Soon it was the men who were pleading for their lives.

I dashed out of my room and gathered all my brothers and sisters into the farthest bedroom, which belonged to Chessa's sons, Felix and Noah.

Lana stared at my blood-soaked pajamas and burst into tears. "She's bleeding. Zenya's dying."

"It's not my blood. I'm all right."

I went back to the door and watched what was happening. One by one, Uncle Kristian dragged our tied-up attackers out of the master bedroom and roughly downstairs. He saw me watching and winked at me.

When Uncle Kristian was finished and he told me I could go in, I went to the master bedroom to find Chessa untying Dad. She'd pulled on a dressing gown. Her hair was in tangles and she was trembling. Tears and blood streaked her face.

When she saw me, she started crying harder. "Baby girl, did they hurt you too?"

I shook my head and explained that there was a dead man in my room and all the kids were safe down the hall in Felix and Noah's bedroom.

Dad was bleeding a lot from a cut on his arm and I helped Chessa clean him up and got the first aid kit. Chessa had been a nurse, and she wanted to give him stitches, but her hands were shaking so hard she couldn't do it. Every time there was a blood-curdling scream from downstairs, she jumped. In the end, she told me how to put in the stitches and I sewed up Dad's arm.

"What's Uncle Kristian doing?" I asked as I worked.

"Finding out who those men are," Dad said through gritted teeth. Chessa had needles but no anesthetic.

I heard the unmistakable sound of a power drill, and then a man's piercing scream.

Dad finally managed a bitter smile. "It shouldn't take him too long."

But Dad was wrong. The screaming went on for hours, long after I finished with the stitches, and we all went to join the kids in Felix and Noah's room. Chessa handed out earplugs but I shook my head. I wanted to listen to our attackers' screams. Every single one made me burn with triumph and pride in Uncle Kristian.

Then it wasn't enough just to listen. I wanted to see.

While Chessa and Dad were distracted, I crept away and sat on the stairs, watching the scene of carnage in the living room below.

Four men were tied to chairs, their bodies slumped and blood oozing from dozens of wounds. Uncle Kristian was in their midst, his face, chest, and hands red with blood, and he stood next to a gory pile of knives, garden implements, and power tools. He sorted through them, picked up a pair of pliers and a buzz saw, and turned toward the nearest man who was conscious.

The men cried.

They screamed and begged.

Uncle Kristian was intent on inflicting as much pain as possible on them and didn't say a word. All the blinds were drawn, but the room slowly lightened as the sun came up. Uncle Kristian glanced toward the windows and then disappeared into the kitchen.

He was back a moment later and put plastic bags over each of the men's heads and tied them tight with twine.

Then he stood in the middle of the room and watched them all suffocate to death.

I came downstairs and joined my uncle, but it took him several minutes to notice me standing there.

He stared at me, his face spattered with gore, and raked me from the top of my head to my bare feet. "You've got blood on you, dandelion."

"So do you."

Uncle Kristian reached out his hand, and I took it. Our tangled fingers were red and sticky, and he rubbed his thumb over my knuckles.

"Did you find out who these people are?" I asked him.

"Oh, yeah. Hours ago." He hunkered down on his heels until he was gazing into my eyes and searched them for a long time. "There is no justice for what happened here tonight. No police. No statements. No courtrooms. Belyaevs don't call the cops. If you were hoping that it was going to be like TV and someone was going to be thrown in prison for what happened to you tonight, then I'm sorry, dandelion, you're going to be disappointed. There's only this."

He gestured around the room at the four mangled corpses. His words were firm, but his eyes were filled with uncertainty. Had he made these men suffer enough for what they did to us tonight?

Had he given me every drop of vengeance that he possibly could?

I reached out and turned his face back to me and smiled. "Why would I need any of that when I have you?"

Uncle Kristian pulled me into his arms and squeezed me tight, and I could feel how much he needed to hear that. My words were everything to him. "You are a Belyaev through and through. Go take a shower. Your uncle will buy you a new dress this week, and we will forget all about these *mudaki*."

I hugged him back, both of us reeking of blood. My hero, who would protect me above all others.

When I was nearly out of the room, he called out to me.

"Zenya?" Uncle Kristian lifted the blood-soaked drill and smiled at me. "Nice work tonight. Be proud of yourself."

I smiled at him from the stairs. "I am."

"Good girl."

He was different with me after that day. He bought me that dress, but he bought me a gun as well. He paid for self-defense classes and taught me more about how to fight with a knife, how to break into various buildings, when to stand my ground, and when to run. He told me more and more about the family business and the way we worked. I was hungry for everything he told me.

"You don't have to choose this life, Zenya," he often reminded me. "There are plenty of other options for someone clever and strong like you."

On the morning of my fifteenth birthday, I broke into Uncle Kristian's house—which he'd bragged to me was unbreachable—and he woke to find me sitting cross-legged at the end of his bed eating a bowl of cereal.

He sat up, bare-chested and rubbing his hand back and forth across his rumpled hair. There was a cut on his cheekbone, and he looked more dangerous than ever. "How the hell did you get in here?"

The moment he claimed I couldn't get into his house, he knew I would either succeed, or my life would take me down a path very different to his.

I chased a marshmallow charm around my bowl with my spoon. "I've made my choice."

I couldn't change that I'd killed a man, and I didn't want to. Going back to being a normal person after seeing what I'd seen and doing what I'd done?

Impossible. I wanted to walk on the wild side with Uncle Kristian forever.

He smiled at me. "Yes, you have. Happy birthday, princess."

And now?

I've been walking for two years without him.

I lift my hand and stroke a finger down the silver chain around Uncle Kristian's neck. "Where have you been all this time?"

Uncle Kristian touches my cheek. My hair. Trails his fingers down my arm as I gaze up at him. "Rebuilding my life."

"But your life was here."

"I have my pride, Zenya. I wasn't going to sit on my hands and wait for your stubborn bastard of a father to forgive me. I've been making my own money. Earning loyalty from my own people." Anger flashes over his handsome face. He went on living without me, but he wasn't happy about it. "Now all that I have, I offer to you. You're the one in charge of the Belyaevs now."

"I'm not. It's still Dad."

He shakes his head. "You're the one who's holding this family together. All I want is to help the one who's leading the Belyaevs, just as I always have."

"Dad is…" I start to say, and then trail off and close my mouth. There's no point lying to Uncle Kristian. I hope with all my heart that Dad pulls through this latest round of cancer, but meanwhile, I am the one holding things together, and I need support from someone who knows what he's doing.

"What do you want in exchange for helping me?"

Uncle Kristian gives me a long look through his lashes. He looks sly, like a fox. "Me? I don't want anything. I'm your family. Your muscle. Your protector. You say it, and I'll do it. Whatever you want, whatever you need."

"You want nothing from me?"

He reaches for his coffee with a smile. "I'm just happy to be home with my family. My life has been unbearable without you."

He's only telling me half of the truth. I can feel it. I twitch open his jacket and look at the label stitched to the lining. "Pining for us in Prada. How you must have been suffering."

He chuckles darkly. "I have standards to keep up." Then he takes my hand and his expression grows serious. "I know you, princess. You're a hard worker and you're making sure everyone and everything is taken care of before you take care of yourself. Someone needs to look out for you, and that's my job."

I flex my nails so they dig into the fleshy base of his thumb. They look good poking into his flesh. He seems to like the sight of it as well.

I lift my eyes to his. "Just so you know, last night, I would have got out of that warehouse alive, injured foot and all."

"Of course you would have." His gaze falls to my mouth. Slowly, he drops his head closer to mine. "But you have to admit, it was much more fun my way."

The kitchen is hushed and the air between us grows hot and heavy. Uncle Kristian is so close that a lock of his hair brushes my forehead.

"I kissed you once, two years ago, and I don't think you even remember," he murmurs.

I didn't, at first. Then a week later when I was staring at the jacaranda in the back garden and thinking about the day he left, a jolt went through me. He kissed my lips. He'd never kissed me on the lips before.

I went over that kiss again and again in my mind in the months that followed, trying to fathom what it meant. He'd been distraught at me crying and wanted to comfort me? He'd simply missed and had been trying to kiss my cheek?

But it hadn't been either of those things. He meant to kiss me, and he wanted me to understand from that kiss that he wanted me. He was asking me to wait for him.

I lift my hand and touch his lips with my finger. "I was crying and you said, *I promise I'll be back.*"

Uncle Kristian groans and takes my face in his hands. "You do remember."

My heart is thundering. He lowers his head and brushes his lips softly against mine. A question. He pulls back and looks into my eyes for the answer.

I feel like I'm drunk as I slide my palms up the muscles of his chest.

Uncle Kristian stands up and grasps me around the waist, perching me on the table. He moves between my thighs and wraps my legs around his hips.

He captures my jaw in his hand and whispers urgently, "Open your mouth for me."

Gripping his waist with both hands, I lick my lips and part them.

"Fuck, princess," he groans, and his lips ghost over mine once more. Not quite a kiss. A sweet torment that makes us both breathe harder and harder. "You're delicious."

I search his face and feel how fast his heart is beating beneath my hands. "You're serious about this?"

"You think I've been playing with you?"

I shake my head helplessly. "This is so insane that I thought it had to be a twisted game."

"Let me tell you a secret. When it comes to you, I'm never playing."

I grip his shoulders hard and whimper. I shouldn't want this man. I can't want this man. Dad's upstairs suffering, and I'm down here almost kissing his brother. He's twice my age, and we're family, for God's sake.

"Uncle Kristian," I whisper. I try to say *don't* but I can't make myself form the word.

He slides his hands around my ass and pulls me tighter against his body. He's looking at me like he's never seen anything so beautiful in his life. With burning lips he plants kisses to my throat, and then moves his lips to my ear and whispers, "Tell me one thing. Last night. Did you enjoy my tongue?"

I close my eyes and breathe hard. It took him a hot second to find my clit and apply the perfect amount of pressure and friction with his wet tongue. There was so much love and adoration in the way he moved against me. How could I not love that? How could I not want that again and again? Even now that I know who it was and that I'm a sick, twisted slut for loving the feel of my uncle's tongue on my sex.

"I need to take care of you in all the ways," he murmurs, his lips ghosting over mine. "I want us to be like we always were, but closer than ever. Family is the most important thing to me."

My family. My muscle. My protector. My…lover?

There's so much about him I don't know. What he's been doing these past two years. Where he's been. Who he's been with. Has there been a woman? He exudes so much sexual confidence, and yet, I've never seen him with a woman. I've barely noticed him even look at a woman, but he must like women if he's touching me like this and burning up against me.

Apparently he likes strippers.

I huff as I remember that photo. Every few months it resurfaces in one of my social media feeds, and I'm filled with volcanic rage at the sight of it. In between wondering whether that kiss meant anything, I've been jealous of that stripper on his lap. That's *my* uncle she's sitting on. How dare she? How dare *he*?

Now I'm supposed to forget all that and welcome him back?

Uncle Kristian pulls back and frowns at me. "What are you thinking about? You're tense all of a sudden."

I suck my lower lip into my mouth and watch him watch me do it. I could forget all about that photo and lose myself in Uncle Kristian's kisses. He'll do whatever I want. I could lay back on this table and ask him to use his mouth on me like he did last night, and he would without question.

I lean back on my elbows, my thighs dragging up his hips and gathering him closer. Uncle Kristian reaches for the button on my jeans with lust burning in his gaze, ready to give me the bliss of his mouth.

But before he can undo my jeans and get his mouth on me, I stop him with a squeeze of my thighs and ask, "Been to any good strip clubs lately, Uncle?"

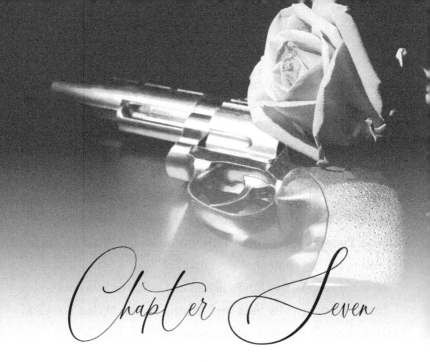

Chapter Seven

KRISTIAN

I glance up in confusion. "Have I what?"

Anger flickers in those jewel-blue eyes of hers, and she digs her tapered nails into my shoulders. The pain is heavenly. I hope she leaves ten little pinpricks on my skin.

"I've never seen you with a woman before, but I guess brunettes are your type."

"Brunettes are not my type."

"That stripper was a brunette," she points out.

"For the record, my only type is…" I run my fingers through her hair, admiring the silky tresses, and then lift a lock to my lips and kiss it. "…you."

Zenya gives me an angry look like she thinks I'm full of shit. She never used to believe me when I told her that she's beautiful, exquisite, entrancing, and now she finds it downright insulting. Like I'm mocking her.

She pushes me away and sits up. "I don't know what you think you're going to gain by coming back here, but if you want me to persuade Dad to change his will to make you heir again, then you're in for a rude shock. I grew up while you were gone. Sixteen-year-old me would have done anything her darling Uncle Kristian asked of her, but I've learned to stand on my own two feet in the past two years."

I cast my eyes over her beautiful face, which is currently blazing with anger and more beautiful than ever. I can see that for myself. I glance at the button on her jeans. I should be going down on her right now and sinking a careful finger into her virgin pussy. I want to explore every single way to make her moan, but apparently she doesn't want to come.

She wants to fight.

Fine. I enjoy foreplay as much as the next man.

I grasp the table either on side of her body and move in close. "I told you. I want to be your protector. You think I came back here for money and power? Sure, I want money and power, but if that was *all* I craved I would have stayed where I was. I was well on my way to becoming *Pakhan* of that last city. The people there were weak. Pathetic."

She narrows her eyes at me. "And how are you going to get money and power here?"

I smile and close in on her mouth for a kiss.

Zenya raises her uninjured leg and plants her foot against my chest, keeping me back. "This is a game you're playing. It's a sick and twisted one, and I'm not playing with you."

I grasp her ankle and massage it. "How about we talk about what you want. I've got your back, and your back only. Not Troian's. Yours. You say beat that man to death? I do it. You want me to tell everyone in this city that Zenya Belyaev rules the streets and break the fingers of anyone who doesn't agree? I'm there. Anything you need. The sky's the limit."

She thinks for a moment. "I want you to admit that what happened two years ago is all your fault. You hurt Dad and me and you're sorry."

If she were anyone else, I'd tell her to get fucked and point out that it took two people to get me thrown out of this family. Apparently Zenya needs to believe that none of this is Troian's fault. Her precious father is at death's door. His are big shoes to fill, and she craves to look up to him and be the person he wants her to be.

So I swallow my pride and my anger and tell her what she needs to hear.

Taking her face in my hands, I look deep into her eyes. "It was all my fault, princess. I take full responsibility for what happened two years ago, and I'm so sorry for the pain I caused you."

"Wow," she whispers in shock.

Her foot slides down my chest. I catch her leg behind the knee and hold it at my hip, moving closer to her. I'm so close to a real kiss I can taste her lips.

"You've changed these past two years," she says. "The old you would never admit any faults. Will you say this to Dad, too?"

I shake my head. "He's not the one who needs to hear it. Don't worry about me and your father. We'll sort our issues out between the two of us."

"Promise you won't say anything to upset Dad," she says anxiously.

"I'll try." Probably. I haven't decided yet whether I want to share everything that happened between Troian and me two years ago with Zenya.

"Swear that you won't. Swear it on my mother's grave."

My jaw clenches. If I do that, my lips really will be sealed. I would never break an oath like that. Is this what it's going to take to convince Zenya that I'm a better man and to accept me as part of this family again?

I gaze into her big blue eyes. Apparently so.

"I swear on your mother's grave that I won't say anything to upset your father. What's more, I swear on her memory that I never wanted to stay away so long. Every day that I was gone hurt like hell, and I never stopped thinking about you."

Zenya breathes harshly and pain fills her eyes. "You better not be telling lies as you swear on my mother's memory or I will never forgive you, Uncle Kristian."

I take her hand and place it on my heart. "It's the truth. I only want to be here for you."

"Do you mean me specifically or the family?"

A smile hooks the corner of my mouth. Does my princess need

to feel special right now? Then I'll make her feel as adored as I know how because I live to spoil her. "The Belyaev family is important to me, but the one I need the most? You, princess. In the last…" How do I put this without freaking her out? "…several years, I haven't touched another woman. I haven't kissed another woman. I haven't even looked at another woman."

Her cheeks flame red and she stammers, "I wasn't asking about anything like that." Then she thinks for a moment and scowls at me. "What about strippers?"

I shake my head. "The boys love strippers so we always used to drink in places like that, but the boys and I do our drinking in bars these days. If they want strippers, they go without me."

Zenya studies me for a long time, a confused expression on her face. "But why would you stay away from other women?"

I slide my hand around the nape of her neck and my lips whisper in her ear, "Because I only wanted you. For me, there's been only you for a long time."

Zenya is silent for a long time, gripping the edge of the table with both hands. "I don't understand."

I pull back and rest my forehead against hers, stroking her cheek with my thumb. "Since the moment I realized you're the only one for me, I haven't wanted anyone else. So I've been waiting for you."

It didn't start as a conscious decision. I've never been short of female attention, and sleeping with one or two different women every week was normal for me for a long time. Often the women would come back for seconds and thirds—if they weren't offended that I didn't remember their names. But then I found myself turning away from flirtatious smiles and hands that lingered on my arm. First I was too busy for sex, and then when I realized a month had passed without indulging in one of my favorite pastimes, none of the faces and bodies on offer held any appeal.

Not that I wasn't ferociously horny. I kept looking for a slender blonde with a pretty, plush mouth and blue eyes that danced with mischief, and I was so frustrated when I couldn't find her.

Until I got it through my thick skull who I was hunting for.

The girl who was right under my nose. Snuggling up to me on the sofa. Begging to drive my car. Doing her homework at the kitchen table. Teaching her younger siblings to read. Working at the Silo. Asking me to practice self-defense with her.

One blood-soaked night changed everything, and there was no going back.

"What moment are you talking about? Do you mean the day you left?"

I shake my head slowly, wondering how much to tell her right now. "Not that day. It's been a long time since you saw me with another woman, remember?"

"Yes, but I assumed that there were other women who you were, you know, with." An adorable blush tints her cheeks.

"Years ago, yes. But then I started feeling very, very serious about someone, and the agony of waiting for her became strangely..." I smile and brush the tip of my nose against hers. "Pleasurable."

Zenya has her hands on my chest, leaning closer, hungry for my secrets. "Pleasurable how?"

"Do you remember a night years ago when you picked gravel out of my shoulder and cleaned all my cuts?"

"Of course I do," she whispers, gazing at my mouth like she's afraid I'll slant it over hers and terrified I won't.

"I like the pain when it's you. I'll endure anything for you."

"How long have you not been with—" She breaks off and sinks her teeth into her lower lip, gazing at me uncertainly. She's dying to ask her uncle about his sex life, but she's still shy about it. "What was the moment you're talking about?"

Isn't she just tormented with curiosity? Her hands are on my shoulders now, and she reaches even higher to twine her arms around my neck. Her breasts press against my chest and her fingers stroke the short hairs at my nape. Her touch feels possessive. Demanding. Hungry to know how long I've been waiting for her.

And I have been waiting for her. I'm devoted to Zenya, and only Zenya.

But this has been my secret for so long, and I'm not ready to give it up. Besides, being left on tenterhooks and thinking about me all day is just how I want her.

I take hold of her waist, help her down from the table, and set her gently on her feet. "You and I have work to do and the morning will have gone by before we know it. Tell me what our plans are this morning. I'm right by your side, always."

Zenya seems disappointed when I stand back and let her go, and I could purr I'm so fucking pleased.

She gazes at me doubtfully. "You want to come with me?"

I put both my hands in my pockets and give her my sincerest look, turning the charm up to a twelve and looking deep into her eyes. "Tomorrow, I want to open that front door and see you smile that big, beautiful smile that means you're happy to see me. I want that more than anything in the world, dandelion. So tell me what you need to make that happen for me."

Zenya looks around the kitchen, deep in thought. Finally, she looks up at me with a determined expression.

"I want to see the bodies."

The watches, chains, rings, and wallets sit in a bloodstained pile atop the table.

I can't show Zenya the corpses of the men we killed last night because they're long gone at the bottom of a lake deep in the woods, but I can show her the things that might identify her attackers, which is what she really wants to know.

I study her beautiful face while she goes through each of the items, talking to me but mostly to herself. "These men were Bratva. Some of them are from Russia, or they spent time there. Look at the makes of their watches. Expensive, too. They're well paid. They probably didn't need to steal my merchandise."

I feel a thrill of pride as she says *my merchandise*. She always used to say *our merchandise* because it belonged to her only because she was part of the family. One day she'll *be* the family. Zenya's getting used to the idea of leading, and a warm, delicious feeling rolls through me. Seeing her in charge is hot as fuck.

Zenya looks up and meets my gaze. "What are you smiling about?"

I smile wider, and my admiration must show in my face because she turns a little pink. "Mikhail and I thought the same thing about your attackers. Bratva assholes."

We're in a room over the warehouse that's currently serving as the Silo. Troian gave his men the okay to let me, Mikhail, and my guys in last night when we were dropping off the merchandise.

"But I still have no idea why I was attacked." Zenya drops the ring she was holding back onto the table and brushes off her fingers before turning to Mikhail. "Thank you for your help last night. I appreciate it."

The dark-haired man standing at my side nods respectfully at her.

Zenya glances at the half a dozen men behind us. "And thank you to all of you as well. Uncle Kristian tells me you're eager to work for the Belyaev family, and we're very happy to welcome you. I'll make sure you meet my father in time, but for now, please let me know if there's anything you need."

Finally she turns to me. "I have a meeting now. I'll see you later?"

"I'll come with you." I start to move toward the door, but Zenya stops me.

"You don't have to. I'm sure you've got other things to do."

I reach up and touch her cheek. "You were nearly killed last night. Do you think your protector has anything better to do than ensure nothing befalls his princess?"

Zenya pulls my hand away from her cheek and glances at the other men. Most of them are talking among themselves. Only Mikhail is paying us any attention, but his expression is carefully bland as if he's never had an opinion about anything.

"I'm used to doing things by myself," she reminds me. "And don't call me princess while we're working."

I pretend not to hear that. "So you weren't going to take Radimir or Stannis or any of the other men with you today if they'd survived?"

She turns toward the other men. "Well, I was, but I can take someone—"

I catch her by the elbow and draw her back to face me. "What's really bothering you? Are you worried I'm going to take control of the meeting and not let you get a word in?"

"I should hope not," she says indignantly.

"Then what is it?"

Zenya pins me with a glare. "I'm not sure how long I can rely on you before you abandon me again."

"I'm not going anywhere, I swear it. You lead, and I follow." I spread my hands and glance down at myself and then back up at her with a smile. "I'm all yours."

Zenya glances at my chest. My hands. My shoulders. Her gaze goes a little unfocused, and I know she's remembering what it felt like to be beneath me on that sofa last night. Touching me. Seeing herself wrapped around me in the moments before I put that blindfold on her. As she sat in my lap with the aftershocks of her orgasm coursing through her, she felt for herself my undeniable reaction to her.

I'm everything she needs.

Her muscle.

Her protection.

Her man, in all the ways.

And she's just so very needy for me.

I dig my keys out of my pocket and nod toward the door. "So, shall we go?"

Zenya nods but doesn't move.

I smile wider and watch her watch me playing with the keys in my fingers, slipping my middle finger into the metal ring and flipping the key over my knuckles. "I'm following you, angel. You're the boss."

"Oh—right." Zenya walks quickly to the door, and I follow her with a grin. It's just so delicious making my niece flustered.

Zenya's meeting is on the other side of town at a private club belonging to one of the Belyaev family's oldest associates, Bohdan Adamovich.

At that time of day, the main bar of the club has only a handful of drinkers, some with cups of espresso, others with glasses of whisky, who probably haven't been to bed since the previous day. Work hours are unconventional in the Bratva.

There are only men here. It's always just men in places like these, unless a woman is serving the drinks. Our lifestyle isn't welcoming to women in charge or kind to them either. As Troian's daughter, Zenya walks in a halo of protection almost everywhere she goes, or she's supposed to, anyway.

Protection and interest. Irritation ripples up my spine as I notice how every man in the room is staring at my niece.

Sweet little Zenya Belyaev is finally eighteen. Old enough to wed.

I hang back for a moment so I can gauge their reactions to her, and nothing I see makes me happy. I step up behind her and cast an angry glare around the room. I recognize many of the men and their eyes widen as they see me.

That's right, you fuckers. Kristian Belyaev is back in town, and Zenya Belyaev isn't looking for a husband. Being with Troian's daughter means that everyone will know I'm back in the *Pakhan's* good graces. Word will spread everywhere by tonight.

Adamovich's man was expecting Zenya, but as he approaches us, he gazes between us in confusion for a moment and then talks to me, announcing that Adamovich is waiting for me.

"You mean he's waiting for my niece," I tell him, and I say it loud enough that my voice carries around the room. Glances are exchanged and a few eyebrows raise.

Zenya Belyaev is old enough to wed, and she's old enough to lead in her father's absence too.

I wait for Zenya to go first, sending the message to everyone watching—and everyone is watching—that I'm here with Zenya and not the other way around.

Zenya might have faltered in the privacy of the Silo, but here her expression is a cool, relaxed mask, and her head is high as she leads the way upstairs to Adamovich's office.

Before I follow her, I turn around and cast a hard glare around the room. Which one of you absolute cunts tried to hurt my niece last night? When I find out, he'll wish he left his intestines on the warehouse floor along with the goons he hired.

In Adamovich's office, I stand by Zenya's chair and face his desk. Adamovich is a short, sturdy man in his sixties with dyed black hair slicked to one side. He stares from me to my niece, wearing an expression of confusion.

"The merchandise you requested is available. We weren't about to source the exact models you requested, but I'm able to provide alternatives." Zenya talks him through the technical details of the radar jammers and detectors and explains why they're actually better than the ones Adamovich was hoping for.

When she's finished, he turns to me. "I'm disappointed that you weren't able to fill my request down to the letter, Kristian."

I haven't said a word since I stepped in the room. I glance at Zenya and see irritation flash through her eyes.

She smiles sweetly at him. "As I explained, the radars and scanners we obtained are newer and better than the ones you requested, but I hope we're able to come to a deal that makes up for your disappointment."

Then she names a price for the merchandise that's higher than the price she told me last night when she thought I was a stranger who could be bribed to let her live, and I have to hide a smirk.

Adamovich clicks his tongue and shakes his head. To me, he says, "I'll pay four hundred and fifty thousand."

I stare at the man without saying anything, and so does Zenya. Finally, when the silence becomes uncomfortable, I ask, "Why are you disrespecting my niece like this?"

The man gapes at me. "What? I presumed—"

"Zenya Belyaev is the one you're meeting with," I growl. "Do her the courtesy of addressing her."

He glowers from her to me. "I would prefer to conduct my business with someone more experienced."

Zenya gets to her feet. "Then I'll stop wasting your time."

Good girl. End this meeting and show Adamovich who's in

change. I turn away and open the door for her, but just as we're about to leave, Adamovich calls out to us.

"Wait. Please, Zenya." He gestures to her chair. "You may sit down."

She stays where she is and examines her tapered nails. They're painted a glossy blood red that's so dark it's almost black. "May I? But the price just went up ten percent." She flicks a dark look at him. "My price. Not yours."

Adamovich's face flushes angrily. "That's the kind of petty behavior I expect from a teenage girl."

"You disrespectful goddamn—" My temper flares and I step toward him, but Zenya stops me with a hand on my chest.

"It's all right, Uncle Kristian," she murmurs, and the chilly expression in her eyes tells me she's got this.

Zenya slowly blinks her lashes at Adamovich. "Would you call it petty that you took advantage of my father's illness two years ago to pay us a far lower price for a shipment than what was previously agreed? He was too sick and foggy in his mind to argue with you, but I know for a fact that you deceived him. I'd call that petty. In fact, I'd call that downright despicable."

Adamovich gapes at her. "How dare you accuse me of such a thing? How would you even know the first thing about my deals with your father?"

Zenya gives him a cold smile. "This petty little girl has been managing her family's stock movements and financial records since she was fifteen years old. My father tells me everything about his deals, and I realized back then how you tricked a sick man. We don't have e-mail records and order forms in this line of work. We only have our word and our honor. I wasn't at those meetings, but I'm here before you now, and I'll be at every meeting in the future. If you want to make deals with the Belyaev family, you're going to have to make me happy to work with you."

Adamovich blusters for a few minutes about how he never deceived anyone, and if there was any mistake it was an honest one.

"Of course it was. We'll forget all about the past as long as you agree to my terms today," Zenya tells him.

Her hand is still on my chest and she's playing with one of the buttons on my shirt. I gaze down at her with a smile.

Adamovich agrees to her terms.

My niece is such a fucking badass.

As we leave his office and head down the corridor, Zenya says to me, "I thought it was too good to be true that you wouldn't steamroller all over my authority back there. I owe you an apology."

"No need to apologize. Seeing my niece take that idiot down a few pegs is the best thing I've seen in two years."

She smiles and shakes her head. "Kristian Belyaev, feminist icon. Who would have thought it?"

"Me? More like you. You were absolutely magnificent." I move closer to her, enjoying that I have her totally alone here. "I hope you're proud of yourself."

She raises her chin and meets my gaze boldly. "Of course I am. I'm a Belyaev."

That daring look in her eyes makes blood rush to my dick. I glance up and down the corridor and take her jaw in my hand, playing my thumb over her full lips. "If you need more of what I gave you last night, all you have to do is ask."

I feel her warm breath against my skin. I stroke her lips again and her tongue moves against the pad of my thumb. I groan and press my forehead against hers. Her back is against the wall, but she's not the one who's trapped.

I am.

Wild horses couldn't rip me from my niece.

I angle my head until my lips are so close to hers that I'm nearly kissing her, and her gaze drifts to my lips. "I know you must be keeping yourself chaste for your husband…"

Me. I'm your fucking husband.

I'm just managing to keep myself from declaring that to her and everyone within a fifty-mile radius, but my resolution is hanging by a thread.

"There are so many things I can drive you crazy with that stop just short of giving up your innocence. And if you don't give a damn about your innocence, I'll happily relieve you of that, too. You deserve everything that's good from this life, Zenya. And I want to give it to you."

"Uncle Kristian, we can't do that," she whispers. Her hands slide up my forearms to cling to my wrists. We're both panting against each other's mouths.

"We can. My tongue was made for your pussy and you know it."

Zenya is plastered against the wall, breathing fast, and her eyes are dilated.

I know her pussy is wet.

I just know she's wet.

Not twenty-four hours since my return and we're moving at lightning speed toward each other, hurtling so fast that our collision is going to be explosive.

My fingers drop to the hem of her dress because I have to know for sure.

Zenya shakes her head desperately.

"Let me feel, princess," I murmur. "If you're not wet, I'll never touch you again."

"I'm not," she insists, but doesn't stop me as I slide a hand between her warm inner thighs. I nearly groan at how silky soft she is.

I wrap an arm around her waist and pull her tight against my body, and her hands land on my chest. With my nose buried in the nape of her neck, I breathe her in. I live to savor this girl. Every second without her felt like eternities stringing together, on and on. With my other hand, I stroke up her panties over her sex. They're made of thin lace and she's soaking right through them.

"Shit, you're not wet," I whisper.

"I'm not?" she replies, and I smile against her throat as I hear her surprise and just a hint of disappointment.

I grind her clit gently with my middle finger, and Zenya gasps and clings even tighter to me. "You're soaking."

I hold my finger up and show it to her. She has enough time to stare at it, and then I put it in my mouth and suck. With a groan, I pull my finger out and whisper, "You taste fucking delicious, princess. I've been starving for you."

Shock and desire have her completely at my mercy. Taking my time now, I lower my hand once more and get my fingers inside her panties, zeroing in on her clit and rubbing her in firm circles.

Zenya's gripping my lapels with both hands and she walks her feet open and arches her back. Her lips are as wet as her pussy is, and each pant she makes is a tiny kiss against my own mouth. I could do so many things to her while she's in this state.

I lift my finger to her lips. "Now you suck."

She opens her mouth and I slide my finger past her lips, up to my second knuckle.

"Good girl," I murmur huskily, entranced by the sight of her lips wrapped around me. The sensation of her soft tongue and the suction of her mouth. Her eyelashes flutter as I praise her. "You're so beautiful when you're horny. I love seeing this side of you."

I'm teaching her that being wet and panting for me is a good thing. No shame.

Only pleasure.

"You're the woman I need. Beautiful. Strong. Clever. Melting to the touch. We can have anything we want, Zenya."

A sound at the other end of the hall makes her jump, and she snaps out of her trance and realizes she's sucking on my finger that's covered in her wetness.

Zenya yanks my finger from her lips and pushes against me. "Please, let me go."

"I don't want anything in return. Just let me watch your beautiful face as you come."

"Uncle Kristian, *please*." Confusion is filling her blue eyes.

Reluctantly, I loosen my hold and she steps back from me so fast that she stumbles.

We stare at each other in silence, her panting with shock and me with my shoulders resting against the wall, my hands in my pockets, and a glower on my face.

"Why did you do that?" Zenya tugs on the hem of her dress as if she can make it cover more of her heavenly thighs. Knowing she's so wet and swollen for me with just a scrap of lace in the way is making me crazy.

"Why wouldn't I?"

She seems to be struggling to find a reason as her jaw works. "I'm your niece. That's all I'll ever be. If you think I can be anything else for you, you're insane."

I throw a challenging look at her. "Who do you want to walk down the aisle toward on your wedding day? Someone who only wants you for your money and power, or a man who's always loved you?"

She stares at me in shock.

Yes, *always* loved her, in one way or another.

Zenya turns and hurries downstairs, disappearing from my sight.

I groan and knock my head against the wall, staring at the ceiling. I can't give Zenya up. I won't.

Seeing her with another man will make me commit murder. If I ever see a man touching her, I'll rip his guts out of his belly with my bare hands.

After a moment, I take a breath and calm my frustration, and follow her. This is a marathon, I remind myself, not a sprint. I can't undo sixteen years of Zenya adoring me as her uncle and two years of pain and loneliness in just one day. I've shown her how much her body responds to my touch, so I'll allow that to soak in for a day or two and then renew my pursuit.

As I emerge into the club downstairs, the first thing I see is Zenya. In another man's arms.

The world turns molten red. Some piece of shit I don't recognize has his arms around Zenya and he's lowering his mouth to hers.

I'm at her side a split second later. "If you kiss her, you're a dead man."

The man lifts his head and scowls at me, and he doesn't let go of my niece. "Who the fuck are you?"

I glance at Zenya and she's wearing a disgusted expression, so different to the desire I saw on her face when she was in my arms.

"Grigor's new," Zenya explains. "He's only been working in the city about a year. His father is Gedeon Kalchik."

I don't care if his father is the King of Olympus. "Get your hands off her," I say through my teeth.

"Your new bodyguard thinks he's hot shit, baby." The man smirks at me, dragging his gaze up my body with an insolent look in his eyes. "Run along, idiot. I'm Zenya's fiancé."

I turn to her and raise an eyebrow. Last night she claimed she was engaged, but I thought it was something she said to throw off the strange man who was making her feel things she'd never felt before. Her shoulders are hunched against this man's touch and her eyes keep cutting away from him. Whoever he is, she's not pleased to see him.

I'm vaguely aware that everyone in the room has stopped talking and is staring at the three of us. No one comes to Grigor's aid. They all know who I am, and they like their blood inside their veins.

I give him a threatening smile. "Get your hands off my niece."

The young man opens his eyes wide and rakes me up and down. "Kristian Belyaev? I thought you were dead or whatever."

"It's whatever."

"Grigor?" Zenya says, looking at me with worried eyes, guessing correctly that I'm about to cause bloodshed.

"Yes, baby?"

"Get your hands off me."

With a sulky expression, Grigor drags his arm from around her shoulders and steps back.

"Grigor is not my fiancé," she explains to me, settling her clothing back into place.

"Only because of a technicality," he butts in, and shoots Zenya a conspiratorial smile. "Zenya just hasn't said yes."

I form my hands into fists. Zenya puts a placating hand on my arm like she's telling me not to worry about it.

"I'll call you. You owe me a second date." Grigor saunters away with a confident swagger, as if it's only a matter of time before he makes her his.

Zenya has her arms wrapped around her body and her expression is downcast. I know that look. My sweet little dandelion looked that way on the worst days of her life. When her mom died. When Chessa's kids were crying for their dead mom. The day I left her. I never wanted to see her look like that ever again.

"Let me guess. That asshole's been harassing you for weeks. Months. You keep saying no but because there's no man around to tell him to fuck off, he's been trying to wear you down."

She presses her lips together and nods.

I wrap an arm around her waist and kiss her forehead. "Your uncle's got this for you, princess."

As I turn toward Grigor, Zenya says quickly, "No, Uncle Kristian, don't—"

"Hey. You." I hear Zenya's exasperated sigh behind me as I follow Grigor. Does she really think I'm going to stand for a complete nobody making her feel like she's prey? "What did you just say to her?"

Grigor turns back to me with a frown on his face. "Huh?"

Another ripple of anger passes through me. "It's not *Huh?* It's *Yes, sir.* You need to learn some manners. I asked what you said to my niece."

He glances between Zenya and me with a confused expression. "I said goodbye. Why are you getting up my ass?"

"She owes you another date?"

A stupid grin spreads over his face. "I took her to dinner and she promised me another date, but she hasn't been answering my—"

"Zenya Belyaev owes you something?"

"Well, yeah, she said—"

I grab him by the hair and pull him back to Zenya.

He grabs my wrist and tries to escape my grasp, but he's got no choice but to stumble over his own feet as I drag him across the carpet. "Ow! What the fuck! Let go of me, you fucking psycho."

I make him straighten up and snarl in his ear, "I told you. Not *you fucking psycho.* It's *sir.*" I make him face her, and I'm not gentle about it. "What does my favorite niece owe you?"

"What are you talking about? Let go of me!"

"Zenya Belyaev, my brother's first and most precious child, the most beautiful woman in this city and heir to the lion's share of the Belyaev fortune, owes something to a sniveling dog like you?"

Grigor finally catches on and gasps, "Okay. No. She owes me nothing."

I shake him so his teeth rattle. "Does she owe you a date?"

"No."

"Did she already turn you down?"

"Well, yes, but—"

"So you didn't listen to a lady who turned you down?" I growl.

"But—"

I shake him so hard his teeth clack together. "You're nothing but a little shit stain, aren't you? Say it."

"What? Seriously, fuck off, man."

He twists back and forth in my grip while I stand there with a hand in my pocket. Everyone around us is staring. I see someone I know across the room and give them a silent hello with a lift of my chin. He replies with an amused smile and toasts me with his coffee cup. Adamovich's bodyguards have appeared, but they'll keep out of this as long as the quarrel stays between me and this little idiot.

I turn back to Grigor struggling in my grip. "I know your father. I know your uncles. They're good friends of mine. How about I throw you into the back of my car, drive you around to them, and tell them how you disrespected my niece?"

Grigor might not understand how dangerous it is to enrage the Belyaev clan, but his family will, and I happen to know Grigor's father has a violent temper.

"You're a nothing little shit stain. Say. It."

Grigor turns red and mumbles, "I'm a nothing little shit stain."

I throw him away from me by his hair. "If I catch you within a hundred feet of Zenya ever again, I'll gut you like a fucking fish. Now get out of my sight."

Grigor stumbles, rights himself, and throws me a dirty look before walking away quickly.

Zenya slips her hand into mine and puts her hand on my bicep, whispering up at me, "You didn't need to do that."

I glance down at her hand holding mine and the corner of my mouth lifts. I suspect she's holding on to me so I don't go after Grigor and beat him to death, but I'm still enjoying this. "Yes, I did. Since when were creeps like that allowed to drool over you and demand things from a Belyaev?"

She makes a rueful expression, and I can guess the answer. Ever since I left and Troian became too sick to remind everyone that we're top of the food chain in this city.

I smooth her hair back and gaze down at her beautiful face. "Everything's going back to the way it was before. In fact, it's going to be even better because all these insolent fucks will learn to pay their respects to you."

Zenya gazes up at me. "Dad thinks I should marry Grigor. Or marry someone, at least. You saw what Adamovich was like. Men in this line of work don't take unmarried women very seriously. Or women in general. But with a strong man by my side..." Her nose scrunches in annoyance.

That's unfortunately true, but that's why she has me. To stand over any dickhead who doesn't give my niece the respect she deserves. "If anyone else takes liberties with you, your uncle will teach them manners until they cry for their mothers."

Zenya gives me an amused look. "You'll have your hands full if that's the case."

Anger ripples through me as I glare around the room. Most people have lost interest in us now that the fight is over, but the few who were still staring look away quickly. "Who's been harassing you? I'll kill them."

She shrugs. "Mostly they want to marry me."

"How many?"

"I've lost count." As she gazes up at me, a smile hooks the corners of her mouth.

I slide my hand around the nape of her neck and pull her closer, murmuring, "Princess, are you trying to make me jealous?"

She gazes up at me from beneath her lashes, a flirty, daring look. It's Belyaev nature to rise to any challenge. "From the look in your eyes, I don't have to try to make you jealous."

"That's right. Every time I think about a man touching you the way I touch you…" I growl, dropping my face even closer to hers and breathing in her sweet scent. "I nearly go out of my mind with jealousy. One of these days, I'm going to kiss you out in the open and make sure everyone in this city knows you're mine."

I drink in the hazy, needy expression in her eyes.

See how different it feels when it's me holding you, princess?

On that day, she'll be wearing my ring and my baby will be in her belly, and the church bells will ring out for everyone to hear for miles around.

She takes hold of my wrist and drags my hand away from the nape of her neck. "I should have been the one to make Grigor whimper and beg for mercy. I'm the next in line to lead this family, not you."

"Fuck yes you are," I breathe. "But it's my pleasure to do that kind of thing for you. Don't take it away from me."

"I don't belong to any man, Uncle. I'm Zenya Belyaev, and everyone in this city is going to kneel to me."

She gives me a push, and I fall onto a sofa and stare up at her in surprise, my hair falling into my eyes.

Zenya smiles at me and folds her arms. "Starting with you."

That's not part of my plan, for me to kneel to her. It's supposed to be the other way around. Zenya Belyaev was supposed to fall in love with me and sweetly hand over all her power to her darling uncle.

But she's changed in the years since I've been gone. She gazes down her cute nose at me with pride burning in her eyes.

"You want me on my knees for you?" I ask slowly, feeling the blood rush to my dick.

"Do you dare, Uncle, in front of all these men?"

Together we glance left and right and see that the whole room is staring at us again.

I, Kristian Belyaev, have never knelt before anyone in my life. Not even my own brother. Troian has always had my total devotion, but I would have told him to fuck off if he asked me to kneel.

But as I gaze up at my niece, I realize it's all I want to do. Every man in this city should drop to his knees the moment she enters a room.

And they will.

Zenya's going to make them all worship her, and I can't wait to watch her do it.

I slide to my knees before Zenya and her eyes flare with surprise. I reach out to take her hand and brush my lips over the inside of her palm as I gaze into her eyes.

"Anything for you, princess."

Chapter Eight

KRISTIAN

*I*t's a special kind of crazy to want to plunge your tongue into your niece's mouth right in front of your brother, but as Zenya takes charge of the meeting, it's all I can think about.

All eyes are on her, and she looks drop-dead stunning with her blonde hair like spun moonlight tumbling around her shoulders and a black minidress clinging to her body. There's a black velvet ribbon choker around her throat, and every so often she touches it with her dark red tapered nails. I'm obsessed with every tiny detail about her. Her lashes. The strands of silky hair by her ear. That choker, which should be my fucking hand as I kiss her roughly.

I shove my hands deeper into my pants pockets and clear my throat to distract myself. I've been semi-hard tending to rock hard ever since she told me to kneel for her. The power of this girl over my heart and body is insane.

Troian's here, of course, and so is Mikhail. We're having this meeting in Troian's bedroom because he was too exhausted from chemotherapy to make it down to the Silo.

Hot, restless desire has been churning through me all week, and now it's reaching a fever pitch. I *need* to feel Zenya's lips against mine. I crave to crush her against my body, ram myself inside her and fill her up. I'm a starving man, and I've been starving for years. Sliding to my knees and pressing a kiss to her palm the other day has short-circuited my brain even more than going down on her did. A primal creature within me has awoken, and he won't be soothed until I've claimed her.

I swore fealty to her.

That girl is *mine*.

Even her own father and Mikhail looking at her makes the monster inside me roar with jealousy.

"Is Adamovich going to pay up, Kristian?"

"Hm?" I tear my gaze away from my niece and turn to Troian. "Oh, of course he will. Zenya tore that man a new asshole and he was as obedient as a puppy by the time she was finished with him. Zenya can handle anyone."

My niece tucks a strand of hair behind her ear and doesn't say anything, but I notice a small smile on her lips. That's right, baby. The Adamoviches and the Grigors of this world deserve to be ground to dust beneath your high heels.

"Zenya's abilities are impressive," Troian says with a smile. "But can she handle her wild uncle?"

I meet her eyes and give her a devilish smile, and her cheeks turn pink. "She's the only one who can."

"Moving on," Zenya says quickly, turning to her father. "The Belyaevs need to make a show of strength. Make our presence known in the world. We've pulled out of a lot of social events these past two years and it's eroded the confidence that people have in us."

I nod in agreement. "You're right, Zenya. Let's make a splash, you and me. Show this city that the Belyaevs are stronger and more united than ever. I'll take you out on the town."

Zenya thinks about this and then says, "Perhaps we could do that, but I have another idea. It's Yuri Golubev's sixtieth birthday party in three days' time. Dad's not strong enough to attend, but I should go and represent us all."

Yuri Golubev is head of the second most important Bratva family in the city. Everyone who's important in our circle will be present. I nod in approval. "Good plan. I'll go with you."

Troian gazes at me in surprise and then laughs. "You're not going to argue that your idea is better? Who are you and what have you done with my brother?"

Two years ago, I would have spoken over everyone. Argued my point aggressively, even if someone else's plan was just as good as mine.

But now it's not important to win. Zenya's what's important. Which is a strange thought to have, considering I came back here with the express purpose of winning everything I want through her.

I flick my gaze to her, wondering if I'm screwing myself by giving up too much ground to her.

No, she'll only fall harder for me if she knows I always have her back. "Zenya had the better idea."

Zenya, Troian, and Mikhail all stare at me in shock.

Troian laughs again. The sound is a lot weaker than it used to be, and it seems to exhaust him, but he manages to say, "This mystery woman has tamed my brother. I never thought I'd live to see the day. You must tell me who she is because I want to meet her."

Mikhail passes a hand over his face like he's silently asking for strength. Zenya's suddenly very interested in her nails. I remember my oath, that I won't say anything to upset Troian, so Zenya's going to have to be the one to tell her father about us.

"She'll reveal herself when she's ready."

"I never pictured you with a shy girl, Kristian," Mikhail deadpans.

"Only in some ways. In others, she's as brave as a tigress. She'll come out of hiding when she's ready."

I notice Zenya is wearing diamond earrings in her ears, the ones I gave her for her sixteenth birthday. She's had an aloof manner with me for days and yet she dressed this morning while thinking about me. I bet she even hoped I'd notice them.

"What do you think, dandelion?"

She looks up, startled. "Me? I have no interest in your love life."

A smile spreads over my face. "I'm talking about the party. You and I can talk about my love life later. I know you're secretly dying to know more about it. Nice earrings, by the way."

Zenya touches one of her earlobes briefly. "You're welcome to come as my plus-one. If it will irritate you to be in my shadow, you're better off just staying home."

"It would be an honor to be by your side. Zenya Belyaev is the future leader of this family and everyone needs to know it."

She gives me a long stare like she's hunting for double meanings or traps. Finally she says, "All right. I'll take you with me if you really can accept that I'm Dad's heir and not you."

"Zenya Belyaev has my utmost devotion and loyalty," I murmur with a charming smile.

When the meeting is over, Zenya and Mikhail leave, but I hang back to talk to my brother.

Drawing over to his bedside, I ask him, "Did you know that men have been harassing Zenya behind your back? I left her alone in Adamovich's club for three seconds and some worthless piece of shit was trying to steal a kiss. I had to teach him some manners."

Troian passes a tired hand over his face and his expression is agonized. "I didn't know that. I hoped I still inspired enough fear in this city that men would leave her alone. I'm so grateful you're back. Protect her, Kristian. Don't let anyone hurt her."

"Oh, I will," I say through gritted teeth. No one's getting close enough to hurt my girl.

Troian's grateful to me, sure. But is he sorry?

I wait in silence, wondering if he's going to bring up what happened two years ago. He needs to be the one to tell her because I can't. She'll rain down hell on her father's head if I speak up, and that falls under the category of me upsetting Troian, something I swore I wouldn't do. Zenya needs to understand that I'm a man of my word.

But Troian can say something to her. In fact, Troian should be the one who comes clean with or without me swearing an oath. It's bullshit he hasn't told her the truth after all this time.

The words burst from my lips despite me telling myself I should shut the fuck up. "When are you going to tell your daughter the real reason I stayed away for two years? She thinks I was worried about you sending an assassin after me."

Troian glowers at me. "Does that hurt your manly pride?"

Yes, of course it does. I'm a proud man, but that's only a small part of it. My lip curls in a sneer. "Zenya should know the truth."

He sighs wearily. "Then you tell her if it matters to you so much."

"So I'm to be the villain again? Why must it always be me and never you?"

He looks away from me and glares out the window. "I was protecting my family from you. She was my only means to keep you away from us."

"But now that it's convenient for you, you want me around."

"If you don't like it, you can leave. I'll hire bodyguards for Zenya to keep her safe."

"Fuck that," I growl. As if bodyguards could give Zenya the protection and devotion that I can give her.

I wait for a full minute, but Troian doesn't apologize for anything. Fine. The truth will come out eventually because I'll force it out. He'll have to confess what he did when my baby starts to show in her belly and it's too late for any more secrets.

I head for the door, but Troian calls my name in a shaky voice, and I turn back to him.

He entreats me with watery eyes. "Please, Kristian. Make sure she is safe. If anyone hurts her, I won't…I can't…" His throat locks up with the devastating thought that he might lose her.

No one's hurting Zenya, but I'm still going to take her and make her all mine, and there's nothing my brother can do to stop me.

I crack the knuckles on my right hand. "You don't have to ask. No one's getting near my girl while I'm around, or they'll pay for it with their lives."

Three days later, I'm standing on the front doorstep of the Belyaev mansion, ringing the bell dressed in a new black suit and shiny loafers, ready for Yuri Golubev's birthday party. I wore a black shirt but didn't bother with a tie. I hate ties. I didn't embark on a life of crime just so I could dress like a Wall Street numbskull.

I've combed my hair back from my face, but as usual, the front locks keep falling over my forehead. With any luck, it will entice Zenya to push them back as she always used to do, tilting her lips up to mine like she's begging for a kiss.

I still haven't had a real kiss from her, a thought that makes my heel tap restlessly on the step as I wait. That brief press of my lips to hers two years ago didn't count. Last week in her kitchen wasn't even close to what I crave. I hope she's wearing red lipstick tonight because I want it smeared all over my mouth by midnight.

When the front door opens, I'm adjusting the silver rings on my pinkie fingers and my heel stops tapping as I stare at her. I give a low whistle as I draw my gaze up Zenya's body, from the red stilettoes on her feet to her bare, smooth legs, the short red camisole dress with feathers around the hem, and then finally, her beautiful face and long, loose hair.

"You look fucking stunning," I breathe.

"Hello to you, too," she says coolly, and turns away and goes to the hall mirror where she picks up a lipstick and reapplies it.

Red lipstick. Just like I'd hoped.

As she's twitching curls into place, I come up behind her and pick up the necklace on the hall table and thread it around her throat. Her gaze flickers between us as I fasten the clasp.

"We look good together, don't we?" I murmur, resting my hands on her shoulders. We look powerful. We look like Belyaevs.

Zenya doesn't say anything, but her hungry eyes devour my face.

"Are you looking forward to tonight?" I ask her.

Zenya turns to me and puts a hand on my chest. "I am, but..." She glances toward the stairs and back to me. "Under normal circumstances, I'd be going with Dad or he'd be coming with us."

I stroke my thumbs along her collarbone and nod. As angry as I am with Troian, I understand how strange she feels.

Distress fills her eyes. "It's a special kind of pain to be stepping into Dad's shoes while he's still living and breathing. I feel like a parasite. A vulture."

"I promise you that when your father looks at you, he feels nothing but pride."

Zenya strokes my chest and whispers, "He's so happy you're back."

Is he? I'm not so sure about that, but I stopped caring what my brother thinks of me when he threw me out of this family two years ago. "How do you feel?"

She gazes up at me through her lashes. "I'm not sure how to feel. You're not the same man you were two years ago."

I take her chin with my thumb and forefinger. "I'm the same man I always was. I'm just choosing to show different parts of myself to you now. You were so young back then. Now, you're…" I smile and let my gaze drop from her eyes to her lips to her dress.

Fucking delicious.

Zenya regards me with thoughtful blue eyes. "You were so wild and unpredictable back then. You're still as dangerous as you always were, but now you seem more focused. I…think I like that about you."

"I aim to please, princess," I murmur, still holding her jaw. Maybe I don't even need to wait for midnight. We're all alone in the hallway, and I lower my mouth toward hers.

Zenya places a finger on my lips. "Don't. I'm trying to talk to you. I still think you're crazy, but I like this new you. The old Kristian would never have walked into a party behind a woman."

I give her a baffled glare. "Since when was I a misogynistic asshole who can't treat a woman like an equal?"

"You were Dad's heir, and you made sure everyone knew it, especially after he grew sick, and it became possible that you would have to step up sooner rather than later. I'm surprised you've accepted me so easily. Surprised, but pleased."

Guilt twists in my belly. It takes me a moment to realize what the sensation is because I've never much been plagued by the emotion before.

"You look good tonight," she whispers, stroking her fingers along my jaw. "But you always look good."

I groan and rest my forehead against hers. "Princess, if you keep paying me compliments and not letting me kiss you, I'm going to burst into flames."

"I can't lose you again," she says, wrapping her arms around my neck and begging me with her eyes. "Don't you understand? One wrong move between us and it will be like Chessa and that photo all over again. Dad's so protective of me, and he won't accept you being anything other than my uncle. He couldn't save Mom. He couldn't save Chessa. I'm all he has left, and he'll shed blood to make sure I'm safe, even if he can't wield the blade himself."

I know she's remembering the assassins Troian threatened to send after me. As if I'm worried about some scavenging little bounty hunters. We can't be lovers because it will upset Troian? Troian might not be around for much longer.

I lean closer and press a kiss to her throat, murmuring, "So under different circumstances, if I were to slip a diamond ring onto your finger and ask you to be my wife, you'd say yes. Is that what you're telling me?"

She breathes in sharply, her breasts pressed tightly against my chest. "No, that's impossible."

"All you say is we *can't*." I kiss her throat. "We *shouldn't*." I kiss her jaw. "But I never hear, *I don't want you*." My lips are close to hers but don't touch, waiting for her to close the gap. "If you want me to stop pursuing you, you're going to have to kill me, because while you look at me with that much desire in your eyes, I'm never letting you go."

Zenya's plush lips resemble soft and powdery rose petals. She stares at my mouth like she's remembering what it can do to her. This girl needs to come so badly she's burning up in my arms.

I dip my head and murmur in her ear, "Let's go to this party and show them all who's boss of this city, and afterward, I'll give you a sweet goodnight. I'll even find that blindfold for you. If you still need it."

Zenya pulls out of my arms, reaches for her clutch with a shaky breath, and takes a moment to compose herself.

I put my hands in my pockets and gaze at her with a smile on my lips. Tonight is going to be wonderful.

Drawing the tassel on her bag through her fingers, she says, "My future husband will have almost as much power in this city as me after Dad's gone. Have you thought about that?"

"It's crossed my mind," I admit, watching her with narrowed eyes and wondering what she's getting at.

She lifts her gaze, and there's a challenging expression in her eyes. "Dad's wishes mean everything to me, and I hope you realize that my ambitions burn as bright and as hard as yours, Uncle Kristian. Right now, I don't trust any man who says he wants to marry me."

I offer her my arm. "My only ambition is to see you in your rightful place, princess. If there's anything I can do to help my favorite niece, all you have to do is ask."

Zenya regards me for a moment and then slips her arm through mine. "Good. So long as we're clear."

A car is waiting for us outside, and we get into the back seat together. The back of my neck is prickling. My niece as my wife, revenge against my brother, and ruling this family. Those are my three secret ambitions, but it seems like Zenya's starting to figure that out for herself.

Zenya leaves her hand lying on the car seat, and I reach for her at the same time she pulls away and holds tight to her clutch. She pretends she didn't see me reaching for her hand, but I know she did.

I grit my teeth. Pursuing this woman is harder than committing murder in cold blood. Actually, murder is a walk in the park compared to claiming a single kiss from the only woman I've ever wanted. If Zenya won't marry me, then I'll lose my chance at all the power in this city and never get revenge on my brother.

But it's not the thought of losing those that makes a black hole open up in my chest. I gaze at Zenya's beautiful profile with the skyscrapers and city lights gliding past behind her. Two years I was banished, and what did I miss the most? Not this city or pissing off my brother, that's for sure.

When we arrive at Yuri Golubev's mansion, I walk around to Zenya's side of the car and hold out my hand to her. She puts her slender fingers in mine and I help her out. A proud smile touches my lips as I drink in the sight of her, head held high, glorious silver-blonde hair cascading down her back, the short cocktail dress showing off her heavenly long legs.

Everyone turns to stare at us as I lead her through the front door and into the house.

Or rather, stare at her.

Kristian Belyaev has returned unexpectedly, but most of the hundred party guests are intrigued by Troian Belyaev's beautiful daughter on my arm. I make eye contact with as many men as possible, silently warning them that this girl is under my protection and they shouldn't get any ideas.

Zenya steps forward first to greet Yuri Golubev. "Happy birthday, Yuri. Thank you for inviting us into your home. My father sends his regards and wishes that he could be here tonight as well."

I take second place, as is right for a man who is no longer Troian's heir. If I don't marry Zenya, I'll always be in second place. And if I persuade her to marry me and then push her aside?

I'll break her heart.

Or she'll kill me.

I hope you realize that my ambitions burn as bright and as hard as yours, Uncle Kristian.

"You remember my uncle, of course," Zenya says, glancing at me as she smiles at our host.

"Hello, Yuri," I say, and he inclines his head in greeting.

Golubev holds Zenya's hand in his, smiling at her with a calculating gleam in his gray eyes. He reaches out and draws a man to his side, one who resembles a younger version of himself.

"Do you remember my son, Zenya?"

Instantly, my eyes narrow.

Zenya withdraws her hand from the father and presents it to the son with a polite smile. "Of course. Hello Jozef, it's nice to see you again. Do you know my uncle, Kristian Belyaev?"

I greet Jozef without a smile and clench his offered hand until he winces. He pays me a fraction of a second's attention before turning back to Zenya with a smile and telling her how beautiful she looks.

I think I've just met the second of God knows how many men who are dying to marry my niece. Watching Jozef Golubev fawn all over her, smile at her, and touch her arm has me itching to cave his face in with my fist. How dare he entertain thoughts of making Zenya his. How dare he even fucking *look* at her. I fantasize about ripping his eyes from their sockets and hurling them to the ground.

Golubev's expression grows serious as he gazes at Zenya, but his sincerity is lacking. "I was filled with sorrow to hear that you were injured, my dear. What a terrible thing when even the finest family in the city is subject to such disrespect."

Jozef's face fills with concern as he gazes at Zenya, and he rests his hand on her shoulder.

His *hand* is on her *bare fucking shoulder*.

I step forward, wrap my arm around Zenya's waist and draw her away from Jozef and back to my side. "It's a good thing that her uncle was around to save her."

Golubev is watching me closely, and for a moment, hatred flashes through his eyes.

Then he's smiling again. "You're staying in the city, are you, Kristian?"

I return his fake smile. "Of course. Protecting my brother's heir is my number one priority." I gaze down at Zenya and feel my smile grow warmer. "Isn't it, princess?"

Zenya's lips twitch in amusement, and she reaches up to brush my hair out of my eyes. "I haven't talked to a man without you breathing down his neck since your return, if that's what you mean."

Her fingers skim past my ear and brush the nape of my neck.

Before she drops her hand back to her side, I take hold of it and press a kiss to her palm. "No, you haven't."

I hold her gaze because I love to look at her, and because I want Golubev, his son, and everyone watching to witness that Kristian Belyaev doesn't give a damn about anyone in this room except Zenya.

I turn to our host. "Enjoy your party, Yuri. There are people Zenya should meet."

As we peel away, I catch the flash of anger in Golubev's eyes and laugh to myself. He'd dearly love to marry his son to Zenya and get his greedy hands on even more power and money. He probably thought he only had Troian to deal with, but there's only one thing worse than an overprotective father.

A jealous uncle.

I walk Zenya deeper into the party guests, and there are people we should stop and talk to, but I keep my arm locked around Zenya's waist and steer her away from anyone who looks like they're about to approach us. Despite what I said, I'm unwilling to share her with anyone tonight, and most of the people who turn her way are men. She's looking dangerously beautiful tonight, and all of them, married and unmarried, are entranced by her beauty.

A man steps into our path, forcing me to draw Zenya to a stop. I glare at the man.

Sergei Lenkov, an arms dealer. He's as tall as I am, with long, dark hair and a thick beard. From the looks of him, Sergei's been hitting our illegal steroids hard.

"Miss Belyaev, how wonderful to see you again," Lenkov says with a sharp smile, completely ignoring me.

I glance at my niece and see she's giving him the smallest smile possible. "Hello, Mr. Lenkov."

"You look beautiful tonight," he murmurs, his eyes roving all over her body. "It would be wonderful for us to meet so we can discuss how better I can support your family's work."

Lenkov sources good weapons, but nothing that I can't get elsewhere, especially if it means keeping him away from Zenya. I've never liked Lenkov because he has a habit of stirring up trouble among the Bratva families. It benefits his weapon sales when we're all at each other's throats.

I give a humorless laugh and pat his shoulder, hard. "Sergei, it's a party. We don't want to talk about work."

Before he can say another word, I lead Zenya around him and into the crowd.

"Asshole," I mutter under my breath.

Zenya gives me an amused smile. "That asshole asked Dad for my hand."

I turn and glare at him. That nobody? Un-fucking-believable.

Three men gaze open-mouthed at my niece as we pass by, so I gather her closer to me and stroke a silver-blonde curl back from her face, murmuring in her ear, "I didn't think I needed to bring a weapon with me to a birthday party. Now I'm regretting that I didn't."

"You shouldn't touch me so much," Zenya says, placing her hand against my stomach, but she doesn't push me away. "People are going to think there's something strange going on between us."

I smile and run the blade of my nose up her cheek, breathing in her delicate scent. "Oh? Like what?"

She parts those lush red lips in a pant. "We don't need any more rumors swirling about the Belyaevs right now."

I bite my lower lip and pull it through my teeth as I gaze at her. I wish it were her lip. She's so fucking delicious. "No one gives a damn what I'm doing to you. If people are staring, it's because you're the most beautiful woman they've ever seen. But if you're feeling so shy all of a sudden, I can fix that."

I lead her by the hand down a corridor and into a side room on the pretense of showing her Golubev's renowned art collection, and the chatter of the party guests disappears behind us.

"Jozef is handsome, don't you think?" Zenya asks conversationally, but there's a smile hovering around her lips as she gazes at an abstract painting in purples and blues.

Instantly my irritation spikes, and I look at her sharply. "He won't care whether you're happy or not. Marrying him is out of the question because he's only interested in your money and power."

"Oh, is he? It's a good thing I have my uncle close by and he has only my best interests at heart," she says, but her tone is ironic.

"I do have your best interests at heart," I growl, squeezing her waist. What I'm doing is for both of us, and Zenya needs me to protect her from the wolves out there. She has no idea what men are really like.

She shrugs lightly. "Maybe you do. But *your* interests are even dearer to your heart."

Zenya detaches herself from me and walks around a vase that's set atop a plinth in the middle of the room, admiring it from every angle. "This isn't much of a party. No one's even playing any party games."

"What would you like to play?" I ask, following her, but she circles around the plinth, keeping herself out of my reach. The energy in the room suddenly crackles. She feels it, too, as her eyes start to sparkle.

Zenya taps her chin and pretends to think for a moment as we circle each other slowly. "Truth or dare."

"All right. I'll go first. How many men want to marry you?"

She laughs. "That's not how the game works. One of us asks *truth* or *dare* and the other gets to choose. And what happened to ladies first?"

I take a quick step toward her, but she flees playfully out of my reach. Suddenly my heart's thundering in my chest. She shouldn't flirt with me like she's prey, or I'll have no choice but to hunt her down. "Then ask me."

"All right. Truth or dare?" Zenya trails her fingertips along the plinth as we circle it together.

I want to choose *dare,* but I can tell from her bright eyes that my girl is hungry for secrets. "Truth."

Zenya glances toward the door to check that we really are alone and then whispers, "How long have you wanted me?"

I grin like the devil. Oh, that secret? She wants to know that secret?

I consider her with my head tilted to one side, wondering whether I should tell her everything because it's complicated and messy, just like my feelings for her. I've got a dozen nieces and nephews, but I've never loved them like I love Zenya. She's always been special. I love her more than my brother. I love her even more than myself.

I stopped admiring Zenya's prettiness as a proud uncle and started regarding her as a force to be reckoned with after the home invasion. I've never been prouder of her than when my beautiful girl killed a man using the knife I'd given her. She knew I was on my way, and I could handle her attacker for her, but she didn't want to wait. She wanted to kill him herself.

Then she came downstairs to stand among the corpses of the men I'd been torturing, her white PJ set and her silvery hair stiff with blood, and I realized she'd been watching me torture them.

Blood, pain, and murder, and she craved to watch.

I didn't want to call her dandelion after that. I wanted to call her princess.

I wanted to call her *mine*.

My daughter? I wondered, puzzling for weeks and months over this strange feeling buzzing in my chest whenever I looked at her.

A few months before she turned sixteen, we were in the pool on a hot summer's day, splashing each other while she squealed. She kept jumping on my back and looping both her arms around my neck while I dove deep, swimming powerfully through the water.

We'd surface and break apart, going back to splashing. Then she launched herself at my front instead of my back, wrapping her slender legs around my torso and climbing my body like a tree.

I was dazzled by the sun on the water. With her arms wrapped around my neck and her smiling lips just inches from mine, I felt a sudden and almost uncontrollable urge to push her against the tiles, cover her mouth with mine, and thrust my tongue deep into her mouth.

I stared down at her in shock.

Oh, shit.

That's what this feeling has been all this time?

I want my niece?

I wrapped both arms tightly around her and squeezed. Zenya felt like heaven in her bikini with her breasts pushed against my chest and her cool, wet skin beneath my hands. I put my lips against her ear and whispered, "You're my favorite kind of trouble, princess."

Her eyes widened. Before she could answer, I dunked us both under the water and got out of the pool.

Not to go and see a priest or a therapist or to give myself a good talking to about the inappropriate thoughts I had of my niece. I drove home and jerked off, thinking about Zenya and her perfect mouth and adorable tits, telling myself I was a twisted bastard for thinking about her like that, but with the full knowledge that it was too fucking late and I wasn't going to stop. By the time the sun set, I'd imagined a dozen different scenarios in which I thrust my cock deep inside her and made a bloody mess of her virginity and my balls were empty.

I hadn't touched another woman since the home invasion. I hadn't even wanted another woman. I thought I was put off going to bed with anyone because Zenya had nearly been raped and it hurt my heart to the point of desolation. Men can be such cruel fucking animals. I saw Chessa in the aftermath of what had happened to her, and it turned my stomach. God knows I never had any love for that woman, but her suffering was brutal.

And yet I hungered for…something. Or rather, someone.

The day in the pool, I realized what it was.

My niece.

My fucking *niece.*

I thought growing up together as family meant you were immune to things like that. I'd held her as a baby, for fuck's sake. But in my heart, there was Zenya as I'd always known her, and then there was Zenya the intriguing and powerful girl who'd killed a man and wanted to help me kill more. She had the same instincts that I did. To protect her family no matter what, and if murder was the way, then bring it on.

The past few years have been agony, but the agony hasn't been denying myself other women. The agony has been denying myself Zenya. Before I was banished, I was always by her side, and she was so fucking delicious. Always smiling at me. Always touching me. I could have persuaded her into becoming my lover when she was fifteen or sixteen. I could have been downright Machiavellian about it and coerced her into my bed, but then what? Eventually, she would have hated her beloved uncle for being a predator and abusing her trust like that.

But she's eighteen now.

Old enough for all kinds of trouble.

I reach out and hook a finger into the neckline of her dress and draw her closer to me. When she's standing in front of me, gazing up at me with those big blue eyes of hers, I murmur, "You're my favorite kind of trouble, princess."

Her eyes widen in surprise, and I know she's remembering being in the pool with me. It's the only time I've ever said those words to her, and I've always wondered if she felt something shift between us that day. If she heard something different in my voice or felt the hungry way I was holding her against me.

"It's been four years since I've touched another woman. I'll wait four more if it means I can have you. I'll wait forever."

Her and me? We're forever.

Zenya swallows, staring at my mouth. "Since the home invasion?"

I nod slowly. I only crave my niece. My heart is true.

But is it, Kristian?

How true can a heart be when it craves revenge?

"Seven," she whispers, gazing up at me.

I frown. "Seven what?"

"There are seven men who want to marry me. Shall I add you to the waitlist?"

My hand slides into her hair, and I grip the silken strands in my fist. Not hard enough to hurt her, but enough to make her mouth fall open to take a panting breath.

"There's no list. There's only me. Now give me those lips."

Without waiting for her reply, I slant my mouth over hers in a powerful kiss. She moans in surprise and clutches my shoulders with her small hands. I wrap my other arm around her slender waist, pulling her flush against my body. Her mouth opens, either in shock or invitation, and I don't wait to find out which as I plunder her mouth with my tongue.

The craving to look at her face overwhelms me, and I pull away for half a second to get a glimpse of her. Then I fist her hair even tighter, tilting her chin up so I can meet her lips with another searing kiss.

When we finally break apart, I press my forehead against hers, panting with victory and desire. She wants me. I can taste it in her kiss. Her mouth was made to be mine, just like the rest of her. We were always meant for each other, and I don't give a damn what the people out there think, what this city thinks, what my brother thinks.

Zenya Belyaev is my woman and no one else's.

She drags her lower lip through her teeth as she gazes at my mouth, her pupils huge and liquid. "I've never been kissed like that before."

I should fucking hope not.

"Kissed how?" I murmur, pressing my lips to the silky baby hairs by her ear. I'm holding Zenya and she's tasting me on her lips. I can barely believe it.

"How I've always imagined a man kisses a woman." She takes a shuddering breath, and I feel her quiver in my arms. "It's terrifying."

"Oh?" I've terrified plenty of people before, but never by kissing them.

"I don't understand these feelings. If you kiss me, or I kiss you, we're supposed to feel nothing. We're supposed to feel squicked out."

I laugh softly. Squicked out. She's so cute. "Who says?"

"It's a law of nature. Of growing up calling you uncle. No one in the world wants this for us. Our family is supposed to come first. My father, my siblings, and all our cousins will be horrified to know what we just did."

Judging from the drunken look in Zenya's eyes, her lecture isn't even working on her. "You can't help what you feel and it's not a crime to want me. Are you wet?"

She gasps and her hands tighten on my shoulders as she practically begs, "Uncle Kristian, *please*."

I slide my hand deeper into her hair. Enough pretending that she doesn't want me. My patience just ran out. "Squeeze your pretty thighs together and tell me how slippery you feel."

With my other hand on her ass, I feel her muscles clench as she does what she's told, and she moans as she realizes she's soaking.

I glance quickly around the room and notice a sliding door into another room. I pull it back and see a small office space and push Zenya into it. The room is dark and far from soundproof, but it will do for what I have in mind.

"Turn around," I tell her.

"Why?" she asks while doing as she's told and glancing at me over her shoulder. Her eyes are huge.

I move her hair aside so I can kiss the nape of her neck and slide my hands down her thighs. Then I begin to draw her dress up her thighs.

"Uncle Kristian—"

"Shh. Close your eyes. Pretend I'm someone else if you want to. The stranger in black who only wants to make you feel good. You liked him so much."

"He was so uncomplicated. I did want him," she says with a whimper.

"He wants you, too." I pull her underwear aside and slide down until I'm kneeling at her feet, her peachy ass in my face. I plant a kiss on her and then sink my teeth into her warm flesh.

Marking her.

Mine.

Zenya's hips wriggle in my grasp. "What are you—*oh God.*"

I part her feet and thighs with my hands and lick her from her core all the way up to her ass. She tastes fucking delicious. I run my tongue over her again, and then concentrate the gentle lashes of my tongue on her tight ring of muscle.

"Seriously, what are you doing?" she whisper-shrieks, panting as her fingers flex against the wall.

I don't bother to answer because it's pretty damn obvious what I'm doing. I'm sure it feels strange to her, but from the way she's breathing and gasping I know she likes it. While she's distracted, I draw her underwear down her legs, help her step out of them, and push them into my pocket.

It's the second time I've gotten down on my knees for her, and I like it here just fine. In fact, I love it. My princess tastes wonderful from down here.

When she's so turned on, her legs tremble in my grasp, and I stand up slowly, getting a good look at the pink burn in her cheeks and the way her lips are parted as she breathes hard. There's a fierce ache in my chest as I witness her experiencing something for the first time and loving it.

Standing behind her, I reach around her for her clit and massage it with my fingertips, watching her eyelashes flutter as pleasure rolls through her.

With my other hand, I stroke her sex from behind and gather wetness on my middle finger. I draw it up and caress the pucker of her ass. And then press lightly into it.

Zenya's eyes open wide. I'm not inside her ass yet, but she just realized it's what I intend to do.

"It feels good, princess," I murmur in her ear. "Promise. Want to try it?"

The color in her cheeks burns harder than ever. She licks her lips, thinking. Her sweet little hesitation has blood surging to my dick, and I don't wait. I push the tip of my finger into her and groan at the tight compression.

Zenya gasps and grabs the wrist of my hand I'm currently using to caress her clit. "What—*ahh*."

"How does it feel?" I breathe in her ear.

She licks her lips, takes a breath, and whispers, "Strange."

My fingers slide from her clit to her inner lips, gathering more wetness. A lot of wetness. The strangeness of my finger in her ass is overwhelmed by the pleasure she feels as I pump my middle finger in and out of her in shallow thrusts. Zenya groans and arches her back, pressing her cheek and breasts against the wall.

"You have no idea how many times I've fantasized about your flesh gripping me," I murmur, staring at myself finger-fucking her ass. "You're mine. Every part of you belongs to me. Including right…" I push my finger deeper and she moans. "…here. I'm obsessed with being inside you, princess. My tongue. My fingers. My cock. My cum. I want to fill you in every place at once. I wish there were four of me so we could all fuck you at once."

Her brows draw up together and she whimpers in pleasure.

Jesus fucking Christ, I need to make her come like this. She's so wet and burning hot against my fingers, and her clit is swollen to the touch. She moans louder as I grind against it. The noises of the party just reach us, which means someone could hear us.

"Hush, princess. Only I get to hear you like this."

I savor the sensation of rolling her clit beneath my fingertips and thrusting into her ass. Zenya moans as I fill her up with pleasure. She's burning in my arms.

I put my lips against her ear and whisper so softly it's barely louder than a breath. "Maybe you want to pretend it's not me touching you right now, but I have to tell you this. You have been my torment since you were fifteen years old. I was never going to show it. I would have rather had my innards ripped out of my body by wild animals than ruin those years for you. But being forced out of the family changed everything. The night in the warehouse changed everything. I want you. I need you. If I have to make you come a hundred times before you beg me to fuck you, I will, and there's nothing you can do to stop me. I'm going to make you crave me as much as I crave you, and that's a promise."

Zenya's hand is gripping my wrist. She pants harder and harder. The sound of my voice and the pleasure rocketing through her has put her into heat.

"You're going to marry me and have my children, and I'm not bothered which happens first. I'll fuck my baby into you right here and now if you give me half a chance."

She cries out and whimpers, "I've never heard you talk like this. I don't even know who you are anymore."

I grin wickedly in the darkness because this is exactly what I want to hear, that she's seeing her Uncle Kristian with new eyes.

Just then we hear footsteps and voices approaching.

"There's someone—" she begins.

"Hush," I whisper sharply, but I don't stop what I'm doing to her clit or her ass. She looks like she wants to argue with me, so I push my finger deeper into her.

I watch pleasure flash over her face and those beautiful swollen lips form the words, *Oh, fuck me.*

We'll get there, princess.

Zenya's eyes flutter closed, and she arches in my grip. I keep one ear on what's happening on the other side of the door as I gaze at her.

"...mess that fucking uncle is making of our plans. Did you see how he's glued to her side? Following his brother's orders, no doubt. At least we know she's still Troian's heir, or Kristian would be forcing her into his shadow by now."

I recognize the speaker as Yuri Golubev, though his tone is as different as it could be from his oily flattery of my niece earlier. His voice is low, but I can hear him clearly.

"I can still convince her to marry me," another man replies. Jozef Golubev from the sound of him.

I go on smiling in the darkness and plant slow kisses on Zenya's throat. She's lost in pleasure once more, her cheek pressed against the wall as she surrenders to my touch. Golubev and his son can scheme and plot all they want. I'm the one who's making Zenya turn into a molten mess, and I'll do it again and again until this girl admits she belongs to me.

"It doesn't matter what that stupid little girl wants, it matters what her father wants. He already refused my proposal to wed the two of you because he says she's too young. She should be running scared after what happened at the warehouse. It should have fixed everything."

Both our heads snap up and we stare at the door. My middle

finger falters on Zenya's clit but I don't stop altogether.

Fixed?

What the hell do they mean, fixed?

Was that attack in the warehouse the Golubevs' doing?

"Now Kristian is a guard dog at her side and Troian must be delighted she's so well protected once more."

"What do we do now? Kill Kristian Belyaev?" Jozef asks.

There's a short silence, and then Golubev says, "You know, that's not a bad idea. With him out of the way, we can maneuver you into his place as her protector."

I bare my teeth in the darkness. They can fucking try.

The two of them keep talking but draw away from the door, and soon their voices fade into silence.

Zenya half turns toward me. "Did you hear that? They—"

But her words are lost in a gasp as I redouble my efforts with her clit and finger-fucking her ass. Golubev and his son aren't ruining the moment I've waited on for years. I would rather cut off my own hands than let Zenya out of this room without making her come.

"We need to discuss what they were talking about," she says desperately, trying to turn away from the wall.

"Not now."

"But they—"

"*I said not now.* Don't fucking fight me," I growl in her ear. "I'm having this from you."

We have all the time in the world to plan our revenge on Golubev and his son, but it took me all week to get my niece this close to heaven, and I'm not giving up now.

Zenya glares up at me in fury but starts closing her eyes for longer and longer intervals. Her breathing gets harder and harder.

I smile as I feel pleasure soften her resistance. "That's it, princess, give me what I want. Good fucking girl. You're so pretty when you whimper for me."

"Uncle Kristian, you…this is…oh *God*." She gives a strangled cry and pushes up on her toes at the same time as her head flies back against my shoulder. Her body bucks in my arms and her eyes are squeezed tight as she comes. Her ass clenches on my finger in time with the waves of her orgasm. I moan and press my face into her neck because it's the most incredible thing I've ever felt.

Sweat breaks out on my brow and my chest is heaving like I'm the one who's flying high on an orgasm. I want more. I need so much more. My fingers don't stop working her clit or thrusting into her ass. "Oh, fuck yes, princess. Give me another. I'm so hungry for you."

Zenya tries to wriggle free of me, her movements frantic as I overstimulate her clit. She's so sensitive after her orgasm and she's bucking like a wild thing in my arms. "It's too much," she sobs.

I put my lips against her ear and seethe, "No. Again."

Her high heel connects with my shin and I grunt in pain but don't let go. I want her a panting, exhausted mess before I'm finished with her. Who knows when I'll have this chance again?

She shrieks angrily in the back of her throat, but the sound turns into a moan as she finally gives in to what I'm doing to her and the intensity breaks through into even more pleasure. This time her climax goes on and on, harder and stronger than the last. My dick feels ready to burst as I stare at her, panting hard. I could just about come from the expression of sheer pleasure and surrender on my woman's face. I've never seen anything so beautiful in my life.

Zenya finally goes slack in my arms. We're both breathing hard in the tiny space as I slowly pull my finger out of her ass, though I don't fucking want to go. Drawing it out feels like physical pain.

Suddenly, Zenya rounds on me and grabs the lapels of my jacket. "Did you hear what they said? They killed Andrei, Radimir, and Stannis. They're trying to force me into marriage."

Zenya's eyes are wilder than I've ever seen before, and her face is lit with fury. "How dare they cross the Belyaevs like this? *I'll kill them.*"

Chapter Nine

ZENYA

I can't sleep.

Heat, anger, confusion, and pleasure keep slamming through me like stormy waves breaking on the shore. I went to bed two hours ago, and I've been tossing and turning ever since.

My heart is blazing.

My core is *aching*.

The Golubevs are going to try and kill Uncle Kristian in order to scare Dad into marrying me to Jozef.

Uncle Kristian made me come twice, hard, and both times I was clenching powerfully around nothing. That's what I'm left with, a feeling of emptiness where there should be *him*.

I groan and press my face into the pillow. I shouldn't even *think* that. I let him do those things to me in a moment of weakness. I teased him at the party, flirted with him, egged him on like a harlot just to see what he would do, and then when he pounced, I didn't whisk myself away from him. I turned into a panting, slutty mess against all his fingers. All his fingers. Everywhere.

And I didn't know men…put their tongues…*there*.

My cheeks burn at the memory and I'm overheating so much I have to throw the covers off. How dare something so bizarre feel incredible.

I could barely concentrate on the revelations that we overheard, then when it was over Uncle Kristian got me out of there so fast my head was still spinning from the orgasms and the words we overheard. Before I could catch my breath, he led me by the hand through a side door and out to the waiting car.

As soon as he pulled up in my driveway, he reached for my hand and said my name, but his touch flooded me with shame and panic. I wanted to fling myself into his arms, and yet, Dad could have been looking out the window right at that moment.

So I ran away and shut myself in my bedroom. My first night out as a grown woman and heir to the Belyaev fortune and power, and that's how I behaved? Getting hot and heavy with my uncle at a party?

Disgraceful.

I huff and turn over onto my back, kicking the blankets off my legs and staring at the ceiling. I completely lost my head. Uncle Kristian was so sweet to me. Kissing my palm in front of everyone.

Holding me out of every man's reach and close to him. Uncle Kristian's possessiveness melted my brain.

And then he kissed me.

I moan at the memory.

That *kiss*.

I was seeing stars it was such a decadent kiss, and then…

Close your eyes. Pretend I'm someone else.

Only, I didn't even try and pretend. I knew it was Uncle Kristian with his fingers between my legs. I *wanted* it to be Uncle Kristian. I'm *sick*. He's the only man I've ever wanted to touch me like that, and he once sat me between his strong arms on a shooting range when I was six years old. *Want to see me hit the target, dandelion?*

I remember that day vividly. The safety goggles were too big for my face. The mufflers were too big for my ears. His eyes were dark and focused like a predator. The gun kicked in his hand when he pulled the trigger, and he hit the very center of the target every time.

I thought he was magical.

All those birthdays. All those Christmases. All those summers. He was always there, making me laugh, holding my hand, drying my tears. There were too many tears. I've always hated crying because it makes me feel weak and like I'm begging for attention. I would run away from Uncle Kristian if I felt like I was going to cry, but he always, always found me.

That day in the pool when I was fifteen. Uncle Kristian and I were playing together, splashing each other and laughing. Our pool is wide and deep and he would dive to the bottom with me on his back, my arms wrapped around his shoulders as he effortlessly swam through the water. His muscles were so strong, I remember that clearly, and holding him like that and drinking in his power was intoxicating. I felt drunk on him. I loved him.

I jumped on him again, wrapping my arms around his neck. I remember my cheek pressed tight against the crossed guns tattoo on his chest. He scooped me close and whispered, *You're my favorite kind of trouble, princess.*

And then he let me go. He got out of the pool and left without looking back.

I felt sad and a little confused, but it wasn't the first time that he and Dad had to leave me without warning. I assumed he just remembered he had somewhere he had to be.

And the next time I saw him? I don't remember. It was probably less than a day later, but it must have been so unremarkable for me that it's become lost in the blur of all the wonderful days spent with Uncle Kristian.

Which means he really did keep it from me that he wanted me.

He always kept it from me until the night in the warehouse.

I frown, thinking carefully. Or did he? Wasn't there something unusual about the night he and Dad were in the motorcycle accident? I was sixteen and people were starting to treat me differently. Not like a kid who needed to be protected and sheltered, but like a woman who had thoughts and ideas that were valuable. Strangers were treating me differently, too. On weekends if I was out by myself, grown men would smile at me. Handsome men with smoldering smiles who must have mistaken me for a grown woman, or just didn't care that I was sixteen.

I was cleaning up Uncle Kristian's wounds, something I'd done dozens of times before, but this time his flesh was so hot and captivating beneath my touch, and I couldn't take my eyes off him.

I was seeing him as a man for the first time, and not just my uncle. He was so hungry for me that the stinging pain of the disinfectant on his cuts was pleasurable because it was *something*. Now that my insides are aching for him, I understand how he felt. Him gripping my hair and pulling it tight in his fist would be a pleasure right now, not a pain.

The door to my bedroom creaks open and softly closes again. I stare at the ceiling, resigned to the fact that a little brother or sister of mine is creeping into my room for a cuddle. Maybe that's what I need to get my mind off my uncle.

A deep voice speaks softly in the darkness.

"Can't sleep?" My mattress sinks, and a huge figure swings his leg over my body until he's sitting astride my hips. "Me neither, princess."

I gasp and reach out in the darkness, and my hands touch a muscular stomach beneath a soft, well-washed T-shirt. Uncle Kristian, dressed in jeans and with his blond hair falling into his beautiful eyes. He's been home and probably to bed. And now he's here at three in the morning.

We stare at each other in the darkness. The space between us is electric and filled with the smell of night air and the delicate scent of flowers. There's a jasmine creeper in the garden below.

"Have you been standing beneath my bedroom window?" I whisper.

"Every fucking night," he says, reaching behind his head to grasp his T-shirt and pull it off in one smooth motion.

I swallow a moan at the sight of his naked torso. His broad shoulders and the muscles of his stomach catch the silvery half-light in the room, and my mouth waters. The man who's so obsessed with me is achingly beautiful. I drink in the ink on his chest, and the long, shiny scars the gravel left on his shoulder. His handsome face. There are fine lines on his forehead. By his eyes. He looks every single one of his thirty-six years. Too old for me, but I don't care. I just don't care. Before I know what I'm doing, I'm reaching for him, and there's a dangerous, hungry expression in his eyes as I stroke his warm flesh.

I hook my finger into the silver chain around his neck and drag him down to me. He moves slowly, dropping onto one elbow and then the other, letting me feel the weight of him on my body.

Anger and desire stream through me. "You did it. You've tricked me into wanting you, and now I'm just as fucked up as you are. I never would have let you touch me like that in the warehouse if you'd shown me your face."

He laughs softly. "Yes, you would. Sooner or later."

"Arrogant bastard," I snarl, even though I know he's right.

He covers my mouth with his in a hard, hungry kiss, parting my lips with his tongue and thrusting deep. I moan against him and arch my back.

This is crazy.

This is so wrong.

Dad and my brothers and sisters are sleeping just down the hall and on either side of my bedroom, and I'm in here with Uncle Kristian. The shock and disgust on their faces if one of them walked in here and caught us would burn me into a pile of cinders from shame.

Uncle Kristian grasps my jaw in his hand and makes me look at him. "I've already tasted you. Your body gave up its secrets to me because you want me too. I know how you sound when you come, how you feel so sweetly clenching on my finger, and I'll never fucking forget it."

We both watch his fingers brush my long hair out on the pillows, the silver ring on his pinkie glinting in the moonlight.

His hand slips down my body, slides over my belly, and curves around my sex. Two of his fingers rub me firmly over my clothes, and the sensation ricochets from my clit and rebounds around my body.

"You deserve something good," he murmurs. "Something just for you. That's why I'm here. Just for you, princess."

Emotional pain slices through me so swiftly that I inhale sharply. I hate it when he reminds me that I'm so unhappy.

"I'll take care of you from now on," he murmurs, brushing his lips lightly over mine. "I'll give you everything you need, and I'll make it so, so good for you." He presses a kiss to my throat.

He pushes his hand down the inside of my pants, and groans when his fingers touch wetness. The most decadent sound I've ever heard. I'm shockingly slippery against his fingers and embarrassment burns in my cheeks.

"Tell me what you need, princess."

"You," I sob, clinging to his shoulders.

Victory flashes through his eyes. "Tell me more. I need my girl to say what's making her pant so hard and get so wet because I've been dreaming about you for years, and I have to know it's not just me who's being driven out of his mind every time we're near each other."

I don't know how to talk about sex and obsession and the darker side of love, but Uncle Kristian makes me want to try. "I can't think about anything but you when you're close to me, and even when you're not. My world feels ten times crazier with you in it, like I'm walking into a lion's den and begging him to eat me alive."

"But?" he insists, slowly circling my clit.

"But…" I squeeze my eyes shut for a second, feeling like I'm standing on a precipice. "I still want you. I want you so much."

Uncle Kristian groans again and slants his mouth over mine in a devouring kiss. His tongue parts my lips and plunges inside my mouth. I open wider and welcome him as I wrap my arms around his neck and my thighs around one of his legs and squeeze. His fingers roll firmly against my clit and white-hot sparks cascade through me.

This man.

He's the only man for me.

Pulling his hand out of my shorts, he grasps the hem of my loose pajama top and pushes it up slowly. Agonizingly slowly. Looking from my face to my gradually revealed flesh. Without thinking twice I flex my back so it's easier for him to move it, and then my breasts are completely exposed.

He dips his head to suck one of my nipples into his mouth, and then the other, and heat flashes down to my core. Wet now, they pucker up and he runs his tongue over my sensitized flesh.

"I've dreamed of you night after night," he murmurs, squeezing me with both hands. "I've been going crazy for you. I need all of you, princess."

He undresses me slowly, pulling the pajama top up over my head, and then edging my shorts down my legs. As he casts them aside, he swipes a finger down my slit and we both feel how wet I am.

His lower lip is softened with lust, and he's breathing harder as he slips his finger into his mouth and sucks. I cover my face at the sight of him because it's so much. I'm racked with shyness. It's *him*. He's terrifying and beautiful and wonderful all at once.

Uncle Kristian gently takes my wrists and draws my hands away. "Don't do that. I want to look at you."

He draws me into his arms, holding me close as I wrap my arms around his neck. My eyes are wide open now and drinking in his face as I press my naked body against his torso. He kisses me with parted lips and our tongues move against each other's. His jeans feel rough against my sex, and he presses the thick rod of his erection into me. His skin is feverishly hot, and I know he's impatient, desperate for me, but he's making himself go slowly. For me. Even though he's waited years and years.

This man is mine, I realize. Completely mine, and no one else's.

It's my touch he craves. I'm the only woman in the world who can fill him with pleasure or inflict torment on his heart. He's laid himself bare to me.

I smooth my hands up his chest, and while his body is familiar to me, the way he moves and sounds is not. As I trace his muscles and the ink on his chest, he whispers my name and lavishes my lips with kisses and bites. I curl my fingers into the waistband of his jeans and pull him closer, reveling in the expression of bliss on his face.

He slides a hand between my legs and rubs my aching clit with his fingers, moving back and forth through my slippery flesh. It's been mere hours since he touched me like this, but my body blazes in response to his touch, and I want more.

"You're the only one who can bring me to my knees," he whispers. "You want me too. Say it. I need to hear it from your lips."

"I want you," I pant, digging my pointed nails into his shoulders and sucking his warm breath down into my lungs. I need more than his breath inside me. I need all of him.

He starts to kiss his way down my body, hungry to taste me once more. His hand is fumbling for the button on his jeans. "Did you save yourself for me, princess? Are you the innocent girl you were when I left?"

I open my mouth.

And then close it again.

When he *left*. Hearing him say that makes rage suddenly boil through me. He left me all alone with a dead stepmother, seven grieving children, and a gravely sick father.

"No. I'm not," I say with relish.

His head rears up and his brows are drawn tightly together. "What?"

"I'm not a virgin," I tell him with a self-satisfied smile. "My hymen? Gone. Obliterated. There was blood. I even had an orgasm."

Kristian stares at me with his hands gripping the bed on either side of my hips, every muscle in his arms and torso bulging. "Don't lie to me."

"I'm not."

"I don't believe you," he seethes.

I shrug, reveling in the anger sparking in his eyes. "Then don't. It's a free country. But it won't change the facts."

Both of his eyebrows shoot up. "Who? Who took you to bed?"

"Why do you want to know?"

Jealousy is roaring in his face. "So I can kill him!"

I sit up and clap my hand over his mouth. "Keep your voice down. There are eight other people sleeping in this house."

Uncle Kristian yanks my hand away and snarls in a whisper, "Why are you torturing me like this? Are you angry with me?"

He's actually *confused*, like it's impossible that I could feel anything but love and adoration for him. I sit up, reveling in my fury. I hate being a trembling waif before him, but anger makes me brave about being completely naked with him. "Little me, mad with big, bad Kristian Belyaev? I wouldn't *dream* of it."

Uncle Kristian breathes hard through his nose. "Who dared touch my girl while I was gone?"

"Your girl? *Your girl?*" I whisper, shoving him, my hair flying around me. "You've got a lovely way of treating *your girl*, abandoning her for two years."

"I was faithful to you," he growls. "Give me his name. I'm going to wipe him from the face of this earth."

"His name is mind your own business, Uncle Kristian."

He seizes my shoulders and pushes me onto my back, and then parts my legs and settles my thighs around him. "It is my fucking business. You better not be telling me lies."

He trails his middle finger down through my sex, and I grasp his strong wrist with a gasp. "What are you doing?"

"Finding out for myself." Uncle Kristian's eyes flick to my face, and then he pushes his thick finger slowly inside me. His expression is intent and he feels around my tight channel carefully before pushing deeper.

Uncle Kristian's mouth falls open. He drags his finger out and then pushes his ring finger in to join it, sending pleasure blazing through my core.

Oh, Jesus. I reach behind me and press my hands against the headboard, needing the stability so I don't fly off into space. Even furious with me, even though he's not trying to give me pleasure but checking whether I kept myself intact for him, the intrusion of his fingers feels amazing.

"What the fuck?" he growls through his teeth, staring at his fingers buried to the third knuckle inside me. Then he pulls them out and stares at them gleaming wetly in the darkness, turning his hand over to check both sides.

"What are you looking for?" I know what he's looking for. I just want him to go on hunting for something that's not there.

"For…" He trails off, presses a hand to my hip bone, and shoves his fingers inside me again, faster and harder this time, then pulls them out and glares at them.

My back arches and I cry out. Panting, I beg him, "Please don't stop."

"Don't stop?" he snarls. "*Don't stop?* You're enjoying this while my whole fucking world is crumbling down? There's no blood on my fingers, Zenya." He leans over me with both hands braced on either side of my head. If he were a dragon he'd be breathing fire.

"Who was he?"

His brows are bunched together at the bridge of his nose. His eyes are flashing. His jaw is flexing. God, he's sexy when he's angry.

And jealous.

And unhinged.

I lick my lips and arch my back. "Are you sure it doesn't make me bleed? Maybe you should try again. Harder. Deeper."

Uncle Kristian growls in frustration and pushes both hands through his hair. "I'll kill him. I'll fucking kill him. How old were you? Sixteen? Seventeen? I waited when I could have made you mine years ago. I fucking *waited* and some piece of shit got to you behind my back."

I wrap my legs around his hips, capture his shoulders in my hands, and drag him down to me. "You shouldn't have left me then," I seethe in a whisper.

Payback is so, so sweet.

His eyes narrow. "I can't believe you're enjoying this."

Why would I be enjoying Uncle Kristian being torn to pieces by something that happened because he walked out on me?

It's a mystery.

"Tell. Me. Who," he growls.

"No." I lick his lips with the tip of my tongue, goading him, hungry for what he might do next.

With his silvery hair falling into his eyes, he shifts down the bed, pushes my thighs apart, and rams his fingers into me again. I yelp at his forceful intrusion and cling to his biceps as he thrusts with his arm, finding a spot inside me that feels like a gateway to heaven and working it mercilessly.

"Give me his name."

"I'll never tell," I manage between desperate pants.

He blasts me with his fingers, ramming them deep and dragging them back and forth over the spot behind my clit. Everything's sliding out of control, and then he dips his head and lashes his tongue over my clit.

"*Tell me who it was.* I won't stop until you give me his name. If you thought two orgasms were too many at the party, I'm about to fucking wreck you."

The pressure feels intense.

The pressure feels *dangerous*.

My orgasm overwhelms me and I soar through it, only to find it's still building toward an alarming conclusion. Oh, Jesus. Oh, *no*. I feel like I'm going to—

Suddenly, I gush over his fingers.

"*No.* Don't—" I sit up and grab his wrist, but it's too late. Together we stare at his wet hand and the sprayed sheets in shock.

Uncle Kristian groans in pleasure. All the anger is gone from his face and he looks entranced. "Fuck, your pussy is magnificent. Has that ever happened before?"

I shake my head, staring down in horror at the dark patch on the bed. "What the hell was that?"

"You squirted, princess. I found the good spot." He slides his hand around the nape of my neck and kisses me deeply. I'm still so confused, but whatever happened, he seemed to like it.

"But what is— I've never heard of— It looks like—" I feel choked up and I can't get the words out. My face erupts with heat. Oh, God, there are even splashes on his jeans. I want to die.

He kisses me again, smiling reassuringly and stroking my hair back. "It's a good thing. A fucking beautiful thing."

I stare at him in confusion. How can he say that when I just lost control of myself?

"If it makes you feel good and isn't hurting anyone else, there's nothing to be ashamed of," he murmurs.

It did feel good, but… Tell that to the sick feeling in my belly.

He gathers me close and kisses the top of my head. "You've got to stop worrying so much about what everyone thinks of you. Where's the fearless girl I've always known and loved?"

I don't think he's talking about whatever I just did all over his hand anymore.

"But what if I disappoint people?" I whisper. "What if it turns out I'm not the person they need me to be, and they don't feel like they can rely on me anymore?"

What if they abandon me and I fall into that black hole that terrified me after Mom died?

It's not a real place. Maybe it's not a rational fear, but it feels real to me. That black hole could appear anywhere, like in the eyes of the people I love, and it might be the last thing I see before they turn away from me forever.

"Then they'll have to deal with it because their disappointment is not your problem if you're only trying to live your life in a way that makes you happy and fulfilled." Uncle Kristian pulls me up onto his thighs with my knees hugging his hips, cradling my naked body against his.

"Look at us," he whispers.

I turn my head and rest my cheek on his shoulder, gazing at our reflections in the vanity mirror. His strong arms are around me and my hair is cascading down my back. The expression in his eyes is dark and possessive.

"I never thought I'd get to hold you like this, princess. I can't let go of you because it will kill me."

I sink my teeth into my lower lip, desperately wishing it didn't look so alluring to be held close in my uncle's arms in the middle of the night.

But we do look wonderful together. Perfect, actually. How can something so perfect be wrong?

Uncle Kristian finds my ear with his lips and murmurs lovingly like he's reciting a sonnet, "I'm this close to eviscerating the next man who looks at you. If you liked whoever got to you before I did, I'm sorry, but he's a dead man. I don't need you to tell me who he is. I'll find out for myself."

My nails dig into his shoulders and I breathe in sharply. "Uncle Kristian…"

Just then, a scream pierces the night.

I lift my head with a gasp. That sounded like Nadia. Memories of that terrible night when our home was invaded by unknown men and my siblings were screaming tumble through me.

Uncle Kristian's up and off the bed before Nadia screams again. I hear him charge down the hall and rip Nadia's bedroom door open. "Nadia!"

I'm tying a dressing gown around my naked body and hurrying after him when he comes into the hall with my little sister in his arms. Chessa and Dad's second youngest, a little girl of just four with golden curls.

"It's all right. She just had a bad dream," he murmurs, sympathy and relief etched on his features. The crying child reaches for me with both arms and he passes her over.

I kiss Nadia's cheek and cuddle her close, rubbing her back and reassuring her that I'm here. "What was the dream about?"

"It was a monster chasing me," she wails. "He was made of purple goo and he had three heads."

"Poor little kitten. It wasn't real. It's over now."

Uncle Kristian is staring at me with an intense expression on his face. Fierce and filled with longing as he gazes at us, as if seeing me hold Nadia is somehow painful. He shoves his fingers through his silvery hair and his jaw flexes in frustration.

A moment later he touches my cheek and presses a kiss to my temple. "I'm going to double-check everything's locked up tight."

"Thank you," I whisper, watching him head off down the hall. I'll breathe a little easier knowing he's certain we're safe. Memories of that night are clinging to me.

All the children were awoken by Nadia's scream. Their bedroom doors have opened and they're emerging sleepily, rubbing their eyes.

"What's wrong?" Lana asks, her face creased and her bangs sticking straight up.

"Nadia had a bad dream, that's all."

A moment later, Uncle Kristian strides back down the corridor and stops by my side. "Everything's locked and the alarm is on."

"Thank you."

Lana frowns at us, taking in my hastily tied robe and bed hair and Uncle Kristian's bare chest and jeans. "Uncle Kristian, what are you doing here in the middle of the night? Where are your clothes?"

He glances down at himself. "I spilled a drink on myself. Zenya and I were talking."

Lana glances behind us at my open door. "In her bedroom?"

She looks more confused than suspicious, but my face still burns hot. "We had a problem at the birthday party we went to earlier tonight. We were just talking about it."

"*U nas s toboy vse yeshche bol'shaya problema, potomu chto ty ne otvechayesh'na moy vopros,*" Uncle Kristian seethes under his breath. *You and I still have a big problem because you won't answer my question.*

Lana whirls to face him. "What did you say?"

"He said goodnight."

"No, he didn't. That's *spokoynoy nochi.* He said something about a problem."

I glare at him, warning him not to say another word. "Uncle Kristian's just worried about work, but he's going home now. Everyone, back to bed or you'll wake Dad. He needs his rest."

One by one, the kids trail sleepily back to their beds. I can feel Uncle Kristian behind me as I take Nadia back to her bed, tuck her between the sheets, and kiss her cheek. After a few minutes of stroking her forehead and talking softly to her, she closes her eyes and falls asleep.

When I stand up and turn around, Uncle Kristian is right there, his arms folded across his bare chest and glowering at me.

"Be more careful what you say from now on," I whisper. "They're not all babies anymore, and Lana's been learning Russian."

"Zenya, tell me—"

"Don't. You've had your fun and now it's over. Go home. I'm going to sleep."

He follows me back to my bedroom door and reaches for my hand. "Then let me sleep here with you."

"I said go home." I close the door in his face. He's too wound up to sleep, and I'm done having the *But who took your virginity, Zenya?* conversation with him.

His growl of frustration travels through the wood. "Give me my T-shirt."

I scoop it up from the floor by my bed. As I stare at the bunched cotton in my hands, a pang of longing goes through me. I want nothing more than to drag that man into my bed and cuddle him close until morning, but what's the point when I can't keep him? I'll only get attached, and then I'll be devastated when I have to give him up. Dad would have the shock of his life if he found out how we've been carrying on. My brothers and sisters would be confused and upset. Everyone's been through enough these past few years. I can't be selfish when I should be thinking of them.

I press my face into his T-shirt and breathe in deeply. How I adore the smell of this man. His cologne fills my nose, but there's so much more than what you can buy in a bottle. What makes me weak at the knees is Uncle Kristian's own rich and powerful scent. His T-shirt is drenched with lust for me.

He's been waiting for me for four years. He hasn't wanted another woman all this time.

I stare at the door with longing. If I open it to him, I'll probably pull him inside and beg him to fuck me. Thick, hot desire courses through me as I picture myself on my hands and knees while he thrusts into me hard and deep from behind. My fingers tighten on his T-shirt and I moan with need.

Desperately, I turn toward my bedroom window, open it, and throw the T-shirt outside. "It's on the front lawn if you want it."

Uncle Kristian huffs in anger, and I hear his feet pounding down the corridor. I stay where I am, and a moment later he emerges onto the lawn, snatches his T-shirt up, and yanks it angrily over his head.

Then he rounds on the house and glares up at me.

I gaze down at him with both hands leaning on the windowsill, the cool night breeze ruffling my hair.

Still glowering at me, he kisses his fingertips. He must be able to taste me on them.

A moment later, he turns and stalks down the driveaway, heading for his black Corvette, fury and jealousy etched in every line of his body.

I know my uncle better than anyone, and he won't rest until he knows who took my virginity.

And kills him.

No man in this city is safe from this night on.

"You look tired, sweetheart." Dad reaches out and swipes his thumb across my cheek, giving me a concerned look. He's seated in an ugly blue chair with tubes in his arm while he receives his chemotherapy infusion. Each appointment takes a few hours, and I always drive him and sit with him throughout.

"I'm fine," I tell him with a wan smile, and then I scoot back in my chair as a nurse arrives to check Dad's vitals and the machine that's delivering his medication.

Truthfully, I'm exhausted. I didn't sleep at all last night after Uncle Kristian went home. I want to focus on Dad's treatment and try to think of what we're going to do about Yuri and Jozef Golubev, but last night's hot and heavy moments have me in a chokehold.

Two words keep resounding through my skull in Uncle Kristian's voice.

You squirted.

I get out my phone and surreptitiously search for *What is squirting?* My face burns as I scroll through the results, clicking here and there and reading.

Apparently, it's not wetting yourself but it is pee? Or it's not pee but it comes out of the same hole? No one seems to have the answer. It's not uncommon, but it's still baffling to me, and it feels shocking and transgressive.

And I did it with Uncle Kristian.

I shove my phone into my bag and cross my legs and arms tightly, trying to think about anything else but the moment Uncle Kristian was angrily pumping his fingers into me and I—my cheeks flush again—*squirted* all over his hand, my thighs, and the bed. When I looked up at him, Uncle Kristian had an expression on his face like it was the most wonderful thing he's ever seen. Apparently, he wasn't expecting it either. But he loved that it happened.

A tingling ache starts between my legs. Remembering that moment with him makes me horny because, of course it does. I dig my nails angrily into my palms. Everything to do with Uncle Kristian gets me hot since he returned.

The nurse walks away and Dad turns back to me. "What would I do without you? Did you talk to Yuri Golubev last night and give him my regards?"

"Um, yes." I decide to leave out the part where his dear old friend is killing our men, intends to murder Uncle Kristian, and is trying to force me into marriage with his son through fear.

"And have you sent money to Andrei's, Radimir's, and Stannis's families?"

"Yes."

I swallow a sigh as Dad recites a list of questions. All the things that I should be doing for the business, family, the Silo, my brothers and sisters. The weight of all his expectations pile up on my shoulders, and I want to shout at him to stop because I haven't got time to breathe, let alone think, but I catch sight of his gray, lined face and force myself to reply.

Finally, Dad settles back with a tired smile. "You're such a wonderful role model for your brothers and sisters. The family is in good hands with you while I'm recovering. I'm sorry I've left you all alone with this."

But I'm not alone. I have Uncle Kristian, though that's been its own special kind of challenge.

"Kristian's been telling me how well everything's been going. I wasn't sure if it was a good idea, the two of you working together, but you seem to be able to handle him. I'm starting to think there's nothing you can't handle."

Haha. Oh, God. Me, handle Uncle Kristian? That man's untamable.

And yet a smile is tugging at my lips because, despite his dangerously distracting presence, I have enjoyed working with him. When we're with the men or at the Silo, Kristian is always by my side, strong and supportive. He's made certain things easier and has given me more confidence. I've always wanted to tell Adamovich that I knew he screwed Dad over three years ago. The unfairness of it *burned*.

And when we're alone, or at that party last night?

You're going to marry me and have my children, and I'm not bothered which happens first. I'll fuck my baby into you right here and now if you give me half a chance.

I squeeze my thighs together. The words he whispers in my ears have me seeing stars. The things he does to me are unhinged. I picture Uncle Kristian down on his knees and kissing my palm, swearing that he'll do anything for me. A delicious combination of loyalty and insanity.

If I did marry Uncle Kristian…

If he were my husband, my protector, the father of my children…

I remember how he jumped out of bed and charged down the hall the second Nadia screamed. How he emerged from the bedroom with her in his arms, relief painted starkly on his face. The man is a villain and a rogue, but his devotion to the people he cares about is breathtaking.

I glance up at Dad, my tongue playing with the corner of my lips as I think carefully. He disinherited Kristian, and he's made it clear that he doesn't want him to lead this family. Would he be angry at the thought of his daughter and his brother leading the Belyaev family together if anything happened to him? If Dad wants me to marry, then wouldn't Uncle Kristian be a better option as my husband than some stranger who only cares about money and power? Wouldn't he be perfect as the ferociously protective father of our children?

A hot sensation takes a swan dive down my body and spreads through my core. Uncle Kristian's baby. My heart beats faster at the thought.

I glance at Dad, gnawing on my lower lip. Anyone I choose, I want my father's blessing.

"Dad. Me and Uncle Kristian…" I begin but trail off and curl my nails into my palm. I can't decide whether mentioning this to Dad right now is a good decision or not.

Dad frowns. "Is Kristian causing trouble? If he's upsetting you or won't listen to your orders, I'll send him away. My brother needs to understand that he's not my heir anymore. You are."

Panic seizes me as Dad threatens to banish Uncle Kristian again. What am I *thinking*? If I open my big mouth, Uncle Kristian will be driven from this city all over again.

I shake my head quickly. "No, nothing like that. Uncle Kristian's done nothing but help me. He's working tirelessly by my side, and his men have been eager to help. I thought you should know. That's all."

Dad relaxes again. "I'm glad to hear it." There's a moment of silence, and then he asks gently, "You missed Kristian, didn't you?"

I grasp the arms of my chair. My feelings are a snarl of complex emotions. Learning that he's wanted me for years is strange.

Learning that he wanted me and still left?

Devastating.

Dad sighs as I struggle to answer. "Sometimes I think I overreacted when I sent Kristian away two years ago. My guilt over Chessa was so raw that I wonder if I treated him too harshly."

I look up in confusion. "Your guilt? But it was an accident that Chessa died. You couldn't have done anything to help her."

Dad gives me a sad look. "Sweetheart, not that. The way Chessa died was a terrible way to go, but I'm talking about the home invasion. I've never stopped feeling terrible about that night."

The night when five tweaked-out assholes broke in and four of them gang-raped Chessa in revenge for Dad killing their boss. I shake my head. "But that wasn't your fault either."

He gives me a sad look. "Wasn't it? It never would have happened to her if she hadn't married me. Chessa was a carefree, beautiful young woman when I fell for her, but by my side, she only knew suffering."

"That's not true. Chessa loved you. The two of you were happy together, and I saw how you made her laugh and made her feel cherished."

"I think about her all the time these days. Because of…this." He glances around at the machine, himself. "I think about your mother. About Kristian. You. There's so much guilt, sweetheart."

He closes his eyes from the pain of it all, and I study him closely. I don't understand why he's being so harsh on himself. Dad's never been the kind of man to wallow in self-pity.

I reach out and cover his hand with mine. "Chessa never blamed you for what happened that night, and she would be sad to know that you're hurting yourself over it now."

Dad takes a shuddering breath and opens his eyes. "I hope I did my best for you after that night, but I feel like I failed you too."

I try to remember when Dad ever failed me. Truthfully, I can't remember anything specific Dad did in the months after the home invasion, and that's fine, because he had to be there for Chessa and the other kids. All my memories are of Uncle Kristian. Helping me grow fierce. Showing me how to make sense of this cruel world and my place in it.

"You never failed me," I tell him, but my words sound hollow.

"Your Uncle Kristian believed that if you wanted to be part of our world then we should open it up for you. At fourteen years old, I thought you were too young for everything that a fully grown Belyaev must shoulder. Shouldn't you stay innocent?" He laughs without humor. "What a stupid man I was, believing that anyone who had to kill to save herself needed sheltering instead of support. Kristian had the right idea all along, didn't he?"

Uncle Kristian was the one who talked to me, encouraged me to defend myself, use weapons, and learn all sorts of important and deadly skills. Now that I think of it, he must have done so much of that behind Dad's back. My heart burns with gratitude because it was what I needed. I needed to feel strong, not powerless. I needed to be anything but that lost little girl standing by her mother's open grave, sobbing her heart out. I wasn't going to let those men make me feel weak and small, and Kristian was there to help me through it.

"This is a hard life, Zenya, and I never even asked you if you wanted it. If you would rather walk away from the family business after I'm gone, you have my blessing."

My eyes widen and I exclaim, "Are you kidding me? After everything I've learned these past few years? I've been working so hard because I want to make you proud of me, but also because there's nothing else I want to do. I'll die before I give it up."

Dad smiles sadly. "You sound just like Kristian."

A terrible thought occurs to me. He's talking about Uncle Kristian so much it makes me wonder if he's having second thoughts. "Are you thinking of changing your will? Do you want him to lead the Belyaev family instead? But I can do this. I swear I can."

He shakes his head. "No, sweetheart. Don't think that I'm talking like this because I'm thinking of changing anything. I would never disinherit you. It's the right decision for you to lead this family after I'm gone. You're steady and thoughtful. Kristian is unreliable and irresponsible, and he always will be."

I wince because that feels unnecessarily harsh. "Actually, Dad, he's been everything I need him to be."

As long as he stays. We're living in a powder keg and things might blow up in our faces one of these days. I pick at a loose thread on my jeans. What if I open my heart to him and then he's just…gone? Even the thought of it fills me with suffocating panic. Why didn't he fight harder to stay by my side? If he loved me so much, why did he leave me all alone two years ago?

I swipe an angry tear from my lashes. What's done is done. He broke my heart, and now I should be protecting it from him at all costs. "Let's not talk about him. You need to focus on getting better."

Dad gives me a long, worried look. "You're angry with Kristian, aren't you?"

I shake my head. "Who's angry? I just don't want to talk about him right now. Ever since he came back, all we talk about is Uncle Kristian."

Dad scrubs a hand over his face and sighs, his expression is more miserable than ever.

A nurse walks briskly over to us. I brought a takeaway coffee with me, and I sip it as she checks Dad's medication and asks him questions about how he's feeling.

Dad's slumped so tiredly in his chair after the nurse has gone that I wonder if he's fallen asleep.

A few minutes later, he drags his eyes open and reaches for my hand. "I love you more than anything, Zenya. You and your brothers and sisters are everything to me. You will take care of them, won't you?"

I nod quickly and reach for Dad's cup of water. I'll agree to anything as long as he stops talking about dying. "Have some water, okay?"

He brushes his thumb over my knuckles and smiles ruefully. "That night changed you. I didn't want to admit it to myself, but after, there was something new in your eyes." He lifts his shoulders and lets them fall, and then switches to Russian. "How could there not be? You'd taken a life, and at such a young age. Younger than me.

Younger than Kristian."

He's right about that night changing me, but it changed me for the better. I became stronger. Focused. More determined. If Dad senses any unhappiness in my heart, it's not because of that night. It's because of what happened two years ago when someone I loved dearly walked away and forgot all about me.

Two hours later, I get Dad home and help him into bed. He's always exhausted after chemotherapy infusion and goes straight to sleep.

It's not until I'm closing his bedroom door and walking down the hallway that I take my phone out of my bag and check the screen. Twelve missed calls. So many text messages. All from Uncle Kristian.

Uncle Kristian: *Zenya.*

Uncle Kristian: *It's your uncle here.*

I roll my eyes. As if I don't know it's him. I can feel his tension and gritted teeth radiating from my phone screen.

Uncle Kristian: *I don't need you to do anything.*

Uncle Kristian: *There's nothing you have to worry about.*

Uncle Kristian: *Just give me his name.*

Uncle Kristian: *Zenya. Answer me.*

Uncle Kristian: *Why aren't you picking up?*

A dozen more messages follow, and I shake my head as I scroll down and read them. If someone leaves for two years without any sign that they're coming back, they don't get to be mad about what goes on in their absence.

Zenya: *Could you chill for half a second? You're going to burst a heart valve.*

Instantly, the three dots appear.

Uncle Kristian: *WHO WAS IT ZENYA?*

Zenya: *Take a deep breath. You are a drop of rainwater falling into a calm sea.*

Uncle Kristian: *Do I have to kill every man in this city?*

Uncle Kristian: *BECAUSE I WILL IF YOU DON'T GIVE ME A NAME.*

I throw my phone into my bag with a shake of my head and go downstairs. My stomach's rumbling, and I need to eat before I can deal with him.

After a sandwich of turkey on light rye with mayonnaise, cucumber, and lots of salt and pepper, I'm feeling better equipped to cope with my uncle's jealous meltdown. I expect that he's sent me another dozen texts, but there's only one from two minutes ago, and it's highly ominous.

Uncle Kristian: *You've left me no choice.*

Zenya: *What do you mean? Where are you?*

Zenya: *Uncle Kristian?*

Uncle Kristian: *I'm busy, princess. Talk to you later.*

Zenya: *Busy doing what?*

Uncle Kristian: *Can't type. Too much blood.*

Zenya: *Please tell me you're joking.*

Zenya: *Oh my God, I hope you're joking.*

Zenya: *UNCLE KRISTIAN PLEASE DON'T KILL ANYONE WHEN I HAVEN'T EVEN GIVEN YOU A NAME.*

I wait for a reply, but none comes. Is he serious, or is he messing with me? What's he planning on doing, driving to every underground club and to the houses of our associates and slaying every man he sees?

Or is he after one man in particular?

My stomach drops as I realize who that man might be. The only man I've been on a date with and the first one to push his jealousy into overdrive.

Grigor Kalchik, the man who tried to kiss me at Bohdan Adamovich's club.

He wouldn't...would he? It was *one date*. Uncle Kristian can't seriously believe that I went to bed with that irritating, sleazy man after one date?

No rational man could think that.

I put my dirty plate in the dishwasher, my mind racing. Uncle Kristian isn't thinking rationally. He's thinking like a jealous lover.

I search through my phone contacts and hit dial.

A moment later, Grigor answers. "Well, hello, babe. Good to hear from you."

My skin crawls at the sound of his smug, oily voice. From the sounds of it, he's not in deadly peril. Yet. "Hi, Grigor, I wanted to ask where—"

"I know," he interrupts me, and I can hear his smirk. "You're dying for that second date. Saturday night just freed up, but only because it's you. You're a lucky woman, Zenya."

I grip my phone hard, silently wishing for strength. Uncle Kristian carries on as if he's God's gift to women, but at least he has the right considering his looks, charm, dress sense, and intoxicating aura. What has Grigor got? Average looks and a below-average personality.

"Listen to me, Grigor. I think you're in danger."

Grigor drops into a dramatic, breathless tone. "Are we role-playing? Hot. What's the game, sexy spies?"

For a man in the Bratva, Grigor is supremely stupid. Either his family hasn't impressed on him how dangerous this life is, or he's never learned to take a woman seriously. The idea of marrying a man like him, let alone sleeping with him, makes me nauseated.

"If you see my Uncle Kristian, run in the other direction. In fact, just get in your car and leave town right now."

"Babe, I'm not in town, but as soon as I return from Vegas I'll—"

He's not in the city? Then there's no point in me continuing this tedious conversation, and I hang up without saying goodbye.

I put my phone face down on the counter and sigh in frustration. Bratva men are so frustrating. It's not just Grigor treating me like I'm a bimbo, Adamovich calling me a petty teenager, or Yuri and his son plotting to terrify me into marriage. Every man I come into contact with thinks he's smarter, stronger, and more capable than me. Even the four men who attacked me in the warehouse called me *girl*. I'm so tired of men not taking me seriously or seeing me as an opportunity for more power. It's *my* power. I'm Dad's heir. I'm going to fight to keep what I have no matter what.

I need a hot shower. The memory of the hospital still clings to me, and I want to burn it from my skin.

I turn around and see a man standing in the doorway, blocking my way.

I jump and suck in a startled breath.

It's him. My stranger in black.

Black sweater, black pants, black gloves, and a tight black mask covering his whole head.

He reeks of blood, just as he did that night.

Slowly, he removes one leather glove and then the other, and I see the flash of silver on his pinkie fingers. He reaches up and pulls off his mask. Silver-blond hair tumbles out and he shakes it back, leveling his cold, glittering eyes at me. There's blood staining his fingers and throat. More blood smeared on his neck.

"What did you do?" I whisper.

"I did what you needed me to do," Uncle Kristian says in a dark voice, strolling toward me.

I take an involuntary step back, my heart beating wildly. He doesn't mean me any harm, I know that, but there's so much malice emanating from him that it takes my breath away.

He reaches out with bloody fingers and captures a lock of my hair, rubbing it gently between his fingertips. His expression softens as he gazes at me. "I killed him for you, princess."

"Who?"

"Yuri Golubev. The man who thought he could murder me and frighten my beloved into marriage with his son."

"He was the one who ordered those men to attack me in the warehouse? The one who killed Andrei, Radimir, and Stannis?"

Uncle Kristian gives a short, angry sigh. "No. Unfortunately, he was not. He only heard about the situation and thought he could benefit from it, but he did intend on killing me. The two-faced bastard didn't deserve to live." Uncle Kristian smiles coldly. "So I cut off his face and fed it to his dogs."

If it wasn't on Yuri's orders that I was attacked, then whose? "Are you sure he's dead? That sounds painful, but is it life threatening?"

"There are more blood vessels in the face than people realize. He bled out, screaming the whole time. I tied a plastic bag over his head when he passed out, just to be sure."

Uncle Kristian's signature move.

He speaks casually, but there's a smile curving his lips. He enjoyed going around to the Golubev mansion and taking his jealous rage out on Yuri.

"And Jozef?"

His eyes flash with malice. "I didn't like the way he was looking at you."

A chill goes down my spine. "What did you do to him?"

"Why?" Uncle Kristian asks sharply, stepping closer. "Do you care about him? Does his pathetic, worthless existence matter to Zenya Belyaev?"

I fix Uncle Kristian with a glare. I won't cower before him or fall over my words rushing to explain myself. I asked him a question, and as someone who answers to me, or is supposed to anyway, he owes me a reply.

Realizing I'm not going to elaborate, Uncle Kristian reaches into his pocket. "I made him watch his father die, and then I made sure it was the last thing he ever saw."

He tosses something white and shiny at my feet. Two somethings that are round with bloody stalks and gray markings.

Gray markings that stare back.

Eyeballs.

Jozef Golubev's eyeballs.

I regard them for a moment, then lift my gaze to Uncle Kristian, who's watching me closely. Is he hoping that I'll collapse or throw up? Is he trying to shock and undermine me or prove that I'm too weak to lead?

No, I realize, as I drink in his hungry gaze. He's hoping that I'm not bothered in the slightest. He wants to know that I'm pleased by his brutal offering and that Jozef Golubev means nothing to me.

I reach out and nudge one of the eyeballs with my foot and it wobbles on the tiles. "Nice work. They deserved it."

Uncle Kristian smiles wider, delighted that I'm pleased.

"But next time, ask me before committing murders and atrocities in my name."

"Of course, princess. Anything you say." He reaches down and scoops up the eyeballs, and then flings them into the waste disposal. The machine grinds noisily as it chomps them up.

Uncle Kristian turns to me with a narrow, angry look. "Was it him?"

"Was it him what—oh." I fold my arms. Again with the virginity thing.

"If it was him, I'll go back for a more intimate part of him and roast it over a fucking fire."

Anger boils through me. "Does it matter to you that much? Am I unclean, despoiled, *ruined* in your eyes? Is this what it takes to make you turn away from me in disgust, the fact that a tiny membrane between my legs isn't there anymore?"

Uncle Kristian shakes his head as he washes the blood from his hands. "You did what you had to do these past two years. You will never be anything but precious to me, Zenya."

He shakes off his hands, dries them on a cloth, and turns to me with glittering eyes.

"What I won't accept, what I will *never* accept, is that there's a man out there walking around with pictures of you naked in his head. Memories of how you look when you—" He makes his hand into a fist and presses it on the counter as if struggling to maintain his composure at the mere thought of another man having sex with me. "I won't allow him to possess what rightfully belongs to me. He needs to die."

"You're insane," I tell him.

He gives a mirthless laugh. "I promise you that given how I feel, I'm acting very fucking normal right now."

Says the man who just threw eyeballs at my feet and fed a man's face to his dog.

Uncle Kristian reaches for my hand and pulls me closer, his voice growing husky. "I want you, Zenya. Marry me and I'll always love and protect you. I'll love and protect our children. You and our babies will be the only ones in the world who matter to me. I will always strive to do what the leader of the Belyaevs asks of me, no matter who he or she is, but I answer first to no one else but my wife. *You.*"

"And if the leader of the Belyaevs is your wife?"

"Then I'm hers to command."

I want to believe him. I desperately want to, but the pain of his absence is so raw and it still bleeds. "I don't believe you. How can I?"

"Because I'm saying it," he snarls. "Does my word as a man and your lover mean nothing to you?"

My lover. My stomach swoops with happiness and alarm, and I yank my hand out of his. Everything's moving so fast. "You should have thought about that before you abandoned me to live on the other side of the country."

"You know I didn't have any choice about that."

"Yes, you did."

"I—" he starts, but then stops himself. His nostrils flare as he tries to control his temper. "I swore to you I would be back and I am. What else must I do to prove myself to you?"

All the hurt, all the rage of the last two years comes bursting forth.

"You could have not done what you did in the first place!" I shriek at him. "You with that stripper on your lap and your hands around her throat is branded on my mind. I'll never forget that. *Never*. And you know what else I'll never forget? Begging you to stay, and you walking away from me."

He seizes my upper arms. "I didn't want to do that! It killed me to walk away from you. I *loved* you. I would have made you my wife years ago if I could."

"Then why did you leave? And why did you stay away?"

He growls in frustration and glances toward the door.

I grab the sides of my head, digging my fingers into my scalp from pure frustration. I want to *scream*. "If you've got something to say, just say it."

"Damn it all to fucking hell," he says through his teeth.

And that's all he says.

Not a word more.

I shove his shoulder with the heel of my hand, and he falls back half a pace. "I wish I'd fucked ten men while you were gone." I shove his other shoulder and watch pain fill his eyes. "I wish I'd fucked a *hundred*." I put both hands on his chest and push with all my might. "*I wish you'd never come back.*"

I turn on my heel and walk out of the room, blinded by tears. I don't mean those words. I don't mean a single one of them, but I'm too angry to take them back. I want to hurt him. I want him to bleed like I'm bleeding.

As I hurry toward my bedroom, he thunders up the stairs behind me, taking them two at a time. "*Hey.*"

By the time I reach my bedroom door and try to close it, he grabs it from me and pushes his way inside.

He grabs hold of me and walks me back against the wall until my back hits it and I'm staring up at him. "You wish I'd never come back? I know you don't mean that."

"I do mean it," I snap at him. My hands grip his shoulders as he leans his body into mine. I hate how good he feels pressed against me.

"You're hurting. That's my fault. Let me make you feel better, baby." He dips his head and brushes his lips over mine. "Take your clothes off and let me ravish your pretty cunt with my tongue. You can dig your nails into my shoulders and tell me I'm a bad man, the worst man, that you hate me, but you have to do it while I make you see stars. If you want, I can find that spot deep inside you with my fingers and you can burst all over my face. I'll drink every drop."

I shudder against him, my eyelashes fluttering as he whispers sweet, dirty, horny words to me.

"Or you can have my cock," he breathes, his tongue flicking my lips. "Let me claim you the way I've dreamed of for years, angel. Do you crave the deep stretch of me filling you up inch by inch?"

How dare he tempt me with that when I'm trying to stay angry with him.

"I don't need you to make me come. I can do it myself."

He chuckles darkly. "Have you been touching your pretty clit and making yourself come? I'm aching to watch you play with yourself, but, princess, just your fingers? Is that all? That's a spoonful of pleasure compared to what I can do for you. I can give you a whole feast."

Arrogant bastard. I'll show him. "I've given myself better than that. Do you really want to know who fucked me before you?"

Kristian frowns, but he moves back as I push him away from me, too curious for answers to fight me. I go over to my bed, reach into my bedside table, and take out a pale pink object that's lying next to the knife I used to kill a man four years ago.

He frowns at the object in my hand, not understanding. Then he suddenly snatches it away from me and studies it with dawning anger. He brandishes the vibrating dildo at me. "Wait. This...*thing* stole what was rightfully mine?"

"I thought it didn't matter to you whether I was a virgin or not?" I taunt him. "I thought what was important was if there was a man who remembers what I look like naked."

Uncle Kristian glares around my bedroom, looking for something. He strides over to my desk and grabs a black permanent marker from a mugful of pens. Fury sparking in his eyes, he yanks the lid from the marker with his teeth and scrawls something along the sex toy. Then he throws the pen aside and hands the pink dildo back to me.

I take it from him and read what he's scrawled along its length.

Uncle Kristian.

My cheeks burn and my lips twitch. This man is outrageous.

"Go on," he says harshly.

I look up at him uncertainly. "What?"

"Fuck yourself with it. I want to see everything I missed."

Chapter Ten

KRISTIAN

Zenya laughs, but I don't join in, and the smile dies on her lips.

I close in on her slowly, taking her shoulders in my hands and walking her over to her bed. "I'm serious. I'm not missing out on one little thing about you. If your first time was like this, then I want to see it."

Her mouth falls open and she drops onto the mattress with a plop. Thoughts are racing behind her eyes as I stand before her. The urge to tell me to get out is strong, but so is the impulse to torment me and show off—the little vixen.

Zenya glances at the vibrator in her hand, smiles, and licks slowly up its length.

Right over my name.

I growl in the back of my throat and reach for her, but she puts a hand on my chest and opens her eyes wide.

"What do you think you're doing?"

I'm about three seconds away from snatching that dildo from her and fucking her with it myself. "I'm helping."

"No, thank you. Stay where you are."

I watch as she slowly takes off her clothes, pulling her blouse off over her head, wriggling out of her jeans, and throwing them aside. Her bra is made from white see-through lace, and I can see her dusky nipples through the fabric. Her panties are the same, and there's a slightly darker patch over her slit.

My mouth waters at the sight. Wet already. Fuck, I'm addicted to this girl.

She takes her underwear off, dropping them over the edge of her bed. Her crumpled panties land on my shiny black shoe.

As Zenya settles back and makes herself comfortable, she closes her eyes. She hasn't looked once at me since she took her clothes off.

She's decided to pretend I'm not here. Torment me. Look but don't touch, Uncle Kristian.

I stay where I am for now, standing by the side of her bed and gazing down at her with my cock getting harder and harder in my pants.

Zenya turns on the vibrator, spreads her knees with the soles of her feet pressed together, and trails the head of the dildo up and down her sex. With her middle fingertip, she slowly caresses her clit.

This must be how she touches herself, night after night. Beautiful eyes closed. Panting softly. When the pink sex toy is thoroughly wet, she pushes it inside her.

I swallow a groan as it sinks into her pussy. That should be me. I want to yank the sex toy out and throw it across the room. It should be *me*. I'm raging with jealousy over an inanimate object.

I wait until she loses herself in pleasure, and then get up on the bed with her.

Zenya opens her eyes and gazes up at me, pleasure, desperation, and hunger in their blue depths. I cover her fingers on the vibrator and squeeze until she lets go of it. I take over for her, thrusting it deep into her pussy and angling it up so it pulses against her G-spot.

Zenya lets out a cry and quickly smothers it, remembering that we're not alone in the house.

"Why did you teach yourself to come like this?" I gaze down at her perfect body. Her adorable tits lifting and falling. Her pretty sex swallowing the dildo and making it shiny and wet.

Zenya licks her lips. "I wasn't going to be afraid of any man my first time."

I thought that might be it. Zenya hates trembling in front of anyone and she loathes feeling out of her depth.

I screw her slowly with the vibrator while her fingers work frantically on her clit.

"I broke my own virginity and screwed myself with this thing so many times that I wouldn't be afraid."

"Am I so frightening, Zenya?" I say, pushing her feet apart so I can kneel between her thighs.

"I—" she begins and breaks off with a gasp. She's getting closer and closer to coming. "I didn't know it would be you."

"I did." I fantasized long and hard about her first time with me. Where it would happen. How I would seduce my niece.

"But I never thought about you like that," she whispers.

"Never, Zenya?"

Zenya grasps a fistful of my sweater and drags me closer to her face. "You were my sexy, dangerous, handsome *uncle*. Anytime I was drawn to touch you or felt flustered by your body or the way you looked at me, I felt strange and restless. I didn't know what was happening to me."

I rake my lower lip through my teeth and groan. "You were on your way to desiring me. Fuck, that's torture to know."

"What would have happened if you'd stayed?"

I brush my mouth over hers, inhaling her intoxicating desire for me. "I had the best intentions, princess. I thought about touching you and kissing nonstop, but I swore that I wouldn't try to kiss you before you were eighteen. I fantasized about strangling the life out of every boy who tried to date you. Slaughtering any fiancé who tried to marry you the night before your wedding."

Zenya laps at my lips with her tongue and asks in a heavy whisper. "What else did you fantasize about?"

She wants the dirty stuff? She can have the dirty stuff.

"Everything. Sucking on your pretty nipples. Spanking you hard when you were sassy to make you cry for me. Breaking you on my cock and seeing it smeared with your blood. Slowly and decadently screwing your tight little ass because I own every fucking inch of you."

I twist the dildo as I push it deeper, making her moan.

"How would you have seduced me?" she asks, clenching and releasing her nails on my shoulder and gazing between her legs as I fuck her with the toy.

"Oh-so sweetly, princess. Touching you. Praising you. Giving you every reason to love and adore your Uncle Kristian until it was you who made the first move on me. If you ran from me in shame and confusion, I would have hunted you down, snatched you against me, and shown you just how much I craved you."

"You always knew where to find me when I ran," she moans.

"My favorite fantasy was being alone with you in the dead of night in some blood-soaked warehouse. Protecting you. Killing for you. Being the man that you admire and desire and having you give yourself to me. Whisper that you want me. Letting me taste you. Own you. That night and every night after."

I move down her body, push her hand aside, and lavish her clit with my tongue.

"So I made it come true."

I keep twisting the vibe and working her with my mouth. "Your pretty cunt is my life. Your desire for me makes me insane."

Zenya clutches the sheets, my shoulders, tangles her fingers in my hair. Her moans reach a fever pitch, and then she throws her head back and pushes her sweet cunt into my face as she climaxes. I go on thrusting with the vibe and working her with my tongue until she collapses back onto the bed.

I draw the vibrator out, switch it off, and smile at my name written along its length.

Better.

But I won't feel like I've claimed her properly until I've fucked her full of my cum. "How did that feel?"

"Amazing." Zenya sits up, scoops her fingers through her hair as she fluffs her long tresses, and smiles a self-satisfied smile. "Sorry if you were hoping I'd be all, *Oh no, the scary man and his thing are toooo biiiig.* You don't intimidate me."

I brandish the dildo at her. It's five inches long and barely wider than a fifty-cent piece. "It's cute you think this is how big I am."

The smile vanishes from her lips. "What?"

"Oh, Zenya. You really think that this thing would prepare you for me? You should have practiced with a bigger dildo."

Her eyes widen. "Are you kidding? I thought the bigger ones were novelty sizes. Jokes or something." Then she laughs in relief and shoves my shoulder. "You are kidding. You had me going for a second there."

I stare at her without smiling and wait for her to finish laughing.

"…Aren't they? Why aren't you saying anything, Uncle Kristian?"

I groan and throw the dildo aside. Fuck, I love it when she's naked and calls me Uncle Kristian. It's so sexy and messed up and cute. She'd better call me that when I'm buried to my limit inside of her.

"I'm bigger than your toy." I push her onto her back once more and pull my black sweater up over my head, revealing streaks of blood on my chest. I undo my pants and push them down, along with my underwear, and drag my cock out, clenching myself in my fist. I've always been proud of my cock. Thick, veiny, and long.

I bite back a groan of relief that I'm no longer being strangled by my own clothing. My balls are aching for release.

She stares at me wide-eyed and whispers, "Holy shit." Then she starts shaking her head and scooches back on the bed. "Uh-uh. No way. Keep that thing away from me. You're a *monster*."

I chuckle darkly. "Don't worry, princess. The way you get wet? I'll fit."

I stroke myself up and down with a wicked smile on my face as I approach her. Grabbing her hand, I wrap her fingers around my girth. Her slender, pretty fingers on my thick, veiny member. I've never seen anything so delicious.

With bright pink cheeks and wide eyes, Zenya runs her fingers tentatively up and down my length. "You're so hot and silky. I felt you that night in the warehouse, but I didn't realize you were this…" She swallows hard. "Big."

I run my fingers through her hair as pleasure races through me. "I need you, princess. I have to make you mine. I've waited so long, and I'm going out of my mind with wanting you."

Zenya gazes up at me, shock dawning on her face. "Oh, God, we're really going to do this. What if we ruin what we have together with sex?"

"Making you mine is not going to change anything except to make me even more insane about you."

Desire swirls in her gaze, but so does fear. "If something happens to Dad, I can't lose you too."

"I swear on my life that I will never leave you."

She shakes her head and panicked words start spilling out. "You can't know that. You might be taken from me, too. I can find another lover or another husband. I won't ever have another Uncle Kristian."

Downstairs the front door closes, and my other nieces' and nephews' voices can be heard in the hall.

Zenya jumps and gasps, covering her nakedness with her arms as if someone's already walked in on us. "There's no lock on my door."

We need to do something about that, but not right now. I glance at the en suite. "Is there a lock on that door?"

"Um, I…" The thoughts behind her eyes rush a thousand miles a minute.

I move closer to her mouth and whisper. "I need to wash all this blood off. I'm going insane for you, but I'm not going to fuck you until you're ready for me. All I crave is to be with you, always, so come and help me shower if you trust me to be alone in there with you."

Zenya bites down on her lower lip and nods.

I stand up from the bed, help her off it, and lead her into the bathroom, locking the door behind us. Our private sanctuary away from the rest of the house and family for as long as we need it. If anyone comes in and sees our clothes crumpled up and tangled together we'll be found out, but I can't bring myself to give a fuck about that when I've finally got my girl. To hell with any consequences. She's all I care about.

I take Zenya in my arms and kiss her, reveling in the sensation of her naked body against mine. It's exhilarating holding her like this at last, and pleasure bursts through me as I lead her to the shower and turn the hot water on.

She gets the loofah and the shower gel and starts to wash me, and the water runs red. The blood of her enemies being washed away by her own hands. This must be how a warrior feels when he returns from battle to meet his queen, and I'm filled with pride and lust.

Zenya rises up on her toes and kisses me. "If we were going to have sex, what would you do next?"

I turn Zenya around and tuck myself between her thighs, the head of me getting slippery at her entrance while my finger works her clit. I can't stop kissing behind her ear, her throat, her collarbone. Every part of her is exquisite.

Zenya reaches behind us and runs her nails up the back of my neck, her breathing unsteady. "You've made me come so many times and you haven't…"

"I'll wait until you're ready for me, princess," I murmur, and she squeezes her thighs around my length.

"Could I have a little more please?" she asks.

She can have whatever the hell she wants. "Do you want to feel the head of me inside you? Just one inch deep. I won't go farther."

Tentatively, she nods. I grab her hands and put them on the glass wall and cover them with my own. With her back arched like this, it takes only a slight movement of my hips for the plush tip of my cock to slip inside her.

I wrap my arm around her waist and drop my head against her shoulder, grinding slowly into her but careful not to push any deeper. The tight grip of her flesh is heavenly torture.

"You tell me how deep you want me, baby. I can stay right here. Or I can give you more."

Zenya pants in time with my shallow thrusts.

"All of you," she finally cries. "I want all of you."

Holy fucking hell.

Yes.

I hit the faucet with my fist and the water shuts off, leaving us in silence as I pull out.

Zenya turns to me in confusion, hurt flickering in her eyes. "Don't you want me?"

"Not here. Out there." I take her out of the shower and over to the vanity. "Put your hands on the marble."

I admire her beautiful body as she does as she's told. Her dandelion silk hair is wet and flows down her back with droplets of water. I lick some from her shoulder with my tongue.

"I want to watch us." I swipe my hand across the condensation on the mirror, revealing both of our naked bodies. Zenya stares at our reflections with huge eyes.

Her eyes get even bigger as I take my cock in my hand and drag the swollen head through her sex and find her tight entrance.

"Please be slow," she whimpers. "I don't know—you're so—"

"I'm not in a hurry," I murmur. "We'll do just the same as we did back there."

I surge forward just a little and stop, thrusting carefully. Without the water running, I can hear every one of her little gasps and me moving against her wet flesh. I wrap my arm around her waist and murmur, "Is that too much?"

Zenya relaxes a little and shakes her head.

"Aren't you so brave for me," I whisper, praising her as I slide a little deeper. She hated the idea of showing any little weakness in front of me, but I love her like this. Her hand clutched tightly over mine, her attention all on me. I pump slowly into her, moving back and forth just a little but working myself deeper and deeper.

Pleasure starts to flood my body, and my next words are a groan. "Princess, your pussy feels like heaven. You're so hot and tight around me."

I slide my hand down her belly and find her clit is so swollen to the touch, and she yelps as I brush my fingers over it.

"How deep are you?" she whispers, her eyes closed.

"Halfway."

"Only half?" she whimpers. "You feel huge. I don't think I can take any more."

I reach down between us to the place where we're joined and run my fingers around my girth, gathering the wetness, and then lifting it to her lips.

"You see how wet you're getting for me?" I ask as she sucks my fingers. "Your body knows there's more of me. Your pretty cunt wants all of me."

While she sucks, I pump deeper into her, and she moans around my fingers.

"You see how well you take me? Such a good girl."

A pink flush stains her cheeks, making me smile. How she hungers to be praised. Out there, she has all the responsibilities on her shoulders, but in here with me, she can let go of all her worries and know she's pleasing me just by letting me spoil her.

I move back a little and grasp her hips with both hands, watching myself fuck her carefully, easing in another fraction of an inch only when I feel she's ready for it.

Every time I glance up at her, I catch her staring at my face in the mirror, but as soon as I catch her eye, she drops her gaze like I've caught her red-handed. "You can look at me, princess. I like when you look at me."

"The expression on your face. It's too much."

"Too much how?"

"That you would look at me like that. Breathless and fierce and tender."

I let go of her hips and wrap both my arms around her, enveloping her with my body and squeezing hard, and thrusting up at the same time.

"Do you know what else is too much?" I whisper in her ear, staring into her eyes.

"What?" she asks, twining her fingers through mine just like she did while we were watching those fireworks on New Year's Eve two years ago.

"Not my cock, apparently. I'm all the way inside you."

Her eyes widen. "You are?"

"Uh-huh. How does that feel?"

"So good," she moans, tilting her head back and flexing her spine to allow me in deeper.

"I told you I'd fit," I growl, and sink my teeth into the flesh of her shoulder. The grip of her pussy on my cock is insane. "Do you like your uncle's thick cock deep inside you, princess?"

Zenya gasps in horror and drops her eyes again.

I take her chin in my hand and force her to look up. "If we're going to fuck, you're going to look at me, my sweet little niece. Whose cock is railing your tight pussy?"

"Don't make me say it, please," she moans.

I grin wickedly at her, moving one hand to her waist and the other holding on to her shoulder as I pump into her in a rhythm that sets my soul on fire. I'm finally fucking my girl like she was made to be fucked. "If you want to come, you will. You're going to love coming on my dick, princess. Whose cock is railing this pretty cunt of yours?"

"Yours."

"And who am I?"

Zenya whispers so quietly that I can't hear her.

I lift my hand and bring it down in a hard spank on her ass, making her yelp. "No. *Who am I?*"

"Uncle Kristian," she whimpers.

"Don't you forget it. I'm not some piece of unworthy trash sniffing around your feet. I'm Kristian fucking Belyaev, second to no man. You and I were made for each other. We belong to each other, and I'm never letting you go." I cup her chin in my hand and force her to look at herself in the mirror. "Now watch while I get you pregnant."

Her face slackens in shock. "What are you—*ahh*."

I find her clit again and rub her vigorously. She heard me. I said what I fucking said.

Zenya's eyes flutter closed for longer and longer as my fingers alternate between rubbing her fast and slow and my thrusting cock forcefully driving her closer and closer to the edge. I can't take my eyes off her, flushed with pleasure and totally lost to everything but what I'm doing to her.

A spasm ripples along my length and then she clamps down on me so hard I see stars. She comes in a long, loud wail that's in danger of echoing around the whole damn house, but I don't care. I'm not hiding anything. I hope Troian wakes up and fucking hears.

My woman.

Mine.

No one else's.

Zenya flattens one of her hands against the mirror to steady herself as I pump faster into her. I cover it with my own and clench her tight as my own climax rockets through me. I fuck her even deeper as I feel my cum shoot up my cock and spill inside her. Where it needs to be at long last.

I groan and drop my head between her shoulder blades, whispering her name and listening to my heart thundering in my ears. I keep thrusting lazily, eager to push my cum as deep as it can go inside her.

Carefully, so carefully, I draw myself out of her and straighten up, holding on to Zenya's waist.

"How does that compare to your little plastic toy?" I ask with a sardonic lift of my brow.

Zenya laughs weakly, still out of breath, and pushes her hand through her damp hair. "You're so much. In all the ways." She flicks her gaze to mine, more daring now. "I liked it."

Hell yeah she did. My girl was made to be fucked like this. Fast and deep and raw.

I run my thumb up her slit and pull her open. My cum wells up inside her and a little of it drips down her thigh. I take a rough breath and commit this sight to memory.

Fucking *finally*.

Zenya Belyaev, a wet horny mess and dripping with my cum.

"Oh fuck yes, your uncle loves seeing you like this, princess," I breathe, dragging two fingers up her thigh to gather my seed and push it back inside of her. I do it a second and then a third time, making sure not to waste a drop, a hot and heavy feeling gathering inside me as I imagine her getting pregnant right this second. I'll be a father by the time I'm thirty-seven, and there's plenty of time for us to have more babies because my sweet girl is just eighteen.

She's going to look so fucking beautiful when she starts to show. I'll hold her bump with one hand while I sink myself into her mouth, her pussy, her ass.

My cock twitches and I feel myself getting hard again. I wonder how soon I can try knocking her up again. The second time might be the charm if it didn't take right away.

Zenya tries to push herself upright and my cum wells up around her entrance again. I stop her with a hand on the middle of her back.

"No," I say sharply. "Stay where you are for five minutes."

Zenya frowns at my reflection. "Why?"

I smile at her in the mirror, my teeth gleaming but saying nothing.

My girl is so disobedient that she ducks out from my grasp and stands up. With a growl, I wrap one arm around her torso and another behind her knees and scoop her up against my chest.

"What—Uncle Kristian!"

I carry her to the bedroom and drop her on the bed. "I told you to stay still. A few more minutes and then you can do whatever you want." Her thighs are sticky with my cum, and I glare at the sight. That better not be all of it.

I get on the bed with her and plant my hands on either side of her head, trapping her in place.

"Out there," I nod at the door, "I follow your orders. In here and in my bed, or wherever I've just fucked you, you follow mine."

Zenya raises both eyebrows at me in surprise. "Aren't you bossy all of a sudden."

She thinks I'm playing some kind of sex game with her, but this is serious Belyaev family business. She could be carrying the next heir to the Belyaev fortune very soon. My son or daughter.

She studies me, understanding slowly dawning on her face. "Wait. You don't have a horny look in your eyes. You're plotting something. What are you—" She gasps in shock and grabs my shoulders. "You're trying to get me pregnant. We didn't use a condom. I didn't think of it. I've never even touched a condom."

And she never will. "I've had blue balls for four years and had checkups in the meantime. I wouldn't put you at risk."

"Have you had a vasectomy?"

I reel back in outrage. "Are you crazy? I want children. I told you already I'm going to fuck my baby into you. Are you on birth control?"

Zenya stares at me with her mouth open. "Yes," she says quickly.

Too quickly.

A smile spreads over my face. No, she's not. We just fucked totally raw, and I want to celebrate by shaking a bottle of champagne and spraying it all over us. "You're going to have my baby, princess. A little Belyaev for us to dote on together and for the whole family to love." I kiss her hard. "You're going to look insanely hot when you're showing. That's how we'll tell everyone that we're getting married. A bump and a save the date."

I reach for her belly but she swats my hand away and sits up.

"Don't even joke about that! Can you imagine everyone's faces if they find out what we just did, let alone if I had your baby? What would Dad think?"

I sit back on my heels and rub my hand over my jaw with a smirk. My cum is dripping down her thighs again but it's been long enough now. My boys will have been eager as fuck to get in her womb. "Troian? He always thought I should settle down with a wife and get my babies into her."

"Yes, but not with your *niece*."

I cup the nape of her neck and draw her closer to me, murmuring huskily, "Why shouldn't I have a baby with my niece? You're the woman I love best in the world. I already want to protect you and keep you close to me forever. Do you think I'll stand by and watch as another man gets his filthy fucking hands all over my most precious girl?"

She struggles with this. "But what if this tears the family apart? Wouldn't it be better if I married someone else? I've got enough choices."

I narrow my eyes at her. "I'm not kidding, Zenya. I'll kill any man who touches you."

"You don't own me," she tells me, grabbing her phone, pulling on her robe, and walking out of the room.

"Oh, yes I do," I seethe under my breath.

Where the hell does she think she's going? I pull on my clothes and stalk silently down the carpeted hall until I hear her talking in one of her siblings' rooms.

"Can I please make an appointment with Doctor Nader? The sooner the better. I can come to his office. He doesn't need to come to the house."

I realize what she means to do in a flood of anger. I reach for the door handle and nearly rip it open, but I stop myself and listen carefully instead.

"Five o'clock? Perfect. Thank you."

I smile darkly to myself.

No, thank *you*, princess.

I glance at my watch as I leave without saying goodbye. Five o'clock is in less than two hours' time, and I know exactly why Zenya's in such a hurry to see the family doctor.

I won't stop her from asking Doctor Nader for birth control and Plan B.

But I will stop him from giving it to her. The real ones, anyway.

I stride down the driveway to my car, determined to move every obstacle out of my way until Zenya is finally mine.

It's time for me to pay a call on the faithful family doctor.

Chapter Eleven

ZENYA

"Is everything all right, Doctor Nader?"

The dark-haired, bespectacled man is trembling slightly as he fumbles to remove the blood pressure cuff from my arm. Normally he's warm and welcoming whenever he sees me, the epitome of calm and collected in his white coat, but today there are beads of sweat on his brow and he can't look me in the eye.

"Your blood pressure is normal, Zenya. There's nothing to worry about."

I'm not worried about my blood pressure. I'm worried about his, but what do I know? I'm not a doctor.

"You wanted to discuss your options for birth control. For someone of your age and in your situation, I'd recommend the contraceptive shot as it lasts for three months."

I blink. I didn't even know there was a contraceptive shot. "I was thinking of going on the pill."

"The shot would be better for you." He runs through risk factors, pros, and cons so fast that I can't follow him. My brain has been mush since Uncle Kristian left. I can't stop thinking about the way he coaxed me so sweetly into letting him fuck me hard over my own bathroom vanity. My first proper time with a man and it was...

Wild.

And dangerously addictive. No pain, only the stretch and burn of his monstrously thick cock and the explosive pleasure of him thrusting deeper and deeper inside me. I don't care what kind of birth control I use as long as I'm protected in case I slip up again. Uncle Kristian is pursuing me hard, and he makes me feel so incredible that I wouldn't be surprised if I'm on my back with him plunging every inch of himself into me again within twenty-four hours. Thrusting hard. Dragging his thickness back and forth against my inner walls. Pinning me to the bed while he fucks his cum deeper into me, hell-bent on getting me pregnant.

I want to slap his face for groaning *good girl* while he was buried all the way inside me.

Slap his face, kiss him hard, and beg him to do it again.

I clench my hands between my knees, my cheeks burning. "Fine. Let's go with the shot. And may I please have a prescription for Plan B? I know, I should have been more careful. You don't need to lecture me about safe sex because I won't do anything risky again."

But Doctor Nader seems too distracted to give me a lecture. More beads of sweat break out on his forehead as he dithers over my request.

A moment later, he reaches for a drawer and his voice is unusually high as he says, "Actually, I keep stock of Plan B in my office. Every other day I have a woman asking for it, and the sooner it's taken, the better."

Doctor Nader drops a blank white box into my hand with a nervous smile. Maybe there's no name on the box because it's generic? I don't know how drug companies work, but I'm sure it's fine. I tuck the Plan B into my handbag for now because I don't have any water on me. "Thank you so much, you've saved me a trip."

"It's no problem at all. Now I'll get you the shot."

He stands up and moves to the other side of the room, getting what he needs, I presume. I'm preoccupied by my own thoughts when he comes back to me with a needle.

"Pull your sleeve up for me. The shot goes into your upper arm."

I stare at the needle. If he sticks that in me, I won't be able to conceive for three months.

Doctor Nader frowns when I don't move. "Is there anything wrong, Zenya?"

But what if I want a baby? A little baby who looks like Uncle Kristian and has his crystalline blue eyes and white-blond hair. A baby he would hold in his strong arms with a gentle smile on his handsome face. My insides melt as I picture him putting his forefinger in the baby's tiny hand and it gripping him with all its might. When it cries, its cries would be loud and demanding, because any baby of his would be strong and spirited.

My heart *aches* as I imagine it.

What the hell is wrong with me? Maybe I'm more like Uncle Kristian than I thought, and I crave to behave disgracefully and revel in everyone's outrage. Or maybe I have a self-destructive streak that's pushing me toward messier and messier decisions.

Or do I want to have Uncle Kristian's babies because I'm in love with him?

I nibble on my lower lip, trying to decide what the right thing is to do. I don't have to have a second shot if I change my mind later, but not having the shot today and throwing away the Plan B would be totally irrational.

I pull up my sleeve, turn my face away, and offer my arm to Doctor Nader. "Nothing's wrong. Give me the shot."

As I step through the front door, the sound of my brothers' and sisters' animated voices greet my ears. Everyone seems to be at the back of the house in the kitchen.

"Is that you, Zenya?" a woman's voice calls amid the sound of clanking dishes and something sizzling. I can't see who it is, but I recognize her voice. Aunt Eleanor, Chessa's sister. She comes over once a week to cook dinner for us all. I'd forgotten tonight was her night, and I'm grateful because I'm so distracted right now, I might put a chicken fillet in the toaster.

"Yes, it's me. I'll be there in a minute," I call back.

Someone strides out of the lounge, snatches my handbag from my shoulder and pulls it off my arm. I whirl around and see Uncle Kristian pawing through the contents. He must have been home and come back again because he's changed out of his bloodied assassin getup and he looks clean-cut in a black shirt and pants.

"What do you think you're doing?" I ask him, trying to take my bag back, but he steps out of reach, still hunting among my lipsticks, tissues, receipts, and keys. A moment later he holds up an empty blister packet, an expression of hurt and accusation on his face. I snatch it back and shove it into my bag.

He doesn't get to feel hurt.

And yet, a pang of conscience slams through me.

Uncle Kristian glares at me. "I thought so. You ran straight to Doctor Nader."

I gaze up at him with my emotions in free fall. I did the right thing, didn't I? He's twice my age and he's my *uncle*. Just because I'm insanely attracted to him doesn't mean I should lose my sense of reality.

Uncle Kristian steps closer and puts his mouth close to my ear. There's a secretive smirk on his lips like he knows something I don't. I must look devastated as he hurries to reassure me. "Don't worry, I understand. You panicked. Next time then, princess."

A shiver goes through me, and he feels it. Glancing left and right, he pulls me into the next room and behind the door. We're hidden from sight but the door is still open. My brothers, sisters, and aunt are just feet away.

But he still kisses me.

A greedy, aggressive kiss with one hand gripping my waist and the other cupping the nape of my neck. Bending me to his body. His desire. His will. He thrusts his tongue into my mouth with a hunger like he's been starving for me for years, not a matter of hours.

Uncle Kristian rests his forehead against mine and whispers fiercely, "I'll never let you go. Never. You've always been mine and you always will be mine." He delivers a final, bruising kiss and disappears.

I stay where I am for several minutes, trying to calm my wildly beating heart. I listen for the sound of the front door closing which means he's leaving, but I don't hear it.

Oh, great. Now I have to try and be normal sitting across from him through a whole dinner.

With a sigh, I plaster a normal expression on my face and go upstairs to see if Dad's awake. He is, and I put away my handbag and help him downstairs.

When I enter the kitchen, I'm hyperaware of Uncle Kristian handing plates and cutlery to my nine-year-old stepbrother, Noah, so he can set the table with them. As he passes over a handful of forks, Lana says, "*Avtobus povorachivayet naleva.*"

The bus is turning left? What?

"*Nalevo,*" Uncle Kristian corrects her, and Lana repeats the phrase without the mistake. "That's right," Uncle Kristian says, and I smile as I realize he's helping her with her Russian. I wonder if Lana is thinking about joining the family business after high school or if she's merely learning about her heritage.

"Excuse me, Zenya," Eleanor says behind me, and I move out of the way as I see my aunt behind me with a dish full of roast vegetables held with oven gloves.

Lana smiles at me. "*Privet*, Zenya. *Ty golodnaya?*" *Hello, are you hungry?*

"*Ona vyglyadit golodnoy*," Uncle Kristian murmurs, a dark glimmer in his eyes. *She looks hungry.*

His tone and the expression on his face catch Eleanor's attention and she peers from Uncle Kristian to me. I'm reminded of how much it would annoy Chessa when we would speak Russian in front of her. Uncle Kristian catches Eleanor's disapproving look and holds her gaze until she tightens her mouth and turns away. It irritated him to have Chessa telling him what to do in this house, and he's not going to stand for it from Eleanor.

I busy myself, pouring cups of soda for everyone on the other side of the kitchen, but I can't help but hear my uncle's voice over everyone else's, laughing and talking with my brothers and sisters like he always used to. It brings back fond memories and makes me smile. We feel like a family again.

When we sit down to dinner, Dad sits at the head of the table and Uncle Kristian takes the place opposite mine. He's so good at pretending there's nothing out of the ordinary about today, while I feel like I'm riding a roller coaster. Upstairs in this very house not long ago, I had sex with a man for the first time.

I glance at Dad, who's talking with Felix about a recent football game and picking at his food more than eating it, dark smudges beneath his eyes. I'm still not sure how he feels about Uncle Kristian being back. I wonder if he would have been allowed to come back at all if Dad didn't believe I needed some strong family support that he couldn't provide. My loyalty to Dad should have me holding Uncle Kristian at arm's length but instead, I'm…

I flick my gaze at the handsome man across from me, only to find that he's staring at me as well.

Adoring him.

"Can we all have dinner together again on the fourth?" Lana asks hopefully, looking from Dad to me, Uncle Kristian, and Eleanor.

I think for a moment, wondering what's significant about the fourth. Of course, it's Lana's sixteenth in just two weeks. How could I have forgotten?

"A dinner? Why would you want a dinner when I've been planning a party for you?" I ask her. I haven't, I've been woefully distracted, but there's still enough time for me to organize everything. Just.

Lana's face lights up. "You have?"

Uncle Kristian turns to her. "Of course she has. I've been helping your sister make the arrangements. Do you remember her sweet sixteenth?"

"Of course I do. Zenya's party was beautiful."

It was beautiful. The house was decked out in silver decorations and white and pink balloons. I had a wonderful night, but the best part of my birthday was actually the next night when Uncle Kristian secretly took me to an underground cage-fighting match. There were no seats, the spectators were all crushed in together, and he stood behind me with his arms around me to protect me from being knocked off my feet. We yelled ourselves hoarse during the fight. He let me choose who to bet a hundred dollars on and my fighter won. The cops raided the place just as the fight was wrapping up. Uncle Kristian grabbed my hand and led me through the panicked crowd and out a side entrance. He didn't let go of me until we reached his car. It was one of the best nights of my life.

After dinner, Uncle Kristian asks me to walk him out to his car. I suspect he wants a kiss goodnight, but I have other ideas.

As he draws me into the shadows beneath a tree and lowers his head to kiss me, I say, "We have a problem."

"Yes, we do," he murmurs. "I'm not kissing you right now."

"A *real* problem. If Yuri and Jozef didn't send those men to attack me in the warehouse, then someone else did. We need to find out who it was before they try to do it again."

Uncle Kristian's hands tighten murderously on my waist. "I'll find out, and then I'll rip every organ from their body and stuff it down their throat. Meanwhile, don't worry about your safety, princess. No one will dare attack you with me by your side."

He tries to kiss me again, but I sidestep his advances and slip out of his grip. "Goodnight, Uncle."

His eyes are bright with determination as he watches me walk back to the house, and I wonder how long it will be until he has me pinned up against a wall again.

Over the following days, I'm professional, detached Zenya, getting through the challenges of work as well as planning a sweet sixteenth. Eleanor helps me by sending out e-mail invitations to all the family, and I ask Lana's best friend at school to make sure all her friends are invited.

Uncle Kristian is always there, helping me, driving me to meetings, backing me up when I need it. Since Yuri's birthday party, men in the Bratva are becoming less likely to automatically start talking to my uncle and ignoring me. I don't attend meetings with Uncle Kristian. He comes along with me.

Officially, no one knows who murdered Yuri and blinded Jozef, but there's a rumor going around that Yuri told Jozef to assault me to make me the laughingstock of the city, and Uncle Kristian violently thwarted them. I'm pretty sure I know who started that rumor, and it's had the benefit of fewer men looking at me like I'm meat.

I'm doing so well at not lusting after my uncle as well, until a week after we had sex, I slip.

And Uncle Kristian is there to catch me.

We're at the Silo late at night sorting through a shipment of counterfeit twenty-dollar bills that's been hidden among bags of pet food. Uncle Kristian tears open a box, and he's showered with dust and fragments of cardboard.

"Ah, fuck," he mutters, brushing dust from his designer black shirt and drawing my attention to his body. Not on purpose, I'll admit. There's nothing sexy about getting dusty, but my body apparently doesn't agree because suddenly I'm biting my lower lip and drinking in his every movement. The long, muscular lines of his body. His hand on his chest where I wished my hands were right that moment.

Uncle Kristian chooses that moment to look up and catch me staring at him. His eyes sharpen and his nostrils flare. He wipes his hands on the seat of his pants and prowls toward me, intent on my lips.

"We should probably…" I begin, backing up because the hungry expression in his eyes is making my stomach flip. He's gone from zero to a thousand in a split second.

He grabs me and slams his mouth over mine, parting my lips with his tongue and sweeping it into my mouth. I moan as he keeps devouring me, wrapping an arm around my waist, and pulling my hips against him. I can feel his rapidly hardening cock against my stomach and my core lights up with desire. *Uncle Kristian wants to fuck you. Let Uncle Kristian do whatever he wants because it will be so, so good.*

"I need you now or I'm going to lose my goddamn mind," he growls, sliding his hand down my ass and pushing it between my thighs to rub my sex.

I melt in his grip, no longer in control of my own body. Instead, I'm wrapping my arms around him as he lifts me onto a box and pulls my underwear aside. One swipe of his fingers across my sex shows him how wet I am.

I've been soaked for hours and denying it to myself the entire time.

Everything starts moving so fast, and I'm swept up in the electric feeling I get whenever he touches me. There's the clank of his belt and the sound of his zipper. I feel the thick head of his cock bump against me, and then he thrusts into me, swift and deep. I cry out and clutch his shoulders. Uncle Kristian's ferocious expression is just inches from mine as he works himself deeper with every stroke, making my tight channel surrender to him. He's kissing me the whole time, hungry, open-mouth kisses, his tongue pushing into me at the same pace as his cock.

When I'm whimpering his name, he slows down long enough to

get his fingers between us and on my clit, rubbing me so that pleasure blazes through me, and I come harder than I ever have in my life.

Uncle Kristian pulls out of me, turns me roughly around so I'm bent over the boxes with my legs splayed, and thrusts into me again.

Then he's drilling into me with his cock with single-minded determination. "This is where I belong. Right here. Deep inside you. My cock. My cum."

To prove his point, he climaxes with a growl, and drives his cock even deeper as he breathes raggedly to catch his breath.

When I try to stand up, he grabs my hair in his fist and holds me in place. "Stay where you are."

"Let me up."

"Not yet."

He's doing it again. Trying to get me pregnant. I run my tongue over my top lip as a swift pang of heat goes through me.

Uncle Kristian laughs softly as he feels me clench around him. "You're a little slut for me trying to knock you up. What a good girl."

He holds me in place for several minutes, occasionally thrusting, before finally drawing out of me and stepping back.

I push myself up and settle my underwear and hair back in place, still feeling dazed by what just happened.

"Take your vitamins. Eat some whole grains," he tells me, tucking himself back into his pants.

What the hell is this man doing? Giving me pre-pregnancy advice?

He kisses me once more and pats my cheek. "And keep being my horny little angel."

Then he goes back to work like nothing happened.

I stare at him and shake my head. Unbelievable.

A few days before Lana's party, he's driving me home from a meeting close to nine in the evening, and the tension in the car is thick around us. He's been touching me all day. His hand on the small of my back as he opens doors for me. Tucking my hair behind my ear as we talk. Handing me my coffee with his fingers brushing mine. Every single touch has my insides lighting up with desire.

When we get to the Belyaev mansion, I turn to get out, but Uncle Kristian grabs my wrist. "Where do you think you're going?"

"Inside. This is where I live."

He glances at the house and then back to me. "Come home with me. Stay the night."

I swallow hard as I stare at his mouth. Every time we've kissed or done anything more than that, he's ambushed me to get what he wants.

"You could just drive off with me," I say, half hoping he will.

"I could," he replies but doesn't move. He's asking me to decide.

Finally, my cheeks burning, I nod. "Take me home, please. Your home."

Without a word, Uncle Kristian starts his car and we race away.

It's been a long time since I've been to his house, but it's just as I remember it. Sleek. Stylish. Just like him.

When we reach the living room, I turn to him shyly. "Can you teach me how to, um…"

He smiles and he suddenly looks wolfish. "Teach you to what? Dismantle a bomb? Snipe from a tall building?"

I could murder him for taunting me like this. "Give you…a

blow job."

He groans and laps at my lips with his tongue. "The nuns at school didn't know what they were talking about. I knew being a terrible man my whole life was going to get me exactly what I wanted."

"Don't bring up nuns when I'm talking about—"

But I can't answer because he kisses me hungrily. "Lay down on the ottoman, princess. On your back. Move along so your head is hanging a little off the edge."

I'm confused as to why I'm doing this, but I lay down and position myself as he says.

Uncle Kristian grabs hold of my throat, squeezing the sides and holding on firmly. "Now open your mouth."

I do as I'm told, and he pushes his middle and ring fingers past my teeth.

"Now suck. That's it," he murmurs lovingly as I close my lips around him, and he slides his fingers deeper. "You see how you don't gag when I hit the back of your throat like that?"

Then his hand is off my throat and his fingers are out of my mouth.

"Sit up," he orders.

Feeling flustered and a little out of breath, I raise myself up until I'm seated before him. Uncle Kristian is still clothed and his erection is right in my face. He waits, a smirk on his handsome face, to see what I'll do next.

This man is not letting me off the hook by being overbearing. Tonight, everything's happening because I want it to happen. Damn him.

I reach for his pants and unbutton them, my tongue moving against the roof of my mouth. I've been thinking about this all day. All week. The sensation of his tongue on my pussy is intensely wonderful, and it surely must be the same for him to feel me lick him. Feel me suck. Occasionally he's sucked gently on my clit and it's made me see stars.

While I undo his pants and tug the waistband of his underwear down, he shrugs out of his shirt and discards it on the sofa. I've never seen his cock this close before, and I stroke my fingers along his swollen, veiny length.

Uncle Kristian groans softly under his breath.

Heat and pleasure ripple through me. I made him sound like that, and I'm the reason his eyes are fluttering closed and his head is tipping back. I love the way his throat muscles flex and his Adam's apple stands out.

My mouth opens of its own accord and I lick him, enjoying the sensation of the ridge of his cock against my tongue. Uncle Kristian sucks in a breath, and in my peripheral vision I see his head snap up and he gazes down at me with laser focus. I open wider and take him in my mouth, sucking him slowly up and down.

"That's perfect, princess," he murmurs through gritted teeth. "Just like that."

Uncle Kristian pushes deeper, and I panic and grab his hips as I feel myself about to gag. He stops and pulls back a little.

"Take your time. Remember how it felt on your back," he murmurs, gathering my hair into a ponytail with his hand.

I lift my chin a little so he hits the same spot as his fingers did, and it's much easier. After a few careful movements, he starts thrusting deeper, taking charge of what's happening.

"You're so fucking beautiful with your lips around my cock," he whispers, and his words of praise twine through me.

I'm fixated on all the little sounds he's making, and my core starts to ache with envy over what he's doing to my mouth. His breathing grows heavier, and I feel him swell against my lips.

"I need to fucking stop. I don't want to stop," he groans.

Why would he want to stop? It sounds like he's having the time of his life.

"Take your panties off. *Quickly.*"

I'm confused, but I do as he asks, keeping him in my mouth while I reach under my dress and draw my underwear down my legs.

"Don't swallow," he growls. "Not a drop. Don't you fucking dare."

I have no idea why this is so important to him, but I'm curious to see what he does next. My hands are splayed on his belly and I can feel his muscles clenching harder and harder. At the same time, his grip on my ponytail becomes ferocious as he steadily fucks my mouth. My eyes are closed. I love this so much. The feel of him filling my mouth. Taking his pleasure.

A moment later, he gasps and his rhythm stutters. Warm liquid that tastes like Uncle Kristian's scent floods my mouth and my eyes open wide in surprise. There's more than I thought there would be, and I nearly swallow automatically before he draws his cock out of my mouth, hunkers down on his heels before me, and grabs my throat.

"Give it to me. In my mouth," he bites out, his eyes burning, before kissing me hard.

He wants his cum back? I part my lips and let it flow into his mouth. He gathers it up with his tongue, sweeping his seed from every corner of his mouth. With his lips tightly closed, he grasps my waist, pushes me back on the sofa and spreads my legs.

He pushes both forefingers into my sex and pulls me open as much as he can, spitting his cum in a long stream straight into me.

"Uncle Kristian?" I say, hands gripping the sofa and staring at him in shock.

He gathers his saliva and cum on his tongue and spits a second time, and I feel it land on my inner lips. Drawing his fingers out, he carefully pushes the warm liquid inside me, so intent on scooping every stray drop into my pussy, and doesn't look up. "Yes, princess?"

"What are you doing?"

He smirks a little, his white-blond hair falling into his eyes. "Me? Don't worry about me. You just lie there like a good girl."

I know what he's doing. He wanted to come in my mouth, but he didn't want to miss an opportunity to fill me up. A swift, hot pang goes through me at the thought. "You're obsessed."

He smiles wider, holding me in place with his hands on my thighs. There's no point even trying to get up for the next few minutes because he won't let me.

"Hungry? I'm starving. Let's order takeout." He pulls his phone out of his pocket and starts scrolling through an app, one hand still gripping my thigh and keeping me on my back. He keeps his weight on me in a way that says, *Don't you dare try to get up until I say so.*

I let my head fall back onto the sofa with an exasperated sigh as he asks whether I prefer dumplings or ramen.

"Is this what people call a kink, or are you seriously trying to get me pregnant? Or is it both?"

He raises one eyebrow at me, and the look in his eyes is devilish. Whatever is going on in his villainous mind, he's not going to tell me. My core is still aching, so apparently being filled with his cum and then held down is a kink, and I've got it.

"I want dumplings," I tell him. "And then you owe me an orgasm."

"Anything for my princess," he murmurs, tapping on his phone with his thumb.

Chapter Twelve

ZENYA

*L*ana's sweet sixteenth birthday party is at home on a Friday night. The house is filled with family and friends and children are running everywhere. My heart bursts with happiness because it reminds me of the parties we used to throw before Chessa died and Uncle Kristian was banished. Before the house grew cold and silent and filled with sickness and tears.

It's taken me all day to decorate the house, welcome the caterers and help them set up the food and drinks, and get myself ready. Eleanor's been here all day helping as well, only driving home briefly to change into a blouse and skirt and do her makeup.

I'm so grateful for her presence here, especially considering Lana isn't Chessa's daughter, but Eleanor's always treated all of Troian's children with love. I'm surprised she doesn't have a family or a boyfriend of her own. She's in her early thirties and her looks are striking. She wears bold colors and lots of black eyeliner, which is so unlike Chessa's soft and romantic appearance. I wonder if Eleanor's rebelling against her traditional family and she's secretly a little wild. I've never known her to bring a man to a party, and I don't know what her type is, but maybe she likes a bad boy.

As she finishes putting out the punch glasses on the drinks table, I notice a red mark on her shoulder, just by her neck.

"Is that a hickey? Wait, that's a bite," I exclaim, but not loud enough for my voice to carry because I don't want to embarrass Eleanor.

She puts her hand to her neck, her eyes going wide, and then she smiles. "Isn't it silly? I feel like a teenager." Her cheeks turn pink and she hurries away, tugging up the neckline of her blouse.

I smile to myself as I watch her go. So Eleanor does have a lover, and a mischievous one by the looks of things. I wonder when I'll get to meet him. I'll have to drop hints to bring him to one of our family dinners.

I'm handing out cups of punch to my brothers, sisters, and younger second cousins when Lana bounds across the room toward me, wearing a glittering royal blue dress that makes her eyes look even bluer.

"What do you think? Is this the party you hoped for?"

Lana throws her arms around my neck and hugs me tight. "It's everything I wanted. *Thank you.*"

I relax a little at my sister's words. I wanted everything to be perfect for her, but there's another reason as well. This might be the last birthday she celebrates with Dad, a thought that's been making my throat burn with unshed tears all week.

Dad and I went to see Doctor Webster a few days ago to get the results of his latest scans. The tumors haven't responded to chemotherapy this time, and worse, they've spread to his liver and adrenal glands. It was gut-wrenching news. Worse was the expression on Doctor Webster's face as I demanded to know what our options were.

It was a short silence, but it rang in my ears until I was deafened. I could barely hear his next words. Just snatches of phrases from my worst nightmares. *Pain management. Palliative care. Quality of life expectations.*

My brain was frozen until I realized what Doctor Webster was gently trying to tell me. Dad's going to die from his cancer, and it will be soon.

Dad doesn't want to tell the kids yet as he's still struggling to find the words to give them such terrible news. I can understand that because remembering the conversation with Doctor Webster makes me break out in a cold sweat and want to scream until I pass out. I haven't even managed to tell Uncle Kristian, and we've been alone together several times since we spoke to the doctor.

As if thinking about him has conjured him into existence, the front door opens, and Uncle Kristian's here. My heart somersaults in my chest, and before I know what I'm doing, I'm walking down the hallway toward him, faster and faster. I don't question it.

I only know I want to be with him right now.

I need his arms around me.

I *need* him.

His eyes widen as I reach him and wrap my arms around his neck and press my cheek to his jaw. He squeezes me hard in return, rocking me a little side to side and then easing me away from him with a concerned wrinkle on his brow.

"Not that I don't love when you throw yourself into my arms, but something's wrong, isn't it?"

I nod, feeling my throat burn again. "Let's not talk about it right now. I just want to pretend everything's okay tonight."

Uncle Kristian glances past us into the living room where Dad's seated on the sofa looking pale and tired. My uncle's lips thin and worry fills his eyes, but he plants a kiss on my forehead. "Of course, princess. Let's enjoy the party. The place looks amazing."

He takes my hand and walks around with me, admiring the decorations and complimenting everything. He tells Lana how beautiful she looks and gives her a birthday present, which is a bracelet of amethysts.

"You gave me diamonds for my sixteenth," I murmur as Lana hurries off to show her gift to Eleanor. "And my fourteenth and fifteenth."

"Ah, well, you're special, princess," he tells me with a sly grin. "Only my best girl gets diamonds."

The two of us wind up in the kitchen, which is always my favorite place at a party anyway. We can hear everyone talking and laughing in the rooms beyond and the music playing. Every now and then, a child runs through or someone comes in for bottles of lemonade or to take a phone call.

My dad's cousin, Helena, is holding her four-month-old, Celeste, while her three-year-old cries that he wants to be pushed on the swings outside.

"Not while your sister is fussing. If I put her in her carrier she'll scream the place down."

"I'll take her," I offer eagerly, holding out my hands for the baby. I haven't had a good dose of baby cuddles in such a long time.

Helena thanks me with a tired smile and passes her over, allowing herself to be tugged out into the backyard. It's dark but all the lights are on in the garden and half a dozen kids are playing on the swings and with a beach ball.

"Are you fussing? Are you a fussy baby?" I murmur to Celeste, planting kisses on the top of her wispy hair.

I look up and see Uncle Kristian gazing at me with the same naked longing that was on his face when I was holding Nadia.

He takes my jaw in his hand and angles his face down to mine like he's going to kiss me.

"Don't," I whisper, aware that people are walking in and out of the kitchen.

"But I need you, angel," he murmurs. "I want to fuck you so bad it hurts. I want your belly full of me right now."

My mouth falls open and I cover the baby's ear. "Stop being horny in the middle of a party. And in front of the baby."

"I'm horny for your whole fucking *soul*," he breathes. "I want to make my life with you. Your baby and mine, can you imagine? Three babies. Five babies. I want a huge family with you. My dick is hard and my heart is soft. You're killing me, princess."

My lips twitch, and I shake my head. I can't even pretend that I'm surprised he's talking like this. "Get a grip. You turn into a hot mess whenever I'm holding a small child."

"Always have, always will," he agrees with a rueful smile, looking at Celeste, and I remember the day I held Danil, standing right here with him on the day Chessa died.

"You thought about it when I was sixteen," I accuse him.

"Yes, I fucking did," he says unapologetically, tucking a strand of my hair behind my ear. "I've been going crazy for you to have my baby for years. Maybe it wouldn't be so bad if I wasn't adopted. I don't know."

That's new. I've never heard him say anything like that before. "What do you mean if you weren't adopted?"

He reaches behind me and props his hand on the counter so his arm is almost around me, and when Celeste and I are close to his chest, he speaks softly into my ear. "You look at your dad and your brothers and sisters and you see yourself, don't you? You recognize your own features."

I think I see where he's going with this, and I point out, "You do look a lot like us."

"Superficially, sure. Same hair. Same color eyes. But my build is different from your dad's. My face is different than yours. I've never not felt like a Belyaev, even when I was banished, but it's always been in the back of my mind when I look around a room full of Belyaevs that I don't see my nose. My chin. No one says, *Oh that's what Kristian was like when he was a baby* or *You get that from your Uncle Kristian.*" He gazes at me with naked longing in his eyes. "I'm starving for it, princess. When I look at my children, I want to see me in them, and I want to see you as well. Your beautiful face. Your lovely smile. Your spirit. Your strength."

His words make my heart feel like it's going to burst open in my chest. I touch his jaw, wishing that I could press a kiss to his lips. "I didn't know you felt this way."

"Well, now you do. I couldn't say it when you were sixteen, but I can say it now." He dips his head lower toward mine, murmuring, "That look on your face makes me think you really do want my baby. Tell me you do. Say it."

Heat rushes up my body.

"I…" *I want your baby, Uncle Kristian.* "I…"

Hunger flares in his eyes.

There's a nagging feeling low in my belly.

A small child pelts across the room toward us and wraps himself around Uncle Kristian's leg, laughing gleefully.

Helena comes toward us with a smile and takes Celeste from me. "Thank you for holding her for me, Zenya. Come on, Anthony. Let's go get some cake."

We're left alone, and Uncle Kristian hasn't moved his gaze from my face. The nagging feeling low in my belly doesn't dissipate, and I realize it's not nerves.

It's something else entirely, and my heart drops.

I look up at him with a cry of dismay and my hand on my stomach. "Uncle Kristian, I…"

He stares from my hand to my face, worry blooming in his eyes. "What's wrong?"

I should be relieved, shouldn't I? Or I should feel nothing in particular, like I do every other month this happens. Guilt and sadness are slicing through me as I gaze into his blue eyes. "I think I'm getting my period."

His face falls. A moment later, he wipes the expression away, but I can still see the disappointment in his eyes. Even though being pregnant would be a disaster, I feel the strangest urge to throw my arms around his neck and tell him I'm sorry. I need to tell Uncle Kristian that I went to Doctor Nader. Do I go back to him for a shot? Do I just leave everything up to fate? Making a decision about this is tearing me in two.

"Are you sure?" he asks.

"I don't know. I'll have to check."

"Come on," he says, taking my hand and leading me out of the kitchen.

"What? No—"

He threads me through the party guests and up the stairs, squeezing my hand firmly. "Too late. I'm already part of this."

When we're alone in my en-suite bathroom, he closes and locks the door behind us and every sound from the party recedes. He takes my face between his hands and kisses me, thoroughly tasting me, massaging his tongue against mine. By the time he pulls away, I'm out of breath.

"I've been wanting to do this all night." He seals his lips over mine again, props me against the vanity, and tugs up my dress. His finger slides along the seam of my sex over my underwear. My core is tingling from his kisses, and I can feel myself slippery against his fingers. Am I wet? Is it blood?

What if I have got my period?

What if I haven't?

Uncle Kristian slips his fingers beneath the fabric and slowly sinks his finger in me, caressingly my inner walls lovingly. I gasp against his lips because he always feels good inside me, no matter the reason.

He removes his finger and draws it carefully out from beneath my dress. We stop kissing and stare at it together. The tip is red with blood.

There's a rueful expression in his blue eyes but he smiles at me and kisses me softly. "It would have been crazy if you were pregnant so soon. Don't worry, princess. We'll keep trying."

"But we—" I was going to say, *We're not officially trying* but desire flares in Uncle Kristian's eyes. He grabs my throat and holds tight as he slants his mouth over mine while he rinses his fingers off in the basin.

When he speaks, there's not a trace of disappointment in his husky voice. "And I love trying with you. I also fucking love period sex. A deep, slow fuck, an orgasm or two, a hot shower, and I'll have you feeling so much better. How does that sound?"

It sounds amazing, but there are eighty people in this house. "We can't do anything like that. Lana's party."

"It will be winding down soon. We'll wait until everyone's gone home, and then I'll take you back to mine."

Period sex. Isn't that messy? Won't he feel weird about it? The level of intimacy we just dove into is off the charts.

He brushes his lips over mine and smiles. "I've been fantasizing about taking care of you like this."

I look up at him, puzzled and pleased at the same time. "You have?"

"Hell yes. I said I want all of you. Let me take care of you now so you'll know I'll be the sort of man who'll go out at three a.m. for cookie dough ice cream and pickles when you're pregnant."

I bury my face in his chest and my shoulders shake with tired laughter. How did we get here? Why am I not shutting down his crazy talk? I haven't thought about the future in such a long time, but that's all Uncle Kristian wants to do.

"Where are your tampons or whatever you use?" he says, opening and closing drawers on the vanity.

"I can take care of it. You go downstairs." I push at his shoulders but he doesn't budge.

"Please, I've always wanted to do this. I told you I'm horny for your whole soul. Your whole life." He looks through the cabinet and comes out with a purple box of tampons and a victorious smile.

I'm going to die of embarrassment as I watch him take a tampon out and study the leaflet.

"Uncle Kristian, you really don't have to—"

"Quiet. I'm reading."

"Healthy relationships have boundaries," I grumble.

"I don't want a healthy relationship. Being insane for you is my love language."

He peers at the tampon and opens the wrapper. His eyes open wide in surprise as he turns the applicator over, examining it from every angle. "Fuck. That's so cool."

With the applicator in one hand he pushes my thigh up. I cover my face with my hands, half laughing, half mortified. "I can't believe you're doing this."

"You're so cute. You really think a little of your period blood is making me squeamish when I've ripped a living man's eyeballs out for you?"

I slowly draw my hands away from my face to find him smiling at me. Carefully, he pushes the applicator into me, depresses the plunger, and carefully draws it out.

"Good girl," he murmurs with a wicked smile and throws the applicator into the trash. "Later, I'm going to take that out and fuck you."

My insides turn molten and my cheeks heat as he disappears into my bedroom and comes back with a clean pair of underwear for me.

When we go downstairs, I'm convinced that everyone in the family is going to see my sheepish, flushed expression and know that I've been doing crazy things with my uncle in an upstairs bathroom. Everyone's having too much fun to notice how close we're standing or how he's always touching me, or that I cling to his pinkie and ring fingers because I'm too shy to hold his hand, but I want to hold on to him just the same.

Eventually, the caterers pack up their trays and clean the kitchen. The guests start to go home, and I help Dad upstairs to bed.

"Did you enjoy yourself?" I ask him as I tuck the blankets around him.

Dad gives me a tired but happy smile. "Of course. Lana had a wonderful time. I'm so happy I got to see that." He reaches up and touches my cheek. "You're just like your mother, sweetheart. She'd be so proud of you."

I wonder what Mom would think of everything I've been up to lately. I hope she'd be proud of everything I'm learning about how to be a Belyaev, even if she might not approve of some of my recent decisions.

But I do remember something. She always liked Uncle Kristian. He made her laugh so hard and she only scolded him a little when he did crazy things like taking me to a shooting range at six years old. Perhaps she wouldn't be surprised to know how much I've come to rely on him lately. How my feelings for him have changed from loving him as an uncle to something more.

I'm facing the very black hole that I've always been afraid of, but it's a little less terrifying with him at my side.

"We have to tell everyone soon," I whisper to Dad. That he's dying. That there's nothing else anyone can do.

He nods and closes his eyes. "We will. Just give me a little longer with them while they're all smiling. That's all I ask."

I blink away tears and nod. I can understand that. Tonight, I want to live in my secret and postpone tomorrow as well.

In my bedroom, I quickly put a toothbrush, some tampons, and a change of clothes into my largest handbag. Downstairs, Uncle Kristian is waiting for me in the silent hallway, and he takes my hand and leads me out to his car.

I take deep breaths of night air as we drive. I love my home, but tonight I'm blissfully happy to be free.

When we're inside his house, Uncle Kristian turns to me with an expression of concern. "How are your cramps? Do you need some painkillers?"

"I just need…" I trail off and go up on my toes to kiss him.

Him.

Just him.

We shower together and I wash my makeup off. Uncle Kristian makes good on his promise and takes my tampon out, which makes me flame with embarrassment all over again, but I'm laughing this time. My laughter turns to a moan as he thrusts two fingers into me.

In bed, or wherever it is that we fuck, he's normally ferocious, but tonight he's slow and careful as he eases his thick length into me. Every sense is heightened as he thrusts deeper and deeper, praising me between kisses and telling me how beautiful I am, how sexy, how he can't help but think about us like this whenever we're together. My blood is all over his cock. All over his fingers as he drags them through my inner lips and around my clit, and he leaves bloody fingermarks on my breasts and the sheet by my head.

It feels…freeing. Everything he's ever done for me makes me feel free, and I don't ever want him to stop.

After he makes me come four times and I'm a panting mess, he climaxes hard inside me, his teeth in my shoulder and one hand gripping the nape of my neck.

With his strong arms around me, his cock still buried deep inside me, he whispers for me to go to sleep and that he's going to stay right here. "I want to stay inside you as long as I can."

I close my eyes and melt into his arms, my body heavy and my mind exhausted. I don't think I'll be able to fall asleep with him still inside me and filled with blood and cum, but only a few minutes pass while I listen to his breathing before I drift off to sleep.

In the morning I wake alone in his bed and find that I'm wearing fresh underwear. My thighs are clean and I have a tampon in again. I smile as I vaguely remember careful strokes of a warm washcloth in the darkness and the rustle of a wrapper, and his murmurs for me to go back to sleep.

I pull on his black shirt from the night before and go downstairs.

Uncle Kristian is wearing gray sweats and nothing else as he stands at the coffee machine. His pale blond hair is falling into his eyes and there's a line of concentration between his brows as he tamps the grinds into the silver holder. Kristian owns an espresso maker that's like one you might see in a coffee shop, only a little smaller.

I remember standing right here just a few years ago and watching him make coffee, dressed in a black shirt with the sleeves rolled back past his elbows. I was fascinated by the sight of the muscles of his forearms bunching and flexing and the sunlight catching the hairs on his arms before I understood what that fascination truly meant. Admiring someone down to every tiny detail speaks of a love that's far more devoted than uncle and niece.

There were bruises on his knuckles. Fresh injuries that were a nasty deep purple and red and swollen at the edges. I stepped forward and took his hand. "You've been fighting again."

He twined his fingers through mine and gave me a dangerous smile. "You should see the other guys."

"Who were they?"

He hesitated for a moment, and I expected him to tell me something vague, but then he squeezed my fingers and said, "Take a seat, dandelion. I'll tell you all about it."

And he did. He placed a latte with half a sugar in front of me and sat down opposite with his double macchiato and related all the details about why he and Mikhail had gone after three brothers on Dad's orders. How they prepared. What weapons they took. How they got rid of the bodies. He talked to me like I was intelligent enough and strong enough to cope with the realities of Belyaev family life.

Like I was his equal.

It was just a few weeks after the home invasion, and I would be lying if I said that night hadn't had any bad effects on me. I saw how Chessa was still suffering mentally and physically. I was awoken almost every night by one of my brothers or sisters having a nightmare. My attacker had been drinking, and if I smelled alcohol on someone's breath, my heart started to race. But not from fear.

From *anger*.

I burned for a way to feel safe in my home again, but safety came from power, and I had none. I was a fourteen-year-old girl. A baby in Dad's eyes who needed to be protected and sheltered even more aggressively than before.

But Uncle Kristian understood. This one conversation was enough to make me feel more in control of what happened to me on that terrible night. Yes, people did terrible things to the Belyaevs, but we retaliated, ten times harder.

As I gazed at my uncle, handsome, brutal, and bruised, I'd never seen a more beautiful and awe-inspiring sight.

Looking at him now with the memories of last night's lovemaking clinging to my body, I feel the same as I did when I was fourteen. That he's the most wonderful person I've ever known and ever will.

Kristian notices movement in his peripheral vision and glances over at me. There's so much warmth that fills his pale blue eyes as he gazes at me, and I'm soaked in happiness.

The corners of his mouth turn up and he says softly, "There's that smile I've been hoping for."

I blink and remember what he said to me the morning after he found me in the warehouse.

Tomorrow, I want to open that front door and see you smile that big, beautiful smile that means you're happy to see me. I want that more than anything in the world, dandelion.

I drink him in with my eyes. From his bed-rumpled hair to all his warm, muscular flesh, the ink on his chest, and the gray sweats slung low and tight around his hips.

I'm so happy to see him that my heart is singing.

He moves toward me as if compelled to do so by an unseen force, gathers me into his arms, and kisses me. His mouth is plush and urgent against mine, parting my lips so he can caress me with his tongue, thoroughly tasting me.

"I want to tell everyone about us," he murmurs between kisses. "I've been keeping you secret in my heart for so long, and I want the whole city to know you're my woman."

I don't know how to answer. I'm only just getting used to the idea of the two of us being closer than uncle and niece.

"Kristian, I—"

His eyes widen. "That's the first time you've called me just Kristian."

So it is. It just slipped out, but it feels natural. "I think I prefer it. Calling you uncle is getting weird, considering everything we've been doing."

He takes my face in his hands and kisses me. "I prefer it, too." Kristian gazes at me for a moment. "I'm going to say something, and please don't think it's because I'm callous. I'm only saying it because I've always believed you're strong, and I don't need to sugarcoat things for you. I want to be honest with you, princess. You don't need the fairy tales we tell your brothers and sisters."

I stroke his face. "It's all right. You can say what's on your mind."

"Troian…" he says, and hesitates, and I can see his reluctance to cause me any pain even if he does think that I'm strong enough for it. "There are two ways we could do this. If you want to wait until your father is gone before we can openly be together, I understand. I'll wait forever if I have to, as long as I can have you like this when we're alone. In the meantime, I'll be by your side always. Your protector and secretly your lover."

I marvel that my proud uncle would consent to be what amounts to a bodyguard and a dirty little secret when he was once heir to the Belyaev fortune. "You would do that for me?"

His eyes are unclouded and sincere. "I'll do it if it's what you want. If it's what makes you happy."

I gently scratch my pointed nails across the muscles of his shoulders, thinking. "What's the other way?"

He strokes his thumb over my cheek. "We don't have to keep this secret. Troian will be happy to know in his final days that you're loved completely and fiercely by a man who will always protect you."

I nibble my lower lip, considering this. Will Dad be happy, or will he be disgusted by the thought that I'm sleeping with his brother and fret that Kristian is trying to maneuver himself into position as head of the family?

Kristian kisses my forehead. "Something to think about. You do what you need to do, and I'll do what I need to do."

I'm still imagining Dad's reaction if I told him the truth, and it takes me a moment to realize what he's said. "Wait, what does *I'll do what I need to do* mean? Are you going to cause trouble and upset Dad?"

He shakes his head. "I promised, didn't I? I haven't forgotten. Actually, I've come to the conclusion lately that I want to do the opposite."

"What does that mean?"

But he gives me a mysterious smile and goes back to making coffee.

Kristian's words in his kitchen echo through my mind every day. Sometimes every hour. That Dad would be happy to know that

Kristian wants to be with me. I vacillate wildly on this, sometimes picturing Dad breaking into a smile if we tell him we're together, and sometimes imagining that he has an instant heart attack or aneurysm at hearing the news.

And my feelings? Do I believe that I would be loved, cherished, and protected as Kristian's lover? Maybe even his wife? Would I feel respected as well as happy? Dad telling me that Kristian was always pushing against boundaries that he set for him haunts me.

The old Kristian was like that.

Is the new Kristian any different?

Kristian.

I adore calling him Kristian.

At first it was only in private, but I found just *Kristian* slipping out at home and in front of our men. Mikhail and the others didn't blink—it sounds more professional if I call him Kristian—but my brothers and sisters have been giving me strange looks.

Lana asked him if she should start calling him just Kristian too.

"Absolutely not," he replied.

"Why not? Zenya does."

"Zenya's special," he said, and gave me a smile that made my insides feel like hot syrup and melted butter.

Every time he takes me in his arms and kisses me, pure bliss washes through my body. It would be so easy to carry on just as we are, working together, being lovers in secret, but the answer to one question has the potential to take that decision out of my hands.

Have his baby?

Don't have his baby?

I don't know, but for once I just want to live in the moment, and that means reveling in the sensation of Kristian filling me up with his cum as often as he can.

And he does. Every day he finds space in my schedule to drive me to his place and fuck me hard. Sometimes fast, sometimes slow. If we don't have long, we're frantic about it, not bothering to undress before he shoves me down over the arm of his sofa and thrusts into me. He always takes charge when we have sex, even if I'm on top.

If we have an hour or more, he takes me to his bedroom and goes down on me lavishly, making me come on his fingers and against his tongue. He loves to watch me on top of him, straddling him reverse cowgirl style with one hand on my waist and the other gripping my ponytail. The spot his cock hits in this position makes me see stars, angels, supernovas, and as soon as I'm finished coming he sits up and pushes me face-first into the bed and fucks me hard and deep until he climaxes.

His favorite thing to do is stay lodged deep inside me and then thrust lazily until his cum starts to well up around his length. Then he draws out and gathers it up on his fingers before pushing it all back inside me, murmuring huskily, "That's my good girl."

Being told I'm a good girl for laying still with his cum inside me turns me into a puddle all over again. I'm a soft, clingy mess who wants nothing more than to be cuddled and spoiled for the rest of the day and night, but I have to snap myself out of it because I have meetings with Bratva men and orders to give to our men. I work with my thighs sticky with Kristian's cum, and the man I'm obsessed with glares over my shoulder at any man who dares to come near me. I wouldn't have it any other way.

Weeks have gone by and Dad still hasn't told the kids about his worsening condition and prognosis. It's his decision and so I keep my mouth shut, but one week turns into two, which turns into four. I keep a close eye on how much pain he's in. He'll have to go into a hospice at some point, and it hurts my heart to think he's suffering just so he can stay with us.

I had a feeling that Lana's figured out what's going on when I found her crying behind the laundry door one morning. She pretended to be upset over a bad grade, but two minutes earlier she'd been in Dad's bedroom. He looks gaunter than ever lately. Our handsome father, turning into a skeleton before our eyes.

Lana deserves some carefree sister time, and on the following Saturday, I take her shopping at all her favorite places. We talk about school, about boys, about who her friends have crushes on. Who she has a crush on.

Finally, when we're walking through the underground parking lot on the way back to my car with shopping bags and strawberry frappés, her smile dies and she says in a small voice, "Dad's dying, isn't he? Like, really dying this time."

My throat locks up, and I don't know what to say. She's just blindsided me with the truth I was hoping to protect her from.

When she realizes I can't deny what she's said, her face crumples and she starts to cry. "It's true. I didn't want to believe it's true."

I quickly put our shopping bags in the trunk of my car and help her into the passenger seat. When I'm behind the wheel, I put our drinks in the holders and just hug her.

A moment later, she's shaking her head and pushing me away. "I'm okay. I'm fine. I'm strong like you are."

My heart crumbles a little more watching her struggle to compose herself. Is this what Dad felt all the times he tried to comfort me when I was crying? Uncle Kristian too? I always told them I was fine and swallowed down my tears, and I just realized how painful it is to watch someone do that.

"I'm not strong all the time. Often, I'm only pretending," I tell her, squeezing her shoulder.

"How long does Dad have?"

"He has a few more months with us," I tell Lana, and watch as she digs her nails into her palms. "It's going to be scary and sad, but I'm here for you. I'm always here for you, and I know you're here for me. That makes my heart a little lighter."

"We really will be orphans this time," she says.

We've already lost two mothers and now we're losing our father as well. We sit on that thought together and there are no platitudes to say. Nothing to take that pain away.

"When Dad's gone, who's going to lead this family? You or Uncle Kristian?"

I take a deep breath and let it out slowly. "Well, that's a good question. First it was supposed to be Kristian, and now it's meant to be me. I wonder if Kristian would prefer it if he were at the head of the family or if he could truly be happy calling me...boss or whatever." He can't call me *Pakhan* as that's masculine. I can't even think what the feminine form would be.

"I think he wants you to be in charge."

I look at her in surprise. "What makes you say that?"

"The other day I asked him if I could learn the family business, and he replied only if you said yes."

I smile at her. Despite the misery in this car over Dad, I can't help it. "He did?"

"He didn't even think twice about it. Haven't you noticed how he's always asking what you think and he actually listens to what you say?"

"How do you know that? Is your Russian that good already?"

"I know that phrase. *Chto vy dumayete? What do you think?* I don't know what you're saying in reply because you talk too fast, but he's always listening to you. It's so different from how he and Dad would talk to each other in front of us. I couldn't understand a word, but they would argue and argue. He likes you better, or he respects you more."

A warm sensation ripples up my body. He does say that, doesn't he? And he listens.

I glance at my sister, my tongue playing over my inner cheek. I'm keeping Kristian a secret like I'm ashamed, but I'm tired of boxing him up with so many negative emotions. The way I feel about him is not normal, but we're not a normal family.

Maybe it's time someone knew about us. It would make Kristian happy to know I've confided in Lana, and I'd have someone who shares my secret.

"Lana," I say slowly. "Since Kristian came back, he and I have been spending a lot of time together."

"No kidding."

"My feelings for him are complicated and so are his feelings for me." I hesitate, wondering how best to word my confession.

Lana stares at me with huge eyes, takes a deep breath, and seizes my arm.

"Ohmygodisheyourboyfriendhashekissedyoutellmeeverything."

"What?"

"*I knew it*," she shrieks. "Well, I didn't *know* it, but I saw the two of you talking in the kitchen on my birthday last month." She stares at my stomach and then back up at me. "Are you having a baby? You were holding Celeste and Uncle Kristian looked so yearning, and then later I saw you touch your stomach."

I stare at my sister. She saw that?

"Please, please, *please* tell me you're having a baby. It would make Dad so happy. Ooh, you could get married. Dad could walk you down the aisle. There's still time."

"Whoa, slow down. I'm trying to tell you that I'm involved with our uncle. This isn't a boyfriend. This is *Uncle Kristian*. Don't you have any complicated feelings about that?"

Lana slumps back in her seat and shakes her head like I'm an idiot. "Why would I? We're not related to him. Uncle Kristian makes you happy. You were miserable when he was banished, and now he's back and he adores you more than ever. It's so obvious whenever he looks at you." She reaches out and takes my hand. "Dad's dying, Zenya. What are you so afraid of? The worst thing is already happening."

"I could lose all of you," I whisper, feeling choked up, but also knowing that she's right. The worst *is* already happening. The important thing now is that we're all here for each other, and my family always has been.

My fear is my worst enemy, but it's all in my head.

My flesh and blood? They've always had my back.

"We want to see our big sister happy," Lana tells me with a smile. "Arron and I often talk about how you protected us all the night of the home invasion. How many other big sisters could have done that? I want to be you when I grow up, you know. You always get to do the cool, edgy stuff. The murder and the crimes at midnight and everyone always telling you secrets. Now you've got the most badass boyfriend in the city. Every family we know is going to be gossiping their envious hearts out. If we were pop stars and not criminals you'd be trending online for literally years over this."

I stare at her with one eyebrow raised. "You're not supposed to know about the murder and the crimes at midnight. That stuff isn't cool, either. It's work, and we actually try to avoid bloodshed."

Lana sighs. "Fine, but that doesn't change the fact that you're always so strong and focused in the face of danger. I wet myself three times the night of the home invasion."

"That's a normal response. I bottle everything up and it's not healthy."

Lana smiles. "So you do have faults. What are you going to do about that?"

I wrap my arms around her and give her a squeeze. "I'm going to tell my beautiful little sister about feeling complicated things for Kristian."

She hugs me back, and we hold each other in silence for several minutes until she asks, "Well, can you?"

"Can I what?"

"Teach me about everything you do. I could be your sidekick."

I laugh and brush her hair back before turning to the wheel and starting the engine. "This life is hard, and you should go to college before you decide anything."

Lana pouts. "But I don't want to go to college. I want to be a badass like you."

As I pull out of the parking garage, I say thoughtfully, "Kristian gave me a present a few weeks ago."

Lana's expression is suddenly pure delight. "Was it diamonds? A trip to Paris?"

"It was eyeballs."

She gags and covers her mouth. "You're kidding. That was supposed to be romantic?"

"He thought so. Bratva men are all unhinged. So, how about college and then we'll talk about whether you still want to be part of the Belyaev crime family?"

Lana shudders and reaches for her frappé. "Okay, maybe college first. Fewer eyeballs." She points her straw at me. "But I might want in later down the track, just so you know."

If she graduates and she wants to work for the family, I won't have a problem with that. What's important is that she has a choice. If I hadn't killed a man the night of the home invasion, would I be where I am today, providing for my siblings and running the Silo?

Every morning I get up and can't wait to get to work. Arranging deliveries of stolen and banned merchandise in the night. Sourcing illegal goods for people in all corners of the country. It gives me a thrill. The same one I feel whenever Kristian kisses me.

I smile at the road ahead. I guess I've always loved the taste of danger.

Upstairs in my en suite, I cast my eyes over the vanity and my reflection in the mirror and remember how Kristian took my virginity—my real virginity—right here. That man is pure, distilled danger, but he loves to show his sweet side to me. I smile as I spot the nearly empty box of tampons in a drawer. I'll have to buy more because I'm due soon.

I frown as I stare at the box, and realize it's been quite a few weeks since I had my period. I got it the night of Lana's birthday, which was the fourth. Now it's the tenth of the next month, which means I'm eight days late.

Eight is a lot. I've never been that late.

The back of my neck prickles as I check inside my underwear. Still no sign of my period.

I'm probably just late.

I try to distract myself by taking the tags off the sweaters and skirt that I just purchased, but my mind won't change track. *Pregnant?* It keeps clamoring at me.

Am I pregnant?

I stare blankly out the window, running a cashmere sleeve through my fingers, imagining cuddling a baby of my own just like I've held so many of my brothers and sisters, but this one's different because it's mine. I couldn't make a decision in Doctor Nader's office. I had to leave it up to fate, and now I have my answer. My emotions are unambiguous.

Disappointed when I got my period.

Elated now I might have missed one.

Finally, I can't stand it any longer and grab my handbag and car keys. Ten minutes later, I'm back in my bathroom with a pregnancy test and I'm peeing on a stick.

I pace up and down the small space while I wait the several minutes it takes for the test to develop. If I am pregnant, my life is going to change. I'll have to sacrifice a lot of time and sleep to look after a baby, but nothing is a sacrifice when it's done for love. I touch my stomach and think, *If you're there, I already love you.*

I remember what Kristian said at Lana's birthday, about craving to look at a Belyaev and see some of his own features, his own mannerisms and personality.

Kristian already loves you, too.

But there are things I'm just not willing to give up. My place in this family, for one. My work, for another. I'm meant to represent my father among the members of the Bratva in the city. They already struggle to take a woman seriously, and I wonder how they'll treat a pregnant woman.

With Kristian by my side ferociously protecting me, and by continuing to prove I'm more than capable of running the family business, the Bratva families of this city won't dare mock me. Will they?

Kristian will back me up, won't he?

Or will he just take over and expect me to stay at home?

Will he be furious when he hears how this happened?

And how is Dad going to take the news?

There are so many unanswered questions, but there's one I can answer right this moment. I flip the test over.

Tears fill my eyes. A smile breaks over my face, and I feel a great rush of happiness. For a few minutes, I ride a wave of pure bliss.

It dims as all my responsibilities come flooding back. I take a deep breath and stare at my reflection in the mirror. I'm going to have to come clean to Dad about everything I've done.

I'll have to come clean to Kristian as well.

And I'm not sure who's going to be angrier.

TROIAN

*C*rumpled pajamas. Hands and inner elbows bruised from hypodermic needles. A scuffed oxygen tank. Never-ending fucking pills to swallow. The trappings of a slow death are banal and ugly.

I wish I'd gone out in a blaze of glory, something violent and spectacular that would tinge the men of the Bratva's faces with awe. A shoot-out with the feds. A high-speed car chase ending in a fireball.

But I was never the glamorous one. That was always my brother Kristian.

It's the middle of the afternoon and there are noises from down the hall. Zenya was out at the Silo, but perhaps she's come home early.

I slide my wasted legs out of bed, grasp the handle on my oxygen tank, and heave myself up off the mattress. I'll greet my daughter on my own two feet for as long as I'm able, and I'm not dead yet.

There's a smile on my face as I shuffle along with my oxygen tank. Making Zenya my heir two years ago was the right thing to do. She has a strong and steady nature like me, and she understands duty, unlike someone I could mention in this family. Not once has Zenya ever complained to me about anything or argued with me merely to hear the sound of her own voice. She's a good, dependable girl, and she's growing into a strong, young woman. I'm proud of her, and I should tell her that more often. I'll tell her right now, just because I can. I don't have time to waste anymore.

But when I reach her open bedroom door, I find it's not Zenya inside. It's Kristian.

He's going through her things and hasn't noticed me yet. He's opening drawers, sorting through her clothes, peering into jewelry boxes. It's infuriating that he's invading her privacy like this, but the prominent emotion to flood my veins is envy as I see him standing tall and strong in his expensive suit. He has the rest of his life ahead of him, while I'm leaning on an oxygen tank in ruins.

It isn't fucking fair.

"What are you doing in here?" I rasp.

Kristian glances over his shoulder and sees me, but there's no flash of guilt in his eyes that he's been caught going through my daughter's things. "Oh, hello."

"I said, what are you doing in here?"

"None of your business." Kristian turns his back to me once

more, continuing to touch Zenya's things like he owns her. His bored, insolent tone makes fury rage in my heart. Kristian didn't come back to this family because he thought he was needed. He came back for his own selfish reasons.

"You treat my daughter like she's your property and you always have."

Kristian lifts his head and stares at the wall, but he doesn't turn around.

"Aren't you going to deny it?" I ask.

When he speaks, his voice is cold and quiet. "You know nothing about how I feel about Zenya."

All the anger, all the envy I've felt toward my brother since we were teenagers gathers in my chest. Kristian the troublemaker. Kristian the charmer.

Kristian the *favorite*.

He exasperated our parents but they still adored him. Women have always fallen over themselves for his attention even though he treats them like trash. He's never sincerely loved another person but himself. I've always suspected that of the two of us, Zenya loves him more. Now at the end, I believe it, and it fucking hurts.

"I know plenty. You've treated Zenya like she's an extension of your own ego since she was fourteen years old. Everything you loved, she had to love too, without ever considering what that girl needed or what was appropriate for a child. She lost her mother. Her stepmother. Her innocence—"

"Her uncle," Kristian growls. He takes something from her dressing table and slips it into his pocket. Turning around, he folds his arms and glares at me. "Thanks to you."

There's so much anger radiating from his eyes that it almost scorches me. Whenever he's been in the same room with me since his return, he either looks right through me, or he's looking at Zenya. His smiles are for Zenya. He treats me like I'm already dead.

"Without you, that girl had space to breathe. You were always a terrible influence on my daughter."

Taking her to a shooting range when she was six. *Six.* Telling her more than she needed to know about the family's true line of work when she was only twelve. Giving her weapons and teaching her how to use them. Letting her see him torture and kill. Daring her to try to break into his home. Zenya always idolized Kristian, and he manipulated her into becoming just like him.

"Without me, she became overworked, stressed out, and miserable," Kristian snarls. "When was the last time you made her smile? When was the last time you opened your mouth and it wasn't to demand something of your daughter? I make her laugh. I make her *happy.*"

My fists clench so tightly they shake. "I'm making sure my heir has everything she needs to step into my shoes when the time comes."

"Bullshit," he says, his voice filled with scathing condemnation. "You use her. She doesn't learn from you. She's your tool. I give Zenya what she needs to survive in this life and protect herself. With me, she flourishes."

"You give her far too much. She killed a man at fourteen because of you."

"And if she hadn't she would have been raped just like Chessa!"

Kristian shouts at the top of his lungs. Suddenly he's breathing hard and his teeth are bared. "Do you think she would have been better off that way? Fuck you, Troian. *Fuck you.*"

Pain rips through me. Of course I don't think that. She's my daughter. My little girl. I didn't want that for Zenya any more than I wanted it for Chessa, but since that night, I've felt my daughter draw away from me and closer to Kristian, and it's not fair. I should have been the one to give her that knife to save herself, yet I know for a fact that I wouldn't have even if she'd asked for it because that's not how I thought you should raise a daughter.

After she killed a man, I still didn't know what to say or do around her. I failed Zenya. I failed her so hard and now I can't help hating the man who's rubbing my nose in all my failures with his mere presence.

Kristian paces toward me, his fists clenched at his sides. "What do I find when I come back here? Zenya's completely unprotected. The men of this city circle her like starving wolves, and you've done nothing to stop them."

"Well, what can I do?" I shout hoarsely. "I'm trapped in this wreck of a body. I let you come home, didn't I? You're meant to be protecting her. Instead, you're back to your old ways, spoiling her and manipulating her into being whatever you want her to be."

"I got down on my fucking knees for that girl. Perhaps I wanted— there was a time when revenge—" He breaks off as he struggles for words. "If you still think I'm here for my own sake instead of hers, you're blind *and* pathetic."

"I'm not as blind as you think I am," I say coldly.

I see how he looks at her.

I see it.

My daughter.

His *niece*.

Lately I've started to wonder if there's something in her expression when she looks at him, and it makes my chest so tight I can't breathe. I won't believe that Zenya wants Kristian in the way a woman wants a man. I refuse to even entertain the idea. If anything twisted is going on, it's all on Kristian's side, and I have to put a stop to it.

"What did you just take from her dresser?" I demand.

Kristian says nothing.

I want him to fight me. Insult me or try to strike me down so I can send him away, but he doesn't do anything but stare at me with pity in his blue eyes.

His pity burns like acid.

I draw myself up as tall as I can. Stealing from Zenya now, is he? "You only returned for my money and power and you think you can get your hands on it through my daughter. If you're thieving from her, you're thieving from me as well. You can get out of my house. You're no longer welcome here. You can leave this city and never come back."

Murder is blazing in Kristian's eyes. My heart races in my chest, certain I'm about to die at my brother's hands. But then he sweeps around me without a word, and a moment later, I hear him descending the stairs at a rapid pace.

When the front door slams, I stagger and grab the doorframe. I picture Zenya's heartbroken expression and hear her voice, but she's not asking me how Kristian could abandon her. She's begging to know how I could banish him. Why I drove my brother away yet again with my selfish pride and jealousy when he's the one she needs, not me.

The house is silent, and I feel the loneliness of failure seeping into my walking corpse.

Chapter Fourteen

ZENYA

The sound of the front door lock clicking into place is like a shot ringing out in the dead of night. The house is silent and I lean against the front door.

It's only been a handful of hours since I found out I'm pregnant. I went for a walk so I could think how best to handle this. I have to tell Kristian. I have to tell *someone*. The pressure is building higher and higher inside me.

"Zenya, is that you?" Dad's shuffling along the landing, and I rush upstairs and help him to descend, carrying his oxygen bottle for him.

"We need to put you in a bedroom on the ground floor," I tell him, but he shakes his head.

"I like my own room. I don't want to move." He studies my face with concern in his washed-out eyes. "Is something worrying you, Zenya?"

I help him sit down on the sofa in the living room, my mind racing. I need to tell Dad, but the first person to know should be the father.

"Let me just talk to Kristian." I take out my phone and call him. He just about always answers by the second ring, but this time it goes to voicemail, twice. I frown and put my phone on the coffee table. "He's not answering."

When I look up, Dad's got a strange expression on his face. Carefully blank, like he's shielding some strong emotions, and apprehension trickles down my spine.

"Do you know where Kristian is?

"I have no idea." But he doesn't say it like he's mystified. He says it with satisfaction.

"What happened? Did you and Kristian have a fight?"

"Why is he Kristian all of a sudden? You always called him Uncle Kristian."

Dad's deflecting, and I feel my blood pressure spike. "Dad. What's happened between you and Kristian?"

Dad's expression turns mulish. "He was here a few hours ago. I sent him away again."

"Why, because I wasn't here?" I ask with a puzzled frown.

"No. For good."

Panic crashes through me and I cry out, "What? Why?"

"The same reason as last time. He tramples all over this family and cares for no one but himself."

"That's not true! If Kristian has done something wrong then he should answer for it, but you can't banish him for no reason."

"He came home for power and revenge. He all but admitted it to me," Dad seethes, his breathing growing labored.

I remember Kristian in the warehouse the night he returned. In the days after. Anger burned in his eyes, especially when he looked at Dad. I felt his hunger for power, and I told him myself that I wasn't going to let him take any from me.

But in the weeks that followed, I watched that anger melt from his eyes. He worked tirelessly by my side; with me, not against me. I would have sensed if he still planned to seduce my position as Dad's heir from me.

"If he returned in anger, he stayed out of love. He's proven to me these past few months that he doesn't care about being your heir or ruling this family. He cares about us."

But Dad won't look at me and he's shaking his head. This rift between them is bigger than what was caused by Kristian's callous moment with a stripper and a tube of lipstick. It's as if Dad lays all the blame over losing his wives and dying from cancer at his brother's feet.

I go to Dad and get down on my knees before him, taking his hands in mine. "Don't do this, please. I need the two of you to be friends now more than ever."

"Kristian and I can never be friends again, and we can't be brothers either."

"But why?" I cry, my voice cracking.

Dad stabs a finger at his chest. "Because I'm the one who always gets hurt, and never him. *My* wife. *My* leg. *Another* wife. *Cancer.*" He seizes my hands and squeezes them in his. "You're all I have left and he wants to take you from me, too."

I stare at him in shameful silence. Does Dad know about Kristian and I being lovers?

Dad releases me and drags a shaky hand down his face. "I'm right, aren't I? Chessa told me years ago, but I didn't want to believe it. Kristian doesn't love you as an uncle, and he hasn't for a long time."

I move back and sit down slowly on the sofa, my heart thundering in my chest. All this time Dad knew? He knew before I did? Chessa knew?

I recall how Chessa's manner turned cold whenever Kristian entered the room, and she told him off for speaking to me in Russian. I thought she didn't trust him because he was wild and unpredictable. I had no idea she thought she had to protect me from my uncle.

"I was so angry after Chessa died," Dad says. "I've never been angrier with someone as much as I was with Kristian, and I wanted him to hurt as much as I was hurting. The only person Kristian cared about was you, and I thought if I separated the two of you, then he'd get a taste of what it's like to suffer."

"But that's so cruel," I whisper.

Dad averts his eyes, but he doesn't deny it. All he says is, "Grief is cruel."

"Is that supposed to be an excuse for petty revenge?"

There's something I still don't understand. If Kristian loved me, truly loved me, he wouldn't have abandoned me, no matter how angry he was. There can be only one reason he stayed away.

He didn't want to.

He *had* to.

My eyes snap to my father. "How did you convince Kristian to stay away for two whole years? He never tried to see me. He never even called."

All the rage and grief dissipates from his eyes as he sits back in his chair. "I told Kristian I put something on your phone. A tracker that monitored all your calls and your location. It wasn't true, but he didn't know that."

The admission that Dad even considered spying on me turns my stomach. "But a bit of software wasn't going to keep Kristian from me. There must have been a reason why I didn't see him for two years."

Dad stares at his hands in his lap. "You were underage. Legally, you had to do as I said. I told Kristian that if he returned or even talked to you on the phone, I would send you to an overseas boarding school to finish high school."

Horror sweeps over me. "You would have sent me away? But then I wouldn't have seen my brothers and sisters. I wouldn't have seen you or anyone that I cared about. I would have lost *everything*."

Being separated from my family has been my worst fear since Mom died. Dad knew that. Kristian knew that. It would have destroyed me to be sent far away from the people I love and so he had no choice but to obey Dad's orders.

Kristian didn't stay away from cruelty or indifference.

He stayed away because he loves me.

Dad rubs his eyes miserably. "Kristian came to me and begged me to allow him to come home. He said he'd do anything, but it was Chessa's funeral and I wasn't thinking straight. The only thought in my head was to be as cruel to him as possible. The shock on his face…I'm ashamed of myself, Zenya. I used you to punish him."

Chessa's funeral was just a few days after Kristian was banished. I doubt he even left the city before returning to Dad, hoping he'd cooled off enough to rethink his threats.

Only for Dad to threaten him with destroying what little happiness I had.

"I love him, Dad," I whisper, getting up and sinking down onto the sofa next to him. "I was shocked when he told me about his feelings for me, but in these past few months, I've realized that I feel the same way. He's my other half. He always will be."

Kristian is dangerous, chaotic, and brutal, but in the life I've chosen for myself and the children I'll bear, I need that in a man.

Dad winces, but I can't bury my feelings any longer to please him.

"I love Kristian and…and I just *want* him. What there is between us, I've never felt anything like it, and I know I never will again."

Dad covers his eyes and sighs deeply. He's silent for a long time before he mutters, "It's the same for Kristian. I've never seen him look at a woman the way he looks at you."

As much as my heart soars to hear those words, it aches too. "You hate this, don't you?"

Dad gazes at me with a hopeless expression. "Do you truly love him? Did you choose him of your own free will? All that man is. All that he has done."

I give him a pitying smile. "Do I really need to answer that question? Have you ever seen me make a reckless decision that I didn't struggle with for months and months?"

I pass my hand over my belly, rubbing it gently. Even this wasn't reckless. I wanted his baby with all my heart, I just couldn't admit it to myself.

"Kristian has only ever loved me. He's only ever seen me for who I truly am. He's far from perfect, but he's perfect for me."

Dad presses his lips together in a white, rueful line. "Then I suppose it's time I got out of your way. I've stood in it long enough."

He stares into his lap for a long time, processing what I've just told him. I wait, holding my breath, waiting to hear whether he'll accept us or banish me along with my uncle.

"Kristian would never do anything to hurt you," Dad says finally. "He'd sooner drive a dagger through his heart than break yours. I've wronged you both so much these past few years, and I know you must be angry with me, but please give me the chance to make things right."

Hope flares in my chest. "How?"

"By giving you my blessing—if that has any worth to you. If it's Kristian you love, then I'll accept it. I won't interfere if he asks you to marry him."

I shoot to my feet, my heart lodged in my throat. Can it really be this easy? Am I in touching distance of everything I want?

"You mean that?"

Dad nods. "It feels strange to say it, but if he truly does love you and you love him, then you should be with him. As hard as it is to trust Kristian, I trust that he loves you."

I drop to my knees before Dad and wrap my arms around his shoulders. Him understanding why we're together even if it doesn't make him happy is more than I was hoping for.

Perhaps Dad will learn to be happy for us in time once he sees us openly in love, if Dad has enough time left.

Only, where is Kristian?

I fumble for my phone and call him again, but again it rings out.

"Try Mikhail," Dad suggests.

"That's a good idea," I reply, dialing Mikhail's number. He picks up right away. "Mikhail, have you seen Kristian? He's not answering his phone."

"Yeah, I ran into him at the Silo about thirty minutes ago. He said he was heading over to Harcross. Is everything all right? He seemed angry."

Harcross is a region of the city to the northeast. I can't think why he'd go over there, but at least he's not leaving the city. "It will be. Thanks, Mikhail. Bye."

I give Dad a kiss on the cheek. "I'm going to get Kristian. If he calls, tell him I'm on my way."

Without giving Dad a chance to answer, I flee out the front door and head for my car. As I get on the road that heads to the northeast, I suddenly remember who lives in Harcross.

Sergei Lenkov, the arms dealer.

Panic tumbles through me. Kristian's angry and he's buying more firepower?

I step on the gas and the car shoots forward. I have to get there as soon as possible. I don't know what his intentions are, but fury and weapons aren't a good mix. Best-case scenario, he's gone to murder Sergei Lenkov for daring to flirt with me at Yuri's birthday party. Worst-case scenario, he wants a new weapon in order to kill his own brother.

Overhead, the skies are heavy with gray clouds that have been threatening a downpour for days. We've been without rain for weeks and the air is dry and dusty. The heavens are teasing us, and the sky is more leaden than ever, but still not a drop falls.

When I arrive in Harcross, I drive up and down the streets, searching for Kristian's black Corvette and trying to remember where Sergei Lenkov lives. It's an upmarket area with lots of expensive cars, and I keep thinking I've found it, only to realize it's a Porsche or a similar make.

Then I spot it. Kristian's car, parked on the street without him in it. I pull in behind the car, get out, and turn on the spot, studying the buildings around me. A spa. A florist. A jeweler. Several mansions.

One mansion in particular looks familiar. I think that's Lenkov's mansion, but I can't be sure. Or is it the one farther down the street? There's another familiar car parked outside, a white Lexus with a gold moon and stars hanging from the visor. Eleanor's car. She must be shopping in this part of town today.

I peer again at the mansions, wondering which one belongs to Lenkov. I've only ever been here once before. Kristian brought me when I was fifteen because he was sourcing some rifles for a friend.

I suppose there's only one way to find out. I take a deep breath and step forward to press the button on the gates.

"Buying a grenade launcher, princess?"

I whirl around and see Kristian standing behind me, his expression unreadable. As usual, the sight of him in his black suit with his white-blond hair spilling over his forehead takes my breath away.

"I'm looking for you, actually. Are you here to see Lenkov?"

He nods at the home a few houses down. "Lenkov lives in that one."

Which doesn't answer my question. His shoulders are tight and so is his jaw, but I can't discern which emotion is making his blue eyes as stormy as the skies overhead.

"Please don't leave," I whisper, my lower lip trembling. "Dad told me everything. How he forced you to stay away by threatening to punish me. I know now that it must have been the worst two years of your life. It was for me too."

Kristian stares at me in silence, taking in my desperation. The tears clinging to my lashes. "I've come to my senses, dandelion. You're never going to be mine."

I step toward him with a cry and grab his shoulders. "Don't say that!"

"It's not what I want, but it's true. You can never be mine." His eyes bore into mine as he inflicts those words on me. Then his face melts into a smile. "But I thought you might do me the honor of allowing me to be yours."

He's reached into his pocket and he's holding something between us. Something that sparkles in his fingers.

An engagement ring.

My hands almost fly to my mouth. I want to gasp in shock, but there's a smirk tugging at the corner of his lips, and he's enjoying himself far too much already.

"I wasn't visiting the arms dealer. I was in the jeweler's." He nods over his shoulder.

I pass from despair to surprise to relief so quickly that I feel light-headed, and then arrive at maddened, exasperated adoration.

Of course he would want to rip the rug from under me with his proposal. The man can't do anything without causing a load of drama.

I put my hand on my hip and give him a sassy look. "Diamonds? How ordinary. I thought you'd propose with a gun."

He smiles and walks me over to his car. Opening the passenger door, he reaches into his glove box and pulls out a polished wooden case. I open it and find a sleek silver revolver nestled in red velvet with a word etched along the barrel.

Pakhanovna.

It's not a real Russian word, but I know instantly what it means. *Pakhan* is what everyone calls my father. It's a term of respect that means boss. In Russia, a woman takes a feminine form of her father's name as her middle name. If we'd followed that tradition here, my middle name would be Troianovna.

I trace the etching with my fingers. Kristian is saying I am my father's daughter. Troian's true heir, and the future *Pakhan*.

Kristian's future boss.

He takes the box from me and lays it on the car seat. The diamond ring is sparkling on the tip of his forefinger as he takes my face in his hands. "What do you want first, princess? For me to pledge myself to you as my future boss, or for me to get down on one knee and ask if you'll take me as your husband? *Pakhanovna's* choice."

"Not for me to be your wife?"

He shakes his head with a smile. "I'm yours. I've always been yours. If I ever forget who's leading this family, I want you to take that gun and shoot it right into my heart."

Thunder rumbles overhead. The clouds are moving so fast they seem to be boiling in the sky. A fat raindrop falls on my cheek. The heavens seem to be aching for us to fall into each other's arms for a kiss, but there are a few things we need to straighten out first.

"You lied to me," I say, another raindrop sliding down my face.

He nods, his eyes filled with regret. "I did. I have been. I'm sorry. I didn't come back here to support you as you stepped into your father's shoes. I wanted you, the city, the money, everything. And I wanted revenge."

I laugh and shake my head. "No, you idiot. What happened to not confessing anything until you know what you're being accused of?" He taught me that strategy a long time ago in case I was ever kidnapped or questioned too closely by an associate. Don't let your own mouth talk you into trouble.

His brows draw together. "What?"

"I'm not talking about why you returned or for what purpose. As I was saying, you lied to me."

He rubs his forehead. "All right, all right. I shouldn't have threatened Doctor Nadar into giving you a fertility shot and pretended that I didn't know that morning-after pill was a fake, but—"

I laugh and hold my finger to his lips. "Are you crazy? Are you just going to keep on confessing to all your crimes when you don't even know what I'm accusing you of? Pull yourself together! You're Kristian goddamn Belyaev."

He grips my upper arms. "Let me get it all off my chest, princess. I'm trying to be a better man for you."

"Screw being a better man. You can do that on your own time because I'm the one asking the questions right now, and I want to know why you lied about the swimming pool. Let's talk about *that*."

He stares at me like he doesn't understand what I'm talking about. "The pool? We haven't been in the pool for years."

"Exactly. That's what I'm talking about—what happened in the pool three years ago. You said that day in the pool changed everything for you, but I don't believe you. That wasn't a special day. That was a nothing day. So when was it really?"

Maybe I looked a little more grown up that day and we were touching each other a crazy amount. But laughter and skin and sunshine aren't enough to make Uncle Kristian fall in love with anyone. He would have fallen in love a hundred times with a hundred women by now if that was all it took. His heart is full of darkness and danger. It must have been something dark and dangerous that made him fall for me.

He licks a raindrop from his lips, and suddenly I want to use our mouths for anything but talking, yet I wait because I want to hear him say it.

"You know what day it was, princess. Or rather, the night."

"The home invasion," I reply.

He nods. "When I busted through that window and saw all the blood and devastation in that room, I was never so afraid in my life. I thought I was going to find my girl broken and bleeding, but instead, there you were with my knife in your hand, and the monster who tried to break you was bleeding out." The corner of his mouth turns up in a smile. "My princess doesn't need rescuing. She's a fucking queen."

Kristian draws closer to me and takes my face in his hands.

"She always has been."

I want to melt into him, give him my lips and my whole heart right this second, but there's more I want to say.

"Dad knew how you felt about me," I whisper. "Chessa told him. That's one of the reasons he sent you away."

Kristian groans and pushes his hands through his rapidly wetting hair. "I knew she knew. I was so fucking angry with her for getting in my way, which is why I celebrated when she died. I wondered if she blabbed to Troian, but I never thought Troian would have believed her."

"Dad didn't want to, but he knew the truth in his heart."

"Don't be angry with him, princess. You were sixteen. In his place, I would have banished me as well."

I touch his cheek, my heart swelling to twice its size. "You came back for me two years ago. Why didn't you tell me? You were there the day of Chessa's funeral, but I didn't see you."

He presses his forehead against mine. "I thought about telling you these past few weeks but then you would have confronted Troian about it. I swore on your mother's grave that I wouldn't do anything to upset him."

Even though it would have been in his own best interests to let that information slip. "You're a villain, Kristian. But you're a villain with a heart."

"Only for you, princess," he murmurs and lowers his mouth toward mine.

I put a finger over his lips, stopping him. "Now it's my turn. I've got something to confess to you."

Chapter Fifteen

KRISTIAN

*J*groan as she prevents me from covering her lips with mine. I'm aching for this kiss, and it feels like I'm never going to get it. "Tell me quickly because I've got other things to do with my mouth than talk." Like getting her clothes off and lavishing my beautiful fiancée with my tongue.

"I went to see Doctor Nader after we first had sex."

I nod impatiently. "Yes, and I got there first and threatened to cut off his balls if he gave you so much as a dried herb that would prevent you from getting pregnant."

"Yes, you said," she replies with a glare. "Why did you do that?"

"You made me swear that I wouldn't say anything to your

father that might upset him. I thought I'd let nature take its course." I smile at her. "A pregnant daughter would get the message across loud and clear."

She pokes me in the stomach. "That's a loophole and you know it."

I take her face in my hands. "You've always wanted to be a mother. I've been aching to get my baby into you for so long. When we both want something so much, why wait?"

Zenya takes a deep breath. "You're not the only one who can play secret little games. Doctor Nadar offered me that fake contraceptive shot, but I refused it. I didn't want to be infertile for three months. I took the Plan B with me, but as soon as I opened the packet, I threw the pill out the window as I drove. I didn't tell you because I didn't know what to say."

I stare at her in shock. And I thought I was the sneaky one.

Zenya gives me a worried look. "Are you mad at me?"

A delighted smile breaks over my face, and I feel all the blood rush to my cock. "You knew that I've been fucking you raw and breeding you this whole time and you didn't do anything to stop me? Fuck, that makes me hard just thinking about it. You really do want my baby."

That settles it. I need to be engaged to this girl. She's going to be my wife and the mother of my children.

Our heads are close together, and I hold the ring between us. "I'm prepared for a long engagement. You don't have to put it on your finger if you'd rather keep us secret. I'll buy you a chain to wear it on."

Zenya's left hand drifts up, her ring finger slightly raised. "Please," she whispers. "I want everyone to know I'm yours."

My heart flares with victory as I slide the ring onto her finger. It's the perfect fit. It should be, considering I stole one of her other rings from her bedroom so I could give it to the jeweler for sizing.

"You'll marry me, dandelion?"

Zenya lifts her eyes from the ring to my face. There's a smile on her perfect lips, and her eyes are glowing. "I'll marry you."

I groan and wrap my arms around her and hold her tight against my chest. She fits perfectly beneath my chin, my little dandelion. Right where I've wanted her to be for years and years. "I don't think I could possibly be happier than I am right this second."

Zenya gives a mischievous snicker. "Want a bet?"

I don't understand what she means until she pulls away, takes my hand, and places it on her belly.

Then she just looks up at me, still smiling.

My mouth falls open. "You're pregnant? *Already*?"

Her lips twitch. "You've been trying so hard, and you know I'm not on any birth control. This is hardly a surprise."

I shout with laughter and hug her again, one hand on her stomach. I'm in there. My precious girl is carrying part of me. "But it is. I've been longing for this moment forever and feeling like it would never come."

I dip my head toward hers to finally kiss her.

"I have another confession," she says.

I growl in frustration. "I don't care if you went back in time and assassinated a president, I need to kiss you or I'm going to fucking explode."

"I love you."

I press my forehead to hers, a smile spreading over my face as my anger immediately dissipates. "I love you too, princess."

"You look like a devil with an angel's smile," she whispers, stroking my hair back from my face. "No wonder I fell in love with you."

"I knew that I was for you and you were for me a long, long time ago, dandelion. I just had to wait for you to grow up and realize it for yourself, and you can't deny I've been a patient man."

She wraps her arms around my neck, smiling up at me. "Tell me again how patient you've been. I think this is going to be my new favorite story."

I brush my lips over hers. Anything for her. "Since the night you killed a man and watched me torture four more to death without flinching. Since you jumped on me in the swimming pool and it was all I could do not to kiss you. Since you picked gravel out of my shoulder and ate me up with your eyes. But really? I've been waiting for you my whole life. Since always, every day, forever and ever. Before I even met you. My queen. I'll always want you and I'll always love you."

"I love you, too, Kristian." She traces a finger down my collar, her smile dimming. "Now all we have to do is tell everyone else. We should gather everyone together because Dad's got some news that's long overdue as well."

I can guess from her expression that the news isn't good. I take her hand and give it a squeeze. "Whatever happens next, I'll be there with you, princess."

The tears fall and keep falling in the living room of the Belyaev mansion. All of Troian's children are gathered on the couches, along with myself and Eleanor, as we listen to my brother reveal that this is it. He's dying.

As much as we've fought over the years and despite all the pettiness of him banishing me, I still love my brother. I've had two years to come to terms with what he did, and while it still angers me, Zenya loves me and that's what matters. Troian is the only brother I'll ever have. A brother despite the fact that we share no blood, and with all the trials that come from having a brother who's a rival, a business partner, and a *Pakhan*.

"Daddy, we don't want you to go," Nadia whimpers, tears falling down her face.

He reaches for her, and Eleanor stands up and places the little girl in his lap. He cuddles her close, his eyes filled with pain. "I don't want to go either, but I'll always be with you. All of you carry a little part of me inside you, and when you feel sad and want to give me your love, you can give it to one of your brothers and sisters. Wherever I am, I'll feel it." He smiles at Chessa's children, the ones he adopted. "I'm so proud of each and every one of you."

My throat burns, and I remember my accusation years ago that Troian found it easy to discard me because I'm adopted. They were words spoken in anger. Troian never loved anyone less just because they didn't share his blood.

Zenya is sitting next to me, and I reach for her hand and hold it tightly. Her eyes are glossy with tears, though they're not falling. I suspect she's done all her crying in the privacy of her bedroom.

Troian stares for a long time at our joined hands. Then his eyes meet mine and my whole body tenses. This is his daughter, and I can only imagine how ferociously protective I'll be over my own daughters. If any man like me comes within a mile of my daughters, I'll probably gut them.

"I'm sorry for what I did to the two of you," Troian says in a shaky voice. "I hope you can forgive me one day for keeping the two of you apart. Grief gave me a kind of madness, and I know everyone in this room will do better than I did."

The kids and Eleanor look between us and Troian, frowning in confusion.

Troian clears his throat. "Kristian and Zenya have some news to share with you all. Some happy news, and I hope we can all be happy for them."

Zenya and I look at each other. What the hell are we going to say?

Instead of words, Zenya blushes and sheepishly holds up our joined hands. I don't know what she's doing until I realize she's showing everyone the sparkling engagement ring on her finger.

There's confused silence in the room.

Then Lana screams. She jumps up and flings her arms around her sister, yelling at the top of her lungs, "You're getting married to Uncle Kristian? I'm so happy! Can I be a bridesmaid? Can I be the maid of honor?"

The rest of my nieces and nephews catch on one by one and crowd around us asking dozens of questions. Troian's smiling. Eleanor's expression is one of blank shock. It takes a few minutes for the buzzing in the room to die down.

To my surprise, all my nieces and nephews seem happy for us, and no one's especially confused by Uncle Kristian marrying their big sister. Love just makes sense to children, but I'm sure they'll have lots of questions for Zenya over the coming weeks. Lots of questions for me as well.

"When's the big day?" Lana asks eagerly.

"We'll plan it quickly," Zenya says, glancing at Dad. "I'll start calling venues tomorrow and see what dates are available."

"There's no need to throw something together so fast that you hate the result," Troian replies. "Doctor Webster says I have at least six months, maybe more."

Zenya gives her father a tearful smile. "I want to ask you to walk me down the aisle if you can. Or I'll walk you. I don't care as long as you're with me. And—and we have some more news as well." She glances at me. "You tell them."

I smile at my fiancée, envisioning how she'll look on our wedding day with her bump showing. "Zenya's pregnant."

Lana screams again and once more we're mobbed with hugs and questions.

Troian's face is slack with shock, and he's trying to get to his feet. Zenya gets up, hurries over, and embraces her father.

"Don't get up. You're happy, aren't you, Dad?"

"Of course I am. Thank you for sharing your happiness with us all," Troian says hoarsely, gazing up at her. "It's given us all some sweetness so that we can swallow the bitterness of my own news. I've got so many reasons to stay with you all as long as possible, and the biggest one is meeting my first grandchild."

"Who's also your nephew or niece, Dad," Lana says, giving Zenya a teasing smile.

I flash Lana a dark look, the little troublemaker, but as usual, my girl is serene in the face of taunts. I'd be snorting like an angry bull if Lana were my sibling.

"Whoever they are, they certainly won't be more mischievous than my sister," Zenya says, and everyone laughs.

Everyone but Eleanor. Her eyes are huge as she stares at the coffee table.

"Eleanor?" I ask, wondering if the news about Troian dying has upset her more than I would have expected.

Her gaze snaps to mine and she stares at me like she doesn't know who I am. Then she looks at Zenya, before turning back to me and murmuring, "Congratulations, Kristian. I'm glad that we can console our hearts with your news."

Finally, she looks at Troian, and her expression is pained. Maybe the fact that she will lose her last link to her sister has reminded her of her grief over Chessa. She still has Chessa's kids, something she seems to remind herself of as she scoops Nadia into her lap and gives her a hug.

Later that evening after we've all eaten dinner together and Lana's demanded to know every single detail about how we fell in love—and we've given eager young ears an abridged version—I follow Zenya upstairs to bed.

"Can I stay the night with the heir to the Belyaev fortune, *Pakhanovna*?" I murmur as I kiss the nape of her neck on the stairs.

She giggles at the name. "You can. We'll have to be quiet, though."

I'm nuzzling her hair when she digs her nails into the back of my hand and calls, "Goodnight, Eleanor, see you soon."

I glance over my shoulder and see that Eleanor has paused with her handbag over her shoulder on the way to the front door. There's an expression in her eyes very much like the one her sister Chessa used to give me whenever she saw me close to Zenya.

Get over it, you sour-faced bitch.

I'm marrying her.

I won.

Zenya blushes and hurries onward. I smirk at Chessa's sister, and maybe it's petty, but I feel a thrill of victory as Eleanor hardens her mouth and strides toward the front door. Then I follow my pregnant fiancée to her bedroom.

As soon as we're alone, I groan and tug Zenya's clothes off, desperate to get my mouth all over her body.

"Shh," she says, hushing me and laughing at the same time. "We still have to be quiet even though we're not sneaking around."

I stop what I'm doing just long enough to jam her desk chair under the door handle, then I get her on the bed with my face between her thighs and go down on her like it's the very first time. I'll never stop being addicted to the way she tastes. The soft cries she makes as I hit exactly the right spot. The way she arches her back the more turned on she gets.

I sit up with my cock in my hand, ready to drive myself into her. Her belly is flat and smooth, but I know my baby is in there. Our baby. Our whole future is right here inside her. Totally vulnerable. The thought makes me freeze.

Zenya has her hands pressed against my chest and she's panting, hanging by a thread as she anticipates me thrusting into her.

"Kristian? Why have you stopped?"

It suddenly feels too easy that I've got everything I ever wanted. What if having sex with her now is what undoes everything? If I'm too rough with her, Zenya could lose the baby and she'll never be able to look at me ever again.

I feel Zenya's hand on my cheek and she draws my gaze up to hers. "You look like you're getting in your own head. This isn't like you."

It's not. I rarely think about the consequences of anything, but I've never had this much to lose before. "What if I hurt the baby?"

Her eyebrows lift in surprise. "By us having sex? I don't think it works like that."

No, it probably doesn't, but there's an ominous feeling in my gut and it's paralyzing me. "Don't you think we've had it too easy and something's going to blow up in our faces?"

Zenya's mouth falls open and then she gives me a severe look. "Kristian Belyaev, we spent the last two years being separated and miserable every second of it, and you think we've had it easy? Are you *crazy*?"

I laugh and shake my head. She's got a point there. "I'm just so stupidly happy right now, and I don't know if I deserve it."

Zenya wraps her arms around my neck and draws me down for a kiss. "I think you do. I think you deserve all the happiness that this baby and I can give you and more. Does anyone else's opinion matter to you?"

No, it fucking doesn't.

I push her thighs up to her chest, line myself up at her entrance and sink into her. She gasps and her head tips back, and I drink in the long, lovely line of her throat, and I can't stop smiling the whole time I fuck her because she's mine now. Mine, and we don't have to hide it anymore. My ring is on her finger and my baby is in her belly and soon the whole world is going to know that Zenya Belyaev belongs to me.

I cover her mouth with my hand as we both climax, because suddenly she's the one who's forgotten we need to be quiet and I have to remind her.

Over the following weeks, I become addicted to touching Zenya. I already enjoyed putting my hands on my woman, but now not a minute goes by in her company that I'm not caressing her cheek, her lower back, her stomach.

Every morning when I wake up with Zenya or pick her up in my car, the first thing I do is get my lips on her mouth and my hands on her belly. I swear that when she's six weeks pregnant, I can feel the tiniest, tiniest of bumps.

Zenya's living at home at the Belyaev mansion, and I did briefly entertain the idea that she would move in with me, but I quickly discarded it. Zenya needs to be with her family, now and after Troian passes, so we've decided that after we're married, I'll move in with all of them.

With Troian's permission, we've asked her brothers and sisters if we can become their legal guardians in the future, and they've all agreed. I think Eleanor found that difficult to take as she's so close to Chessa's children, but it would hurt them all so much to be separated from each other. Legally, they're all Troian's children, which makes them mine and Zenya's responsibility after he's gone as we're his next of kin.

Eleanor doesn't say anything, but Zenya sensed her grief and reluctance and hurried to assure Eleanor that she can be part of the children's lives as much as she has always been.

By Zenya's tenth week of pregnancy, we've made all the wedding plans. We're to be married in two weeks' time, just after her twelve-week scan.

Troian's health hasn't deteriorated any further, and I hope for his sake and Zenya's that he'll be able to walk her down the aisle as planned. We've moved his bedroom into the downstairs study because he can't manage the stairs any longer, but he can still walk without getting too out of breath.

I drop Zenya off at the Silo one morning, and Mikhail eyes me from the doorway before following me out to my car.

"Look at you, Mr. Family Man," he says, a taunting smile on his lips. "What happened to the Kristian who told me, *This will all be mine, the city, the daughter, the power*?"

I push my sunglasses over my eyes and grin at him. "It *is* all mine. Everything I wanted. I've just reordered my priorities a little."

"No one's calling you *Pakhan*," he points out. "Are you going to be all right with that for the rest of your life?"

"Zenya's dropped the *uncle* and just calls me Kristian. Soon I'll be called daddy. That's more than enough to be getting on with. Watching the assholes in this city bend their knee to my woman? That's something money can't buy."

Mikhail stares at me in shock. "Fuck, you really do love her."

"I really do." I pat his cheek and then turn away and get into my car.

There's a smile on my face as I head to my own house. Ambition has been a big driving force in my life, but I don't need to be leading the Belyaevs to feel like a man. Zenya makes me feel like a man every day when she allows me to love and protect her.

Nothing, it seems, can break my happy bubble. I park in my driveway and get out of my car and stretch my arms overhead.

I sense movement behind me and see a flicker out of the corner of my eye.

Pain explodes on the right side of my skull. I've been hit with something hard and heavy.

Zenya. If I pass out, what if someone hurts Zenya?

I stagger onto one knee and struggle to hold on to consciousness. If anything happens to me, Zenya and the baby are in trouble.

I fight it as long as I can, but I'm hit a second time.

My knees buckle. I hit the ground, and the world goes black.

I wake up with a pounding head and it's difficult to breathe.

I can't see.

Am I blind?

I blink several times and realize that my eyes are gummed together. It must be coagulated blood gluing my eyes shut, and I tilt my head and drag my face across my shoulder.

That unsticks my eyelids and I can finally take a look around. I'm bound to a chair, the ropes brutally tight across my chest. The room is dimly lit, but as my eyes adjust, I can make out the floor. The ceiling.

A man in front of me perched on a table.

A big man with tawny, tangled hair and tattoos on his biceps. His arms are folded loosely as he grins at me like he's warmly greeting an old friend. "Kristian. It's been ages since we talked."

"Lenkov?" I say, and the sound of my own voice sends splinters of pain through my skull. Sergei Lenkov, the arms dealer. The last time I saw him, I was giving him a death glare at Yuri's party for smiling at Zenya.

Is that what this is about?

I pin him with a glare, fury racing through my body. "You can't have her. She's mine."

Sergei tips back his head and laughs. "Zenya? Your pregnant little uncle-fucker? You couldn't pay me to marry that slut." He enunciates every word with delight.

My eyes narrow and my jaw clenches. He'll pay for those insults. Maybe I'm the one tied to a chair right now, but he's the one who'll die screaming. I quickly glance around the room. There are no windows, so I expect we're in a basement. Probably the basement of Lenkov's own house.

"Besides, I've got someone else," he says slyly.

"Congratulations," I seethe, tugging at my bonds to test how tight they are. I'm not getting loose anytime soon, and I huff in anger and glare at him. "Well? What do you want? Money? Get on with your threats and demands, I've got shit to do."

"Me?" Sergei asks with a grin, pointing at his chest. "Not me. Her."

Someone strides forward out of the shadows behind Lenkov. A woman with honey blonde hair, pinched cheeks, and dark eyeliner smudged like she's been rubbing at her face. Her fists are clenched at her sides like she's this close to snapping, and she clutches a knife, which trembles in her grip.

I frown as I recognize her. Eleanor?

What the fuck is Chessa's sister doing here?

I glance from her pale, furious face to Lenkov's grinning one. I couldn't pick two people less likely to be working together in the whole city. Less likely to even *know* each other. A vicious arms dealer and Chessa's legally employed and totally unremarkable sister.

"What's going on here?" I ask, my eyes narrowing at Eleanor.

"You shouldn't have come back," Eleanor seethes. "I wouldn't have had to do anything if you hadn't come back."

I keep my mouth closed but my thoughts are racing. I've messed up Eleanor's plans by rejoining the Belyaev family, apparently, but I can't fathom what plans Eleanor can have that involve me. Her priorities have always been her nephews and nieces and seeing that they have someone to keep Chessa's memory alive. That's what she wants, and I'm not stopping her.

"But no," Eleanor continues. "Back comes Kristian with his smirks and his threats and his chaos, only this time he doesn't flame out and ruin everything for himself. He makes Zenya and Troian happy."

"You don't want me to make Zenya and Troian happy?" I ask slowly, beginning to get an inkling of where this is going and not liking it one bit.

Eleanor starts slapping the blade of the knife against her thigh she's so agitated. If she's not careful she's going to cut herself. "Those people deserve to suffer hell on earth for what they did to my sister, and they'll get there soon. That's a matter for another day, but what I want right here and right now from you before I kill you is to admit that you murdered Chessa."

I'm so caught off guard by the accusation that I burst out laughing, but my humor is short-lived as anger takes its place. "Chessa choked on a fucking dumpling. Yes, I celebrated, but because I was happy to be rid of that woman breathing down my neck, not because I did her in."

"Don't lie to me," she cries. "Sergei sent me that photo of you at the strip club choking the stripper with Chessa's name written on her. Troian didn't see that for what it was, but I did. *A confession.*"

I glare at Lenkov and he dips his head in an ironic bow. So it was him who took that fucking picture and ruined my fucking life, nearly for good. He must have been in the club at the same time as me and my crew, and I didn't notice because I was so drunk.

I swing my attention back to Eleanor. "Why the fuck did Sergei Lenkov have your number?"

Lenkov smirks at me. "A beautiful woman like Eleanor, why wouldn't I be courting her?"

Eleanor simpers at him. Stupid fucking woman. There wasn't

one sincere word that Lenkov just spoke. There's only one thing Lenkov cares about, and I know it because I used to be just like him. He craves power, and having someone he can influence within the Belyaev family circle must have been too good to pass up. No wonder Eleanor's never brought a man to a family party. She's been sleeping with Lenkov for years and he must have insisted she kept it secret.

I relax back in my chair as if I'm enjoying myself and smirk at Eleanor. "Screwing this cold bitch in exchange for gossip? You poor man. I hope she at least came through with the goods now and then."

Lenkov laughs. "The real pleasure is disrupting your family's power in this city. It's good for business to have everyone stabbing each other in the back. The news that Zenya Belyaev was gang-raped in a warehouse and that her family couldn't protect her was going to be the tipping point that plunged this city into chaos." The smile drops from his face. "But you ruined everything."

Rage boils through me. I can still picture those four *mudaki* advancing on my niece, laughing at her. Intent on hurting her in the worst ways possible, and all because of these two people in front of me. I wrench my wrists behind my back, but the ropes don't give even a fraction of an inch.

"Kristian Belyaev returning and taking over as *Pakhan* is not part of my grand plans. I don't make as much money when the Belyaevs are keeping everyone else in line."

"I'm not going to be *Pakhan*," I growl at Lenkov. "Zenya is the one in charge."

"Oh, don't worry. She'll die, too. Eventually."

"Shut up about Zenya! What about my sister?" Eleanor shrieks and brandishes the knife at me.

Eleanor doesn't intimidate me. I've been beaten and stabbed plenty of times in my life, and I made my peace with pain and death a long time ago. The only thing they could threaten me with is hurting Zenya and my baby, and Zenya's not here.

But they can't be allowed to kill me and go after her.

I look between the two of them, feeling sickened as I wonder how to play this. So this is what happens when a twisted need for revenge meets a manipulative psychopath. They must have been meeting and plotting behind our backs for years and we had no idea.

I give Eleanor a deadpan glare as my head pounds with what's probably a concussion. Even from beyond the grave, Chessa is giving me a headache.

"Listen up, idiot," I seethe. "I didn't like Chessa, and she didn't like me, but I didn't want her dead. I just wanted her to leave me alone."

"And why was she so preoccupied with you, Kristian?" Eleanor asks, getting even closer with the knife. "Because Chessa knew you were screwing your underage niece. Grooming and coercing her and forcing her against her will, and so you killed her for getting in your way."

"For fuck's sake. I'm a killer, so I must be a rapist as well? I suppose you think I torture small fluffy creatures for fun in my spare time. Has it ever occurred to you, you stupid fucking woman, that I'm a violent asshole to everyone *except* my family, because those are the people I actually love?"

I glare at her in disgust as she struggles to comprehend this.

"You threatened Chessa and her children," she points out. "She told me all about it and showed me the bruises you left on her arm."

If Zenya talks to any man but me tonight, I will make you cry, and that's a fucking promise.

Am I really tied to a chair because of something I said at a New Year's party two years ago? "For fuck's sake, Eleanor—"

"I've heard enough from you," she screams, demented from grief. Sent mad from her craving for revenge. And I thought Troian and I were the vengeful ones in the family.

"Gag him," she snaps at Lenkov, who glares at her until she adds in a wheedling tone, "please gag him. I don't want to hear his voice a second longer."

Getting grudgingly to his feet, Lenkov shoves a rag in my mouth and ties another over it so I can't spit it out.

Eleanor steps toward me, brandishing that wickedly pointed knife. "It's all your fault I have to do this. You could have stayed away, and I wouldn't have had to kill Zenya because the universe was already making her suffer. No beloved uncle. Troian dying a slow and painful death. It was wonderful to watch them get what they deserved. I only wanted one more thing, for that bitch to be gang-raped like my sister was, but no, you had to come back and save her, and then make her *happy*."

She says that like I've committed a disgusting crime.

"Belyaevs don't deserve anything but suffering for what you all did to my sister. Raped by criminals. Murdered on the floor of her own kitchen. You disgust me. I'm going to kill you and watch your precious Zenya suffer for the next few months wondering where her man is. Before she has a chance to give birth to your brat, Sergei will make sure she's hit by a car or drowns in the pool. It will be easy," she says, trailing the tip of the knife down my chest, hard enough to break the skin. "After all, I can get into that house whenever I want. I could even make her sick if I wanted to. Not enough to kill her, but I could poison her for fun and watch her suffer. I could do it next week. Tomorrow. Slip something into her coffee and make her afraid for the baby as she vomits her guts out."

Pain slices through me as I imagine Zenya, stricken by shock over my sudden disappearance, accepting a hot drink from Eleanor. Her expression is sympathetic but her eyes are lit with vile, vindictive delight.

I wrench again at the ropes, and Eleanor laughs like she's never enjoyed herself so much in her life. She wants me to lose my shit and scream uselessly with this gag in my mouth. I can't get out of these restraints.

I don't have a weapon.

I can barely think with all the rage swimming in my skull.

Eleanor steps back and turns to Lenkov. "Hurt him. I want to see him bleed."

Lenkov steps forward with a glower at her ordering him around again, but he can't resist some violence. He grabs a handful of my shirt and raises his fist. I glare up at him and picture the blood pouring from his throat and the life draining from his eyes.

He did this. Eleanor might be unhinged from grief, but Lenkov has been the one pulling her puppet strings and feeding her misery for his own ends.

Lenkov draws back his fist.

A voice speaks from the darkness on the other side of the basement. "Touch one hair on his head and I'll rip your balls off and make you eat them."

Zenya walks out of the shadows, a gun in her hand pointed straight at Lenkov.

Her short cream dress clings to her small bump, and the sight of her, armed and pregnant, sends pride, love, and fear bolting through me. She shouldn't be here. She's in danger because of me.

She came for me.

My heart convulses in my chest and my throat burns. I was going to fight with everything I had, but for a moment there, I felt so fucking alone.

Zenya has her attention on Lenkov but there's still Eleanor with that knife. She recovers from her shock and starts edging toward Zenya, hungry to hurt her. Too impatient to wait.

Zenya notices and gives her a withering look. "Bitch, please. Back the fuck down."

As if on cue, Mikhail and several more of our men step out of the shadows behind Zenya, and I take a shaky breath through my nose. She brought backup, thank fuck, but I'm still tied to a chair while Zenya is in the same room as these assholes.

Lenkov stands back with his hands raised, his expression resigned. "I'm out, Eleanor. This whole thing is a headache and your pussy's not worth it. I was having fun, but playtime's over. Shut the door on your way out."

He turns toward the door to leave the Belyaevs to what he's decided is our family squabble.

Zenya levels the gun at him. "Take one more step and you're dead. I haven't finished with you."

"I didn't do anything to you, you stupid bitch. I was just having fun," Lenkov seethes.

"Setting four men on me to kill my people and rape me? Yes, so much fun. Mikhail, could you please disarm Eleanor and untie my fiancé?"

Yes.

Fucking untie me.

Rage is boiling through me and there's something I need to do.

"*Da, Pakhanovna*," Mikhail replies. A few of the men have picked up on my honorific for Zenya and started using it. He twists the knife from Eleanor's grip and uses it to cut away my gag and untie me.

I spit the rag out of my mouth, wrench the knife out of Mikhail's grip, and stride toward Lenkov. Rage builds inside me with every step. He called Zenya a slut and an uncle-fucker. He tried to have her attacked in the most brutal way possible. He dared to plot behind the Belyaevs' back and undermine our authority in this city for his own gain.

There's only one way this can end for him, and it's going to be my way.

Lenkov's eyes go wide, but he hasn't got time to do anything or say anything to defend himself. With a yell of rage, I plunge the knife straight into his throat. He grabs hold of me, and we hit the ground together. I go on stabbing him over and over in the neck and chest, blood spraying all over me until I know he won't survive.

I sit back on my heels and fling the bloody knife into the corner, my chest heaving. Eleanor is a viper, but she wouldn't have been able to do any of this without Lenkov. With my teeth bared in a snarl, I watch him bleed out and the light leave his eyes.

There's a short silence in which the only sound is my ragged breathing.

And then Eleanor wails and clutches her head. "He's dead, he's dead. You killed him."

"He's no fucking loss," I say, getting to my feet.

Zenya is gazing at her with a mixture of horror and pity. "How could you do this to us? Chessa didn't blame our family for what happened to her the night of the home invasion, so why should you?"

"Because it never would have happened to her if she hadn't married one of you!" Eleanor shrieks, demented from grief and the scent of blood and gunpowder. "You're all sick and twisted and you'll pay for your crimes in hell."

Eleanor screams and lunges for me, her face twisted in hatred and her nails raised to claw my face.

A gunshot explodes and the sound ricochets off the concrete walls.

As Eleanor staggers and falls to the ground, I see Zenya standing there with smoke rising from the barrel of her gun.

"Nice shot, princess."

She raises her gun with a smile. "I learned from the best." Her smile fades as she looks at Eleanor, and I know she's wishing she didn't have to kill her step-aunt, but if she hadn't, I would have. I can't live on the same planet as someone who fantasized so thoroughly about hurting my woman and baby.

I wipe the blood from my face with my sleeve, glancing from one dead body to the other. Fuck, that was close. That could have been so much worse.

"We'll go upstairs and check that there's no one else in the mansion," Mikhail says, and leads the other men upstairs, mostly to give us some privacy, I expect.

"How did you find me?" I say raggedly, taking the gun from Zenya and sweeping her into my arms and holding her tight. I'm covered in blood and it's soaking into her clothes, but I know she doesn't care.

Zenya threads her fingers through my hair, gazing up at me with a desperate expression, assuring herself that I'm all right. "You weren't answering my calls. No one knew where you were, and Mikhail found spots of blood in your driveway. I panicked, but then I remembered some strange things I've noticed lately. Since we announced we were engaged, Eleanor has been staring at us in a way that made me wonder what was going on in her head. A hickey on her throat at Lana's birthday party, and I saw her car parked outside this house the day we got engaged. Eleanor has no good reason to be hanging around Lenkov unless she was using him to hurt you, so I took a chance on you being here."

"Thank fuck you did," I breathe, resting my forehead against hers and holding her tight.

"She blamed the Belyaevs for Chessa's suffering and death, didn't she?" she asks sadly.

"She did. Apparently, she's been enjoying watching us tear ourselves apart and suffering these past few years, and she didn't like seeing us putting ourselves back together."

"Let's never let anything like that happen again," Zenya says, gripping my shoulders and gazing into my eyes. "I want us to be strong together from now on."

"Always," I whisper.

Zenya gives Eleanor's body a sad look. "I liked Chessa. I liked Eleanor as well. My siblings have already lost so much and now they've lost their aunt. She should have thought about them while she was constructing her horrible plan."

I gaze down at Zenya's beautiful face and remember how close I was to choosing revenge over love. I'm ferociously glad the woman in my arms was able to pull me back from the edge by reminding me of all the reasons I love her. Revenge wouldn't have made me happy. Revenge is poison.

I stroke her cheek with my knuckles, murmuring, "You saved my life, *Pakhanovna*. It's supposed to be me protecting you, remember?"

She turns her face up to mine with a beautiful smile on her lips. "I wanted to return the favor, my handsome stranger in black. Have I told you lately that I love you?"

"Tell me again," I demand, hungry for her.

"I love—"

I slant my mouth over hers in a demanding kiss and breathe in sharply as she opens her lips for my tongue. She tastes like everything I crave.

Blood and danger.

Steel and bullets.

That's what our love is made from, and I'll never let go of this girl as long as I live.

Epilogue

ZENYA

The night Kristian and I first made love after I told him I was pregnant, I thought he was silly for freezing up and worrying he would hurt the baby. As I walk up the aisle on my father's arm in the vaulted church, I understand what he was really worried about. That we didn't deserve our happy ending. We hadn't bled enough or fought enough or beaten our enemies back.

And he was right. At that time, there were still enemies circling us in the shadows, hungry to tear apart our happiness, but now we've defeated them. He and I fought to be together, and as we fought, we fell in love.

I smile at Kristian as I walk slowly by my father's side, my long white dress brushing along the floor, and he returns my smile with glowing eyes. He wears a gray suit and a black shirt, but no tie. When he glimpsed a hint of the lace on my wedding dress after a fitting, he had a crisis over his own attire, saying he would wear a tie, after all, because he didn't want to let me down.

"You could never let me down," I told him, kissing him and smiling. "Besides, the bride won't look traditional either. I will be so goddamn pregnant in that dress."

"Even better," he said with a devilish grin, and kissed me harder. "All right. A bump for you and no tie for me. We'll do this our way."

Dad is gripping my arm tightly and leaning on his oxygen tank, but he's smiling as the music plays. There are so many happy, smiling faces around us, and I drink in every sound and sight. It's the wedding day that I've been dreaming of, and there are tears on my lashes as I kiss my father's cheek, help him into a seat at the front, pass my flowers to Lana, and join Kristian at the altar.

Kristian doesn't care that the priest is waiting or it's not time to kiss me yet. He takes my face between his hands, touches my curls, my neck and shoulders, my waist, and finally my bump.

"I love you," he breathes, drinking me in, and presses a soft kiss to my lips.

And that's the most important moment of our whole wedding day. Not our vows, not the party. That quiet moment with Kristian at the altar when he shows everyone we care about that I am his and he is mine. Forever.

Demyan Troian Belyaev is born five and a half months after our wedding at two in the morning, and he fills the birthing suite at the hospital with his strong, indignant cries. Kristian is the first one to hold him, and he gazes down at his son with the most beautiful smile I've ever seen touching his lips.

He lays the baby in my arms and presses a kiss to my sweaty brow. "You're amazing, dandelion. Look what you made."

"We made," I whisper, marveling at our son's tiny, beautiful face. I've never seen anything so wonderful in my whole life. My head and Kristian's are bent over the baby as we gaze at him together.

I insist on being discharged as soon as possible because there's someone Demyan has to meet. Eight hours after I've given birth, I leave the hospital with my baby in my arms, and Kristian drives us to the hospice to see Dad because we could no longer take care of him and manage his pain at home.

It hurts so much to see Dad so weakened in his bed. With all the emotions and baby hormones circulating through my body, I don't sob as I sit at his bedside, but the tears flow down my cheeks while I smile through them.

"He has your eyes, Kristian," Dad says, his bed raised so he can sit up with Demyan in his thin arms.

Kristian swallows hard and squeezes my hand. A moment later his voice is husky as he asks, "Do you think so?"

Dad smiles and stroke's the baby's cheek with a finger. "And I think he has my nose."

I gaze at Demyan and realize that Dad's right. Demyan is a perfect blend of mine and Dad's features and Kristian's as well.

Kristian blinks hard and his jaw is tight. His happiness at finally hearing something he's always wanted to hear is bittersweet.

Dad passes away just two weeks later. He was only forty-two, and even though I knew it was coming, I cry so much. So do my brothers and sisters, and for once I don't run away and sob by myself because I think I have to be strong for them. I'm with them, and when that first storm of tears has passed I have them all in my arms to ease the hurt.

Kristian is there to hold me too, and for me to hold him, and the grief is stark on his face. As much as they fought, he and Dad loved each other.

I cling to him tightly and whisper, "I'm happy we were all together at the end. I don't think I could have done this without you. Our family wasn't meant to be in pieces."

"Never again," Kristian says and holds me back as hard as he can, and I can feel how determined he is to keep us all together, now and always.

I catch the scent of blood in the air before I see him. Strong arms wrap around me from behind and Kristian buries his face in my neck and breathes me in like he's been gone for weeks instead of a matter of hours.

"Mm. I missed you, dandelion."

I look down at his hands, which are spattered with red. "What are you covered in?"

He chuckles darkly. "The blood of your enemies."

I stand up from my laptop and walk into Kristian's open arms, smiling up at him. His eyes are lit with blue fire and there's a smear of blood on his jaw. This handsome man can still take my breath away after a year and a half of marriage.

As I wind my arms around his neck, I purr, "You found them, my love?"

"Of course I did. Anyone who disrespects my *Pakhanovna* deserves to die."

Anger flashes through me at the memory. Mikhail and two of my men were forced off the road and nearly killed last month. It was only thanks to Mikhail's expertise with a gun that he managed to fend off their attackers and escape injured but alive.

He and Kristian found out who was responsible and hunted them down mercilessly. Every now and then, people get it in their heads to test my authority in this city and attack my people, but they always die screaming.

I brush my lips over Kristian's. "Thank you, my love. We missed you while you were gone, too."

My husband kisses me hard and then turns to where Demyan is playing with blocks on the living room floor. He hoists our fourteen-month-old into his arms with a smile.

"Did you miss Daddy? He missed you, too."

Demyan is delighted to see his father, and I admire my dangerous husband holding our baby. Then I check the time. "You have just enough time to wash up before dinner, and we can tuck the children in together before going out."

"Perfect." Kristian kisses me before handing over the baby and heading toward the stairs.

I open my mouth to call out to him, but hesitate, wondering whether to tell him my news now or later when we're alone.

Later. I want him all to myself when we talk.

I head to the kitchen to check on dinner. Arron has finished his homework and he's setting the table, and Felix takes Demyan for me while I take the casserole out of the oven. Lana is away at college but everyone else is living at home, and I love having my family around me. Kristian and I have been able to balance our work life and home life in a way that we're both happy and fulfilled. We have help from a nanny at home for the younger children so we both have equal time to devote to work.

My favorite part of the business has always been the figures and the deals, while Kristian is my enforcer. He couldn't give a damn about spreadsheets, but he's excellent at reading people and protecting me.

With nine people around our table—ten if Lana is home— dinners are always raucous affairs and my favorite time of the day. My eldest siblings argue good-naturedly about sports or music, and the little ones talk about school. There are often some squabbles, but Kristian is excellent at mediating those, distracting everyone with stories, or simply heaving whoever is throwing a tantrum over his shoulder and walking around with them until they're giggling and have forgotten what they're upset about.

Family is everything to us. Our big, noisy, messy table is what I look forward to coming home to, and with the way Kristian's been determined to get me pregnant again lately, we're going to need a bigger table.

After we've eaten, my older siblings tidy up the kitchen with Kristian, and Giselle, our nanny, takes the younger children upstairs for baths.

I return to my laptop to finish up the spreadsheet I was working on, and thirty minutes later, I'm ready to head to the Silo. First I make the rounds of the bedrooms and kiss Micaela, Nadia, Danil, and Demyan goodnight, and remind Arron, Felix, and Noah that the video games are to be switched off at ten and then it's bedtime. The three eldest boys are all addicted to a car racing game, and they play it together every night.

Kristian meets me downstairs and takes my hand as he leads me out to his car. I'm humming softly along to the radio as we drive, one of my hands dawdling in his lap. I love his thighs. I love his whole body, actually. His mornings are spent in the gym with his men where they work out and spar, and I join them three times a week so that I stay strong as well.

We work for an hour and a half in the Silo, going through the merchandise and discussing our business contacts. I'm smiling on the inside the whole time, wondering when to tell him my news. Now, or when we're at home?

When we're finished, I hook my finger into the neckline of his shirt and draw him down to me for a kiss. "Shall we go home? I wouldn't mind getting my husband into bed."

Kristian glances around with a smirk on his lips. We're totally alone. "You know I've always loved a warehouse late at night."

He picks me up with an arm under my knees and carries me upstairs to the office where there's a sofa and lays me down on it. His mouth covers mine in an insistent kiss, and I unbutton his shirt while he pulls off my jeans and underwear. There's a light in his eyes, and I know he's anticipating the moment he can fuck me full of his cum.

As much as I love that too, I have some news for him.

When he pulls off my shirt and bra and I'm naked beneath him, I whisper, "I have some news."

"That you're adorable and sexy and all I can fucking think about?" he asks, sucking my nipple.

"I took a test earlier."

He freezes and draws away from me. "Are you…?"

I nod, smiling up at him. "You're going to be a daddy again."

Kristian's eyes go wide. "Oh fuck yes, oh hell yes. Really?" He kisses me breathlessly over and over as I laugh and tug at his belt and pants. He's hard as a rock as I draw him out, and I lovingly run my nails across his balls and the underside of his cock.

"Yes, really."

"This is wonderful. Did you just find out? Another baby. I can't wait until you're showing again," he murmurs, kissing down my body to my stomach.

Kristian loves my body when I'm pregnant, marveling at every change that I'm going through and preening that it's because of him.

He looks up at me with a devilish smile. "That means I can come wherever I want."

"You always come wherever you want," I point out. It's just that when I'm not pregnant, he's obsessed with finishing inside me.

Kristian moves down my body and lashes my clit with his tongue. With the hush of the warehouse around us, I'm reminded of that first night with my stranger in black. My reaction to him is as electric as it was then.

"Do I want you to swallow me down like a good girl?" he murmurs as he goes on licking me. "Or should I stripe your pretty tits with my cum? No. I know."

He turns me over onto my knees, spreads me open and spits on my ass. "Who's my sweet little slut who loves a cock in her ass?"

Heat floods my body. Me. I do.

Kristian licks me from my clit all the way up to that tight ring of muscle, smearing my wetness about, then using his fingers to do the same thing.

With one swift thrust, he buries himself in my pussy, making me gasp. He carefully pushes a finger into my ass as he fucks me, and then another, and I feel my cheek melting into the sofa, groaning at the twin sensations.

"You're my *Pakhanovna* out there, but you're my dirty little bitch in here, aren't you?"

"Yes, I am," I moan into the sofa cushions.

I'm so close to coming and Kristian is always eager to push me over the edge, but when he fucks me in the ass, he prefers to torment me and make me wait for him.

He draws his cock out of me and his fingers from my ass, spits on me again in a way that makes my stomach swoop, and then I feel the broad, plush head of his cock pushing against my ass. He groans as he sinks into me and starts to fuck me slowly.

"Princess, you're so fucking perfect and tight around me. God, I've craved you like this. Totally at my mercy."

My fingers brush my clit but he grabs my hand and pins it

behind me.

"What do you think you're doing? You don't come until I say so."

I'm so close that a few swipes could send me over the edge. Kristian fucks me deeper, holding me on a knife's edge between pleasure and release. It's not until he's groaning my name that he releases my hand and uses his own fingers on me to bring me to climax around him. I take advantage of being alone for a chance to yell as loud as I please. Then he's fucking me swiftly, chasing his own orgasm and finally feeling it surge through his body.

He stays where he is for a moment before slowly and carefully drawing out of me and giving my ass an appreciative spank, which makes me gasp and laugh. "That's my good fucking girl."

Kristian pushes himself back inside his pants and does up his belt while I pull my underwear on, and then he sits down on the sofa and reaches for my hand. I go to him. I always go to my beautiful man, and I drink in his handsome face, the aftershocks of my orgasm circling through me.

In the darkness of the warehouse, he draws me up onto his lap so I'm straddling him. He cuddles me close, kissing my neck and smoothing my hair down. And he can't stop smiling.

"Dandelion, are you happy? Do you have everything you want?"

I press my forehead to his and wrap my arms around him, thinking about the life we're building together and our growing family.

"Everything," I whisper.

Out there, I'm his *Pakhanovna*. He is loyal only to me and fiercely protects all that is mine.

In here, he's my world, and I am his.

THANK YOU FOR READING BRUTAL CONQUEST! IF YOU ENJOYED THIS BOOK, PLEASE CONSIDER LEAVING A REVIEW ON AMAZON AND GOODREADS.

ACKNOWLEDGMENTS

Thank you so much for reading *Brutal Conquest*. I always have fun writing my books and this was no exception, but I particularly enjoyed exploring the impatiently-waiting-for-her-to-grow-up trope because it's a favorite of mine. Anti-heroes who pine and suffer for their girl are just so delicious to me!

I was inspired to write an uncle/niece pairing by Daemon and Rhaenyra and *House of the Dragon*. I immediately fell in love with Daemon Targaryen with his warrior braids, incendiary temper, and indulgent horny uncle vibes. I just adore that grimy hunk of bastard. Rhaenyra Targaryen is my favorite kind of heroine. Sweet, smart, willing to do whatever it takes to follow her own heart, and able to bring the most intimidating, chaotic man in her life to his knees.

I was also inspired by that classic uncle/niece pairing, Hades and Persephone. They too have a rocky beginning marked by push-pull, manipulation, and surrender, before they become boss-ass bitches ruling the underworld at each other's sides.

Thank you to Evva for sliding into my DMs and suggesting a niece/uncle book when I was flailing about #daemyra. Once I saw Matt Smith's sleek and dangerous red carpet looks, I couldn't get the idea for a mafia alternative universe out of my head.

Thank you to Darlene for the eyeballs scene. You have all the good ideas, lovely! I'm always excited to hear your opinion and excellent thoughts.

Thank you to Jesi, beta reader and designer of the gorgeous special edition covers for this series. They are absolutely stunning.

Thank you to Arabella, my beta reader and wonderful fellow author.

Thank you to Crystal, Daniela, and Nouha for being a final set of eyes when I needed you.

Thank you to Xenia for checking over my Russian and being an amazing person all these years.

Thank you to Heather, my editor. You are my biggest cheerleader and the best editor I've ever had.

Thank you to Rumi, my proofreader, for catching all my flubs and making me laugh.

ALSO BY LILITH VINCENT

Steamy Reverse Harem

THE PROMISED IN BLOOD SERIES (complete)

First Comes Blood

Second Comes War

Third Comes Vengeance

THE PAGEANT DUET (complete)

Pageant

Crowned

FAIRYTALES WITH A TWIST (group series)

Beauty So Golden

Steamy MF Romance

THE BRUTAL HEARTS SERIES (ongoing)

Brutal Intentions

ABOUT THE AUTHOR

Lilith Vincent is a steamy romance author who believes in living on the wild side! Whether it's reverse harem or M/F romance, mafia men and bad boys with tattoos are her weakness, and the heroines who bring them to their knees.

Made in the USA
Las Vegas, NV
11 November 2023

80656806R00203